Setareh

Doctrine

By Mark Downer

OLD STONE PRESS

Setareh Doctrine
By Mark Downer

© 2021, Mark H. Downer
All rights reserved.

For information about special discounts for bulk purchases or autographed copies of this book, please contact John H. Clark, publisher, Old Stone Press at john@oldstonepress.com or the author, Mark H. Downer at mark.downer@landstarmail.com

Library of Congress Control Number: 2020922811

ISBN: 978-1-938462-47-4 (print)
ISBN: 978-1-938462-48-1 (eBook)

Published by Old Stone Press
an imprint of J. H. Clark & Associates, Inc.
Louisville, Kentucky 40207 USA
www.oldstonepress.com

Published in the United States

Author's Note

Setareh Doctrine is a work of fiction, but the unique cast of characters that make up the Themis Cooperative are by design a creation of names and personalities from a long list of real acquaintances that I want to thank for being a part of my life experience. Some will recognize the resemblances and hopefully enjoy the portrayals. The mission of these "heroes" is as the name of their co-op implies. Themis is an ancient Greek Titaness. She is described as "the Lady of good counsel", and is the personification of divine order, fairness, law, natural law, and custom. The world is a dangerous place. It has its share of bad people and evil exists everywhere. Heroes of good are needed, so there will be many more opportunities for the Themis Cooperative team to administer the natural law of justice in a series of future adventures.

Prologue

Nolin Lake, Kentucky, October

Jake Woods secured the Cobalt R-5 to the dock and stepped back aboard to retrieve his windbreaker along with the Beretta M9 pistol from the glovebox. He took one last cursory look inside the boat before climbing back out through the open bow and heading up the three-tiered level of wood steps. The steps gave way to a steep, rock laced trail that eventually plateaued to the small backyard of his beloved cabin built into the hillside above him. The climb proved taxing to even those in the best of shape, and for a well-conditioned and exceptionally fit 75-year-old Woods it was proving more difficult every year, but he relished every step. This was his sanctuary, and he wasn't about to let the sands of time stand in the way of this indulgence.

He brushed back on his full head of silver hair as he entered the house on the lower level and took the staircase up to the main floor of the three-story log and stone structure. Depositing his Patagonia fleece pullover and windbreaker on the rustic hook by the front door, he pulled off his well-worn Red Wing boots and made a beeline for the bar.

Along the way he returned the pistol to the top drawer of an old secretary desk and glanced out the rear window to the fading daylight giving way to a fiery orange fall sunset in Central

Kentucky, the glow reflecting in a long blazing streak off the water of Lake Nolin.

Sliding his sock feet sideways to the rebuilt antique sideboard, repurposed with an ice machine, mini refrigerator, and ample storage for plenty of distilled spirits, he removed a cold bottle of water for immediate sustenance, and spent the next few minutes concocting a Bookers Manhattan straight up, stirred not shaken.

He turned toward the large creek stone fireplace with thoughts of a roaring fire for the cool October night, and froze abruptly as he came within a few feet of the oriental gentleman seated on the couch in the great room.

"Good evening Mr. Woods."

Woods eyed the older man with a trained suspicion and panned the room for any additional threats in hiding. Finding none, he returned his gaze at the man and offered an impersonal reply, "Good evening to you. Who might YOU be?"

"My name is General Tzu Huang. I am the former Deputy Minister for the Ministry of State Security, People's Republic of China," he replied in almost perfect English.

"General," Woods nodded as he sidled slowly backward to the desk and removed the Beretta once again, "Long title. Pleased to meet you in person, as I'm well aware of you and your reputation. What the hell are you doing here in my house in the good old U.S of A.?"

"There's no need for the weapon, I'm quite alone."

"You'll have to excuse me, I'm a Reaganite, trust but verify."

Huang smiled and nodded. "If you'll make one of those for me," pointing at the manhattan, "I have a story to tell you. I thought it important to present it to you in person."

* * * * *

After nearly ten minutes of dead air, as Woods tended to his guest's request for a cocktail while downing his first and chasing it with a refill, he delivered on a now robust and crackling fire. Another five minutes were devoted to exploring the first and second floors in his commitment to verifying Huang's claim of solitude. Satisfied as to no immediate threat indoors, he returned to the bar, stirred up another batch of libations and topped off their glasses, his third and Huang's second. Returning to his worn brown leather chair opposite Huang, he propped up his socked feet on the matching ottoman. With lingering doubts about the General's continued insistence of aloneness, Woods' senses remained on high alert, vigilant to his surroundings and any noises other than the popping logs, the Beretta lying softly in his lap.

"These are quite tasty." Huang projected a raised eyebrow in approval of the bourbon concoction.

"You know what they say about manhattans and martinis, General?"

Huang shook his head, "I don't know the saying."

"They're like women's breasts, one's not enough and three's too many."

Huang snickered, "Sounds like a Chinese proverb."

"Doubt it," winked Woods.

"Then you need more than one woman."

Woods chuckled. "I think on that one I can give Chinese attribution." Woods offered up an open hand, "Please, storytelling is a lost art, tell me your story."

He twisted and pressed his back into the chair as Huang waited for him to get comfortable.

"You were on a mission once," Huang sighed, "Cambodia, springtime 1970. I know, because I was there, too."

Woods eyed the large cocktail shaker of extra manhattan resting next to him on the oak lamp table and thought it a smart move that he brought it with him from the bar. He recalled with remarkable clarity events that the General's story was now revisiting.

* * * * *

Mondulkiri Province, Cambodia, May 1970

Captain Jake Woods, 3rd Force Reconnaissance Company, III Marine Amphibious Force, walked through the wall of sandbags and knocked on the rotting piece of plywood substituting as a door. Not waiting for a reply, he wrestled it open and entered the steaming Quonset hut at the northeast corner of the O Rang airfield, temporarily being utilized as HQ for 1st Brigade, 1st Air Cavalry.

The entire area around O Rang was a pigsty, but a really busy one. Chinook CH-47 and Bell UH-1 Iroquois helicopters swarmed in and out of the airfield like agitated bees at the hive, the latter mode of transportation being Woods' ferry into this forgotten part of the world. Recently captured from the Viet Cong and regulars of the People's Army of Vietnam during Operation Rockcrusher, the airstrip, along with Fire Support Base DAVID three klicks to the northwest, was being reinforced and resupplied in full by the 1st Brigade and the 11th Armored Cavalry Regiment. They were to be the jumping-off point for further incursions into Cambodia as a part of the elusive hunt for the communist headquarters of the Central Office of South Vietnam.

Woods was the son of a small-town dentist and stay-at-home mom from Bardstown, Kentucky. A three-sport high school star and all-state baseball player, he earned a baseball scholarship to the University of Kentucky and enrolled in the campus ROTC program as a way to afford school in Lexington. He fine-tuned his leadership skills as an All-SEC pitcher and Marine officer in the making. After graduation, he was assigned to Camp Lejeune, NC where he was commissioned a Second Lieutenant with 3rd Force Reconnaissance Company.

He was shipped off to replenish the Company's forces in South Vietnam in the fall of 1966, and distinguished himself in several campaigns at Khe Sahn, the Hill Fights, and in ongoing reconnaissance of the Cobi Than Tan Valley and Quang Tri Province. Along the way he earned a battlefield promotion to Captain and was awarded a Bronze Star and Purple Heart. Then in November 1969, when 3rd Force Recon was placed under Third Marine Amphibious Force, with the goal of deactivating 3rd Force sometime the following year in 1970, the CIA came knocking. Their overture was convincing. They pushed him into a whole new realm of covert action and intelligence gathering, including multiple black operations and two assassination missions. His latest operation placed him in this miserable armpit of the world known as Cambodia.

Now, looking over the assemblage of staff purposely milling around the long open space of the hut, Woods lightened his load as he slung his rucksack to the ground. He leaned his M16A1 rifle and additional M40A1 Sniper rifle against the loaded pack. Removing his soft boonie hat, he engaged a corporal seated at a table tapping furiously on a typewriter. "I'm looking for Colonel Justice, Corporal, any idea where I can find him?"

Looking up, the enlisted man jumped to attention in response to Woods' question, "Yes, sir. He's in the curtained area on the right, just past the map table. I believe he's expecting you, Captain."

Without hesitation, Woods pointed to his equipment on the floor and gestured to the corporal with a nod of his head, "Keep an eye on my gear." He immediately moved on past a knot of officers hunched over a large rectangular wooden table in the center of the hut adorned with several maps highlighted in an array of arrows and other military deployment symbols in a variety of sizes, shapes, and colors.

Colonel Justice was seated behind a make-shift desk of two empty diesel drums and more plywood. Two worn wooden chairs facing the Colonel's desk were occupied by an Army Lieutenant and an ARVN Captain.

They all rose to their feet in unison as Woods drew back the curtain and said, "Knock, knock," and stepped in to greet them.

"C'mon in Skipper," Colonel Justice returned Woods' salute. "We've been expecting you."

"So, I hear."

Colonel Justice continued with introductions, "Captain, this is Captain Dae-Ho Park ARVN Special Forces and 1st Lieutenant Colin Patterson U.S. Special Forces."

Handshakes were exchanged all around, and Woods pulled over a folding metal chair found behind one of the multiple curtain panels creating the illusion of privacy.

With everyone seated and introductions dispensed, Colonel Justice didn't waste any more time, "So...Captain Woods I understand you have a special mission that you need to accomplish. Per orders from on high, these two gentlemen are here to assist." Justice leaned forward with both elbows on the desk, his left fist clenched and covered by his right hand, his index finger extended up as if it were the front sight post of his m1911 pistol, as he placed Captain Woods squarely in his sights. "I also understand it's not for me to know what you guys are up to, direct orders from way, way up the chain. But having said that, this whole thing smells like something from the dark side. You may be some badass from Recon, but I also know a 'spook' when I see one.

"I'm on record with not being real comfortable dropping you guys in behind the line where you want to go, especially as 'hot' as this push has been. It's crawling with 'gooks'...VC and Regulars.

Regardless, I've got my orders, so you're set up with our best chopper jockey Lieutenant Clint Fogle, and he along with Park and Patterson here will get you to your desired infil. Patterson has the best SA on some of the target area from his recon patrol last week and can help with current enemy positions, but that is fluid. Park has been in and out of this area for years on ARVN black incursions and understands the terrain and the civilian locations. I got somebody tracking Fogle down on the flight line now, and he should be here shortly. When he shows up, the three of you can get with him on the latest updated maps outside to determine your LZ. Any questions?"

The other three exchanged glances at each other in a visual query of who might speak first.

Lieutenant Patterson didn't wait for the others, as he addressed Woods, "Are you able to provide any mission details? Might be nice if we know what we're getting ourselves into."

"Not a lot of specifics," replied Woods. "We're going in to recon the area for signs of any mass genocide, specifically through non-violent means. We will be looking for any intelligence we can gather on the possibility of Chinese military and scientific involvement in the vicinity. That's about all you're cleared for. However, I'll go one step further, and probably not a revelation to either of you, we have our suspicions that chemical or biological agents have potentially been introduced recently."

Park interjected in a remarkably impressive grasp of English, "Rumors have been persistent in the region for months that entire villages have disappeared. No bombings, no bullets, just wiped out and the bodies nowhere to be found."

"Those are some of the answers to questions we're looking for," Woods acknowledged. "We're not there to make enemy contact. In fact, we don't want anybody to know we're there." He turned to Colonel Justice, "And that's why we will only be three strong. We need to go in-country and stay as long as we can…undetected. I'm confident based on what I've read about both of these men's histories and capabilities," Woods nodded his head in the direction of Park and Patterson, "we can get those answers and get out safely."

A half hour later, Lt. Clint Fogle banked his "Huey" away from the O Rang airfield with a northwest heading, deeper into the Cambodian hills and jungle. He looked like he still belonged in high school chasing girls and footballs back in his hometown of Macon, Georgia, but he was easily one of the most talented and experienced of 1st Air Cav's pilots. In his 11 months of flying missions, he had recorded over 1,200 combat flight hours, received 19 Air Medals, and had a Distinguished Flying Cross to his credit. He had seen his fair share of hardship and lunacy over the last year, but he was surprised to be driving his three passengers this deep into the shit. He looked at his co-pilot, Warrant Officer Justin Jordan, gave a little wink as he reached down and jammed in an eight-track tape and pulled down his shaded visor.

In the back of the fuselage Specialist (SP4) James Garcia, safely restrained in the aircraft by a "monkey harness," sat holding an M60, belt-fed, 7.62mm machine gun supported by a tow strap spanning the cabin door. He looked up front and offered a thumbs up as the opening strains of the Rolling Stones' *Gimme Shelter* belted out over a set of dual speakers mounted behind Garcia's head.

Woods was seated on a canvas bench facing forward, staring at Patterson and Park on an opposing bench, hot and humid air whistling into the cabin around the pilots' doors. In the middle of the deepest hell hole in all of Southeast Asia, he couldn't help but chuckle to himself as he closed his eyes, the soothing cadence of the thumping rotor and the percussive voice of Mick Jagger belting into his ear. The comic relief soon gave way to a subtle chill down his spine, as he couldn't help but agree that a storm was threatening his life today. If he didn't get some shelter, some safety soon, somebody, maybe even he, might truly fade away.

* * * * *

Once they reached the coordinates the group had decided upon earlier at O Rang, there were a couple minutes of discussion between Fogle, Park and Woods as they chose a landing zone just over a small range of hilly terrain and in an open field adjacent to an "L" shaped tree line. It would provide enough cover they could get into quickly and out of sight. They also agreed to a touch and go.

Fogle signaled two minutes to the group with an ironic "peace sign" of index and middle finger. They pulled on their packs, replaced hats with helmets, and checked weapons. Following Woods' lead, they readied themselves on the edge of the open door with feet dangling below to the landing skids. Fogle's descent was fast and steep, then he abruptly pulled up with the tail end slightly down and he hit the knee-high grassy earth with barely a bump. All three jumped to the ground in order back to front, as Fogle accelerated up and away nose down, exiting as quickly as he entered.

Woods looked straight ahead to the edge of the jungle, approximately 100 meters in front of him, Patterson to his left and Park to the right. Cradling his rifle under the right arm, Woods raised his left arm and waved two fingers at Patterson to spread out and move forward. He looked right for Park to repeat the same directions, but Park was already moving double-time in an almost ninety degree heading from Woods to the other shorter wood line.

Within 50 meters of the heavy cover, Woods started to get a bad feeling, his sixth sense of trouble metering up in his brain. He looked to his right again and noticed Park had virtually evaporated out of sight. Woods stopped, knelt down, and inserted two fingers into his mouth and let out an ear shattering whistle at Patterson advancing on his left. He held up his left fist in the air as an order to halt, that was immediately obeyed. The air was still and quiet, the slight chirp of birds and the receding whomp, whomp, whomp of Fogle's Huey banking off to the southeast the only noise breaking the silence.

Woods lifted his M16 up to his shoulder and adjusted the parallax on the Colt scope retrofitted to the top carry handle. With the image sharpening, he scanned the thick growth of bushes and trees in front of him. Nothing out of the ordinary. On his second pass he froze as movement caught his eye. The slight back and forth of a heavily camouflaged NVA pith helmet, and then it stopped. Woods made a slight adjustment for range and then let loose a quick burst on the target. Branches and bushes splintered all around the area, and the helmet disappeared from sight.

All hell broke loose in reply. The entire tree line erupted in the distinctive rat-a-tat sounds of AK-47 fire, shredding the grass all around him. One round knocked him to his knees as it tore into his flak vest just above his left shoulder, tearing the top layer of flesh with it, and another grazed off his helmet as he fell to the ground. Shaking off the ding to his senses, he righted himself on one knee and reached around to the side of his pack, yanked away two smoke grenades, pulled the pins on both, and heaved them one right after the other toward the tree line. Green smoke billowed out, briefly obscuring them from the enemy's sight. That wouldn't last long. They had maybe 30 seconds to fall back in the field and try to get help from Fogle's weapons. Over the reduced barrage of gunfire, he heard two more smoke grenades thump and hiss to his left, which told him Patterson was still in the fight.

Almost two miles out, Chief Jordan spotted the smoke and saw tracer fire raking the field they just left. "LT, we got problems," he mic'd in over the noise of a new tape of the Animals Fogle had punched into the player for the ride home. "The LZ is lit up like the Fourth of July. Smoke is out."

"I'm on it," Fogle replied, banking back to the east on a heading that would take them straight down the line of trees still erupting with tracer and smoke.

Woods army-crawled toward Patterson's last position with bullets thudding into the ground and whizzing all around him. He let out another finger-to-mouth whistle to alert his position to Patterson, just before the two men nearly slammed into each other.

"What the fuck is this welcome party," yelled Patterson, blood all over the left side of his face, and a portion of his left ear dangling against his cheek.

"We need to crawl back as far away as we can! Park has the damn radio. Hopefully, Fogle will see the smoke. Let's move."

Patterson rolled onto his stomach, "Park bolted off in the other direction, and I never saw the son of a bitch come back."

As they reversed themselves on their bellies, they heard the chopper, and then the ground behind them exploded in a hail of 7.62mm rounds scorching the earth. Through it, emerged two NVA soldiers that materialized out of the grass and smoke, stumbling over Woods as they ran right into him, oblivious to his whereabouts. One landed headfirst, and before he could recover was hit with three rounds to the chest and neck by Patterson. The other stumbled briefly but turned in time to get several rounds off in the direction of Patterson, with an extended volley firing harmlessly in the air as Woods stitched across the man's waistline with a burst from his M16.

"Oh shit," screamed Woods, as he barrel rolled over towards Patterson, letting off more random bursts in the direction of the charging NVA.

Patterson was moaning and unable to move or utter any discernible words. One round had gone through the flak vest, which was worthless at point blank range, tearing into the right rib cage. Another went clean through the right shoulder, and a third bullet had torn off the right cheek.

After entering the fray on an 80-knot dive, and the 'gooks' pouring out of the tree line in pursuit of Woods and Patterson, Lieutenant Foglesprayed the field in front of their position with dual automatic M60 machine guns, one of two signature weapon systems of the Iroquois' configuration. After cutting up the majority of the advancing enemy, Fogle pulled up and banked 90 degrees right, hovering about 20 meters off the ground and facing the jungle about 50 meters away.

"RPG 12 o'clock dead ahead," Chief Jordan screamed out, as a Soviet made RPG-2 rocket propelled grenade streaked right at them and sailed off less than ten feet left of the cockpit as Fogle slid their bird to the right. Seemingly oblivious to the incoming fire pinging off the metal hull of the helicopter, Specialist Garcia was busy picking off the retreating soldiers still in the field with the door gun. Fogle sighted and triggered off both sides of the Iroquois' dual XM 157 rocket launchers. As a full volley of 2.75" rockets streaked forward to his target, Fogle hammered the auto M60s again, adding to the conflagration as the entire tree line detonated, and was systematically shredded from the blast of rockets and deafening drone of automatic gunfire.

Woods wasted no time in throwing out the last two of his smoke grenades while the heat was being poured out from Fogle's gunship. He got to one knee, pulled Patterson up and over his shoulder and threw all caution to the wind as he stood and sprinted toward the chopper suspended in midair, spewing out fire like a mad dragon.

Jordan pointed off to Fogle's left hand side, as Woods, with Patterson slumped over him, broke through the smoke and into the clear.

"I got him JJ," Fogle barked into his mic and yawed the chopper sideways with Garcia's side facing the fire. "Keep pouring it on Jamie, we're out of here in ten seconds," Fogle sat the skids down hard to the ground. Specialist Garcia was still laying down a withering cover fire, as Chief Jordan climbed out of his seat and reached the open side door the same time Woods did. Jordan grabbed at Patterson as Woods propelled him into the chopper and onto the floor, bullets popping off the interior and one slamming into Jordan's right hand, mercifully saving one more round from piercing Patterson's blood-soaked torso.

Woods was barely in the door as Fogle pulled up and away from the expanding enemy fire, Garcia grabbing him by the back of the vest and yanking him onto the fuselage floor next to a battered Patterson and an irate Jordan screaming obscenities at his mangled hand. Green smoke cylconed around them as the chopper ascended to safety.

As they reached a cruising altitude out of range of the gunfire, Fogle punched his speed to 200 knots on a southeast heading and radioed in to the 45th Surgical Hospital at Tay Ninh to alert they were in route and had wounded. He did the math in his head…they were 15-20 minutes out. As Jordan climbed back into the co-pilot seat and wrapped his hand with a loose tee shirt, Fogle looked behind him at the carnage and estimated Patterson didn't look like he had 15-20 minutes.

Garcia was out of his harness, had broken open the medical kit, and was slipping and sliding all over the place as blood and brass casings mixed together on the floor. He handed two compress pads to Woods, who was still seated on the floor cradling Patterson between his legs and arms. Woods placed each of the pads on the shoulder and torso wounds and applied pressure with both of his hands, while Garcia wrapped Patterson's head with the remaining pads and gauze.

Garcia sat back on the bench and stared out on the now peaceful green canopy passing below them. *How can this place be such a fucking nightmare?*

Woods leaned back against the other bench and listened to the casings roll back and forth melodically as he maintained as much pressure as he could on Patterson's wounds, his life bleeding out on the floor in front of him. *Where in the hell was Park...where did that son of a bitch go?* In the background, he realized the 8-track was still playing, Eric Burdon and the Animals. He laid his head back and exhaled audibly, mimicking the song in his own mind, *I gotta get out of this place, if it's the last damn thing I ever do.*

* * * * *

General Huang finished his story, and the abrupt silence in the room shook Woods out of his reflections and back to his present circumstance. He sighed and tilted his head slightly, staring blankly at the Luxardo cherry swimming in the remaining bourbon, vermouth and bitters mix as if it was some crystal ball about to give forth answers to questions unresolved. "That's a story I remember well, General. All too well. However, that's also a story that has no resolution...at least not a good one as I recall."

"I knew you would remember," replied Huang, "but I thought it worth reciting, as you are wrong about the ending...it dovetails into what your notable commentator Paul Harvey famously used to ponder... 'the rest of the story'."

Woods set his glass down and eyed Huang with a look of skepticism.

Huang continued, "I was an intelligence officer in the People's Liberation Army, working covertly and in conjunction with the

NVA and Khmer Rouge on a biological weapons program." He paused to take a sip of his drink and gather his thoughts.

"In early 1968, we uncovered some obscure information that led us to the awareness of a young Korean teenager who had some involvement with the Japanese Unit 731 during their occupation of our country in World War II. For the sake of his own survival, the boy was forced to collaborate with and assist a very nasty Japanese doctor by the name of General Daichi Arakawa. I would surmise his life was most likely contingent on him also being Arakawa's sex toy.

"Arakawa was one of the leading architects of Japan's Unit 731 Biological Field Testing, and responsible for the deaths of thousands of local Chinese from the Manchuria region. In some cases, entire villages had been exterminated at his personal direction. Arakawa was executed in the Pingfang District in July of 1945 as he was attempting to escape the advancing allied armies converging on his position. It was unclear whether he was killed by your American soldiers or by one of our NRA officers, but his death was confirmed, and the young boy was turned over to a company of U.S. Army Rangers operating in the area. Arakawa was the personification of evil and I'm quite sure he resides in the same hell as his peer of that time, Josef Mengele. We believed all of the General's hideous secrets died with him, but there were always some lingering doubts.

"At some point an old case file on Arakawa came to the attention of our intelligence analysts with the Central Investigation Department in the early 1960's. They worked to confirm the Korean boy's identity and after conducting an exhaustive search, we were able to locate him, now a Doctor of Biology at Kim Il Sung University in Pyongyang. With the help of the DPRK, we surreptitiously removed him and his family to mainland China.

"After interrogating him, we were able to learn the depth of his knowledge, and with the help of his wife and daughter in our custody, convince him to lend us his expertise. We began utilizing him late in 1969 in experiments with a virus strain he had developed from his knowledge of working with the infamous Arakawa many years ago during his incarceration in Manchuria. I, along with a small PLA unit assisting me, was tasked to provide security to our biological team assisting him with introducing this man-made, natural viral strain into remote villages in central Cambodia, determining the efficacy of the virus, along with antidotes and therapeutic applications with the ability to treat and neutralize its effectiveness.

"We were several months into the testing and became aware of the United States Army's knowledge and interest in activity that was taking place in our area of operation and were specifically alerted to your suspicions and operational actions through an informant who had a vested interest in not only the program, but in the Korean scientist running it."

"Park," muttered Woods.

"Yes, Mr. Woods, Captain Dae-Ho Park. He had been working with us for about a year. He was an easy convert once we were able to initiate contact. The Korean scientist running the program was his father, Dae-Hun Park.

"After he hastily provided us with a general understanding of your mission, we arranged the ambush of your landing party with the NVA, and the defection of Captain Park to our scientific exercise. Obviously, we failed in our attempt to kill you and your comrade, but Park was able to escape to us without further incident. We assumed he would go on to be listed as MIA and forgotten. I would be remiss if I didn't offer congratulations to you on your miraculous escape." Huang raised his glass in salute, to which Woods returned an insincere nod.

"Our team and Park were realizing significant results with introducing the virus, eliminating entire groups of exposed and infected people, complete villages were eradicated in whole. However, the lethality of the virus and the inability to effectively create any type of antidote or medical treatment and cures, became troubling. It was an unpleasant, rapid death once exposed, usually inside of a few days. If it got outside of our control, we could have potentially created a genocidal pandemic that we would not have been able to stop.

"The whole thing was sickening and quite insidious. Moreover, it was incredibly dangerous. It was beginning to scare even me. That was enough for me to communicate to the Central Commission that we shut down the program and cease any further operational activity. After returning to testify in front of them and present my findings and assessment, they agreed. Furthermore, because of his proprietary knowledge of the virus and its structural composition, we were instructed to eliminate Park and his son. We were successful with the father, but Captain Park proved much more resourceful. Before we could terminate him, he escaped into the countryside after killing several of my soldiers."

Woods grabbed the shaker from the table, gave it a brief back and forth and poured the last of the ration into Huang's glass and then his own. He lifted open the humidor on the coffee table and pulled out two Oliva Connecticut Reserves. Clipping both and lighting one for himself, he passed the other cigar and lighter to Huang, who repeated the process.

"Thank you, Director," Huang said through a blue haze of smoke.

"I haven't been called Director in a while. Slight clarification for you...Deputy Director."

"Your tenure as Deputy Director of the Defense Intelligence Agency and head of its Clandestine Services Organization was well documented and well respected in our country, as well as by me personally. We have crossed paths many times over the years, all experiences that were quite formidable."

"Likewise, General," Woods exhaled a small cloud above his head. "It's been a compelling story so far, and one I recollect rather unfavorably, so where are we going with this history lesson?"

"History has a tendency to repeat itself Mr. Woods, and what transpired in Cambodia over 40 years ago appears to have risen from the ashes."

Woods shifted uneasily in his chair. "You have my attention, General."

"As you know, China has a long-standing relationship with the Islamic Republic of Iran. More like a mutual arrangement. As you are probably also aware, they provide us large amounts of their oil, and in return we pay them for it…and we also provide some other intangibles. Most notably, and to most of the world anonymously, we offer nuclear expertise to their fledgling nuclear program.

"With our access to some of Iran's top scientific programs and personnel, we have very well-placed assets that actively gather intelligence to help us in our relationship. It has come to our attention that Iran has biological programs they are developing in conjunction with their nuclear intentions, but they have allowed the nuclear program to dominate the news cycle in order to deflect any attention on the others. Recently we have gleaned information about another program, biological in nature, that is relatively new and, so far, very much 'top secret.' A Korean scientist is working on a project under deep cover, and we were able to secure a number of photographs of the person in question."

Woods was now upright, leaning forward on the front edge of his chair, right hand rubbing at his chin.

"You may know where this is going?" continued Huang.

"A pretty good idea."

"I don't subscribe to coincidences, and my curiosity got the best of me. I had photos of both Parks, father and son, from our Cambodian files. I was curious, so I processed Dae-Ho Park's photo with the mystery man through our facial recognition software...."

"A match." Woods finished Huang's thought.

"It's him," Huang nodded. "I'm convinced he is working in concert with the Iranians on the same virus."

"Okay, let's say it's him, and he is involved...why are you here? Why don't you take care of this again, like Cambodia, but don't miss this time?"

"Ah, Mr. Woods, if it were only that easy. Our country is far too dependent on the energy Iran provides to us, and our government would never jeopardize that relationship with a sanctioned, covert action on Iranian soil. My government has turned a blind eye to Iran's biological programs and has no knowledge of Park's existence or cooperation. Frankly Mr. Woods, just between us old adversaries, they also have no knowledge that I am here visiting you."

"Well then, let's try this again...why are you here?"

"I'm here, Mr. Woods, because I need your help. What the Iranians are doing in conjunction with Park's assistance is cataclysmic. I've witnessed it firsthand, and I can honestly say I'm disgusted by our participation...my participation before, and I won't make the same mistake twice. Park and his virus must be eliminated quickly before it can ever be introduced.

"The consequences could be devastating. My only hope is that Park, like his father, is maintaining a proprietary control of the makeup and structure of this virus. It must, and I can't stress this enough, it must have a treatment protocol, therapeutics, vaccine, or an antidote, some sort of remedy before it is activated into the population. That's what I hope Park is involved in currently. If he's smart, he will control the structural composition because his life would be worthless if the Iranians were to gain an understanding of the makeup."

"General, you're making this out to be Armageddon, end-of-the-world stuff. I was made aware of the genocidal nature of whatever biological agents were being introduced back in Cambodia, but they didn't express the level of concern you're indicating," said Woods, as he made his way over to the bar again, a trail of smoke following him. He helped himself to another water and offered the same to Huang, who declined.

"Your intelligence gathering was obviously ill-informed. It's far worse than you can imagine." Huang dropped a manila envelope onto the ottoman as Woods returned. "The notes from the original testing in Cambodia are detailed in there. Simply put, this Filoviridae virus is a highly contagious, viral hemorrhagic fever. Its transmission is not only through bodily contact, but airborne as well. In this particular virus, respiratory contact with an infected person is highly lethal, and as a weapon of mass destruction, it can be used in aerosol dissemination. If that's not enough to frighten you, this should. The time from exposure to death is 72 hours or less. Unhealthy victims were known to die in 24-36 hours. And I presume you're familiar with the symptoms of hemorrhagic fever."

"My understanding is it's not pleasant," answered Woods.

"Correct, but actually more like horrible. Once contracted, a severe fever develops within several hours, along with muscle aches, fatigue, dizziness, and loss of strength. White blood cell and platelet counts decrease rapidly. Reduced blood clotting ability leads to bleeding under the skin, in internal organs, and eventually from orifices like the mouth, nose, eyes, and throat. It progresses to shock, nervous system malfunction, seizures, delirium, comas, and finally into renal failure."

"Not pleasant."

"Not pleasant at all, Mr. Woods."

"So, General, one last time, Why…Are…You…Here?"

"To ask for your help, Director Woods," implored Huang. "I'm asking you and your government to take Park out."

"You realize I've been retired for nearly three years, General. I don't do this shit anymore."

"You underestimate yourself, Director. You still have the contacts, particularly in the intelligence communities. You have the ear of a number of current government officials at the highest level. If you recognize the threat, which I'm sure you do, you can help. If not you directly, you can muster the assets necessary to pull it off," Huang sighed heavily and emptied his glass in one last gulp, "and I will help you."

Chapter 1

Washington D.C.

The Delta Boeing 717 touched down in a light rain at Reagan National just before noon, and after a quick taxi to the gate, Jake Woods departed through the jetway into the terminal, eventually making his way to the main ground transportation area. A young lieutenant approached him from the bank of glass exit doors and saluted. "General Woods, I'm Lieutenant Anderson, I'll take you to the DDIA sir. Any checked bags?"

"Thank you, Lieutenant, no this is it," Woods gestured to his leather duffle on his shoulder. "I may be long in the tooth Anderson, but I think I can handle this myself."

They climbed into the military sedan double-parked just outside the main terminal building and headed for the airport exit and the thirty-minute trip to Joint Base Anacostia-Boling. Through the misty drizzle, Woods nostalgically looked over the Potomac at the 900-acre military installation, home to the Defense Intelligence Agency main headquarter facility, ironically just two miles directly across the Potomac from the airport but 13 miles on a circuitous route up toward the National Mall and then back south.

* * * * *

Woods was escorted into the office of the Director of DIA and the door closed behind him.

"Good God Jake it's good to see you."

"You too, Mike, it's been a while." Woods walked toward the large Kneehole wood desk, as the DDIA moved from behind it to greet Woods with a two-handed handshake and a hug.

"It's good to see you. You look great, retirement seems to fit you."

"You're headed there soon, Mike. It will be good for you as well," as Woods sat in the offered leather chair.

"So, you were pretty coy over the phone…what's up with the personal visit?"

Woods waved his right hand into the air, "Are we private here, anybody listening in?"

"The office is secure, just you and me, what's up?"

Woods leaned toward the desk, "I have a story to tell you." He recited it from the beginning, without interruption, from 1945 to today.

* * * * *

"Whoa!" the DDIA leaned back in his chair and elevated both of his feet onto the antique desktop. "That is quite a story…one that leaves us in a bit of a quandary."

"I would agree, Mike. Where do we go with this? It's clearly a threat, a big-time threat."

"Definitely a threat and will need some attention…highest level. I'll have to run it over to the DNI, and if James agrees, we can share it with NSA and take it on up to POTUS. Just a warning Jake, this Admin is skittish when it comes to Iran, and if you haven't noticed we have an election coming up. Don't know why, but POTUS and his team think they can negotiate with these idiots. The

Mullahs are crazy-ass liars, and this shit you've told me…well, let's put it this way, it wouldn't shock me if this stuff is sanctioned from the top."

Woods dropped a large manila envelope onto the desk, "It's all in there, Mike. I thought you'd need a report with all the details I just recounted." He anticipated the DDIA's need to push this up to the Director of National Intelligence, before it could get clearance from the National Security Advisor and the President himself. "You need to impress upon our folks that this is bad stuff. I'm not sure how they would use it, but for starters, it wouldn't take much to turn Israel into a wasteland without the nuclear Armageddon everybody is afraid of. If you need me to detail this personally up the chain, I would be happy to give them my two cents worth!"

It was clear the DDIA was onboard with the gravity of the situation. "I'm with you Jake and agree, I'm just telling you that when it gets to the White House, any green light to action will be a hard sell. I'll give it my best shot."

"I know you will Mike." Woods rose to leave, "I'm staying at the Mayflower if you need me. I'm not leaving until I hear what they say."

The DDIA touched his phone, "Elaine, will you please get me the DNI on the phone, tell the office it's urgent, and patch me through if necessary."

"Yes, sir," came the intercom reply, "give me a few minutes."

Woods waved off the DDIA as he started out from behind his desk, "I'll let myself out. You take care of talking to DNI." Reaching the door, he turned back to his old friend who was already picking up the phone in response to Elaine's response and instructions, "Good luck, and keep me posted."

Chapter 2

Washington D.C., the following evening

The dining room at The Palm was busy as usual. The bar was even busier, but it was a short two blocks walk north on Connecticut from the Mayflower, and Woods had arrived early enough to get a prime bar stool along the iconic bar. His wool Camel Hair sport coat protected an empty companion stool, much to the chagrin of several patrons bellying up to the well-worn mahogany fixture.

He was enjoying his second Makers Mark Manhattan and making some light small talk with a pretty female staffer for a Congressman from Colorado, when he spotted the guest he had been waiting for. Politely excusing himself from the conversation, he stepped to the corner of the bar and gave a two-fingered wave at his quarry, who reciprocated an acknowledgement and proceeded to work his way through the crowd congregating at the entrance into the bar area.

Woods waited until a few feet separated the two, and he lunged forward and gave a big hug to his son, Major Matthew Woods.

"Hey Dad, how's it goin'?"

"It's going good, how are you?" as Woods released his son and pushed him back arm's length so he could admire the handsome young man decked out in his starched Army Service Uniform, complete with newly adorned oak leaves.

"All good Dad. Happy to be out and looking forward to a big steak." Matt Woods followed his father over to the two stools. At six feet and two inches, lean and muscular, his dark hair and complexion were the spitting image of his mother. At 31 years of age, his youthful looks belied his active combat history as a UH-60 Blackhawk pilot in the 1st Battalion, 160th Special Operations Aviation Regiment based in Ft. Campbell, Kentucky. He and several other company commanders were on a goodwill visit to Walter Reed Hospital as part of a Wounded Warriors initiative and was genuinely shocked and delighted when he had heard from his father by phone on a concurrent visit to DC.

"A big juicy steak sounded good to me too. Glad you could get away." The young staffer had suddenly lost all interest in the elder Woods and was now eyeing the young Captain as if he were on the menu.

"How's Mom?" He politely nodded at the young woman surveying him from over his father's shoulder and gave a casual wave of his index finger to the bartender who was already moving in his direction. "I'll have one of those also," pointing at his Dad's chestnut colored cocktail.

"She's wonderful. She took the opportunity to spend some time with your Aunt Ruth at the condo while I'm visiting here. She sends her love. You look good son; the promotion fits you well. Enjoy your cocktail for a few, our reservation isn't for another 20 minutes."

Both spent the next 30 minutes catching up while battling off the advances of Brook the staffer and her newly arrived and even more attractive friend Alexa. They were able to appease the two with a promise to return to the bar after dinner, Woods knowing full well he would be headed to bed, Matt weighing his options.

* * * * *

Comfortably ensconced in one of the leather benched booths, they finished off two medium rare filets with a bottle of Silver Oak Cabernet and thoroughly enjoyed father-son conversation from nearly five months of not having laid eyes on each other. Matt ordered a single key lime pie dessert with two forks, satisfying the late-night sweet tooth gene they both shared.

"So, what are you really here for Dad?" inquired Matt. "You were pretty vague over the phone."

Woods sighed and began to recall the story he had told the previous day at the Defense Department, a story that he never had ever spoken to anyone in his family before. The dessert was gone, along with two glasses of Fonseca port by the time Woods had finished.

"Wow," exhaled Matt, "that's got the making of some serious shit, if they ever have the ability to use something like that. In that crazy sand pit, they could introduce it, and it's possible you'd never be able to prove it originated with them."

"Precisely! I was thinking the same damn thing. That's why it's critical for the President to do something." Woods looked away and pondered that statement.

"You don't think they will," Matt interrupted his thoughts.

"No, I don't think they will. This administration has demonstrated itself over and over again to be overly cautious and skittish when it comes to confrontation. I'm holding out a sliver of hope they will do the right thing, step up to the plate, and figure out how to mount an effort against this. The problem is it looks like an equally soft admin is about to be elected."

"Well, you left it in good hands with Mike, he'll know how to run with it," Matt encouraged him. "They can't just ignore it."

"I'm hoping you're correct, but you know me...the old officer in me says what are the contingencies? What happens if we do nothing and they get their hands on something like this? Something the world has never seen before." Woods' words trailed off as the two of them sat in silence staring at two empty glasses of port.

Chapter 3

Office of the Director of National Intelligence, McLean, VA

The adjoining SCIF or Sensitive Compartmented Information Facility, designed as a secure room in which classified information could be briefed and discussed, sat next to the main office of the Director of National Intelligence. It currently was empty except for Woods and the DDIA. Both sat in a stunned silence, the dissenting results of their just completed meeting with the DNI, National Security Advisor and Vice Chairman of the Joint Chiefs of Staff, barely having had time to sink in.

Woods had arrived at the Liberty Crossing Intelligence Campus with a mixture of excitement and optimism after the call to his room at the Mayflower earlier that morning. The conversation was short but requested his presence at a meeting of the three top Intelligence officials reporting directly to the President, indicating to Woods that his concerns had reached the office of POTUS himself. All of this within 24 hours of his conversation with DDIA, it obviously touched a nerve somewhere.

Unfortunately, the nerve must have belonged to someone other than the DNI, NSA, JCS, and the President because he and the DDIA sat dejectedly after a forty-minute question and answer session, seemingly orchestrated more for show, instead of a substantive threat assessment. The "intelligence" in the meeting seemed to have never arrived with the high-level personnel. It was clear to Woods after the final judgement came down that the answer had already been reached earlier and this was nothing more than a meeting of appeasement. Threat acknowledged, thanks for bringing it to our attention.

Woods looked at an equally puzzled DDIA, "Seriously, they're worried about upsetting ongoing nuclear negotiations with the Iranian government? What the fuck, Mike, we seem to be damn near to capitulating on the hard line when it comes to their nuclear ambitions, so are we simply going to concede the biological discussion as well? What do we think we're going to accomplish negotiating with these idiots anyway? Does this administration honestly believe we can trust these people? We're talking about the ability to introduce an unknown, undocumented biological Armageddon onto the world," Woods ranted angrily, "And with something like this, they can potentially pull it off without anybody being able to tie it back to them. What in God's name does it take to convince our own people that these nut jobs will do almost anything to accomplish their goal of a new Muslim Empire?"

The DDIA shuffled in his seat, crossed his arms, and shook his head back and forth in his own display of disbelief, but agreeing in sentiment to Woods' outburst. "You're preaching to the choir, Jake."

Woods wasn't finished. "The sooner we understand there is no real government control in Iran, it's a religious fiefdom, the sooner we don't negotiate squat with them. The radical mullahs are the control, and they are hell-bent on creating a new Persian order, a Shia Hegemony, with them at the top. Hell, they already control a large swath of the region through proxies in Yemen, Syria, and Lebanon, and they're making massive inroads into Iraq now that they're dominated by a Shia government. We don't seem to give a shit!"

"You get much louder Jake and everyone who left a few minutes ago will probably hear you in the parking lot."

"I sure as hell hope they do!" Woods yelled at the metal security door still open to the hallway from where everyone had departed.

"I'm not sure where we go from here, Jake. I'm not finished yet either. I may be out of office shortly, but I can damn sure raise some stink in the meantime. The only problem I do see is if we go public with what we know, the crazy bastards will take this program even further underground than it already is and deny everything. We have no hard evidence and it would be another case of WMDs in Iraq, we know they had it, we just couldn't find it and prove it."

Before Woods could reply, a young staffer knocked on the open door as he entered the room. "Your car is ready for you gentlemen; I'll be happy to escort you down to the lobby."

"Well, Jake, I would say that is our encouragement to pack our things and go. My guess is your loud opining may have touched a nerve."

Woods laughed at the irony, as he stood to follow the young man out. *Finally touched somebody's nerve, just not the one I was hoping for.*

* * * * *

The ride back to the Mayflower was mostly in silence. The two men rode together in the back of the black, armor plated Suburban, each staring out opposite windows at the overcast coated landscape of northern Virginia.

As the Custis Memorial Parkway gave way to the Theodore Roosevelt Memorial Bridge leading into downtown DC, the quiet was broken by the chirping of the DDIA's personal cell phone. There was no incoming number or identification of any kind displayed on the screen, and with a disapproving glare he declined the call, sending it to voicemail. Ten seconds later it rang again, same absence of caller detail, and he looked questioningly at Woods who was staring back at him. He swiped the face and answered.

The call lasted one minute and fifty-eight seconds and ended with his reply to the one-sided conversation, "Yes sir. Understood."

He looked at Woods and a smile broke out on his face, "You're not going to believe this."

"Try me, I feel like I've seen it all today," replied Woods.

"That was the DNI. He says he and the Joint Chief spent a very unproductive meeting at the White House last night. They disagree with the decision, and he says he couldn't agree more with the loud speech you gave in the open SCIF after they left. He said something about the walls being soundproof, but not the hallway. He agrees with our assessment that something needs to be done. Unfortunately, it's nothing either of them can directly or even indirectly sanction. However, he is willing to put us in touch with someone who can help, if we are willing to, as he put it, 'tackle the issue head-on. Totally off the books…as black as it gets'."

"I'll be damned, my faith is somewhat restored."

Chapter 4

Nayband Wildlife Sanctuary, South Khorasan, Iran

The very uncomfortable heat of the day had given way to a cooling dusk breeze. Dae-Ho Park emerged from the obscure stone building constructed into the craggy hillside of an isolated outcropping of mountains situated in the middle of an open plain in northeastern Iran. He gazed out onto a desolate, barren parcel of earth guarded by the Nayband mountain range to the northwest, the Hazaran massif due west, the Jebal Barez range to the south, and sand and scrub surrounding all the immediate other points of the compass.

The Nayband Wildlife Sanctuary is the largest of all the wildlife sanctuaries in the Islamic Republic of Iran. Situated among the rough eastern landscape of the second largest nation in the Middle East, it is made up of mountains, and hilly sand-filled desert plains, with an abundance of animal species and scattered pockets of human civilization in small towns and remote villages.

Park could hear the muted thump of the rotors emanating from the inbound helicopter taxi come to retrieve him from the isolated test lab well hidden behind the dilapidated building in his shadow. In reality, the modern biochemical lab was located not only behind but below his feet as well, in a two story, 700 square meter concrete bunker. The building, carved out of an abandoned mining site, was just window dressing, a perfect disguise to the evils that were being concocted within.

Park stood in the protection of the building as the Italian made Augusta-Bell AB 212 landed on the opposite side of the single-story structure, blowing dust and dirt into a mini sand storm that dissipated as the Pratt & Whitney Canada PT6T engines decelerated to a slow whirl. Park was joined by two Iranian officers, both decked out in full dress uniform pompously adorned with ribbons and medals as they exited the single entrance door. They were followed by another middle-aged man of Middle Eastern descent, who casually threw his Saville Row suit jacket over his shoulder as his sweaty white dress shirt, sleeves rolled up, collected the flying dust like metal shavings to a magnet.

The rotors crept to a slow crawl, enough to allow them all to climb into their transport with a minimal amount of prop wash. As they strapped in, the engines accelerated to lift speed as the chopper rose from the lunar-like surface and banked to the south en route to a small estate outside the city of Ravar, about 140 kilometers away in the Kerman Province.

Inside the loud passenger quarters of the AB 212, Dae-Ho Park reflected on another unsuccessful day working to develop a vaccine or a treatment protocol for one of the greatest biological threats the world had thankfully never seen. His companions were both unimpressed and furious with the progress of Park's mission to make sure, if the cataclysmic release of the virus ever occurred, there would be a workable antiviral treatment to contain the damage and a corrective mechanism developed to either prevent the onset or reverse the epidemic spread of the deadly bio-weapon.

Park had been actively testing options for nearly four months and was keenly aware of what it took to control and prevent the virus. His father had been clear in the antidotal composition and regimen. However, he was stalling for time and refused to create mass quantities of the virus until he allowed for the discovery of a successful prescription for containment and prevention. He knew the consequences of not having them in place, before the controlling powers proceeded with any type of deliverance, were horrendous.

The whole process of testing was deeply disturbing for Park, as the sadistic Iranian officials responsible for establishing the project had been delivering a steady stream of live human test subjects, all suffering very horrific deaths. Twenty more pathetic prisoners had been delivered to the facility the previous day, and the majority, if not all of them, would be dead within the week.

Park had recently been forced to concede some of the successful test outcomes they had achieved so far, but only as a show of some progress toward a preventive vaccine and antidote. As the managing director for the entire testing program, he was able to control and make sure from the beginning that every one of the different antiviral methods and controls they were pursuing up until the last few days had all, eventually, been dead ends. However, his scientific filibustering to slow the process had reached its end. Tomorrow, he would be starting afresh on a new and very positive direction for a preventive treatment that would ultimately lead to a simultaneous final phase testing on the one promising vaccine compound. The end result would be a 100 percent success.

Park couldn't help but wonder when he achieved that success, the incredible carnage that was about to take place. He had been told very little of the eventual use of the biological agent, but his imagination was running rampant. The obvious importance of their objective and the delay in implementing it was presenting a threatening backdrop to Park's work, and he had surmised this was not going to be just another product added to a biological stockpile for deterrent or defensive purposes, or even as a bargaining tool in the world of WMDs. He had an innate sense this was being developed from the beginning for use as an offensive weapon. Regardless of the financial windfall they were bestowing upon him for his services, Park remained at the mercy of the Iranians and Revolutionary Guards Commander Nasser Togyani specifically, but his conscience and the immorality of his actions were weighing heavily on him and had him growing restless about continuing his efforts. Consequently, and disregarding the fear he realized for his own safety, he finally mustered the courage to offer a threat of his own, "Provide me with the ultimate motive for having this virus, or I stop what I'm doing!"

One of his accompanying passengers, or handlers as he preferred to view them, had reluctantly agreed. Commander Togyani had finally divulged his intention, over dinner this evening, to provide him, and the others currently onboard the helicopter with the end game... the intentions of how the virus would be utilized.

As the helicopter descended to a large walled courtyard adjacent to the multi-story stone and stucco villa, Park couldn't help believe tonight's dinner would be enlightening.

Chapter 5

Washington D.C.

Woods had checked out early from his room at the Mayflower so he would have several hours of leeway before his returning flight to Ft. Myers, Florida at 16:35. The uncertainty of the immediate future, the knowledge of what was at stake, and the uneasiness of how to initiate the undertaking at hand weighed heavily on him.

He had been looking forward to catching up with his wife Ann in Naples and knocking off the rust from his golf game. It had been almost two weeks away from his better half and over a month since he had seen his clubs. That grand hope appeared fleeting, as the mixed sense of guilt and anxiety of being sucked back into the "great game" besieged him. In spite of the emotional roller coaster and formidable task at hand, the phone call he received last night certainly seemed worth a few hours of diversion before heading south.

He left his bags at the concierge and requested a taxi to pick him up at 3:00. He handed a ten-dollar bill to the young man behind the stand and wandered down the long ornate Grand Promenade to the nearly empty Edgar Bar and planted himself in one of the totally empty rows of barstools. He ordered a Bloody Mary and settled in with ESPN SportsCenter and an overly attentive but highly attractive female bartender with an opinion about all things Washington Redskins.

The phone call from the man who identified himself as Winston Cromer came late the previous evening, and was brief. Cromer alluded to an inquiry he received from mutual friends of both him and Woods, friends in high places. They suggested that it might be mutually beneficial if the two of them got together. It was by happenstance that Cromer was in town for a meeting of his own and thought it would be a great opportunity for them to meet face-to-face before both flew away to parts unknown.

A quick Google search last night on Woods' iPad revealed this Winston Cromer as a 63-year-old American hedge fund manager and founder of WRD Capital, based in Danbury, CT. His net worth was estimated to be $13.8 billion as of 2014, ranking him two spots outside the Forbes 100 richest men in the world. The only son of a middle-class family from Richmond, VA, Cromer was a graduate of the Wharton School and spent nearly 20 years on Wall Street as a trader and portfolio manager. In 1994, he started WRD with $15 million of his own money, and today his firm managed nearly $20 billion in equity. Woods couldn't help but be impressed, but what would Cromer want with Woods. As his second drink arrived, so did a sleek black Mercedes-Maybach S600 sedan outside the Mayflower front entrance.

The right rear passenger door popped open as the valet hurried over to meet the door handle at the same time the tall, silver haired man exited the vehicle unassisted. The casual attire, of immaculate quality, complemented the confident stride of the man as he walked directly to the front door, nodding at the valet and indicating his intent to only be there for a short period of time. The driver signaled the valet over to the window, tipping him handsomely. The driver clearly indicated his intent to double park right where he was and welcomed the reaction of the valet as he directed him to the curb.

Winston Cromer entered the Mayflower hotel and strode up to the concierge desk and inquired about the location of the Edgar Bar. The young man stepped out from behind and escorted Cromer several steps down to the hall and pointed to the double door entrance further down and to the right. He suggested that Mr. Woods was in the bar waiting for him. Cromer palmed a $20 bill into the young man's hand and headed in the direction he indicated.

After a handshake and courteous introduction, both men slipped into a secluded corner booth, with instructions to the bartender to leave them alone until further notified.

Before Woods could begin the process of satisfying his curiosity, Cromer jumpstarted the conversation, "I'm sure you have lots of questions for me. Who am I? Why did I contact you? What do I want? Blah, blah, blah. However, if you don't mind, let me see if I can't give you a quick summary of answers and intentions, and then you can ask me anything you want. Work for you?"

Woods nodded, "Fire away."

"I'm assuming you have already done your homework and have a short bio on Winston Cromer, so I won't bore you with my background, other than to tell you I believe deeply in America and her long-term future.

"Over the years, I have developed some very important and influential friends in the conservative realm of politics and our military. Several of those friends reached out to me and gave me a synopsis of a theoretical situation involving a highly respected and decorated patriot, who is interested in the well-being and continued safety of our country. For reasons that man is most certainly aware of, those same friends are constrained in their direct support and understandably feeling helpless in their ability to further his cause. I, on the other hand, am not. Additionally, I have the financial and material resources to offer unlimited support to that cause. How am I doing so far?"

Woods was having a hard time suppressing the smile on his face at the presentation Cromer was offering. "You're doing very well, please continue."

"Thank you," Cromer nodded approvingly. "I, too, am a patriot Mr. Woods."

"Call me Jake please."

Cromer nodded again in acknowledgement, "Jake, simply put I want to help. I've been told enough to understand the issues you have brought to my friends' attentions and the consequences that are at stake. I have been provided a very thorough portrait of who you are, your background, the commitment and service you've given to this country, and to say I'm very impressed would be an understatement. I am honored to offer my assistance and would be grateful if you would give me the opportunity to help you tackle," Cromer hesitated in thought, "this most delicate mission, if you will."

"I'm impressed with the offer, and I appreciate your patriotism, but there has to be something else I'm missing? What I'm talking about tackling, if I indeed agree to take this undertaking on, has enormous risks. This isn't a stock or a company that can be invested in, bought, sold, broken up for profit. This is life and death. This has incredible world-wide implications. If this blows up, there are chances you will go down with the ship. You have nothing to gain and lots and lots to lose. My biggest question is why?"

"I hate terrorists. I abhor terrorists. I despise terrorists. Iran is the biggest sponsor of terror in the world," Cromer paused to compose himself, "and terrorists took both the loves of my life. My wife and daughter were killed in the 7/7 London bombings in 2005, killed by an Islamist terrorist who detonated himself on the number 30 double decker bus in Tavistock Square. I don't give a shit about the consequences to me. I just want to get even. I want justice for them," Cromer averted his eyes toward the ceiling, "and this is the type of help that I can offer, to help fight back."

Woods sighed deeply, "That's a pretty good why. I could definitely use the help you're offering, and I would also be honored to accept it from you."

"I'm grateful Jake. Thanks!" Cromer stood and offered his hand, which was accepted without hesitation in a handshake by Woods, who also received a credit card in the exchange. "My good friends call me Cromes. Please call me Cromes."

"Okay Cromes, welcome aboard. For the record, there's no question I accept the errand at hand. This is critical, too significant and far-reaching to even consider saying no."

"Agreed!" Cromer turned to leave, "By the way this isn't my first rodeo with the same friends. That card gives you access to eight figures of resources. There's more where that comes from, but I do appreciate you operating in a more efficient manner than our government does. I also have a Gulfstream G550 that will be made available to you 24/7. I have your cell phone and email address, so I'll be in touch."

"Thanks." Woods offered a thumbs-up and caught up with Cromer as they exited the bar and headed down the hallway, "Cromes, as someone once said, I think this is the beginning of a beautiful friendship."

Chapter 6

Naples, FL

The warm morning breeze off the Gulf of Mexico drifted through the open French doors, spreading the aroma of a fresh brewed cup of coffee resting in the left hand of Jake Woods. His other hand was busy swiping across the iPad resting on his knee, dissecting the news of the previous day.

His wife Ann was up and away early from their beachfront home this morning, supplementing her daily spin class routine with a hot stone massage. She had given her weary husband the green light to join friends for a late morning tee time at the Twin Eagles Golf Club's Talon course, but after his bombshell weekend at the lake and the subsequent whirlwind trip through the nation's capital, golf was the farthest activity from his mind.

Given the adventure that lay ahead and the incredible stakes involved, his concern was how to break the news to his wife that he'd been unofficially called out of retirement. To say she would not be happy might be the understatement of the year, but for now he was following through with the trip back to Florida to keep up appearances. He would have to come clean with her soon, as the ability to relax during his time home had evaporated when General Huang dropped this shit sandwich in his lap.

The chime of the doorbell and authoritative knock on the door quickly broke the temporary tranquility of the moment. Woods reached the door on the second ring and pulled it open as the chiseled Army Major was about to repeat his fist-filled rap again.

"Good morning Major, what can I do for you?"

"General Jake Woods?" the Major asked as he snapped to attention.

"In the flesh."

"This is for you," as the Major handed over a 9 x 12 white envelope, nearly covered in its entirety with security tape.

Woods accepted the package and glanced out at the white Chevy Tahoe with government plates in the drive, the motor running and a disinterested corporal behind the wheel. "I'd offer you a cup of coffee, but it looks like your mission here is short...correct?"

"Yes sir. I was told to deliver this to you personally."

"Mission accomplished, Major."

"Thank you, sir, and a pleasure to meet you. Thank you for all of your years of service," as he stepped backward off the front porch and delivered a very smart salute.

"Likewise, Major," Woods returned the salute and watched as the two soldiers backed out of the driveway and disappeared down the palm lined street.

Woods retrieved a pocket knife from the corner of the kitchen countertop, as he returned to the comfort of his sitting room and coffee and proceeded to remove two nondescript manila file folders from the envelope. No letter, no note, no nothing accompanied the folders identifying the sender. He peeked into both and immediately discovered they were filled with generic copies of electronic military personnel files. He set the bottom one aside and opened the other.

Accompanying a picture was a description and service history for a Major Blake Ferguson, 1st Special Forces Operational Detachment-Delta, retired. A brief scan of the pages left Woods impressed.

After completing his four-year Army ROTC commitment at the University of Alabama in 2000, and graduating with a mechanical engineering degree, 2nd Lieutenant Ferguson volunteered assignment to the Rangers, and upon arriving at Fort Benning, was singled out for and completed sniper school. Woods raised an eyebrow and nodded his head in appreciation. He continued.

Ferguson's 3rd Battalion was part of the initial airborne assault spearheading the support of ground forces in "Operation Enduring Freedom-Afghanistan." After distinguishing himself with multiple citations in Afghanistan, his battalion was employed in March of 2003 on the airborne assault in Iraq to seize Objective Serpent in support of "Operation Iraqi Freedom." He returned to Afghanistan in December 2003, and Woods sifted through a long list of multiple operations through March 2008, with responsibilities involving special reconnaissance, intelligence and counter intelligence, combat search and rescue, personnel recovery and hostage rescue, joint special operations, and counter terrorism. He had reached the rank of Captain in early 2005. There was a note in the record that indicated he was passed over for the Distinguished Service Cross in 2007. Cited for gallantry in action leading his recon team during an ambush involving a large number of hostile forces in Nuristan Province, he disregarded his own wounds while personally recovering and treating three severely wounded soldiers.

Woods muttered quietly to himself, "What the fuck? How do you get dissed for that?"

An additional note below the after-action summary indicated the mission had been disavowed. Woods shook his head and scratched at the stubble on his chin. *Had to be his first foray into the covert world. Bastards. Typical of the spooks to suppress that one.*

Obviously, the relationship with the Intelligence community wasn't ruined over the snub. After a brief reassignment to the Regimental Special Troops Battalion in April of 2008, he attended assessment and selection for 1st Special Forces Operational Detachment-Delta. He completed the six-month training program and began operations with Joint Special Operations Command by the end of 2008. From the heavily redacted entries of the last page in the file, it was abundantly clear that now Major Ferguson had been elevated to a tier one operator and involved and responsible for some very serious shit up until his retirement in July of 2013. Woods couldn't help but think it was C.I.A. *Smells like Specials Activities Division work, probably Ground Branch.*

In nearly 13 years, Ferguson had pretty much done and seen it all in the pile of sand that was the Middle East. The hand written post-it note affixed to the inside back of the folder, listed a last known address in St. John, VI.

Woods closed and dropped the file to the floor, leaning back in the plastic wicker recliner to let his mind take it all in. *Why in the world would he retire? He had to be in line for Lieutenant Colonel and on a fast track for Colonel?*

* * * * *

After a brief respite in the bathroom and refill on the coffee, Woods returned to his seat and dug into the second file. The good vibes started early as he recognized multiple Marine Corps letterheads on the enclosed files. Master Sergeant Clay Wright, 1st Special Forces Operational Detachment-Delta, retired.

Woods nearly burned his lips as he fumbled the coffee cup away from his mouth. *Another Delta by way of the Marines.* A big smile reappeared quickly. Wright was a Recon Marine.

Joining the Marines in September 2001 at the age of 23, with a newly minted MBA degree from Virginia, he was obviously one of the thousands of young men that felt the burn of 9/11, and he enlisted in the Marines. Following basic training at Paris Island, SC, Private First class attended the Marine Corps School of Infantry and volunteered for Amphibious Reconnaissance.

After excelling at Amphibious Reconnaissance School, Wright completed Basic Airborne, Freefall, SERE, Combat Dive School, and the Scout Sniper Basic Course, and was assigned as a Force Recon Operator in early 2003 to the 1st Force Reconnaissance Company just before the Invasion of Iraq in March 2003.

He participated in the battle of Nasiriyah and supported the rescue of PFC Jessica Lynch. In 2004, he deployed in support of the 11th MEU participating in the Battle of Najaf and was attached to Regimental Combat Team 1 for Operation Phantom Fury, commonly known as the Battle of Fallujah.

In 2005 through 2006, Wright participated in numerous campaigns including Operation Matador in the city of Al Qaim and Operation Sword in the town of Hit before finally becoming a part of the newly constructed Marine Corps Special Operations Command (MARSOC) in late 2005.

Throughout, Wright was involved in direct action, special and deep reconnaissance, counter-terrorism, counter-insurgency, hostage rescue, interdiction and clandestine operations.

The next entry on his record was his interservice transfer to the same 1st SFOD-D in early 2006 and completion of his six months training at the end of the summer. Then came the same lengthy list of redacted entries, interspersed with assignments in Afghanistan, Iraq, and Syria, that abruptly ended in his retirement in July of 2013.

Woods had a double take on the date listed. He quickly picked up Ferguson's file and sifted through to the last page and mumbled out loud, "Retired July 2013". *What the hell, that's no coincidence.*

Another post-it notes square attached scribbled with "Deer Valley Ski Instructor".

Chapter 7

Beirut, Lebanon

Abbas Abdul-Mahdi shifted anxiously in the soft leather chair and eyed with suspicion all of the international melting pot that was the lobby of the Hilton Beirut Habtoor Grand. Sweat dotted his forehead and trickled down his torso turning his underwear into a damp dishrag that threatened to saturate through his cream linen suit. He dabbed the handkerchief to his face but had no solution for the other end, even with the Hilton air conditioning functioning to a comfortable 23 degrees Celsius.

The man known as the father of all third world biological weapons programs, and at one time labeled by many western intelligence agencies as one the most dangerous men on the planet, was in reality experiencing his own bout of danger induced angst. It was truly a bit of a role reversal for the once fearless, western-educated, Shiite Iraqi scientist. Ironically, this was the same man who sold the idea of an Iraqi biological weapons program to the Sunni dictator Saddam Hussein, and was rewarded by the "Butcher of Baghdad" for his work in biological weapons, specifically the development of anthrax and botulinum weapons. He was over a decade removed from those heady days.

After escaping the collapse of the Iraqi regime in 2003, Abdul-Mahdi slipped into Northern Syria, where he had been living a reclusive, underground existence. As the convoluted mess of the Syrian civil war escalated, he was inadvertently discovered during an intelligence sweep, as a part of a successful and highly publicized rescue mission of a downed Russian bomber pilot by the Iranian Quds Force. Accompanying the elite Iranian squad in the search operation were soldiers from the Lebanese "Hezbollah" Special Forces and commandos from the Syrian Special Forces. It was an officer in the Hezbollah personnel who recognized their find, and without alerting the significance, he was able to exert some not-so-subtle influence to a reluctant Abdul-Mahdi and spirit him off to Lebanon.

However, his surreptitious disappearance was short lived. Not long after his extraction, the Iranian Supreme Leader became aware of Abdul-Mahdi's existence and angrily demanded his immediate delivery to Tehran. His biological warfare knowledge and abilities were very much in demand, and as much as Hezbollah's leadership was interested in utilizing those skills in their own jihad, there was no denying the request of the terrorist organization's mothership.

After a significant debriefing from the military intelligence apparatus of Hezbollah, including a personal interrogation by the infamous Abdullah Ataya, head of Unit 133, whose mission is to mount terror attacks on Israel's West Bank, Abdul-Mahdi was taken without warning from the plush Mediterranean villa that had been home for the last several weeks of his removal from Syria. Brought to Beirut for an overnight stay in the Hilton, he had just been informed by the Hezbollah handlers who had made the trip with him, and were clearly nothing but thugs in his opinion, he would be boarding a private jet destined for Tehran. There would be no customs clearance.

While the diminutive one known as Nasri, who appeared to be in charge, was checking him out of the hotel, two other oversized muscled brutes camped out with Abdul-Mahdi in the lobby, and a fourth was dispatched for a car to drive them to the airport. The fear of the unknown that was Iran was taking its toll on him mentally and physically.

The foursome exited together as the white, four-door Mercedes sedan pulled up to the curb. Nasri placed the luggage in the trunk, two others went into the back seat, and Abdul-Mahdi took the front passenger seat. The burst of air conditioning was a welcome relief. Nasir nodded and waved them away, as he remained behind.

Turning west onto Camil Chamoun, they passed under the Elias El Hrawi Highway and turned into a small alley. From behind, the largest of the thugs that had no name, placed a nylon garrote over the head and around the neck of Abdul-Mahdi with the precision and speed born of experience, and before Abdul-Mahdi had the chance to utter a scream, the massive assassin pulled it taught and backwards so violently that he lifted his victim out of the seat. Abdul-Mahdi grabbed in vain at his throat and kicked at the dashboard and windshield as he felt his eyes nearly popping out of their sockets. The struggle only sped up the end result, as the lack of any oxygen soon slowed his futile thrashing, his vision blurring, then turning black as the life of one of the most dangerous men on earth was extinguished.

The lifeless body was dragged into the back seat, stripped to the underwear and stuffed into a black plastic body bag, while the car pulled out of the alley and returned to the Hilton. As it pulled to the curb, another man dressed in a Nike sweat suit, and one who could easily have been mistaken as an identical twin of the recently deceased passenger, accompanied Nasri to the same passenger door, shook hands, and sat in the same comfort of the air-conditioned front seat.

Chapter 8

Near Ravar, Iran

With the engine turned off, the rotors slowed and the hurricane of debris from the hard pack landing pad started to settle and dissipate. The occupants waited for the clearing air before exiting the craft and into the respite of the manmade oasis of the Villa Behesht.

Park was the first to enter the walled, open air courtyard that served as the entrance to the estate. Revolutionary Guards Commander Nasser Togyani eased by a stationary Park, who had stopped to admire the lush greenery, blue chip tiled walls, and an abundance of waterfalls with miniature pools that simultaneously took the edge off of whatever might be ailing the mind. Togyani escorted Dr. Malik Abbaspour through the gardens and beyond the large wrought iron and glass double doors standing open as a welcome to the home's most important guests.

There to greet them was Major General Hassan Firouzabadi, Chairman of the Joint Command Headquarters, who provided brief instructions and directions as to the living arrangements on the second floor. Brigadier General Farid Seyyedi, who shared no love or respect for Firouzabadi and wanted nobody interfering with his turf as commander of the Defense Ministry's Special Chemical, Biological, and Nuclear Industries, was less polite as he bumped through Park in a hurry to his preordained sleeping quarters.

The owner of the house had been paid handsomely for the lease of the property and was told in no uncertain terms he could expect not to return for weeks if not months. The two servants and cooking staff had been retained and were busy preparing cocktails and dinner, while the four travelers adjourned to their private bedrooms upstairs. Sufficient security beyond the walls was being handled by a company of Revolutionary Guards, handpicked by Togyani himself.

* * * * *

The rack of lamb and squash dinner was spectacular. The three bottles of Château Mouton Rothschild had set a relaxed tone for the most part, and there was a mutual feeling of agreement among the three believers in the room that Allah would understand and forgive them of their intemperance, given the great circumstances that weighed upon them. The elephant in the room remained. To address Park's ultimatum, the party of five moved from the dining room to a secure billiards room in the basement that had been swept for any electronic eavesdropping, and a scrambler was mounted on the roof of the villa to jam any outgoing signals.

The billiard table was not going to be used for sport this evening. Laid across the green felt, as if in a military strategy room, was a map of the Middle East, from Turkey to the north down to Yemen in the south, with Egypt over to Iran spanning west to east.

Everyone stood as they gathered around the table, and an eerie quiet settled over the group.

It was Togyani who broke the chill. "Gentlemen, all of you are aware that we are conducting top secret biological testing at the facility we attended today, but none of you," Togyani eyed Park, "has been briefed to the detailed extent of what we are attempting to accomplish with a fully functional and controllable viral weapon.

"The state of the Middle East is in major flux. To put it bluntly, the region is on fire. Political instability fueled by years of American influence and ever-increasing violence at the hands of Sunni terrorists funded by the corrupt Saudi Princes is causing a rot in the heart of the Muslim world." He motioned to the map, specifically pointing at Syria and Iraq. "The Sunni Revolt and the unprecedented growth of Daesh, the Islamic State in Iraq and Syria, the burgeoning Muslim Brotherhood, and remnants of Al-Qaeda continue to fracture the Islamic faith, creating volatility across the entire region. Marginal governing entities and their political will are about as stable as the breezes that blow them.

"Iran is the guiding light for the entire Middle East. It is Allah's will that we lead. We are on the verge of negotiating away our international sanctions with the 'Great Satan' and their pathetic allies in the UN. They have turned their tails from our part of the world, thanks to the weakness of their President and puppet administration. We are on the cusp of being the lone Islamic nuclear power in the Middle East to thwart the occupying Zionist regime to our west. Lastly, we are the last great hope for all of the Persian people and have the will to act on behalf of them. United, we will return Iran and Persia to its rightful place atop the world."

The room's occupants were both captivated and mesmerized with Togyani's fantastical oratory. It was clear he possessed an unwavering faith of which he spoke and a fundamental belief in his own superiority supported by his military rank and influence, and it came through loud and clear. No comments or conversation interrupted.

Togyani reached under the table and retrieved a corrugated shipping tube and removed a rolled up transparent film. "What we are proposing is a new Persia." He unrolled the film and placed it over the existing map. "Gentlemen, behold the Setareh Doctrine."

A large asymmetrical star covered the map with each of the five points ending in a country that was now highlighted in yellow. Starting at the top of the star and moving clockwise: Syria, Iraq, Kuwait, Jordan, and Lebanon were all engulfed in a map that included no reference to their current borders but included them in a single state that added Iran to the east. In all caps "PERSIA" rested squarely in the middle.

The room remained silent, everyone avoiding any semblance of eye contact, the comprehension beginning to sink in.

"Our goal with Setareh is to reshape the great Persia and save the region from what surely is going to be a bloodbath of its own making."

Park offered the rhetorical question, "And you're planning on using the virus to make this happen?"

All eyes looked at Togyani. "Yes, in the name of Allah, all praise be his name. We will never lose faith in our commitment to His will."

He let the reference to God hang in the air. "We will use the virus to create the conditions to take control of these regions from the corruption of the infidels and Zionists.

"Let me explain," he continued. "We will dispatch the chosen martyrs, each an infected time bomb, to initiate an infiltration of the lands of the infidels and the Zionists' puppets. Each of the chosen *Shahids* will be provided strategic targets within each country. Infiltration will be facilitated by our military and political surrogates in each of these lands, who will then be afforded our full covert military support and the unequivocal backing of the Islamic Republic, as the recognized local government proxy to step in during the power vacuums that will take place as each country struggles with the epidemic.

"Having an antidote in place, we will fake a period of time for discovery of the cure and treatment. For purposes of deception and the greater good, we must include portions of our own country in the devastation."

The fervor and boldness of Togyani's descriptive details grew as he exuded a growing confidence and could envision the resultant glory. "The blame will be easy. We will lay it at the feet of the Sunni dogs in Syria and Iraq. We will frame the viral program as a byproduct of a hidden Saddam Hussein WMD that had been smuggled into Syria during the Gulf War and now has showed up in the hands of those terrorists who maintained no control over it. The evidence to support this accusation will be easy to manufacture and substantiate. It will start and emanate from Syria.

"We can claim exposure to something eerily similar in the *First Persian Gulf War* with the Ba'athist pig Hussein, and reveal that we had diligently worked on cures and antidotes to the symptoms then. Our expertise and experience with the virus then will easily offer instant credibility when we claim the discovery of the antidote now. We will then be in a position to hold hostage what remains of the broken countries, utilizing military intervention, or in some cases direct coups by their surrogates, in the name of saving lives and maintaining safety and stability of a disintegrating security situation. Not one of our enemies will dare intercede or send troops into harm's way without the ability to understand or control the situation and keep them safe. Our most conservative estimates are to be in control of the entire region within four to six months."

Park was having a difficult time breathing. The pallor of his face was evident, and the dinner and wine were turning to bile in his throat.

Firouzabadi finally spoke, "Is the Supreme Leader aware of this Doctrine?"

"He's aware of the program and the goal but not all of the details," replied Togyani. He looked at Seyyedi, who confirmed with a vigorous nod.

"Why not Israel?" inquired Abbaspour.

"We do not want to strike specifically at the Zionists in order to discourage any direct American military intervention. It is our belief the Great Satan would not react or retaliate as quickly to an unknown disease sweeping across other countries, until it was too late and Setareh was fully in motion. Ultimately, Israel would be squeezed and marginalized by a new and larger Iran, and in a no-win position in the long term.

"Bahrain, UAE, Qatar, and Oman would be part of the "Dhil", or tail counter strike, after the results of Setareh are in place. This would be through traditional military pressure and intervention and nurturing the growing Shia influences that are in place. The Royal Families and their self-indulgent governance are on borrowed time as it is. The populations and puppet governments they control grow increasing restless and are looking for openings to end their reigns. Their eventual capitulation would give us total control of the Persian Gulf and subordinate and make irrelevant Saudi Arabia and Yemen as the only remaining Arab countries in the Middle East to the south of a greater Persia. With the Houthi's increasing dominance, Yemen would also only be a matter of time before they fell within our satellite. Beyond the ideological cleansing and Shiite restoration of the region, the companion piece is the command and control of a geopolitical zone that incorporates the vast majority of the entire oil and natural gas producing lands in the Middle East. We will be the only truly Muslim superpower in the world."

The tacit approval exhibited by both Firouzabadi and Abbaspour, and what he assumed was the previous knowledge and backing of Seyyedi, sent cold chills down Park's spine. *What have I gotten myself into? This is a nightmare, and I'm going to be responsible for helping facilitate it.*

Togyani obviously sensed the distress, "Dr. Park, you have other questions?"

Park was speechless. With a blank stare, he focused on the diabolical map in front of him.

"We have an agreement Dr. Park. You are being paid an obscene amount of money. If your conscience is having second thoughts, the end result will not be pretty for you or your daughter. Do I make myself clear?"

"Yes, crystal clear Commander," Park recovered. "You can count on me to uphold my end of the bargain," he lied.

Chapter 9

Coral Bay, St. John V.I.

The balmy tropical air cycled through the convertible jeep as it wound down the switchbacks of Centerline Road. The late afternoon view down the mountain and into Coral Bay was magnificent, crystalline azure water bordered by lush green bumps of island masses leading the eye out of the bay to open waters. Anchored boats of all shapes and sizes dotted the picturesque inlet from shoreline to shoreline.

Jake Woods negotiated his way past a donkey, which appeared to be challenging two locals on bicycles for control of the descending left lane. At sea level, he waited on a small herd of goats to cross the road and then entered the parking lot of Skinny Legs Bar & Grill.

The colorful open-air establishment was very much as he expected it to be from the description of the most helpful receptionist at the St. John Yacht Charter Office on the other side of the island in Cruz Bay. He settled into an empty bar stool, ordered a Red Stripe and inquired with the tanned and tattooed, buxom barmaid sporting the skimpiest of halter tops if she knew of a charter boat captain by the name of Blake Ferguson.

Her chuckled response, "Everybody knows Blakie," was accompanied by a wave of her index finger in the direction behind

Woods at a two-top wood table flush against the outside wall of the t-shirt adorned gift shop. Dressed in island casual, consisting of cargo shorts, a loose-fitting flowered shirt, ball cap, and Sperry boat shoes, he looked like a million other modern captains of the Caribbean. However, his youthful, rugged looks belied his 38 years of age. Short, reddish blonde hair was just evident beyond his hat, and his tan square face was illuminated by a pair of piercing blue eyes. Two-day-old stubble covered a chiseled jaw, while exposed muscular forearms and calves gave an indication that the man was still in impeccable physical condition. Woods inquired about and requested an appropriate drink be forwarded to the occupant.

"Is this seat taken?" inquired Woods, after meandering through the main floor.

Blake Ferguson looked up to acknowledge the greeting, placed the iPad he was scrolling through on the table, and motioned to the empty seat opposite him.

"Thanks!" Woods sat in the white plastic chair, as another skimpily clad waitress winked at Ferguson and delivered a cocktail of Cruzan Dark Rum, lightly splashed with pineapple juice and ginger ale and adorned with what looked like half a lime.

"Thank you, Sharon!" Ferguson returned the wink. "I see Michelle has already provided you with my favorite cocktail. Was she helpful with any other information about me or my boat, or should I assume your presence opposite me is going to present a Q and A?

"The 'Broken Flip Flop' moniker for that concoction was all the intelligence I could gather from her."

Ferguson acknowledged a reply with a slight nod of his head, with an immediate understanding this man was not here about a boat charter. An open palmed gesture was his invitation for Woods to continue the conversation, "What I can do for you Mr...."

"Jake Woods, Mr. Ferguson, General Jake Woods...quite obviously retired." Woods answered the rest of his inquiry for him. "I have a story to tell you, and I'm here to see if you can help."

Ferguson's recognition of his guest was instant, but he gave no outward indication. He knew the name and had heard stories about the man. "How long is this story General?"

"It'll take us well into dark," as Woods looked over his shoulder at the setting sun cradled on the western horizon.

"In that case, let me introduce you to the Skinny Legs very famous burger." Ferguson waved at Michelle behind the bar, held up two fingers, placed them into a stirring motion, and shouted over the growing happy hour throng, "Another round and two menus."

* * * *

"That's a hell of a story General," after a mostly uninterrupted monologue from Woods and a completion of dinner, "but nothing surprises me regarding the lunatics in that shithole area of the world. I get the feeling you're about ready to tell me about the 'how I can help' part, and it doesn't involve captaining a sailboat."

Ferguson tried to order a fourth round, or it could've been a fifth, Woods had lost count and waved him off. The move from Red Stripe to the Broken whatever was making a significant dent in his sobriety, and in spite of the incredible burger that was helping soak up the local island cocktail, their discussion was far too important to let alcohol cloud either of their judgments...even more so given his impending query.

"You're correct Blake. What I'm asking of you...is to help me avert this looming disaster." Woods looked for some reaction from Ferguson, but got none. "I think it's safe to say given this little slice of heaven you have going on here that you would be giving up a lot, once again, and I mean a lot, to help your country. Only this time, there will be no formal recognition. Only a very few people are going to know the sacrifice you make. You would be even more off the books and outside the grid than you ever were before.

"I have been extended the privilege and opportunity, so to speak, without written authorization or orders, to take covert action against the people and facilities responsible for this bio-terror, and I'm looking to assemble the best people I can to fulfill that mission. We have the financial backing we need, and we have some very limited help from our Intelligence services, but for all intents and purposes we don't exist. We are on our own.

"You will be paid a serious amount of money for your efforts, but if I'm guessing correctly, money is not the reason you did what you did before, and if you say yes, would probably not be why you would do it again. Regardless, you will be significantly rewarded for laying your life on the line, and my hope is that might provide some incentive, along with your natural instincts, to come on board."

Ferguson remained passive and poker faced as he heard Woods out. He circled his glass on the table, stirring what little drink he had left. "Why me?"

"You came highly recommended. I've read your file, and it only confirms that recommendation. You're one hell of a soldier and must have been one hell of an operator."

"If you read my file, then you know I got out," Ferguson hesitated, "rather abruptly."

"I'm aware of that. Do you want to discuss it?"

"No."

"Then neither do I."

A lingering silence came over them, while a steel drum band began beating out a calypso tune in the outdoor courtyard below their perch.

After a few minutes, Ferguson spoke first, "Why do I want to leave this?"

"You shouldn't," said Woods, offering nothing else.

"I know it's a dumb question given time is of the essence, but theoretically speaking, if I were to entertain your offer, and I'm not saying I would, how much time do I have to make a decision?"

"I'm flying out tonight to meet with another gentleman about his interest tomorrow. Theoretically speaking...is 24 hours enough?'

"Yes sir. You have a number?"

Woods slid him over a card with his cell number listed.

"If you don't mind me asking, who else are you talking to? Do any of them come highly recommended?" Ferguson mocked somewhat sarcastically.

"As a matter of fact, yes, and only the two of you made the cut. You might know him...Clay Wright." Woods was hoping for the desired effect. What he got was a suppressed chuckle from Ferguson in return.

Woods stood, "It was a pleasure Blake Ferguson. Thanks for your time, thanks for your service, and thanks for the hospitality of St. John."

"Likewise, General. It's been an honor. Thanks for considering me...I think. It does say a lot, and I appreciate your trust."

They shook hands, and Woods made his exit by way of Michelle at the bar, where he paid the tab and left a more than generous tip.

Ferguson couldn't help but laugh at the circumstances that just landed on him like a 400-pound gorilla. Indeed, he loved St. John and the casual lifestyle it afforded and had grown accustomed to the carefree existence. However, deep inside there was still the lingering need for something more, steadily nagging at his soul?

Once a soldier, always a soldier, and there were many days Ferguson had to admit he missed the adrenaline rush of the action, the camaraderie of his fellow warriors, and as ridiculous as it sounded…helping serve justice on the evil that existed everywhere in the world. Ironically, he thought, if only Woods knew of this inner conundrum. If he had even been aware of the lack of any meaningful relationships in Ferguson's life, either with family or a female partner that he could expect to share the rest of eternity with, the General would have thought him easy prey. He snickered to himself and admitted that he probably already knew. He became even more suspicious that Woods probably was aware of his financial predicament in paying off the loan on his Robertson and Caine Leopard 46′ catamaran. He was already five months in arrears and didn't see an obvious way out of the mounting income to expense dilemma he was facing in the sailboat charter business. If it were bought and paid for, the decision would be more difficult.

By the time Ferguson stepped out into the gravel parking lot, Woods was hanging up from his call to the pilot of Cromer's G550, on standby at the St. John airport, and pulling out toward the restaurant exit onto Centerline Road. Ferguson stepped in front and brought the jeep to a halt. He sidled around the vehicle to the driver's side, looked Woods in the eye, and with his own determined squint, winked and nodded, "You can count on me General."

"I knew I could."

Chapter 10

Park City, UT

Woods stopped to admire the oil and watercolor compositions in the Artworks of PC Gallery window, as he used the ploy to catch his breath on the walk up the steep grade of Park City's Main Street. A November early snow was falling, and after another 30 yards up the sidewalk he entered the No Name Saloon and made for the long bar that ran the entire length of one wall in the shotgun style tavern. The happy hour crowd had yet to emerge and the local ski bum masquerading as a bartender threw a paper coaster at him, landing it just in front of Woods' hands, signaling his inaugural experience at one of Park City's favorite local watering holes. After an inquiry of his patron's taste buds, Bones the bartender introduced himself and popped the top of a bottle of a Polygamy Porter, placing it squarely on the coaster in one continuous motion. Woods nodded his appreciation.

"Bones, I'm looking for someone in particular, and the Deer Valley Ski Instructor's office said I would probably be able to find him here any time after five o'clock. His name is Clay Wright. Any chance you know him?'

"I know him well pops, and he's throwing shuffleboard." Bones pointed at the long shuffleboard table on the opposite wall.

"He's the one in the camo hat. Looks like he might be dry, he's headed back this way."

Clay Wright approached the bar and shook his empty bottle of Polygamy Porter at Bones in a plea for another. Tall at six-foot-three inches, he sported a pair of well-worn jeans, hiking boots, and a green fleece pullover with Deer Valley Ski logo stitched in yellow, his long wavy black hair flowed out from underneath the UVA Lacrosse ball cap. A long tan face with dark brown eyes was accented with a well-groomed full beard and mustache, tell-tale signs of salt and pepper adding a sense of maturity to his 37 years of age.

"Are you Clay Wright?" inquired Woods as Wright leaned into the half empty bar, two stools away.

"Who's asking?"

"My name is Jake Woods. Any chance we can talk?"

* * * * *

The No Name was living up to its reputation nearly two hours of storytelling later, as the congregation had nearly tripled and the Thursday evening co-mingling of the sexes was in full swing. The warm fire consuming the large stone fireplace near the front entrance of the bar was removed from the standing room only crowd by handrails, guarding a recessed floor area adorned with well-worn soft seating. The separate space had offered a nice respite for the conversation between Woods and Wright in a fatigued, but incredibly comfortable brown leather couch.

Having listened intently, Clay said, "General, I can't say I'm not flattered that you, and obviously others, think I'm capable, but I'm not sure I'm your man for this. That's some pretty heavy shit you're facing, and I've been out of the action for a while. I don't know what you've been privy to, but I had a not so glorious exit out of the community so to speak. Frankly, I'm not sure I'm mentally ready. I can tell you that the thought of avenging that outcome, regardless of the enemy or mission, with another bite at the apple is appealing...but I just don't know," Wright's voice trailed off as he shook his head with a wave of negative memories flooding his head.

"There have to be some other pipe hitters out there that you can rely on, lots of good guys I worked with that are still in the game. Besides, even though things could be better, I have a pretty good thing going on here in Park City."

"By the looks of this, and the fact you get to teach snow skiing for a living, I can't disagree."

An awkward silence lasted for several minutes as a hand full of eligible young women hovered over the two of them, eyeing an opportunity to break into the conversation with Clay Wright.

"Look Clay, as I told the other operator that is coming on board to help, this is all about helping your country and potentially stopping a low-level Armageddon. If these assholes are successful in what they're planning in the Middle East, there's no telling what they might do to us and others. They are the largest and most formidable sponsors of terrorism in the world, and for reasons beyond my comprehension, our country has shown a willingness to appease them at every turn. It has gotten us nothing but a black eye, potentially allowed these thugs to become a nuclear power, and what appears to be a biological terrorist threat beyond imagination.

"You're not going to get any recognition for the sacrifices you would be making. This op is so far off the books, it can't be found...and there's a number of reasons for that, all of which I'm sure you understand. There would be no love from anybody worth a shit, with only a few people that know what we're actually going to do, but the impact you can make would be immeasurable. You will be compensated like you've never been before. Your future years will be worry free, but as I surmised with another young man, something tells me you wouldn't do this shit for money, you would do it because you're a Patriot and it's the right and moral thing to do. If you're anything like me, you do it for the traditional virtues of God, Country and Family...in that order."

Wright nodded his understanding. "When do you need an answer?"

"Twenty-four hours. I need to get the rest of the team in place." He handed his card to Wright.

"If you don't mind me asking, who's the other gentleman that has joined the posse?" Wright asked.

"Blake Ferguson. I believe you might be familiar with him."

"You're one sly son of a bitch, General. You know I can't say No to him. He saved my life, not just once. He's definitely committed?"

"Yes, he's flying up from St. John to Washington as we speak. He is bringing a list of people that are available that he thinks can help. If you're in, I would ask you to do the same. If you're not, let me know of another incredibly talented operator that you mentioned would be out there and available, because you and Blake are the only two names they gave me. I'm assuming there's a reason for that."

Woods hailed their waitress and handed her a $100 bill and instructed her to keep the change, and then fished out a $50 bill from his money clip and commanded her to personally pass it on to Bones at the bar with his "thanks."

He grabbed his coat, shook hands with Wright and left him to the any number of pretty young women that saw their options open up with his departure.

"Thanks, General, I'll be in touch."

"Looking forward to it."

Woods stepped out into the cold wind and accumulating snow, thankful for the downhill return walk to his rental car. Salt Lake City airport and the Gulfstream were less than an hour away. Just after passing the same art gallery as before, a text chimed into his phone. He removed the phone from his coat pocket and smiled as he read it...

I'm in General! Tell me when and where to report.

Chapter 11

Tehran, Iran

It was well after midnight when a black Mercedes limousine pulled up to the curb in front of the Chinese Embassy at Danesh, 73 Ave Aghdasiyeh on the northeast outskirts of Tehran, Iran. The driver idled the engine for an additional five minutes before a beautiful, long-legged Asian female emerged from the rear door adjacent to the Embassy sidewalk. She tugged tactfully at the scarlet red, full-length evening gown that clung to her lean five-foot, seven-inch frame, melting the eyes of the driver watching intently in the rear-view mirror. The sexy silk fabric accentuated her light peach skin and jet-black hair that had fallen to her shoulders from an elegant updo earlier in the evening. She leaned back into the open door with a deft exposure of ample cleavage for the occupant still inside, blew a kiss, then turned and strutted toward the doors leading to the People's Republic of China's safe haven inside.

The driver remained in park, watching with continued interest until his passenger had entered the gated facility. He stepped out briefly to open the same door, looking inside to check on the remaining passenger splayed fully naked on the leather seats inside, just this side of consciousness. He mumbled something incoherent and massaged a red lace thong stretched around his throat, a small trophy for the hour-long debauchery that had taken place on the ride back from the formal state dinner function earlier that evening.

The driver had seen it before from General Amir Javadi, his disgust in the repeated drunken behavior of his boss he felt sure brought shame upon him as well in the face of Allah. The General was a disgrace thought the soldier, both to the military and Islam. Regardless, duty led him to pick up the remainder of the man's black-tie outfit strewn across the interior bench seats, piling them in a corner next to the empty bottle of Bollinger champagne. He tossed a set of keys, cell phone, and wallet that were variously stuffed between seats or scattered on the car floor into an equally empty ice bucket on the small bar.

He returned to the driver's seat and pulled away from the curb to deliver Javadi to his home only a few blocks away. He lamented the need to help dress the general and escort him into the house and was hoping that he could avoid yet another encounter with his wife or children waiting up for him.

* * * * *

Lei Lau entered the embassy and after being passed through security made directly for the guest quarters located on the west wing. She removed a pair of four-inch stiletto high heels and walked barefoot through the long, marbled hall that spilled into a common sitting area. Tzu Huang rose from one of the large overstuffed couches and greeted her with a hug as she made her entrance. There wasn't a soul anywhere within eye or earshot.

"You look beautiful this evening Lei Lau. I trust you persevered through your evening."

"Duty calls...most unpleasant with the boorish Javadi, but understandably necessary. I believe I have something for you that will hopefully help address your concerns," as she returned the hug and gave Huang a small peck on his left cheek. She slipped a cloned cell phone into his hand, a move that would have been unnoticeable to the naked eye, even if any were around.

Lei Lau's stunningly beautiful exterior was equally matched by her significant intellect, as evidenced by her Master's Degree in Chemical Engineering at Peking University and PhD in physics at the Institute of Physics. All of her abilities were in high demand upon graduation in 2012, and she was ultimately recruited into the General Staff Department's Second Department, 2PLA, as an intelligence officer, also offering her a civilian engineering post to provide cover. She was most recently assigned to the newly created Central Military Commission, which is tasked with overseeing all of China's nuclear weapons programs, and she was placed on temporary assignment as an advisor with the People's Republic of China's delegation to Iran providing ongoing assistance to Iran's nuclear programs.

Her association with General Huang began almost ten years earlier while she was a new student at the university in Beijing. Always trolling for talent in the University, Huang had recognized her budding abilities, and after much effort, was able to enlist the young and impressionable Lau into the Intelligence Branch of the Ministry of State Security, where she became one of his most prized agents helping to keep tabs on his own government.

Through sheer coincidence, she alone was responsible for uncovering the information related to Park's existence in Iran and a possible top-secret biological program that he was spearheading somewhere in the country. Huang's recognition of, and divulgence of his personal history with Park to Lau had also convinced her of the dangers of such an unchecked program in the hands of the deranged leadership of Iran. Additionally, it served to cement her commitment to helping in whatever way she could to destroy the program, or certainly those involved with it.

Through ongoing contact with Javadi, who was the designated liaison from Iran's Ministry of Defense and Armed Forces Logistics and along with the Revolutionary Guards were the primary caretakers of the Iranians' military nuclear program, she was able to gather and develop some low-level human intelligence on Iran's nuclear practices and intentions over the last five months. Furthermore, while actively seducing him for nearly two months, she uncovered some hearsay and innuendo, about what she later surmised to be a most authentic "classified" biological program.

The activities of the covert organization dubbed Special Chemical, Biological, and Nuclear Industries, which had been created through the Ministry of Defense and was responsible for overseeing Park's program, were the one area she was having difficulty breaking through with anything concrete. What little information she had obtained was passed down to Huang, who in turn had been able to connect the dots to Park and subsequently confirm his existence as the principal involved. However, Javadi's limited knowledge and restricted access to the program itself was not leading to any substantive intelligence. Lau was beginning to feel that any further pushing of Javadi for information outside his bounds of knowledge and clearance would make him suspicious and compromise her position. On top of that, she had grown sick of the sexual encounters with the man and felt she was reaching her limit in that regard as well. She communicated both scenarios to Huang before retiring to one of the apartments within the Embassy she had called home over the last seven months.

Huang slipped out a secure rear entrance of the Embassy and walked a half block north down Firouzbakhsh Street. He sat on a bench perched under a canopy of mature beech trees and removed a secure satellite phone, dialing a number in the United States from memory.

Chapter 12

Themis Cooperative Offices, Alexandria, VA

A warm fire blazed in an old red-brick fireplace radiating heat into the large conference room on the second floor of the renovated four-story boutique office building in Old Town. The entire structure was compliments once again of Winston Cromer, who also volunteered the young information technology expert, whose small frame was swallowed by the large leather sofa hugging the wall, opposite the large bank of shaded windows.

Blake Ferguson and Clay Wright were both taking turns alternating hugs and kisses with Elaine Scruggs, who had just entered the room, a genuine affection emanating from all of them. Jake Woods remained seated at the head of the long ten-seat walnut table with matching cordovan leather chairs, admiring the love between them, and invited young Isaiah Taylor off the couch, indicating a seat next to him.

There was a knock on the door and the last member of the team that Woods was expecting today entered. "Apologies for being late Jake, and I hope you don't mind, but I told your receptionist I would find my way up. I had one more housekeeping detail to clean up before I could officially join your endeavor," Sheri DeHavilland gave a casual wave to everyone else in the room, "I'm all good to go now."

"No worries Sheri, I wasn't actually expecting you until later, but glad to hear you're on board, and welcome."

The six of them settled at the table and turned to Woods as he rolled his chair back and away to the side to open up for everyone a line of sight to the large video monitor mounted on the wall. He keyed a wireless remote at the laptop on the table and the screen came to life with the grainy image of Dae-Ho Park.

"Before I get started, I want everyone to know that all of us in this room have been briefed on why we're here and what the mission is. What we don't know is how we're going to conduct it to a successful conclusion. This room comprises what I would call our direct operations team, or to coin a phrase...the 'Accounts Payable Department'. We have others helping out in the background with our financials and contacts to public and private resources, and we're expecting one more member to be added soon, but for the most part, we are it. You are all volunteers for this mission, and it has been made abundantly clear to all that whatever we say...whatever we do...we do it in complete anonymity. To put it bluntly, we don't exist.

"You're not going to sign any waivers, releases, acknowledgements, etcetera...nothing that would indicate what we are doing, who we're working for or with, or in any way could implicate the United States Government in our activities. The old rules of enforcing national security have been rewritten with regulations and oversight, and the shortcuts most of you are familiar with, under which our government used to operate, don't exist anymore. So, in their world of multiple intelligence organizations, laws, executive orders, warrants, rules of engagement, congressional oversight, etcetera, etcetera, this administration claims their hands to be tied. The reality is, given the ideologies and the current cast of governing characters involved, they don't have the cojones to touch it.

"In our world, none of these vagaries exist, so we are not constrained by politics and the moral shades of gray that cloud and paralyze decisive action for the good of our country and the world. That is the domain that we will operate in. Nobody is going to acknowledge us, so don't expect anybody to help us or come to our rescue. Nobody is going to get in our way either. Somebody will prosecute us to the fullest extent possible, lock us up, and throw away the key if we fuck it up." Woods grabbed at a lukewarm cup of coffee and circled it over the table surface. "Everybody understand? We're clear on this?"

Nods of acknowledgement came from everyone.

Woods continued, placing both hands on his chest, "I'll start the introductions. My name is Jake Woods, and I will be the CEO and Chairman of this lovely little cooperative. The only thing that means is I will try to assume all of the risk if the shit hits the fan. I will do everything I can to insulate all of you from jeopardy, but there are no guarantees. Since I don't believe in dictators or authoritarians, I fully expect this organization to function as a full-blown democracy and all of us to have a say in how we conduct operations. If you don't like something we're doing, speak up. However, don't just offer up complaints. Be ready to offer options and solutions. Having said all that, I will be the final arbiter and ultimate decision maker on all matters. Hopefully, I've earned that for being the oldest turd in the room."

Chuckles and snickers came from the group. Woods looked next to him and signaled Taylor that it was his turn for introductions and beckoned him to stand.

"Good morning, my name is Isaiah Taylor. I'm not really sure how I got here or why he thinks I can help, other than Mr. Winston Cromer made it happen, and I owe him a lot. So, with that in mind, and the information that was passed along to me regarding the bad guys and the crazy shit we're chasing, I'm willing to do whatever it takes to help all of us succeed."

Woods interjected before Taylor could sit. "Isaiah here is too modest. He holds a Masters of Information Systems Management at Carnegie Mellon University, graduating summa cum laude. I've been told his skills in the world of IT and computers are extensive and 'mind boggling'. A little too far reaching for some, but we are blessed to have him."

Taylor laughed. "Thanks for the glowing recommendation, but one of the other reasons I am here, which I failed to mention, probably the primary one, is about a second chance. For the sake of full disclosure, and the far-reaching issues General Woods alluded to, I've been a bad boy.

"My roommate at Carnegie and I did something stupid...but what we thought was a good idea at the time." With a shrugged expression of innocence, "It also was fun. We agreed to help one of my roomie's attorney friends, who was part of the court appointed team of bankruptcy lawyers hired to sort out the financial mess left behind when Bernie Madoff was arrested and his firm collapsed. They had been working on asset recovery for nearly six years and hit a couple of stumbling blocks. We performed what we thought were a few white hat hacks, very successfully I might add, to the tune of just over $3.7 billion recovered. There were a number of people that were very happy to get some of that.

"Unfortunately, the whole process ran into some serious trouble with the Securities Investment Protection Corporation. They came to the conclusion, regardless of our successes, that what we were doing was out of bounds and threw us under the bus to the Securities and Exchange Commission, who eventually had us drawn and quartered in front of the FBI.

"Mr. Winston Cromer, who took a personal interest in us, because I was a close friend of his daughter, came to my rescue and peddled some heavy-duty influence to keep us out of jail. We were placed under his supervision, working for him in different capacities since that event, as part of my probation and rehabilitation process. In all honesty when he told me about what the General is trying to accomplish, it really got my juices flowing. It's a little scary, but I'm really looking forward to it."

As Taylor sat, a light golf clap came from Ferguson who added, "Sounds to me that if this whole thing implodes, maybe you have the chops to hack us out of it."

Woods interjected, "Thanks, Isaiah," and motioned to Elaine Scruggs.

Elevating her five-feet eight-inch, 135-pound lean and fit runner's body out of her chair, she brushed back her shoulder-length brown hair around one ear and flashed a beautiful smile that complemented her overall, little-to-no-makeup, natural attractiveness, "Good morning, I'm Elaine Scruggs. These two knuckleheads know who I am," pointing at a smiling Ferguson and Wright, "Since I managed to keep their butts out of harm's way more often than not.

"For the benefit of General Woods and Mr. Taylor, since I apparently came recommended by these same two knuckleheads, I am Captain, US Army retired. I did two tours in Afghanistan and was an Explosive Ordnance Disposal Technician. After an accident blinded my right eye and caused some nerve damage to my right fingers, they shuffled me into Communications on my way out the door. Since I cut my teeth on armaments, which I have a pretty solid understanding of, and can shoot or demolish just about anything we carry into combat...and regardless of Blake's sniper prowess and good looks, I can still outshoot his sorry ass with my left eye."

Ferguson nodded his agreement, as Scruggs sat back down. "Don't let her good looks deceive you folks, this is one tough lady, and I'd travel into harm's way with her any day of the week."

Woods reclaimed the meeting before either Ferguson or Wright could introduce themselves, "Blake and Clay, no need for you two to expound on your backgrounds and exploits, as I'm aware that Elaine knows all of your dirty laundry and I've read your files. Same goes for Isaiah. I gave him all three of your names as an introduction to the team he would be working with, and he's already hacked into the DOD and read your files as well. I gave Olivia the sordid details of you two as well."

Woods gestured to DeHavilland, who rose up her petite five-feet four-inch frame and took a step back from the table. Casually dressed in a pair of tight-fitting designer jeans, plain white blouse and suede ankle boots, her well-toned 120-pound body and flawless complexion belied her forty-something age.

Brushing a hand through her short blond hair, she scanned the room with her penetrating blue eyes, "Hello to all, I'm Commander Sheri DeHavilland. With apologies to the Army testosterone in the room, I'm a Chief Medical Officer and trauma surgeon in the Navy Reserves, compliments of the Uniformed Services University of the Health Sciences in Bethesda and over fifteen years of field service. My expertise is epidemiology, with specialized training and experience in disease prevention and tropical medicine. One tour on a hospital ship in support of Operation Iraqi Freedom and two tours in the NATO Role III Multinational Medical Unit combat hospital in Kandahar for Operation Enduring Freedom went a long way to honing my surgical skills.

"Following my sandbox duty, I went into the Reserves and joined a humanitarian stint with the World Health Organization, assisting in the West African Ebola virus epidemic in 2014. Judging by all the youth and vigor in the room, I'm guessing Jake needed someone closer in age to join this circus."

"Oh yeah, you look way over the hill Commander," snickered Scruggs, "I can only hope my next decade has me looking as smokin' hot as you."

Wright, Ferguson, and Isaiah all looked at each other nodding in agreement.

"We concur with that assessment," confirmed Wright.

DeHavilland returned to her seat, a slight blush formulating in her high cheekbones.

"I'm feeling younger already. If you all don't mind if we get back on track," Woods said sarcastically, "I know that there is one other young lady Blake and Clay have recommended, and I have made inquiries into my old contacts at Mossad to see what can be done to reach out to her. I should have an answer for you soon."

"Already have one General, and she's a go. I got a text back from her last night," announced Ferguson.

"Don't be too surprised General, they have a little history...actually, some very hot history. They are both on each other's speed dial," interjected Wright as he beamed a toothy grin at Ferguson.

"Hooah," said Woods with a chuckle. "Still...might be beneficial for us all if I get some official OK. Are you guys good to work together? I don't need any personal feelings clouding judgment here."

"All good," replied Ferguson. "She's a close friend, but beyond that she's one hell of an operator and really knows her shit around every sand pile over there."

"Ditto, she's outstanding and would be one hell of an asset in that area, and more importantly to this team," added Wright.

"Okay, we can sort out the details of bringing her here later; let's get back to the immediate matter at hand," said Woods. "This is Dae-Ho Park," pointing at the face of a forty-something Korean man on the screen. "He would be probably twenty-five years older than this picture. Our only mission is to figure out how we get to him and the program he's running…and terminate both.

"He's in Iran somewhere, we know that. Where he is, and where his program is, we don't know. We have an active People's Republic of China asset in Tehran that is trying to help locate both, but is not having any luck. That same asset does have an unwitting source," Woods changed slides to reveal a still frame picture of an Iranian military officer, "one General Amir Javadi, attached to the Ministry of Defense and Armed Forces Logistics, who is well connected to complementary nuclear and chemical military programs, and our asset believes that Javadi could help lead us to the info we need to uncover Park. By tomorrow, we will be in possession of information cloned from Javadi's cell phone, and Isaiah, I want you to dissect every tidbit of information and find us something we can use."

"Yes sir, "came a sharp reply from Taylor.

"Did I hear correctly, that we have a Red Chinese agent assisting us?" questioned Wright.

"Yes, and from what I hear from General Huang, she is quite formidable.

"Now, from the rest of you I need ideas, suggestions, and anything that you think will help us jumpstart the mission. I think it's safe to say, Blake and Clay, that you two should begin preparing for infiltrating Iran. I know you both can speak passable Farsi, which is half the battle inside, but we will need to get you both growing some facial hair and working on your best tans. What I do need from both of you is what you will need in-country to surveil our targets and your plans for infiltration and exfiltration. You'll be pleasantly surprised at the armory and equipment storage facility that Elaine has created in the basement. It has about every toy your heart will desire.

"Everyone has an office space in the building, and with Isaiah's oversight yesterday, we should be as technologically advanced as money can buy. Our receptionist is my niece, Courtney. She's fully vetted, but I'm bringing her along slowly with more details of what we're doing here. You two," waving his finger and training an evil eye at Ferguson and Wright, "stay away.

"We've done our best to soundproof the building and have signal jamming in place. We're operating on what I've been told is a very secure server, and encrypted landlines and cell phones have been issued to you and are waiting in your offices now. However, I've found in my world nothing is secure anymore, so be diligent about how you operate.

"Any questions?" Silence dominated the room. "Good, same time here tomorrow morning with updates. Let's get to work, people."

Chapter 13

Tehran, Iran

In the heart of downtown Tehran's 12th District, the team of four IRGC Guards quickly escorted Abdul-Mahdi from the exit of the third building of Parliament, hustling him to the curb of Baharestan Street, where they all were whisked away in a pair of identical black, Mercedes S-Class 550 sedans.

His meeting with Ahmad Jannati, the hardline conservative chairman of the Assembly of Experts, had gone as expected. It was Jannati, with a push from Nasser Togyani, who had encouraged the Supreme Leader to extradite Abdul-Mahdi to Iran and then spearheaded his return. As the newly elected leader of the deliberative body of Islamic theologians, known as the 88 Mujtahids, who were responsible for electing and removing the Supreme Leader of Iran and supervising his activities, he recognized Togyani's request as an opportunity of adding the expert scientist to the undeclared program of Dae-Ho Park and increasing the multitude of devices that improved his stature as the potential successor to the 77-year-old Khamenei.

The two-car convoy raced south on Persian Gulf Highway 7 en route to the city of Qom, 150 kilometers to the southwest. Abdul-Mahdi, or who ultimately now passed as him, sat back in the luxury of the rear leather bucket seat and exhaled visibly as he closed his eyes. For the first time since arriving in Tehran, Ibrahim Abood had a surge of confidence. He had just passed the first of what he thought to be several major tests of his identity. His impersonation mission to infiltrate Iran's revolutionary regime, and certainly the most ardent ideological and financial supporter of Hezbollah, was designed with the hope of penetrating the upper echelons of the Special Chemical, Biological, and Nuclear Industries in the Iranian Ministry of Defense.

With Iran's direct political control waning, and the bulk of financial support transferring from explicit government contribution to flowing more from religious organizations, Hezbollah's leadership was increasingly finding it imperative to gather and disseminate human intelligence on their maternal country's government activities. Of even more importance was keeping tabs specifically on any developments of Weapons of Mass Destruction and how they might benefit their terror activities against Israel.

Born into a wealthy Shia Lebanese family in 1976, Abood's father was a major real estate developer and property owner, including multiple hotels and business districts in Lebanon and Syria. Graduating with a Bachelor's degree in Chemistry from American University in Beirut and a Masters in Accounting at Long Island University, he followed his father into the family business as expected. What wasn't expected was his sudden disappearance after Israel's invasion of Lebanon in July of 2006, commonly known by the Lebanese as the July War.

For several years leading up to that incursion, Abood had gradually been falling under the influences of Hezbollah agents who had been actively recruiting the unmarried Abood and taking advantage of his proclivity for partying and concurrent alcohol and drug use. Initially interested in Abood for his family's money, Secretary-General Hassan Nasralleh personally identified his underlying intellect and powerful knowledge of chemistry and biology and pushed hard for Abood's direct enlistment into the jihad full time. Nasralleh was sure both tools would be in demand politically and militarily.

Regardless of his personal weaknesses, Ibrahim found the radical teachings and doctrine of anti-Semitism and the mission of destruction of the illegitimate Zionist state of Israel to be to his liking. He proved to be an easy convert after the Jews invaded his homeland again, destroying a number of properties he actively owned and managed for the family, during the heavy bombing and artillery focus in the south. He had witnessed enough and, with no warning to family or friends, walked away from his comfortable lifestyle to join the Jihad Council, Hezbollah's paramilitary wing.

Even as an untrained volunteer, he distinguished himself in active combat and ambush missions against the Israeli Defense Forces in and around the Bint Jbeil region, ultimately participating in the Battle of Wadi Saluki, where he suffered severe shrapnel wounds from advancing IDF tanks at the strategic wadi crossing. With a ceasefire instituted shortly afterward, he spent months recuperating off-grid while becoming increasingly involved in the activities of Unit 133, eventually rising to senior commander.

His room at the Al Zahra Hotel in Qom was heavily guarded and room service delivered his dinner early. His guest later that evening was to be an IRGC Commander by the name of Nasser Togyani, who he was told would arrive later that evening to provide him with direction on where he would be located to best help provide his biological and chemical weapons expertise. While waiting on his high-level handler, he relaxed on a stack of pillows propped against the headboard of his bed, beginning his mental preparation for the second significant test of competence in his transformation to Abbas Abdul-Mahdi.

Chapter 14

Themis Cooperative Offices, Alexandria, VA

As Adina Margolis entered the office of Jake Woods, accompanied by Ferguson and Wright on opposite arms, it was easy to see why Blake had a thing for her...she was stunning. Only five feet three inches tall and probably a hundred pounds soaking wet, she lit up the room with her long wavy brunette hair, olive skin, curvaceous figure, and electric smile of pearly white teeth.

"General Woods, I'm Adina Margolis," introducing herself as she reached out to shake hands in a confident strut to his desk.

"Yes, you are," replied Woods standing and making his way around his desk and stacks of unopened boxes to return the handshake. "Welcome. Blake and Clay have given me a short briefing on you and your skills, along with some additional and very gracious insight from your most favorite, albeit retired, Mossad Director Danny Yatom, but none of them told me that you were strikingly beautiful. I count Danny as a dear friend, and I would have expected him to enlighten me beyond your incredible service to your country."

"Flattery will get you everywhere General. However, I've had time to get all of my makeup on, my hair curled and I wore my Spanx and the loosest fitting outfit I could find just to keep everyone confused as to the extra pounds that won't go away now that I'm approaching the big 4-0. Regardless, thank you for the compliment and the welcome."

"Shit girl, you're frickin' 36 and still smokin' hot. Anyway, forty is the new thirty, so we all got that to look forward to, some sooner than others." Wright chimed in.

The four of them found spots on chairs and sofas scattered around the large, but still sparsely appointed office that Woods occupied, and proceeded to delve further into Margolis' background and expertise.

Born a strange mix of a Christian Iranian father and Jewish Spanish mother, Margolis grew up in a life of privilege in Athens, Greece. Her father was a senior executive of Dynacom Tankers and personal friend of billionaire shipowner and founder George Prokopiou. Their wealth allowed Margolis to travel the world with her mother and two younger brothers and afforded her the opportunity to pick an education that fit her wishes.

Graduating with a Masters in International Relations from the London School of Economics, she found herself pursuing a young Jewish engineer she met in London to his graduate assignment in Tel Aviv. It was there that her lover ultimately confessed his long-time involvement in the national intelligence agency of Israel known as Mossad, and the bug of intrigue bit the young Margolis.

Even though that relationship eventually failed, her interest in his profession did not. Much to the chagrin of her father, she herself joined the brilliant, but fearsomely effective and sometimes ruthless intelligence service. Swiftly rising through the ranks of the Research Department, charged with intelligence collection, she later transferred into the Collections Department, where she became responsible for covert espionage operations and counterterrorism. Her abilities in the Middle Eastern theatre and her unconfirmed work in the Kidon, an elite group of expert assassins, made her a star in the intelligence community, not only in Israel but internationally as well.

"Adina…I hope it's okay if I call you Adina?" queried Woods, as she gave an affirmative nod. "Your reputation and accolades are off the chart young lady. I can't tell you how impressed and excited I am to know that you are willing to help us in our little adventure."

"From what I've been told General, I, as well as my superiors, am glad to be of assistance. This is a top priority for all of us. For the sake of appearances, I will tell you I have been counted as terminated from Mossad for a bevy of psychological reasons. So, I am officially known as a 'loose cannon' and not to be trusted by anyone within the service, except for a few nameless individuals that will be tasked to provide whatever assistance we may need. I believe that was a request you made of my office, to insure plausible deniability for them as well."

"Correct, and thanks for taking one for the team. Hopefully we can render this mission a success and you can once again regain your mental faculties and return to your lofty status back home."

"Like I said, I'm happy to do it. I trust these two gauchos with my life," Margolis patted the knee of Ferguson and winked at Wright simultaneously, "and definitely would do anything to help if they asked."

"Well then, I trust they have briefed you on the specifics of the mission?" Margolis again nodded her assent. "I also trust, from what I've been told, that the three of you have determined a feasible way of infiltrating the border and positioning yourselves to move about inside Iran," Woods visually surveyed the three of them.

It was Ferguson who spoke first, as the others willingly deferred to him. "We covered a lot of scenarios but believe this one to be the best option. It's by no means an easy in, but we all think it's imperative to have transportation when we hit the ground. That will also allow us to armor up heavy. If we have to go in on foot or

HALO jump into the middle of nowhere, it's whatever we can pack on our back. That's not going to cut it. We also considered motorcycles, but we figured having Adina all hijabed up and driving her own dirt bike, didn't quite fit if we run into any bad hajis."

"You know I can handle a motorbike better than you Blake, even with a scarf over my face."

"No doubt," chimed Wright, extending and receiving a left-handed high-five with Margolis.

"You two couldn't ride your way out of a paper bag," Ferguson replied, dismissing them both with a wave of his hand. With an exaggerated clearing of his throat, "As I was saying…the best option we decided on was to chopper in with a four-wheeler strapped to the belly. We can tight-rig a quick-disconnect Heli-Strap to a Morattab Pazhan Land Rover, go in 'nap-of-the-earth' at night, drop, and be mobile in under a minute. That will minimize time over hostile territory for the helo, and give us a set of wheels we can load up with the proper amount of equipment and armor we need to stay in-country for a bit."

Wright added, "We've researched several mining and engineering companies operating in central and southern Iran, and we're confident we can doctor it up as a company vehicle to represent a business entity of our choosing. Along with the proper matching credentials passing us off as engineers, should give us some cover to move about, until we can settle into someplace that allows us to go underground a little bit better."

Margolis said, "I've worked the southeastern border region of Iran, specifically in the Sistan and Baluchestan Province bordering Pakistan, and there are some holes in the border wall Iran has been building, all below Taftan. It's an area of major smuggling routes and we can utilize some of the barren or rugged terrain to our advantage."

"An NOE incursion in that region will require one helluva pilot, but it can be done." Ferguson interjected. "We can bring the chopper out of Kandahar and take it down to the old camp Gecko, which I think goes by Firebase Maholic now. We can use the secluded space there to equip it, out of sight from common eyes. Once we're ready to go, we fly out south toward Rudbar, jump the border, and negotiate the northwest "Triangle" portion of Pakistan just west of the Mud Volcano area. It's approximately 150 kilometers max over Pakistani airspace, similar to the Bin Laden timing, but much more desolate. There are a few places we can jump into Iran from that 45-klick area anywhere south of the RCD Lake desert to the mountains below Jâlq. Eight to ten klicks in and the same back out.

"We're still working on the best opening along the Border Road where most of the wall, both manmade and natural, is being constructed. We're getting some damn good satellite data from Isaiah, and Adina has some old contacts with the Jaish ul-Adl, a Sunni insurgent group that operates in that area and that intel is helping us narrow down the best way in. By the way, that Taylor kid is incredible. He's snooping in some very interesting National Intelligence sites as if he has a security clearance access. He can get into about any site that's off limits. It's frightening, the shit he can uncover. I have a new appreciation that there ain't nothing safe or private in this world."

Woods immediately knew who had the mastery to pilot a helicopter under these circumstances, but also realized what the implications of his involvement might have on his career. *Maybe Matt could recommend somebody else to handle this.* He knew if and when he asked him, knowing the mission, Matt would be the first one to volunteer.

As if reading his mind, Ferguson interrupted his train of thought. "We may have overstepped our bounds General, but we're quite familiar with your son. We know he's one of the best jockeys in the service, and we also know he's one of the top go-to guys for Special Ops. He's hopped a lot of operators that Clay and I are both still very close to, and after reaching out to some of them that are active, he's the first name they all throw back. I hear that the stealth Black Hawk project is back and active, and he was piloting one of the modified 60s on the Syrian Raid in July '14 looking for James Foley. That's some heady shit! Probably not who you wanted to hear we would like to chauffeur us in but should make you proud regardless. My guess is he can recommend somebody that could do the job. As a side note, don't know if you have any pull at that level, but it might be worth asking Special Operations Command if we can commandeer one of the stealth units to pave our way in. It sure might make it a little easier."

"He won't bother to recommend anyone else; he'll be the first to volunteer," replied Woods. "It's okay. Without meaning to sound braggadocious, I'm not sure I trust this to anybody else. I just need to rig it so he doesn't take the fall if it goes to shit. I'll make some calls and see what kind of assurances I can get, before I talk to him. I'll also reach out to see what SOCOM says about the stealth program and if we could simply 'borrow' one of the available units."

The conversation distinctly added to the weight of the task at hand, and that had Woods increasingly feeling the growing anxiety of the mission. He stood and walked to the window and looked out on a gray, misty day, the remnants of a light snow from the previous evening still covering the ground. He rubbed his chin in contemplation, "What are your thoughts if you get situated safely inside?"

Wright looked at both Margolis and then Ferguson, "Well, chief, that's where we were hoping you might be able to help. We want to get in direct contact with the PRC asset. You said she's one tough cookie and apparently has the best intelligence going, and that seems to us," he looked again at both Margolis and Ferguson for affirmation, and received it, "that she is the link to get us started on the hunt. I'll lay odds that she can also help find us a hole to hide in. What are the chances of making that happen?"

"Don't know until I ask, but I suspect very good. General Huang pledged his support when he brought this adventure to me, and his girl clearly is knee deep in the shit, so I would hope her availability and access is on the table. I'll have you an answer on that by the end of the day."

"Excellent!" exclaimed Ferguson, "I think that gets us started. On the back side, I'm not sure where we might extract, since we have no idea what the future holds when we find this Park character or the facility housing his operation. We can certainly pack enough explosive ordnance with us to take down a sizable building, but if it becomes anything bigger, we're going to need access to delivery options on cruise munitions or guided missile via drone. We can stay and paint the targets either way. Getting out will probably depend on where geographically the targets are eliminated. We'll come up with extraction contingencies based on north, south, east, and west. It looks like Iraq, Pakistan, Afghanistan, Turkey, and maybe even a water evac in either of the Gulfs might be options."

Woods returned to his seat from the window and jotted a couple notes on a legal pad in front of him. "I'll get an answer on your ferry ride and crew and the availability of the PRC agent. The three of you get with Elaine and requisition everything you need, no expense spared. That includes whatever vehicle you want to drop in with, and talk to Isaiah about the vehicle markings and the legal registrations you'll need to make yourself street legal in Iran. Also, have him develop some iron clad credentials for the identities you plan to assume. Have him forward all of the details on your aliases to me. I know a few people retired from the Farm that can help forge the finished documents. Make sure the comms equipment you need is state-of-the art. I want us able to communicate with each other securely while you're in-country." He glanced up at the group and, before having to ask for understanding, got a nod from everyone in return.

"Elaine already has an incredibly impressive armory built up in the basement, along with all the tactical gear you will probably ever need." I know each of you has a shop credit card, so I'll let you guys determine the fashion statements needed to move around in Iran, not my strong suit, and anything miscellaneous you might need on the open market."

As he stood in an obvious sign of dismissal, Woods said, "Meet back here tomorrow at noon. I'll have lunch catered in. Give me a status report and estimated time of departure. I would expect it to be within 72 hours. Understood?"

Wright stood and saluted, as Ferguson and Margolis said in unison, "Understood General." Everyone could feel the weight of the operation in motion. The countdown unofficially had begun.

Chapter 15

Setareh Laboratory, South Khorasan, Iran

Blood oozed from the eye sockets, mouth, and nostrils of what once was the healthy young adult Jordanian male, now nearing death as his body alternated between involuntary convulsions and near lifeless tranquility as he lay strapped to the gurney. Two lab-coated spectators, standing in safety outside the airlock of one of 12 test rooms in the physical containment level 4 (PC4) facility, tapped notes into their Microsoft Surface PCs, as Park wandered in the sterile corridor behind them, speaking monotone into his iPad mini.

This would be their fourth subject to die today, but this particular one had survived nearly a week with one of the most recent antiviral concoctions Park had created in collaboration with the two new arrivals forced upon him over the course of the last week. The latest addition, Abbas Abdul-Mahdi, recognizable to Park after a brief Google search of his name, clearly revealed trouble for Park's assignment. The notorious scientist was a walking database of all things biological, particularly in the world of weapons of mass destruction. Togyani had clearly brought the best pressure he could find.

The next room held even more promise. Human subject #87, ensconced in Test Room #9, had succumbed immediately after introduction to the virus through airborne transmission; however, after being administered the "newest" AV formula within twelve hours of exposure and ten hours of exhibition of symptoms, was now showing signs of responding positively to the treatment. As of this morning, she was improving and showing signs of potentially a full recovery.

Park completed the conversation with his Apple device and exhaled noticeably, casting a forced smile at the two scientists interfacing in front of him. He had reached the end of his stall tactics. The two "science minders" as he was loath to view them, particularly Abdul-Mahdi, had clearly been added to the process to speed up results, and Togyani was effectively calling his bluff at not being able to create a vaccine and antidote, or successful treatment protocol.

The solution was not complicated, and it wouldn't take them long to identify it once on the right track. His father had entrusted the simple, natural secret to him in the jungles of Cambodia, before the Chinese had unceremoniously shot him dead, execution style in the back of the head, thinking they had killed the knowledge of the virus along with him. He couldn't help but think the same fate probably awaited him once the ability to disseminate the virus, and how to control and combat it, were understood and the processes in place. That time was quickly approaching, and for the first time, the reality began to sway him to thinking of another process…was there a way to sabotage it.

The money he had wanted and needed in return for his services in creating the virus, the amount eagerly agreed upon by Togyani and the Mullahs, was safely ensconced in a secure Swiss account that would help care for his ailing daughter. It would be up to him to make sure she was stashed away and safely guarded in a high-security location, until she could pass in a peaceful death.

*How did I let myself get involved in this shit? Nothing but pure greed. I love my child and wish her all the peace she can have, but I will be forever linked to this insidious Armageddon. Greed, plain and simple...greed...greed...*Park shook his head in disgust and walked down the empty corridor towards his office, the echoes of his shoes clipping against the sanitized floor, the echoes of the impending disaster striking at his brain.

* * * * *

Approximately 90 kilometers to the north of the clandestine lab, in a suffocating bunkered recreation center-turned-war room, made only bearable by the rattling strains of an air conditioner that was losing both battles of cooling and cleansing the fetid air through a single large vent in the wall, General Togyani huddled with one of his commanding officers overseeing the military-style training facility located in the barren land northeast of Nay Band, Iran. Dubbed the Setareh Support facility, SS for short, it had been created solely for the training, operational support, and implementation of the Setareh Doctrine.

Standing side-by-side, the two men jostled in unison around the room, addressing a series of maps, layered upon each other and occupying all four walls of the large rectangular building. In total, the maps represented all of the major metropolitan areas and the barren lands surrounding them to the west, occupying every square mile within the Setareh Doctrine field of operation. All of the same information was stored electronically in a more modern workable format, but Togyani was old school and wanted everything visible in one place. Touchable. Tangible.

Accessing the latest notes and computer models derived from the infectious disease experts in General Seyyedi's Tehran office, both Togyani and General Nuri Massoud were engaged in intense discussions plotting and assessing the latest placement of the two forms of assets, human and mechanical, the latter to be deployed as back-up for any failure by the former, but both a part of the Setareh launch.

Constructed from scratch in conjunction with the Setareh bio lab, the training camp housed nearly 1,000 jihadist trainees all enlisted for Setareh's martyrdom. Undergoing weapons and tactical warfare training, ironically, they were also receiving strenuous physical conditioning, ultimately to be utilized as sacrificial human vessels introducing the fatal plague to come.

The categorization of the men and women into organized units was based on countries of origin or geographic regions associated with the individual so-called soldiers. They would be re-deployed into the same areas to wreak a form of Armageddon on their own people, and in some cases family and friends. It would be of no consequence, because the additional radical Islamic religious brainwashing all of the camp's jihadi soldiers had undergone created a small army of mind-numbed robots capable of anything they would be ordered to do, all in the name of Allah.

The electronic beep of the entry door keypad being utilized interrupted their deliberation and was followed by the intrusion of a young Chinese man, entering with none of the military discipline the two senior soldiers were accustomed to being afforded. Togyani welcomed the civilian with a hypocritical smiling gesture of acknowledgement, masking the contempt he held for the electronics engineer from Shanghai.

Wang Wei was the director and engineering wizard responsible for the mechanical failsafe portion of the Setareh virus transmission. If the human bombs failed to wreak enough havoc in their areas of responsibility, Wei's automated army of machines would rectify the lack of destruction.

Wei looked just old enough to be out of high school, but at thirty-five years of age he had spent nearly a decade with Yuneec International Co. Ltd. and was on the design team responsible for creating the world's first ready-to-fly, out-of-the-box drone, the Typhoon Q500 quadcopter.

It was his whiz-kid persona, and bullet-proof belief in his intelligence and immortality, mercilessly teamed with his relentless penchant for gambling and over-the-top lifestyle, that led him to be saddled with the albatross of inconceivable debt to some of the more unsavory characters in the Chinese underworld. He was the perfect target for the Iranian Intelligence Agency's claws, when they were tasked with finding a candidate to devise the drone program that Togyani had in mind. Money, and lots of it, cured Wang of his indebtedness and easily lured him into the clutches of Togyani. His task was to develop a fleet of autonomous, unmanned aerial vehicles capable of flying through obstacle-ridden environments to pre-programmed GPS targets.

"Ahhh…Mr. Wei, how goes the delivery of our armada of flying artificial intelligence?" asked Togyani with a hint of sarcasm.

Wei's limited understanding of the Persian language understood about half of the question, and the confusion on his face made it clear.

In broken English, Togyani repeated his inquiry.

"It goes very well, General," Wei responded, "We have sixty percent of the five thousand units we ordered delivered to the camp, and we can expect the balance within the next ten days. We ran test flights on twelve units going to Tehran, Isfahan, Bandar Abbas, and Mashhad, all going through rigorous geographic, topographic, and climatic conditions, and all reached their targets within three meters. The dispersal retrofits expelled the perfume as loaded, and the explosive charges virtually disintegrated every one of them. I was told the remaining pieces were so minute they would provide no forensic evidence."

A devious smile emerged on Togyani's face, an imperceptible twitch of his lower lip, signaled his unbridled joy. It was all coming together nicely. "And you have enough of the aerosol and explosive retrofits for the entire lot?"

"Yes, sir. Everything is here. We're just waiting on the remaining units to arrive. We can have the entire fleet assembled and ready for programming within two to three days of the arrival of the remaining drones."

"Thank you, Wei. If you'll leave us now, we have much work to do."

As Wei exited, both men took a break from the wearisome work of designing a model of genocide, seating themselves in the folding metal and plastic chairs surrounding the long spartan table dwarfed in the middle of the room. Both men sampled the contents of a perspiring cooler of bottled waters.

"Are we close General?" inquired Massoud.

"Very," replied Togyani quickly. "All the pieces here are nearly in place. The additional personnel at the lab seem to have done the trick. It's been quite amazing to see how quickly progress has been made by Dr. Park on the treatment and prevention protocols."

"So, your suspicions about his knowledge of them all along may have been accurate?"

"Possibly...actually more than likely. No matter, we have ultimately reached the same outcome, without having to coerce him physically. That was a direction that may have never yielded what we wanted from him. In the end, money talks, along with a little help from the introduction of peers into his lab. The bonus from the additional minds is that they appear to have realized, and in some instances, been able to control the duration of infectiousness, which will greatly aid our ability to manage the outbreak. It won't be easy, but it can be done," Togyani cocked his head with a perverse grin worthy of the devil, "and, Nuri, it's coming soon."

Chapter 16

South of Sistan-Baluchistan Road on the Iran and Pakistan Border

The lunar and weather gods had been kind, as the night was pitch black. A new moon and cloud cover from an approaching cold front forced the ceiling down to 3,500 feet, and the modified MH-60M Black Hawk helicopter had flown the majority of its 500-kilometer journey south below the clouds in a little over two hours. As it slipped from the pseudo friendly confines of Afghanistan into Pakistani airspace northwest of the Mud Volcano area, Captain Matthew Woods adjusted his heading slightly to the southwest, to traverse the desert area triangle just outside the maximum long-range radar coverage emanating from the Karachi Sector West operating field.

Hiding time was over. He was now approaching the outer limits of coverage about 100 kilometers north of the designated insertion point, along the border of the Sistan and Baluchistan Provinces of southeastern Iran and southwestern Pakistan. Woods would now have to begin what was technically referred to as terrain flight.

He brought the specially modified chopper down from the safe confines of the wide-open air space to no more than 60-70 meters over the rolling terrain with little noticeable change in the 130-knot speed. He would maintain the contour flying while taking full advantage of the integrated avionics system's night-vision-compatible cockpit features, including four 6-by-8-inch full-color multifunction liquid crystal displays that provided aircraft flight, mission and sensor data. The feedback gave him a moving map display, an Engine Indication and Crew Alert System known as EICAS, advanced hover and landing cueing, electro-optical video display and forward-looking infrared commonly referred to as FLIR video display. He would need all of the high-tech gadgetry, as he would spend the next 45 minutes trying to hug the variances in landscapes to make him more difficult to spot from the Iranian radar reports.

Woods engaged his microphone and alerted his co-pilot Chief Warrant Officer Andy Thomas, "Make sure all Threat Detection is engaged, AT."

"Roger that," came Thomas' swift reply as he activated the Infrared Jammer, Laser Detecting Set, and Radar Warning Receiver.

His next comments were for the remainder of his passengers, the two-man crew seated immediately behind him, who would act as gunners and insertion support when it was time to drop off their cargo, and Ferguson, Margolis, and Wright, who were all seated together on the forward-facing bench. "Ladies, strap 'em up real tight, we're about to go NOE in 15 minutes, and it should be better than "The Beast" at "King's Island.""

Nap-of-the-earth flying in the rugged southern Taftan Mountain range would be an adventure in traversing eight to ten kilometers of 1,500-meter peaks and valleys. It would be quick, but it would be treacherous. Woods was about to earn his pay, in a job that paid him nothing. When his dad called him nearly 48 hours earlier, he wouldn't have had it any other way.

* * * * *

Less than a day after their last meeting with Jake Woods, the final operational details for the mission had been fleshed out between Ferguson, Margolis, and Wright over beer and pizza. After no objections and a complete sign off from Woods, Elaine Scruggs and Isaiah Taylor had gone to work on the details the following morning. With a little help from a number of her friends still active at the Main Operating Base Kandahar, part of the International Security Assistance Force Southern Regional Command installations in Afghanistan, Scruggs was able to assemble entire wardrobes, for what she referred to as the "three stooges," providing each with the comforts of local Iranian fashion. Additionally, through some extraordinarily good luck, a "very close" DIA agent friend, still operating out of Fire Base Maholic, not far from Kandahar City, was able to provide a late model, white Morattab Pazhan 3000 "Landy" Iranian SUV, recently confiscated in a successful government forces raid on a Taliban smuggling operation. Multiple vehicles were offered, and all were accepted, as reward for the precise and fruitful intelligence supplied. Taylor had expertly created the appropriate engineering decals, Iranian plates, and registration that would adorn their new possession.

Isaiah also found that creating the personal and professional credentials proved much easier than anticipated, as he was able to gain access to a significant number of legitimate Iranian identities and photo identification with which he was able to come surprisingly close to the now bearded Ferguson and Wright. Margolis was much easier, with the ability to hide her behind the Muslim hijab. Taylor was most proud of his ability to create Wright's Iranian alias from an actual mining engineer from Neyshabur.

Scruggs' skills at appropriating the list of weaponry Moe, Larry, and Curly had requisitioned had surprised even them, especially given they were already in her possession in the subterranean arsenal she had been working on since her arrival. Jake Woods' connections to the active duty brass in both the DIA and US Special Operations Command, had greased the skids for acquisitions that otherwise would have been off limits to anybody else asking.

The laundry list, a fraction of the depot Scruggs had accumulated, included 60 pounds of C-4 M112 demolition blocks with detonation cord and blasting caps, advanced tactical and secure satellite communications gear, L-3 AN/PVS-31 Binocular Night Vision Devices (BNVD) with headgear, two Remington Modular Sniper Rifles (MSR) with thermal imaging and night vision scopes, two FN MK 46 Light Machineguns (LMG), with Surefire tactical lights and IR lasers, three Daniel Defense MK18 suppressed assault rifles with two H&K M320 grenade launchers, four Glock 19 hand guns with suppressors, a SOFLAM PEQ-1C Laser Acquisition Marker, three SafeGuard StealthPRO body armor sized accordingly, and enough grenades and rounds for what she thought would be 30 minutes of survival at high rates of fire. She offered up a silent prayer that it wouldn't come to that, as she packed everything into the false bottoms of three metal crates that totaled the size of a small coffin, the top portions adorned with miscellaneous engineering tools and equipment. She would personally deliver the packages to Andrew Air base to the attention of Major Matthew Woods.

Woods had been killing the better part of the afternoon waiting patiently at the private hangers at Andrews for arrival of the personal parcels, almost 24 hours after asking for, and receiving, "urgent" orders to provide night flight training to the pilots at Kandahar Air Field. His orders reflected that his expertise was "badly needed", even though every Chinook and Black Hawk pilot at Kandahar had enough qualified night hours and could pretty much fly the birds in their sleep.

His Dad had been correct. When offered the chance to fly the mission himself, or recommend a pilot that was capable, he laughed off the insult and went to work pulling strings at USSOCOM to get his ass to Afghanistan as fast as possible. For the higher-ups that approved his request, and offered back channel assurances to Jake and Matt on any unanticipated consequences, the "classified" understanding of a clear and present danger had been all they needed to grease the skids for his abrupt re-assignment.

After the arrival of Elaine's disguised weapons cache, Woods observed them as they were loaded into the baggage hold of the Gulfstream G550 registered to WRD Capital, but had come with a special military flight clearance. As he boarded and settled into one of the plush leather seats of the spacious cabin area, a lovely young lady in black slacks and a sheer cream-colored blouse, her auburn hair fashionably drawn up into a high ponytail, appeared almost out of nowhere with a chilled manhattan served "up." "A little birdie told me that newly minted Army Majors were partial to these," as she handed him the cocktail with a seductive wink.

"Actually, I prefer red-headed flight attendants, but seeing as this is already in-hand, I'll try to make do with the drink."

"Be careful what you wish for soldier, we have a long flight ahead of us, and you appear to be my only customer," as she disappeared behind a curtain in the forward galley. "Besides, I've been told I'm a handful, so you'd need both hands," came the sultry response.

* * * * *

Executing with honed precision the more intense NOE technique flying, Woods traversed the nine kilometers over the Pakistani border into Iranian airspace, made even more interesting with an SUV strapped to the bottom of the bird. It had indeed been a roller coaster of ups and downs with the slight acceleration and deceleration to manipulate the natural obstacles that looked as if they could jump in the helicopter door if open.

Maneuvering up and over two mountain peaks and valleys, he finally banked and dropped into a dry river bed, then negotiated a northwest heading for a small remote village less than five kilometers ahead. This was the drop zone. His time inside Iran was being counted down in minutes by Thomas.

"We're here ladies," Woods called out abruptly with no warning, as he pulled back on the cyclic stick and brought the vehicle to a sudden stop and hover. That was all the indication needed for the two crew chiefs, Staff Sergeant Bruce Brewer and Sergeant First Class Luke Trent to instantaneously spring out of their seats, opening the cabin doors on both sides as a sudden sand storm escalated from below the rotor whirling beast.

Remaining tethered to the bird, both stepped out onto the wheel assemblies as Woods adjusted the collective bringing the belly down into the grainy cyclone. When they were only a few feet from the ground, Trent gave a quick thumb down hand signal across the cargo bay to Brewer, and they both disconnected what the Knoxville born and raised Brewer called the best Appalachian engineering he had ever seen. The one release for each side liberated a jerry-rigged web hammock that let the Morattab Pazhan fall to the ground less than a meter above the ground.

Woods pulled the chopper forward and laid it on the ground as Brewer and Trent retrieved the cargo strap, and the "three stooges" hopped out of the doors onto the hostile and desolate ground of the Islamic Republic of Iran. Scurrying out from the prop wash, Ferguson gave a quick salute to Woods, who returned the favor.

With both of his crew chiefs safely back inside, Woods was already airborne in retreat on a slightly different course than he had arrived, while Ferguson, Margolis, and Wright made their way to the dust-covered vehicle. They were mobile in under a minute and bumping along down the river bed to an area due south toward Road 92 as Woods reached Pakistani airspace and headed north for the relative comforts of Kandahar. The whole insertion took less than eight minutes. Two hours later, Jake Woods received confirmation from his son-the engineers had landed, successfully found the mine, and were headed into the shaft.

Chapter 17

Tehran, Iran

The late model JAC Refine crossover that Lei Lau commandeered from the Chinese embassy motor pool was one of the more popular brands and models of Chinese automobiles in Iran and blended in well with the late afternoon Tehran traffic. The benefit of modern Iran, unlike several of her Middle Eastern Muslim neighbors, was that women were allowed driving privileges, so Lau was free to move about the country by her lonesome.

That had proved to be exactly the freedom she needed over the last week while surveilling the daily activities of General Amir Javadi. Having mixed in another sexual tryst in a local posh hotel two evenings previous just to keep up the pretense of interest and to further glean as much information from the pathetic excuse for a father, husband, and military man that he was, she had been able to create quite the dossier on the General.

Today's mission was different. General Huang's orders had changed the game entirely. Per his conversation the previous evening with Jake Woods, her assignment had turned from surveillance and intelligence gathering activities to participating in a fully engaged covert military operation. The most peculiar aspect, of which she still was trying to wrap her mind around, was assisting an American special operation infiltration team that had just been inserted into southern Iran.

Her journey today was to follow through on securing one of the seven safe houses Huang had established since he had approached her with their joint endeavor with the Americans over two weeks ago. Having learned the approximate area the Ops team had entered the country, she was going to be headed to a small farm house on the southwest side of the town of Surmaq, located in the Central District of Abadeh County, Fars Province. The isolated residence was hidden from view from the main highway 65, behind three mature fields of cherry, fig and date trees. It had been well tended to by an elderly local family, who had received a windfall of nearly fifty times their property value and decided it would be wise to take the Euros and run. Rumor had it they had relocated to Morocco to be closer to their son's family. The new owners would be an engineer based in Isfahan and his wife.

With a population of just over 3,000, the rural and weather-beaten town of Surmaq was somewhat centrally located in the country, offering the advantage of an equidistant jump point for wherever the operation required them to go. It also sat just south and west of some of the most rugged and desolate land of Yazd Province, giving some possible area to get lost if it became necessary.

Under the guise of taking a short holiday to visit the Parishan Lake area, she directed her vehicle south on the Persian Gulf Highway 7 for the nearly 700-kilometer journey to meet some "friends." Her mind couldn't help but think this was going to be a journey she might never forget.

Chapter 18

Southeastern Sistan and Baluchestan Province, Iran

With headlights off and utilizing his BVND headgear to illuminate the night in a neon green, Wright negotiated the four-wheel drive Landy southwest through a very narrow dried river bed that Ferguson labeled more like a "creek" while navigating from the passenger seat. The terrain was bumpy at best, and their travel was slow going without the benefit of the vehicle's lights. Ferguson also had his night vision on as well and was busy watching their flanks and six. They had traveled a little over four kilometers since insertion and had approximately 20 kilometers left until they spilled onto Road 92 that would lead them northwest into the heart of Iran.

Their route was intentional, avoiding any of the small clusters of nondescript housing and remote villages that were sparse in the mountains that made up the southeastern tip of the Makran range. The goal was to remain out of sight and undetected until they could reach 92 just south of Kalporagan, navigate north on the highway, and then utilize their identification and credentials as consulting engineers and geologists contracted by the Salderah Mining Company if detained or questioned. The province held important geological and metal mineral potentials such as chrome, copper, granite, iron, lead, zinc, tin, nickel, platinum, gold, and silver, which would help support their interest and presence in the area.

As Wright edged over a small incline, he was greeted by half a dozen men standing in their path, all brandishing Kalashnikov rifles, one of them slashing at his throat with a free hand in an apparent signal to either stop or turn off the vehicle. He and Ferguson yanked off their NVDs simultaneously, as each man slipped a suppressed Glock into their waistbands, untucked shirts concealing the exposed grips.

"Shit," muttered Ferguson.

Margolis popped her head forward between them from the back seat, "What's up?"

"We got company," Ferguson nodded ahead.

Throat slasher, who appeared to be in charge, had already walked forward toward the driver side barking in a language that neither Wright or Ferguson recognized.

Margolis came to their rescue, "It's some sort of Persian, but probably Baluchi. I recognize enough of it to translate his desire for us to 'turn it off and get out'."

Wright killed the engine, opened the door and extended his hands up and out in a show of submission, as he exited the vehicle positioning himself behind the driver door to provide concealment. Ferguson mirrored Wright also appearing to surrender and exit the vehicle. Margolis connected the veil on her Hijab to cover her face, exited the Pazhan on the driver side, and spoke to the angry man in a calming Persian dialect, "Who are you, and why are you treating us this way?"

The man lowered his weapon, scratched at his long, soiled beard as he eyed her suspiciously, and replied in a more recognizable Sistani Persian easier understood by Margolis, "We will treat you any way we want. This is my land, and you are trespassing. We are confiscating all of your belongings, and only I will decide if you live or die in the process."

Margolis walked forward to confront the man, "You have no right to take our things, you are not the law," demanded Margolis.

The man eyed her quizzically. "I am the law in this territory, and anybody who comes through here uninvited must answer to me." His demeanor changed from angry to tyrannical, as he was not going to tolerate a woman speaking to him in this way, embarrassing him in front of his men. "Step away from me or I will shoot all of you."As the smuggler boss raised his hand to hit Margolis, Wright determined that the diplomatic approach had failed, muttering to Ferguson, "I've got the left three..."

Wright drew his pistol and as the barrel cleared his beltline it snapped directly toward the upper torso of the smuggler boss. Ferguson's peripheral vision registered Wright's draw and he reached for his own Glock 19, prioritizing his set of smugglers in a microsecond. The middle smuggler first with both hands on his rifle and his shoulders hunched forward, next the smuggler on the left standing flat footed lazily carrying his AK by the pistol grip, then the smuggler on the right with his AK still slung over his shoulder walking towards their SUV a few meters further back from the group.

Oblivious to his impending doom, the smuggler boss reached the apex of his back-hand windup, as Margolis, hearing Wright's declaration to Ferguson, raised her hands to her face and fell to the ground in a defensive move that took her out of the line of fire.

Firing his first two shots, Wright instinctively aimed his rounds into the chest of the head honcho, as Margolis scrambled to her feet and started for the rear of the SUV to seek cover and retrieve additional firepower. The surprised man, his glossy eyes growing wide and his raised arm dropping to his side, tilted as his legs collapsed underneath him.

Wright snapped his eyes left past one of the smugglers, who had dropped his rifle entirely due to surprise, and on to another of the bandits who was mashing the safety lever on his AK down to full-auto. Wright extended his arms, aligning his sights for a head shot, and squeezed off a 9mm slug that ripped through the right temple of his second target.

Simultaneous to Wright, Ferguson sent two rounds into the chest of the middle smuggler robbing him of every ounce of resolve he had mustered to face the trio of strangers getting out of their SUV. Ferguson then whipped his eyes to the smuggler on his left as the man began to raise his rifle attempting to level it at his hip.

The big boss man was now splayed out on his back, his breathing accelerating into short wheezes, futilely clutching at his chest with his hands as Margolis rounded the back corner of the SUV, instinctively reaching out for the door latch just above the license plate.

Ferguson's next two rounds on the smuggler to his left were hurried to ensure the man wasn't able to get a burst off. The first round sent a shock wave of pain through the smuggler's body as it tore through his abdomen, fragmenting as it impacted into a lumbar vertebra severing the man's spinal cord. The second round scorched through the smuggler's chest as it impacted into the man's sternum sending shards of copper and lead through his lungs and heart. The near instantaneous drop in blood pressure combined with the searing pain and paralysis were enough to ensure the smuggler's burst would be completely ineffective. But Ferguson opted for insurance as he raised the sights of his Glock, now slightly blurred from the heat emanating from the suppressor, aligning his third shot as close to the center of the smuggler's head as possible. The 9mm hollow point round impacted midway between the crest of the smuggler's cheek bone and the tip of his nose, sending fragments of bullet and bone through the inside of his skull negating any chance his brain could signal his finger for a trigger pull on his AK.

Wright swung his pistol back to the right and down to the broad sided ribcage of his third smuggler who had turned and dropped to a knee bending over to retrieve his fallen rifle. Wright's mind subconsciously focused in on the vital heart lungs and spine as the smuggler contorted into an open posture. Wright double tapped his third smuggler with two 9mm rounds that penetrated just below the man's armpit less than two inches apart and bore through the breadth of his chest cavity.

The boss's wheezes were short and rapid as dark circular stains began to expand in diameter across the man's light-colored clothing, two holes high and close together at the top of his chest.

Margolis ripped open the rear hatch of the SUV, overcoming the drag of the pneumatic pistons on either side of the door, and reached for the MK 46 Light Machine Gun.

The boss's unseeing eyes remained open as his body's capillary and venous blood flow ceased in response to the rapid drop in blood pressure. His wheezes slowed and became shallow.

Ferguson transitioned hard back to the right and stabilized himself against the SUV as he sent three rounds into the last smuggler. Frozen still from the sudden shock of overwhelming violence inflicted on the rest of his party, the last bandit standing hadn't even managed to unsling his weapon.

The smuggler boss's conscious thinking had ceased without affording him an opportunity to regret his decision to confront the strange trio in the SUV.

Margolis pulled the MK 46 out of the cargo bay and yanked the charging handle to ready the machinegun. Shouldering the weapon, she lunged out laterally from the rear of the SUV sweeping the area beyond the front of the vehicle to search for any remaining hostile targets.

The whole episode took less than five seconds.

"Damnit, that was a lot of noise," Wright said, kicking at the others to see if there were any signs of life. "We need to get this cleaned up quickly and get the hell out of here. Hopefully there's not any more from where these came from."

Ferguson started dragging bodies up the side of the scraggly slope out of sight from where the Landy sat. "Strip them of anything valuable. We'll have to make it look like they ran into the wrong band of smugglers."

They took a worn haversack off one of the dead men and put everything they could find out of their pockets, along with watches, rings, two necklaces and a few bracelets into the bag. They removed a couple pairs of boots that were in reasonably good shape, pocketed a handful of currency, collected all the weapons, and proceeded to pile up the bodies face down in a crevice, behind a pile of scrub and small outcropping of rocks.

After consulting the map, they agreed that a few miles north on Road 92, just above the town of Saravan, they could dispose of the weapons and jewelry in the Matein River. They needed to move fast and get to the main roadway as soon as possible. They estimated negotiating the remaining rugged terrain wouldn't take as long now that a faint dawn light was looming over the mountains to the East, and the terrain would soon flatten out as they now chose a more northwest path, which would intersect them with the Sistan-Buchestan Road. It would at least provide them with an actual paved, two-lane feeder road leading to 92, and with any luck and no more delays, they would make the highway by sunrise.

Chapter 19

Surmaq, Iran

One hundred meters in front of them, the flashlight blinked on and off three times as promised, and Ferguson crept the Landy down the hardpacked, sandy dirt road just southwest of the small town of Surmaq, Iran. At the candle burning post lamp, he directed the vehicle through a narrow, double-door, wooden gate carved out of a six-foot stone block wall and into an open-air courtyard. A circular driveway brought the vehicle up to a one-story farmhouse built from the same earth it sat on, a red tile roof offering some color relief to the overall image. The wall continued around three sides of the structure, connecting to the two corners behind, effectively enclosing the entire house. Small gates in both of the back walls, flanking each of those corners, led out to a large orchard that stretched well beyond the diminishing natural light, fading into the darkness of the oncoming night sky.

From the time they found their way onto Road 92 early that morning, the 1,300-kilometer trip to the north had taken nearly 16 hours. Successfully disposing of the items confiscated from the smugglers they encountered, the trip had thankfully been uneventful.

Stopping briefly for fuel, they made contact with Woods via one of their encrypted Iridium Satellite phones. Taking no chances with security, Margolis did all of the talking in a pre-arranged Kurdish dialect, reflecting the success of their mining excursion. Details of the minerals and suspected quantities summarizing in a prearranged code the details of their mission progress. A deceptive reply in Kurdish also provided them a phone number to the Moghaddam Hotel in Birjand, where they were to rendezvous for additional supplies and receive their new assignment and location of their next mineral research project in the South Khorasan province. Details and quantities of the supplies were coded specifically to indicate the actual phone number to Lei Lau and coordinates to the location where they were to meet their PRC contact outside of Surmaq...just under 1,000-kilometers west of Birjand.

A brief call to Lau, who was expecting on her secure phone a cryptic message in Kurdish that she could translate, established a time frame for their arrival and a signal confirmation of the correct location and her identity.

Lau closed the gates behind them and jogged up to the dust covered SUV as it came to a halt outside the front door.

"Good evening," Lau offered with a slight bow, as she met Ferguson exiting from the driver side.

"Good evening to you. You must be the famous Lei Lau," Ferguson smiled in return, offering his hand, which was quickly accepted. "For the sake of brevity and operational security, call me Bashir, and this is Asma," gesturing to Margolis who was exiting on the same side.

"Howdy," came Wright's smiling greeting from across the hood. He flipped open his wallet to reveal his Iranian National Identity Card, "I go by Cyrus."

Lau nodded to all of them, "I'm sure you do," she mumbled sarcastically under her breath, leading them to the front door and then escorting them inside the modest little home.

"I have already prepared a little something for you to eat, as I'm sure you're tired and hungry from your journey. Whenever you'd like to grab any of your gear, there are three bedrooms," she pointed them to a hallway off to the left side of a cozy and very rustic great room. Accented by a multi-beamed ceiling and exposed stone walls centered around a mantled fireplace, the dimly lit room was furnished with a reasonably new set of matching twill couch and chairs settled on a large Persian rug. "The master has a queen bed that Asma and I can share, and the other two rooms have single beds that will accommodate each of you gentlemen."

Lau retreated to a kitchen in the back of the house and could be heard moving pots and pans around, as the smell of something really good trickled out to also greet the three travelers. They all nodded in a silent agreement of their hunger, with Wright and Ferguson both simultaneously remarking on Lau's fluent grasp of the English language as they all retreated outside to the car to retrieve what they needed overnight.

* * * * *

Seated around the living area of the great room, after a very tasty meal of stir-fried vegetables and shredded lamb over rice, introductory pleasantries and more definitive details regarding each of the lives in the room were revealed. With the polite banter completed, they deferred to Lau for an up-to-date status of Park and his activities as a second bottle of French Bordeaux, compliments of Lau's provisions, was opened.

"Unfortunately, I still do not know of the whereabouts of the lab that Doctor Park and his associates are working from. It is without question a top-secret project from the chatter I pick up from the Iranian personnel I affiliate with on the nuclear side, which is the area of expertise for why I'm here, and from my intimate conversations with General Javadi. It is being kept well under wraps.

"I have been able to determine that the participants affiliated with the project are Brigadier General Farid Seyyedi, a commander in the Defense Ministry, Dr. Malik Abbasspour, Joint Command Chairman Major General Hassan Firouzabadi, and Nasser Togyani, a commander in the Revolutionary Guards.

"A unique organization in the Ministry of Defense, established to coordinate chemical and biological activity only, is being directed by Seyyedi, with help from Dr. Abbasspour who had been running the operation from its inception six or seven years ago. Its mission is just as it might appear...to build and enhance an infrastructure of biological weapons capable of mass destruction. It has the authority to purchase or develop the expertise, technology, or even the physical stock to produce chemical and microbial weapons and their delivery mechanisms. They have received cooperative assistance over the years from a number of countries, with Park being one of their direct hires, and I hear he did not come cheap.

"Major General Hassan Firouzabadi, I understand, takes part in some of the regular meetings with Park, particularly early in the process. However, based on his regular appearances in Tehran, I suspect he's not involved with the day-to-day activities at the lab facility, unless it's very close to Tehran, which I doubt."

"And why would you doubt it's not close?" inquired Ferguson.

"I will get to that. Let me finish the ones involved first."

Ferguson nodded in understanding and gestured for her to continue.

"Nasser Togyani, who leads the Armed Forces Command Strategic Defense Directorate, appears to be the one overseeing Park, as his position has him managing all associated government run biological related programs. He's a radical, but he has the power of the Revolutionary Guards behind him and the blessing of the Supreme Leader, so he's untouchable.

"Then there is Park. I know you all have been well briefed on him. He's a mystery man to everyone I have spoken to, and any questions about him seem to elicit not only fear, but complete denials as to any knowledge regarding him or his existence. Javadi is the only one that has been willing to acknowledge him, speak about him in generalities, and understands his mission."

"I understand you have been utilizing your feminine powers of persuasion," Margolis winked at Lau in a uniquely female-to-female moment of understanding.

"Javadi is pathetic. He's like a dog in heat, and his alcohol consumption, regardless of its immorality to his Muslim faith, is atrocious. So, it's been relatively easy for him to be my best and most reliable source of intelligence.

"As to your question of the lab being close to Tehran, Javadi has intimated that 'Park's experimental laboratory,' as he has referred to it, is out in the 'middle of nowhere…for sake of safety as much as security.' Plus, I have heard that Park doesn't stay in one place very long, and according to Javadi, he's been whisked away by helicopter on the two occasions that the General has divulged his existence in Tehran."

The room went silent, as everybody digested what passed as an intelligence briefing.

"So, where do we start?" Wright broke the silence. "I'm thinking Javadi is our best angle, but it sounds like Togyani is a pretty important piece, albeit a nasty one."

More silence. The burning wood of the fireplace and gurgling refills of two glasses of wine producing the only noises in the room.

"I do have something else I just learned in the last week about my friend General Javadi that I hope might be of interest. Besides his penchant for alcohol, he also has an interest in women other than me."

"How so?" asked Ferguson.

"He not only visits a brothel on a regular basis, we have discovered that he actually owns part, or most likely, all of it. The business is operated by one of his brothers, but I think that is a front to protect his significant position within the government. Prostitution is still illegal, but there are so many corrupt officials involved in it, it's a joke as to any application of justice. You can also get around it through the Islamic practice of *sigheh*, or temporary marriages. They can be for days, weeks, some apparently apply the practice as a matter of hours. It's even encouraged by the clerics and is merely viewed as allowing contractual short-term relations between both sexes. The wife, as temporary as she may be, can expect a dowry as payment, which can also be in cash. It's quite the operational model for legalized prostitution."

"That is actually very interesting and has a whole host of applications," suggested Wright. "Crazy question, but have you been inside?"

"No, but General Huang, my commanding officer, has. He tells me it's quite the place. Not only are there Iranian girls, some as young as early teenagers, but they appear to have a sex slave operation going, as they have a selection of young immigrant girls from the Eastern European countries as well…Russians in particular."

"Well, well, well," Wright rubbed his chin in delight. "We may have the makings of something here."

"I would agree," Margolis added. "There has to be an angle to get to Javadi. Our only problem is how much does he know. We could be spinning our wheels with him, only to have him be as in the dark as everyone else."

"I think he knows, in fact I'm almost certain he knows more than he's telling me," said Lau. "He's bragged about it before as if it proves his significance, but then he goes quiet very quickly, probably realizing he's said too much."

Ferguson sat quietly, a smile growing on his face.

"So, what's up with you? You look like the cat that ate the mouse," demanded Margolis.

"I think Lei is right. I suspect Javadi knows a lot, or at least enough to get us in the right direction. His involvement in the brothel business can come in handy, but the fact that he visits there makes him an easy target."

"You're thinking snatch and grab?" asked Wright, nodding his own head in agreement to the question.

"I am. If we can get him to a safe house and interrogate him, we can squeeze something out of him. Hell, with a little help from Isaiah, we could even cook up a little blackmail, introduce a little history with the CIA, bank accounts overseas, international sex trafficking, multiple wives…we've got a lot to choose from."

"I like it, I really like it," Margolis chuckled.

Lau put a damper on the enthusiasm, "Getting him will not be easy. He's always well-guarded by a four or five man heavily armed security detail."

"I'll bet they aren't in the same room when the humping is happening," laughed Wright. "And he really shouldn't be trading in Russians, they can really get very angry when their baby sister disappears into an Iranian brothel."

Ferguson leaned over to give Wright a high five, "Dude, I really like your style. It's perfect, Ivan."

Margolis and Lau both shared the same perplexed look as they eyeballed each other, then watched Wright and Ferguson begin speaking to each other in Russian.

They both turned and raised their glasses in a toast to the two women, "Nazdorovye!" they shouted in unison.

Chapter 20

Villa Behesht, near Ravar, Iran

Another splendid dinner had been consumed in the palatial 14-seat dining room at the beautiful villa, and with the wait staff dismissed, Togyani, seated pompously at the head of the table, stood to address the group. He took the time to scan the table and stare directly into the eyes of the eight guests at the table.

"Gentlemen, as we will hear shortly from Dr. Park, we are very close to the final stages of establishing and controlling the vehicle that will make the Setareh Doctrine...a new and greater Persia...and the creation of the most powerful Muslim nation in the world...a reality."

Park swallowed a large gulp of the expensive Dom Perignon Brut champagne that Togyani had flown in for the evening's meal and had just been distributed to everyone to accompany his bombastic, self-congratulatory crowning achievement of how to manufacture and control the extermination of millions of people. He took another gulp as he watched the others focused on him in apparent rapture or disgust, it was hard to tell.

As Togyani rambled on about the virtues of Islam and the great things they were going to accomplish through the genocide of over thirty percent of the Middle East, he had the table turn their heads to the far end opposite him, where a large, wide-screen computer monitor began playing a presentation of how it would transpire.

"We have once again been blessed with the stupidity of President Assad's recent use of chemical weapons against his own people, which only enhances our ability to construct and lay the blame for Setareh at the feet of the imbecile and his stockpile of WMDs smuggled out of Iraq," acknowledging Abdul-Mahdi, the latest guest to be added to the architects of Armageddon.

The presentation offered up a detailed execution of each individual to be infected and where they would be located, on which date, and similar data on the multitude of drone vehicles that would complement, if necessary, the martyrdom to gain the desired exposure. As the dots for each were placed into a map, each subsequent slide produced a progressive expansion of a red cloud, starting from ground zero in Syria, to engulfing the large geographically strange star pattern that it was named for. Times and dates were also advanced accordingly.

As Togyani droned on, the nods and smiles of approval around the table gave way to the bile rising in Park's throat.

"At this point, we will offer up to the world and our neighbors the solution, the cure. Recognizing the virus for what it is and understanding how to treat it from having seen this nightmare before, brutally thrust upon the Iranian people by Saddam and his regime in the mid-1980s at the height of the Iran-Iraq war, we will be the savior. Feigning possession of limited antiviral and antidote stockpiles previously produced and still available, and endowed with the ability and understanding of how to produce more, it will position us in total control of saving the destiny of millions, but only under the conditions of our choosing.

"The great Satan and their allies, along with the UN will object, but by then we will already have dispatched our vaccinated troops into the affected areas to restore order and establish control of the remaining populations. Apparently, according to Dr. Park," Togyani gestured to Park, consuming his third glass of champagne, "the vaccination is quite elementary and straightforward, as is the treatment protocol if it's managed in time, so we suspect the world will find a solution quickly, but by then it will be too late. We will have achieved domination and sovereignty over the lands and institutions we want and need, and the new governments will be installed under our direction."

The final slides showed the large cloud halted by a series of blue lines that encapsulated it, and then the slow recession of the cloud as a series of green arrows with Iranian military units and battle groups listed pushed into the cloud, creating a competing green cloud consuming and overlapping nearly all of the countries of Syria, Iraq, Kuwait, Jordan, and Lebanon.

"Again, the great Satan and their puppet regimes mired in servitude, and the toothless bureaucrats of the UN will rattle their sabers, and demand our withdrawal, but it will be fruitless. We will hold all the cards."

Abood was having a hard time remaining calm as Togyani laid out the Doctrine. Trying desperately to maintain his composure as the renowned Abdul-Mahdi, he couldn't help the rush of excitement washing over him with his inclusion in this process. The entire operation of infiltrating the inner workings of the Iranian biological WMD program had happened so much faster, and to this point had been remarkably easier, than he or Hezbollah could have imagined. Mahdi's expertise in many of the processes at work, masked by the reality of Abood's rudimentary knowledge, had yet to be fully tested by anyone and appeared to be accepted without any skepticism. His name alone had brought him to this magical point.

After a grand champagne toast to the success of Setareh, a truly ironic gesture of alcohol consumption under the assumptions of mercy and blessings of Allah, Park's message to the group at the end of the evening seemed anticlimactic. He made clear they had indeed reached the milestone of a vaccine and successful treatment and a specific cure if delivered within thirty-six, and in some cases forty-eight hours of contraction. What they still had not been able to control was the timing of the onset of symptoms from the time of exposure, so the initial introductory phase of the process remained 'timing critical' for Togyani to make the viral growth work in the geographic progression he needed. Park seemed to take some solace in the knowledge that this component of the plan made it that much more difficult for the man to plan the commission of mass murder on a scale that had never been seen before.

Chapter 21

Charmshahr, Iran

Wright guided the Landy into the neglected and abandoned brick warehouse through a pair of sliding metal doors. Ferguson quickly pulled them closed behind him, as Wright brought the vehicle to a stop in the middle of what once was a car parts distributor.

The interior was as dark as the night outside, and neither had any intention of illuminating their presence to anyone nosey enough from the smattering of industrial neighbors around them. As their eyes adjusted to the deficiency of light, Ferguson noted the darkened silhouette of a vehicle outlined against the wall opposite the office, and was certain that Lau and Huang had managed to uphold the only request made of them before leaving the warm confines of their farmhouse to this commercial dump. The late model Mercedes sedan, rented through a shell company with its roots in Saint Petersburg, Russia, sat amongst the stacks of broken wooden pallets and the remnants of metal racking disassembled in several piles that stretched to the rear of the building.

Without a word, overnight gear in tow, they blindly made their way into a cinderblock office on the ground floor, windows blacked out per instructions, as a large rat stopped to scrutinize the intruders and then scurried past them to the far end of the 2,000 square meter building. Once inside the room and the door closed, a lone overhead light switch was activated to reveal three cots, a folding table, and four chairs in an otherwise musky and blighted interior.

It wasn't much to like, but it was exactly what they expected and geographically where they wanted to be. Wright, Ferguson, and Margolis all agreed the small village of a few hundred in the Behnamarab-e Jonubi Rural District, Javadabad District, Tehran Province was the perfect choice for the second safehouse recommended by Lau and Huang. Only 90-kilometers south of downtown Tehran's Central District 10, they were within an hour's commute to Javadi's brothel, located in an alley off the corner of Shadab Street and Mehr, well disguised in the basement of the Mehr Café that fronted Shadad Street above.

The café was a well-known and popular eatery, centrally located in the business and residential portion of the Bazaar District, just west of Honarmandan Park and north of the trendy, historical 30_Tir Street. The popular Qods and Mehregan Hotels were conveniently located in the same block, and through a well-compensated hotel staff, patrons were always guided to the café, and for a select guest list, to the deliciously illicit enterprise below.

Within the confines of the derelict old warehouse office, all three took a short break to snack on cheese with a loaf of bread and use up the last of the water bottles they had purchased on the trip to the farmhouse. Margolis fired up the Toughbook laptop that had accompanied them on the trip, established a secure connection through one of the satellite phones, made her way through a maze of proxy servers, and logged on to a Google account with a French IP address. She typed up an email requesting the help they needed regarding a General Amir Javadi, saved it in the Drafts Folder, and shut down the account.

Ferguson and Wright took over the computer once she was finished and were busy looking at several maps of Tehran and identifying routes in and out from the location of the brothel. They had already worked through an operational plan between the three of them on the drive up from the farmhouse and would spend the rest of the evening hammering out the details. Per a conversation between Lau and Margolis earlier in the day, Lau would join them at the warehouse in the morning with photographs of the city block containing the brothel, as well as surrounding blocks on the east, west, and south of the area. She would also have recommendations for her and Margolis to set up and serve as spotters.

"When it's time, I think we can back right into the dead-end alley over on Shahrivar, park the car on this corner where it can't get blocked, and come out the same way," Ferguson pointed to the back-door entrance to the brothel that descended below street level and then fingered the dead-end street corner approximately 15 meters to the east. "One right turn and we're headed south on Shahrivar Street, left on Arak and right on Qarani Street. From there we're two miles from the switch. If Lau is correct and Javadi's driver drops him off through the dead-end alley off Mehr Street, returns an hour later, and all of the General's security goes inside with him except for one at the door, then we can neutralize the outside man and can keep all of the collateral damage inside the brothel. We lock up the girls and other customers inside, and nobody will see us come out on the back side."

Wright smiled and shook his head, "That's a lot of 'And's' and 'If's' to all go our way. On top of that, for appearances sake, we'll have to take a couple of the girls with us. What do we do with them?"

"Why not let Lau handle them," Margolis interrupted. "After we meet, you can pass them off to her. And she can process them home through the Chinese Embassy. I would think they keep their mouths shut if it means them finding a way home out of the shithole life they are currently living."

"Agree. Come on Clay, what could possibly go wrong in a brothel, in the middle of Tehran, in broad daylight, with a couple hookers on our arms for escorts?" Ferguson's pointed sarcasm was accentuated with a shit eating grin.

* * * * *

Nearly thirty-six hours had passed since Ferguson, Margolis, and Wright had hunkered down in the Charmshahr warehouse. Based on Lau's surveillance of Javadi, his bi-weekly visit to satisfy his carnal desires at his "den of sin," as Margolis had taken to calling it, was on for later that evening. He would arrive after the Sunset Prayer, known as *Maghrib,* which would put him there approximately a half hour after sundown, and per his routine would leave precisely two hours later, dutifully returning to his wife and children.

With the evening's sunset scheduled for 19:13, they formulated their plan for being in place no later than 17:00, less than three hours away. The Mercedes was loaded with the equipment they would need, the balance of their other gear went back into the Landy.

The three of them had all accessorized their local outfits with the CIPS Communications Kit. The covert-in-plain-sight system was similar to standard earbud earphones with microphone, commonly used with cell phones, linked with a tactical radio connected to a mini-PTT, or Push-to-Talk, finger ring. They all ran through a com check to make sure they were linked up and on the same frequency. An alternate emergency frequency was determined in case things went sideways. Margolis easily concealed her equipment under her *chador* headscarf, wool jacket, and jeans, but Wright and Ferguson would keep their gear hidden under their tailored two-piece suits with open collared dress shirts, compliments of Lau's visit to the local men's haberdashery earlier that morning, and employ the equipment when out-of-sight.

In addition to their tactical communications, they would each keep a suppressed Glock 19 concealed at the small of their backs, Wright and Ferguson with additional magazines. Margolis added one of the MSR night vision scopes.

Ferguson and Wright would take the Mercedes. In the Landy, Margolis would pick up Lau at a rendezvous point in a secluded area a couple blocks north of Mehr Street at 16:00, coordinated a couple hours earlier on a wrong number call placed to Lau's secure cell phone from a burner phone, now a pile of plastic fragments mixing with the debris of the warehouse floor. After determining their spotting locations per Lau's earlier surveillance, Margolis would deposit Lau on the west side of the brothel, park the Landy approximately a mile south of the block in the alley behind the Ferdowsi Square shopping mall's food court, walk to Shadab Street, and set up in her spotting position east of the brothel. Lau would proceed to her position and have no direct communications with the other three, so she would only be there to observe and report back to Huang "if it all went to shit," as Wright had expressed.

After Ferguson and Wright would enter through the back-alley brothel entrance, Margolis would break off her overwatch and all communication, walk the mile back to recover the Landy, and drive to meet Ferguson and Wright in the circle drive of the Park-e Shahr, another half mile further to the south. If they didn't show up within a half hour of breaking off coms, then she would return to the farmhouse and organize an immediate exfil from there.

Since Wright and Ferguson would not be willing to expose their ear pieces to anyone upon entering the brothel, they would go silent and on their own the second they entered.

Chapter 22

Tehran, Iran

"Contact," came Margolis' voice into the ear pieces of Wright and Ferguson. "Driver is pulling into the alley, and I count three, four...no wait, five goons exiting the car. Target is now exiting and entering through the back door. One goon on guard outside the door, all the others accompanied target inside."

Wright started the Mercedes and pulled out into light traffic headed north on Nejatohalli Street. As they made a righthand turn onto Shadab, Ferguson depressed his finger switch, "Has the driver vacated?"

Margolis replied, "Driver and vehicle are gone. I say again, driver and vehicle are gone. Your alley is clean."

Ferguson gave Wright a thumbs up, and in a central Russian dialect any Muscovite would be proud of, asked, "You ready Boris?"

"Let's do this Vlad," came an equally fluent reply from Wright, backing the Mercedes into the empty Sharivar street alleyway adjacent to the Mehr Street alley.

Exiting the car, they both advanced through the trees that covered the twenty-five feet of greenspace between the dead ends of each alley. Approaching the guard at the front door, they gestured with a nod, and Ferguson offered a greeting, "*Dobryy vecher,*" to help establish their bona fides.

The guard eyed them with suspicion and gestured with his hands upward and into a surrender motion to both of them. Ferguson stepped forward and to his left, raising his arms, he placed his hands on his head preparing to get frisked. As the guard reached with both hands toward his torso, Wright stepped in quickly behind him and in one coordinated motion slapped his left hand across the man's mouth and plunged a Smith & Wesson half-serrated black steel tanto-style knife into his throat. Ripping to his right it severed the carotid artery, both jugular veins, and incapacitated the larynx. Wright held the big man up straight as a silent death came quickly. He lowered his lifeless body into a seated position on the steps and wiped the bloody knife on the guard's pants. Ferguson placed the dead man's arms across his lap and propped his back up against the wall of the stair well. They both took a look around for any prying eyes and entered the door.

Inside, the large single room entry hall had the feel of a high-end American strip joint. Dark, accented abundantly in brass, enveloped in subdued lighting filtered in multiple colors, loud music cascading from ceiling speakers, but classically adorned in Persian rugs, the entire room was smothered in a fog of syrupy tobacco smoke. A hookah pipe was actively in use in one corner, while two other corners were occupied by makeshift viewing areas made up of large overstuffed pillows, accompanied by antique French sofas and chairs. Each area was stocked with scantily clad women of the evening, all waiting to see if their loathsome disposition for the next hour was to be with the one man in each setting debating and negotiating for their services.

As they moved past what appeared to be an Olympic weightlifter posing as a bouncer, and into the thick of the sex bazaar that was taking place, an older woman, caked in make-up and perfume, but thankfully dressed in a more age-appropriate outfit, approached and spoke in a broken English, "You here for lady comfort?"

Ferguson shook his head negatively and replied in Russian, "We don't speak English, do you speak any Russian?"

"I speak a lot of languages," came the reply in a better version of Russian than English, "but we offer comfort to everyone from all over the world."

"We've heard you may have Russian girls here. We would like to meet Persian girls also."

Wright took note of what appeared to be two of the "goons" Margolis counted guarding the hallway that extended beyond the back wall. No sight of the other two. He meandered past the knot of three pipe smokers and took a nonchalant glance down the hall containing three doors on each side and a single door at the end. As if on a Saturday stroll in the park, he nodded at the two gargoyles flanking the hallway and eyeballed the remaining two goons guarding each side of the door at the end of the hall.

With the outer two guards taking a keen interest in his movements, he retreated to look in on one of the cluster of girls, noticing an Asian woman, what looked like two very young bleached blonde girls with Eastern Bloc features, and several of Middle Eastern descent. He returned to Ferguson, still negotiating with the Den Mother.

When he concluded his conversation, Ferguson stepped over to Wright and as they both gestured toward both sets of women, "I've bartered for us both to have one each of the young blonde Ukrainians and one each of the two Iraqi ladies seated with them. Our lovely Madame volunteered that her best Russian girl was with her special guest as usual. They are in the back room."

"I noticed," Wright said. "I spy two Ali Baba's at the entrance to the hallway, two in the back of the hallway, and the bouncer. Five total, that look right to you?'

"*Da, verrneyy,*" Ferguson replied loud enough to keep up appearances.

"There are no other exits I see in the main room, so I'm assuming any other exits out of here besides the front are down the hallway somewhere. If you take your two bimbos and start down that hallway, I'll give you three seconds, and the back two are yours. You'll need to hold off any stampede coming toward you trying to escape. I'll get near the front door, and I can take the other two out at the entrance to the hallway, and I should be able to incapacitate Andre the Giant at the entrance. We'll need to move quick before someone discovers our handiwork outside."

Signaling a thumbs up, Ferguson pulled out a wad of Iranian Rial notes, and peeled off a handful that he turned and handed off to the Madame, who was having difficulty maintaining her composure at the excessive amount beyond their negotiated rate.

Ferguson simply smiled, while she led him by the hand over to the two he selected. He explained that he would go first while his friend waited, but not to let the other two selected go with anyone else. She shook her head in understanding and eagerly pointed the ménage á trois to the hallway and barked out a room number to the girl she called Katerina.

Wright positioned himself closer to the front entrance and within a few feet of the bouncer, providing for a clear line of fire to the two guards at the hallway entrance. Both he and Ferguson had been in these situations before, and he had already started the mental process of controlling his breathing and adrenaline, as he knew Ferguson was doing the same.

After Ferguson disappeared down the hallway, Wright counted to three and pulled the suppressed Glock 19 from his waistband and executed a four round box engagement. Centering his first chest shot on goon number one on his left, he transitioned right for a center chest shot on goon number two, lifted straight up to a head shot on the same stunned face, and then transitioned back left for a final head shot on goon one before he hit the ground.

With the advantage of shock still prevalent amongst the guests, he turned and drove a full kick into the right kneecap of the bouncer, that gave an inward snap of bones and ligaments sending him plunging to the ground. On his way down and for good measure, Wright slammed the butt of his pistol onto the back of his head, knocking him out cold.

Concurrently, Ferguson had made it about halfway down the hallway flanked by his two escorts guiding them with a hand on the back of each of their necks. He got to his three count as he pulled his pistol using the escort on his right to screen his draw, while he maintained the large smile so common among the regular clientele to keep the guards at the end of the hall on their heels. Ferguson gripped the neck of the escort on his left and slammed her across the hallway into the one on his right as he extended his pistol out into his line of sight. Noticing bulges disrupting the fit of their button-down shirts and assessing them to be wearing body armor, Ferguson opted immediately for single head shots to each, dropping them like skyscrapers collapsing under their own weight during demolition.

Back in the main room, Wright looked at the Madame as the panic and screaming began to set in and yelled again in Russian, "Tell everyone to shut the fuck up! And keep their faces on the ground."

She complied, but with very little conviction as she cowered in fear kneeling on the floor.

He yanked her to her feet and repeated his instructions, commanding her to be louder. His eyes darting to the front door waiting for any activity from outside trying to enter.

The Madame yelled out twice again, and Wright screamed the same in Russian at the top of his lungs, holding his pistol in a retracted position at the center of his chest like a tank turret.

"Tell them to lie down with their hands behind their heads," Wright instructed her again. "NOW," he shouted at her when she hesitated. The crowd was beginning to comply, most of them kneeling and dropping to the floor. One of the smokers decided he would try to dial out on his cell, and Wright fired off another round just over the man's head and eyed him intently, shaking his head back and forth. The phone dropped to the floor immediately.

As Ferguson reached the door at the end of the hall, he fired two rounds into the door handle, stepped over the two dead guards he disposed of earlier, and launched himself into the door as he rolled into the room on the floor. As he popped up with his pistol forward, a fully nude Javadi was pulling a cell phone from his pants pocket draped over the footboard, while a beautiful young naked girl, on her knees in the bed whimpered and drew the sheets around her.

Ferguson pointed his gun at Javadi and said, "Put it down...slowly." He looked at the girl and placed a finger to his lips, "Shhh...I'm not here to hurt you, I'm here to help you. Be quiet and do as I say. What's your name?"

"Oksana," came a muffled response, as Javadi obeyed the command and slowly raised his hands to his head.

"Put your clothes on General, you're coming with me. You, too, young lady."

"You can't do this! You can't get away with this! Do you know who I am?" barked Javadi.

Ferguson planted two rounds into the wall just over Javadi's head.

The message seemed to work as he began dressing in earnest. The young girl, completely naked but following his command, had certainly done her best to distract Ferguson as he eyed her slipping back into her mini tube dress and heels.

When they marched out into the anteroom, Wright had the Madame walking around the prone patrons collecting their cell phones and personal items. He had collected the two young Ukrainian girls, Katerina and Natalya, and was busy explaining to the Madame in no uncertain terms, "If anyone affiliated with this establishment, or anyone else in this backward sandbox of a country ever tries to kidnap, trade for, or any way imprison another young girl from the Motherland of Russia, we will be back. And if we return, we will not be so kind to the rest of you. Do you understand?"

The Madame, tears streaming down her face, shook her head so hard in the affirmative, he thought it might pop off her neck.

As Ferguson stepped out of the hallway with Javadi, he passed Oksana off to the other two Ukrainian girls and then drove an elbow into the general's kidneys so hard it sent him to the floor gasping for air. As he zip-tied his hands behind his back and stuffed his own sock into his mouth, selling the façade of a Russian mob hit, Ferguson shouted, "This pig is one of the owners. We will deal with him as we do with any other swine that decides to steal our Russian women. A bullet in the brain is too easy, he will be begging for just that when we get through with him. Nobody leaves here to follow us."

Wright grabbed the bag of cellphones and wallets and looked at Ferguson, motioning to the door with his head, "We need to go, NOW. Nobody else ever entered, but when I peeked out the door, the other guard was gone."

They herded the three young blondes together and told them in unison, "We're taking you home. You're getting out of here." They all smiled and were more than happy to oblige with the directions to get out of the building.

As they exited, they both noticed the missing guard and the smeared blood trail up the steps.

"Shit," they both muttered in unison. Ferguson led the girls up the stairs and Wright brought up the rear, their eyes looking all around for the trouble they knew was probably waiting for them. The ladies sandwiched in between them were helping a clearly anguished Javadi along. As they stepped through the trees and reached the Mercedes, Javadi went into the trunk, and the girls were directed to the back seat.

"Pssst," came a whispered noise from the bushes.

Wright dropped to his knee and pointed the gun toward the brothel, and Ferguson leveled his at the trees in front of them.

"Try not to shoot me," said Lau, "I'm coming out."

"Damnit girl, you can't do that shit, we're already a little jacked up."

"I can see that. Nice looking dates. If you're searching for the guard by the door, I thought he looked a little out of place slumped over and bleeding all over himself. I dragged him off into the bushes. He's over there."

Wright visibly relaxed, smiled at Ferguson, and placed the Glock back in his waistband. "I knew I liked this détente shit, especially when the spies come as pretty and helpful as you."

"I'll take that as a compliment...I think. I have another bit of help to offer. Asma and I had a conversation about your unwanted long-legged liabilities. I have a vehicle around the corner. You give me the three ladies, and I'll drop them off at the Russian Embassy. I have a Liaison Officer there that has been much more than friendly at some of the joint social functions, I'm sure he will be more than happy to help."

Ferguson slammed the trunk on Javadi and nodded at Wright, who returned the gesture. "Works for us. Only one problem, I think a couple of them are Ukrainian."

"No problem, I have friends there as well. They will be well taken care of. You two need to get out of here. I'll see you again at the warehouse."

"Looking forward to it," replied Wright, as they were already climbing into the car. Pulling away they could see Lau hustling the girls through the tree line and into the waiting SUV.

Chapter 23

Tehran, Iran

In central Tehran, within blocks of the action at the brothel, Togyani and generals Firouzabadi and Seyyedi exited the Beit-e Rahbari, or House of Leadership and the official residence of the Supreme Leader, and climbed into the waiting limousine.

Their one-hour conversation with the Supreme Leader and Ahmad Jannati had been profoundly contentious. With the intent to be more of an update and status of Setareh to the ruling power structure, the ensuing discussion about pushing forward with implementation was raucous, to say the least. Everyone agreed the timing was ideal, centered around Assad's most recent release of chemical weapons, but the sheer magnitude and consequences of the endeavor had weighed heavily and generated second guessing from the Supreme Leader himself. Concessions from the American administration were beginning to appear as if they might actually become a reality, and relief of the crippling sanctions in place for years were perceived to be a part of that grand bargain. With regards to a firm decision on proceeding forward or remaining on hold until the details of a treaty could be worked out, he acquiesced slightly and offered there would be a verdict forthcoming within the next few weeks.

Togyani could barely contain his fury. Indecisiveness was a trait he was unwilling to tolerate. Jannati was in agreement and clearly sided with a decision to proceed as well. He was convinced any negative fallout would clearly take out Khamenei and leave him in a position to ascend to the top, and any outright success of the Doctrine would be easy for him to reap the rewards, as he could step forward with the credit in making it a reality, ultimately strengthening his position of power.

Firouzabadi and Seyyedi were split in tepid support, both taking risk-averse positions near the middle, with the latter general slightly more confident and vocal for the option of proceeding forward. However, in an acknowledgment to who was ultimately in charge, both indicated their willingness to stand behind whatever decision was handed down by His Eminence. It appeared neither was enthusiastic to be responsible for authorizing the scourge that was sure to follow, but they were also both interested in the power they enjoyed and were certainly prepared to back the choice either way in order to sustain their eminent positions.

Togyani eyed both of the generals suspiciously as they all seated themselves in the back of the luxury vehicle for the ride back to their respective residences. "The timing of Setareh should never have been in doubt," he suggested. "I'm disappointed that both of you did not vehemently support the initiative to launch now. Delays will only create problems for us if we don't take advantage of the conditions that have been handed to us by the stupidity and arrogance of the Syrian President."

"It's not your decision Commander," barked Firouzabadi. "The judgment must come from our Supreme Leader, and he will make it. You gave him the facts, now let him determine the outcome."

General Seyyedi leaned forward to face Togyani, placing his hands on his knee and offered in a calm voice, "I am confident he will come to the same conclusion we want Commander. Exercise patience for another week or two, and you will have the honor of helping create the next great Persia."

Chapter 24

Chamshahr, Iran

Amir Javadi sat naked in the middle of a utility room in the abandoned warehouse back in Chamshahr, flex cuffed to a metal chair, shivering from a chill in the air. Margolis and Ferguson both sat at a small wooden table off to the side that housed only the open Toughbook, marveling at the criminal and treasonous history of deceit and malfeasance Isaiah had managed to create from thin air, to mark Javadi as a dead man in the eyes of the Iranian government. A standing Wright pulled the sock out of the General's mouth eliciting a spittle laced cough and curse.

"Good evening General," Wright said in English, "Nice of you to join us."

Javadi jerked his head up in shock, "You are American?"

"I am. And you're an Iranian, and you're in big trouble," came the reply accompanied with a wink.

"I will personally execute you when you are captured as a spy," blustered Javadi in a bold but nervous bluff of reasonable English.

"Really? Come on now, you might want to re-evaluate your situation here. If I were you, I would be volunteering a little cooperation in the hope you're not a dead man in the next few minutes. By the way, I am impressed with your grasp of our language."

More expletives ensued in Javadi's native Persian.

Wright chuckled and then reached down and grabbed Javadi's pinky finger and snapped it sideways to a blood curdling scream. "Do I have your attention now, General?"

Javadi coughed and spit more obscenities as Wright reached for the other pinky.

"NO. Please no, wait! I'm listening. What do you want?"

"I want your cooperation General. I will ask you questions and you will provide me answers, truthful answers, and if you don't...well, I can go through your fingers first, then your toes, and will work my way up to larger appendages. Do you understand?"

"Yes, I understand."

"Excellent. Let's not beat around the bush, as we say in America. We need information on a covert biological program your country is working on with a Korean national by the name of Dae-Ho Park. You're familiar with him and this, correct?"

"I don't know of this man, and I don't know about our biological programs. I am attached to the Defense Ministry and work in our nuclear and chemical programs."

"Damnit General," sighed Wright, "I don't have time for this." He pulled out his suppressed Glock and spit a round into the top of Javadi's right foot."

Wright held onto his shoulder to stop the screaming Javadi from tipping over the chair as he thrashed his body around from the pain.

"There were two wrong answers there. Would you like me to go to the other foot, or can you make a correction?"

"No, no, please! I know him. I helped recruit him and turned him over to the Revolutionary Guard and Special Ministry."

"Excellent, now we're getting somewhere. We seem to be developing a rapport...an understanding, correct?"

"Yes, yes, I think we are," whimpered Javadi.

"Good. Because here is the real incentive General. I'm just the messenger. My colleagues over there," Wright gestured to Margolis and Ferguson, "administer the real pain."

Ferguson looked at Margolis, "Why don't you explain to the good General what's happening here."

Margolis stood with the laptop and turned the screen to face Javadi. "General, it seems that you have been a very bad and busy boy. In addition to the business venture in illegal sex trading and brothels, that apparently are conveniently overlooked by your superiors, we have created quite a history about you. It is filled with specifics indicating you have been working for some time as an informant to the American Central Intelligence Agency." Margolis pointed to the screen, "We have established multiple accounts that are registered in your name throughout the world that have been funded by front companies of the CIA. We have fabricated phone and email conversations between you and operatives working under the same acronym. We even have composed recordings from same said operatives who have mentioned you by your given name, by your code name, and the treasure trove of information you have provided over the years at dead drop locations corresponding to your much-detailed travels outside of Iran. There's a lot more out there we have constructed on you mister, with mountains of detail and corroborating evidence." Margolis offered a glimpse at the computer, "Have a look for yourself, if you don't believe me."

The puzzled look Javadi initially displayed soon gave way to a submissive resignation.

"As you can see General, you have a big problem. We've managed to make you out to be a traitor, and I think you know what happens to traitors. Are you getting the picture?"

Javadi's head drooped and slowly nodded.

"Good. So, here are your three choices, General. First, my friend here can slowly extract the information we want as he continues to break you piece by piece and selectively shoot your body parts, but he won't kill you. Mind you, at some point you're going to wish he would.

"Second choice is we can perform a lot of the items from the first choice and drop you back onto the street, where you will be found, treated for your mangled wounds, and then when they find the traitorous evidence we will selectively leak, you will be arrested, and the same shit only worse will be performed on you until you are dead.

"Or the third option is you can cooperate fully and give us the information we want. We will let you back out onto the street and essentially hold your life in our hands. If you decide to run, we will not help you, and I suspect you will not live long in retirement trying to elude your government's assassination assets. If you stay, the same intelligence agency referenced previously will be in touch, and you will work with them until they can determine a safe way to get you and your family out and into an identification protection program. We want what you know General, so I'm not bullshitting you when I say we want to get you out, but it will have to be on terms that will get you, and your family if you want them, out of Iran alive. I hope you understand the three choices."

Ferguson offered an ominous warning from the shadows, "Choose wisely, Amir Javadi, your life depends on it."

Chapter 25

Themis Cooperative Offices, Alexandria, VA

Jake Woods settled into the high-back leather executive chair, stretched his legs onto the desk in front of him, and opened the envelope Elaine Scruggs had handed him in the hallway earlier. In it were the new proofs for business cards, letterhead, and a company brochure for the new legitimate business entity they were now operating under, the investment firm known as *Themis Equity Cooperative.*

He smiled at the irony of the name. Themis was the ancient Greek Titaness, described as "the Lady of Good Counsel," and was the personification of divine order, fairness, law, natural law, and custom. He nodded his head approvingly at the symbol associated with her...the Scales of Justice, that were being prominently used in the TEC logo and throughout the promotional and support materials he was holding. Themis embodied all the characteristics that he hoped his cooperative collection of experts could provide in this mission and, if successful, hopefully beyond.

Isaiah knocked and entered simultaneously, "Sorry to interrupt, boss, but I think you want to see this." He placed his notebook on the desk and swiveled the screen to face Woods. They're making some serious progress."

Woods began reading the email "Draft" on the screen.

Update Wednesday 23:00 local time. Target Javadi safely captured and back at safe house. The following is summary of his knowledge of Daeho Park and Park's program from his interrogation:

Javadi claims to only have met Park once on a recruiting trip to an island in the South China Sea. He says nobody seems to know anything about him. He's a mystery man. His handler is a senior Revolutionary Guards commander, Nasser Togyani, who is in charge of the directorate pursuing weapons of mass destruction in the Armed Forces Command headquarters. It's well known that Togyani is hands off to everyone. He has the blessing of the Supreme Leader, but he's a radical and there are concerns for him from many of the moderate voices in the Parliament and even the Assembly of Experts. He is coordinating the biological activities of all relevant organs. He claims that if you find Togyani, you find Park. Also rumored to be involved with Togyani are Major General Hassan Firouzabadi, the chairman of the Joint Command headquarters. Javadi says both are known to have been working with a specialized carve-out organization dubbed Special Chemical, Biological, and Nuclear Industries, set up in the Ministry of Defense. This entity is also involved in chemical and biological activity. Brigadier General Seyyedi is in charge of this organization. His predecessor was a Dr. Abbasspour, who had been appointed by Rafsanjani, and who is no longer seen, but is assumed to still be active. This organization is in charge of arming the regime with microbial and chemical bombs and has been strengthened during Rouhani's presidency. The organization is also responsible for procuring technological needs of microbial and chemical weapons as well as chemical and microbial bombs. A number of foreign microbial weapons experts from China, North Korea, Pakistan, Russia are cooperating with the Ministry of Defense of the Iranian regime. A number of them have been hired by this organization. The Biological Research Center of Special Industries Organization is located at Shahid Meisami, Martyr Meisami complex on Special Karaj Highway, but Park's program is way off the books and there's no known definitive location on his laboratory and testing facility.

Park didn't stay in one place long when he first arrived in Tehran, but apparently, he hasn't been seen there in weeks. Javadi claims he has heard that Togyani has been taking regular excursions to sites in the south. He also knows through the Defense Ministry office, and conversations with General Seyyedi, that he and General Firouzabadi have traveled for several meetings to a villa in the Kerman Province. Not sure where, but he believes it's near Zarand or Ravar.

Isaiah's work on creating Javadi's alternate life was instrumental in him talking. We are keeping him securely incarcerated in current safe location until we either: a) dispose of him, or b) if our spooks want him, and they have the assets to get him out, we can tell them where their people can find him. We promised his release, but we can't risk it while we're still hunting target and in-country. Same goes for "b" above. They will have to wait to get him when our mission is complete, if he survives. He understood the smear we have on him, and that we can release it to the right people at any time, making him a dead man, but I still don't trust him, or trust that his people won't kill him anyway for being so stupid. If it's the latter, he would sing like a canary. Please pass on to appropriate agencies that if they want him, he wants out as soon as can be arranged. He seems to be more interested in himself than his family. He has lots of intel/knowledge to offer and suggest efforts be made to get him out alive if possible.

Awaiting orders, but recommend you see if we can find satellite reconnaissance of the Ravar and Zarand areas of Kerman P. and if they can isolate any activity at a "villa" in the area. No telling how many sites he has to research, but sooner the better. We think getting to that area ASAP is best option, unless Lau can turn up any information about Togyani and his whereabouts.

Standing by.

BF

Woods looked at his watch and did the math in his head. He looked back at Isaiah, "This came in a few hours ago?"

"Yes sir. We thought you would want to respond with orders."

"I need you, Elaine, and Sheri to be ready to start analyzing satellite imagery. I'll make some calls to DIA to see what we can get out of their National Reconnaissance Office. They will…"

"Sir," Isaiah interrupted, with a slight contortion of his face as if in discomfort.

Woods rolled his eyes, "You didn't?"

Isaiah sheepishly nodded, "I did. We all thought we should be proactive and get a jump on it. I think we already know what we're looking for." He threw down a file of 8 x 10 black and white images.

Woods opened the file and started to filter through the photos.

Isaiah advanced close enough to look over Woods' shoulder. "It's called Villa Behesht, just northwest of the city of Ravar. We processed and reviewed a week's worth of data, and there appears to be consistent helicopter traffic in and out of there, and Elaine and Sheri both say it looks to be well guarded."

"Does the NRO know you've been in their computers?"

"I can't be certain, but I don't think so. I was able to use an individual's access that works at the Fairfax HQ and is part of tasking for the EEC…the Evolved Enhanced CRYSTAL satellite or "Key Hole." She has a need to be in there and should have no clue I was in on top of her. There were no re-tasking or special requests, so shouldn't be any red flags raised for security and they wouldn't have any reason to be suspicious of her."

"Holy shit man, you're unreal. Do you know how many serious criminal violations you just committed…we just committed?" Woods asked rhetorically. "Remind me to make sure in the future that we get you legitimate access to a number of our assets spread across our Intelligence Community acronyms and certainly anything the NRO can offer. I don't need us both going to prison, and something tells me we're going to need as much real time imagery as we can get. I'd like to get us set up with eye-in-the-sky ability outside in the commercial market, and, hopefully, even when we make that happen, my old friends will still give us clearance to play ball with their eyes legally.

"Will you please see what you can come up with on the helicopter or helicopters at this villa. Where are they coming from and where are they going?" Woods studied the smile on Isaiah's face, "You're already on it?"

"Yes sir. We should have something for you shortly. I've also taken the liberty to arrange a contract with Skybox, and I'm in the process of having the right equipment installed here this afternoon to have that up and running within the next 24 hours."

"You're awesome, Mr. Taylor. Leave me this workbook, please, I'm going to respond with orders to the troops. I just create another 'Draft,' correct?"

"Correct. When you're finished, just close the account, do not send it. I'll come back up and add the images of the villa as attachments. They know to check back within the hour."

Woods dismissed Taylor with a laugh and a thank you, and began dissecting the images in front of him. He pulled the laptop forward within proximity of the keyboard and began typing.

Chapter 26

Near Ravar, Iran

Ferguson and Wright both lay prone on the rocky dirt ground, Ferguson surveilling the Villa Behesht through a NightForce T-82 spotting scope, while Wright maintained situational awareness of their immediate surroundings. They had just hiked up and over a steep foothill to the south of the villa, finding cover on one of the many rock ridges surrounding a large portion of the out-of-place modern desert dwelling, and now enjoyed a bird's eye view from nearly a hundred meters above.

Having driven nearly twelve hours south from the interrogation at the warehouse, Margolis had checked them all into the Akhavan Hotel in Kerman, approximately 95 kilometers to the south of Ravar. Spending a few hours of the afternoon catching up on sleep, the three engineers then drove the 135 kilometers north on Road 91 to survey the land in and around Ravar. As the sun began to disappear over the Jebal Barez mountain chain to the southwest, Wright and Ferguson let Margolis drop them off southwest of town, while she took the Landy back south to refuel. They made their way on foot to the current observation nest.

It was quite a structure built into the severe slope of a hillside. A series of four large, rectangular smooth-faced boxes, stacked and cantilevered, made up the living quarters. The natural open spaces the offsets created offered multiple decks, incorporating a pool and waterfalls, with small pockets of lush greenery giving the entire residence a sense of a multi-terraced oasis. It was a geometrically modern offering situated into a wilderness of dirt, rock, and scrub.

Lights all over the structure began to kick on as dusk settled in. The helicopter was settled in on a landing pad to the north of the building, and several uniformed guards, all armed with Heckler & Koch MP5 machine guns, were relieved by fresh sentries bearing the same weaponry and clothing of the Islamic Revolutionary Guard Corps.

"IRGC, maybe Quds Force," muttered Ferguson. "I count eight total that are active. Looks like they replaced all of them."

"Affirmative," replied Wright, as he took a turn with the scope. "Have to be at least one or two pilots in there as well."

"Boys, I'm gassed up and waiting for your orders," Margolis spoke into their earpieces. I'm two klicks east of where you got out, same dirt path we came in on."

"Roger that. Are you by your lonesome?"

"Totally, getting towards pitch black. Just taking in the stars, they're incredible out here."

"Hold tight, we are evaluating target and searching for our boy."

"Roger. I have news from the boss that just came in. Waiting to hear back from CIA, but they have indicated they want the General. Trying to find out if they can handle him. We also have two suspected locations for what could be the lab, and the other a military training facility. Both are close. They are working on oversight capability."

"Roger. That's good news. Give us a couple of hours to digest this little bit of nirvana in the middle of nowhere."

"Take your time." Margolis leaned back on the hood of the dusty vehicle and gazed up into the constellations that were like white fireflies growing more intense against the charcoal sky.

* * * * *

Back at the hotel, where they continued their discussion on the lack of any visual evidence of Park during their initial stake-out of the villa, Wright lost out in a game of rock, paper, scissors.

"Shit, gonna be a cold night. Okay, Blake you drop me off tonight, I'll wait out the morning to see if Park, or anybody else, comes or goes. Hopefully, somebody we want gets on that helo for a ride."

Margolis had seated herself at the small wood desk and pulled up the latest communication from the Co-op on the Toughbook, in what could best be described as the most up-to-date pictures available of Park, Togyani, Firouzabadi, Seyyedi, and Abbaspour that had come to her from Isaiah. They were the players Javadi had named and would be the only group of tangos they had to go on. Additionally, satellite images and construction blueprints of the villa were also downloaded, as well as a number of surveillance photos detailing two locations not far from Kerman, with geographic coordinates for both.

Ferguson plotted both sites on a map spread out on one of the two full beds in the cramped room and compared the aerial images with each. He drew a red circle around the general area for each.

"So, this clearly looks like a heavily guarded camp of some kind," mused Wright as he studied the images. "Hundreds of soldiers, barracks, centralized operational facilities. No armor to speak of, with very few signs of mass transportation at all. This area over here has the looks of what probably is a training ground?" pointing at an area on one of the pictures.

"I agree" said Ferguson. "According to home base, this site hasn't received nearly as much helicopter traffic as the other location."

Margolis clicked to another image of what showed a cluster of three small shabby structures, situated at the base of a steep mountain wall, all constructed of the same dirt and stone from the isolated barren wasteland it resided in. "This looks like nothing, but my money says there's more there than meets the eye. That's where Isaiah says he has evidence of regular helicopter traffic coming and going."

"If there's something else there, it's really well camouflaged because I can't see squat, other than that oversize cluster of outhouses. Can you zoom in a tad bit more?"

Margolis, clicked in response, but the image just got grainier with no improvement.

"We need to get eyes on that spot, and I vote that we visit that one first. If we're looking for a top-secret lab, that would have a bunch of nasty virus shit in it, I'm with Adina. I'd put it right there in the middle of b.f. Iran," said Wright.

"I agree," concurred Ferguson. "The best I can tell is we're about 150 klicks from the outhouses and 225 from the military bunkhouses. If Adina goes with us, we can drop you off in a few hours to reconnoiter the villa, and then we'll head north up 91 toward Nayband and see if there's anything that resembles a way east into the hinterland. It looks like an off-road adventure. My guess is we may have to hoof it some of the way, given that a helicopter is being used to ferry in and out of that area. We can circle back at first light and grab you on the way in."

Wright finished memorizing the names and faces on the screen and loaded up a small pack with water and one of the MSR Mk 21 sniper rifles, grabbing both a heat imaging and night scope to complement the Schmidt & Bender 5–25×56 PMII optics already mounted. For backup, he hip-holstered one of the Glocks and added one of the MK 18 assault rifles. He confiscated a quilt from one of the beds in the room that had a monotone color very similar to the stone ground he was heading back to, and wrapped himself in it.

"Jeremiah Johnson, the Mountain Man himself," Ferguson laughed.

"Somebody has to do the rough stuff, while you two pussies...sorry no offense to you Adina, take a Sunday drive in the country."

"No offense taken."

"Speak for yourself, Adina, I'm highly offended. It's getting a little testy. We could all use a little shut eye, and we'll go in two hours. Mountain man," Ferguson gestured to the one missing the cover, "that one is yours. The two you-know-what's will bed down in this one."

For purposes of further irritation, Margolis and Ferguson both giggled like teenagers as they both jumped on top of the bed together and spooned up close.

Chapter 27

Villa Behesht, Iran

Sitting up with his back to the headboard, and both hands forming a steeple under his chin, Togyani pondered the recent phone call just received from his office in Tehran. Amir Javadi had been kidnapped at gunpoint and had yet to be found, or any ransom demands offered for his release.

According to eyewitnesses and a personal recitation of events by the officer in charge from the Criminal Investigation Police of NAJA, he was forcibly taken by a pair of Russians, apparently intent on rescuing several East bloc girls that were a part of a brothel, in which Javadi was not only visiting, but appears to have some ownership stake in. He was still alive when abducted, but threats were made by his captors that most everyone believed to indicate he would be tortured and killed. It's assumed he was taken from the scene in a vehicle, but no witnesses could confirm a make or model, and there has been nothing more on his whereabouts. His body guards were all shot and killed, by what can only be described as very proficient shooters. Any additional physical evidence was being examined and ballistics results were being expedited.

Togyani was aware of Javadi's well-deserved reputation for overindulging in women and intoxicants and believed his immoral and shameless practices would eventually lead to his demise or removal from his rank and office in the Defense Ministry. He couldn't help but feel a slight bit of satisfaction that it had come to a violent end. However, his concerns gave him pause as to the amount of confidential government knowledge and information the man possessed. Even in the hands of their Russian ally, it could have a negative effect if he truly fell prey to a pair of Russians. What if it were pro-western Ukrainians or even others posing as Russians. The timing and consequences were troubling him.

He insisted to the Captain in his office that he be kept up-to-date daily on the investigation, and if Javadi were to turn up, he be the first to know. He personally wanted an opportunity to interrogate Javadi if he were to miraculously survive his ordeal. After he hung up, he made a personal call to Brigadier General Hossein Ashtari, the current commander of NAJA, expressing in no uncertain terms the national security implications surrounding this case and his desire to be kept informed of all developments surrounding Javadi's disappearance.

He thought about using Javadi's abduction as an excuse to place an additional call to the Supreme Leader to voice his apprehension, but in reality, to parlay that into an inquiry if any decision had been made regarding Setareh. He looked at the clock, realizing it was too late in the evening to bother the head of state at this hour and understanding the need to control his patience a little longer.

He would require even more patience to focus on a demanding day tomorrow, that would be a final review of Park's program regarding the pharmacology of the successful antidote and the delivery, dosage, interaction, and treatment protocols developed to meet the narrow window for remedy. The information would be forwarded immediately on to the Special Industries Group's Viral Laboratory for mass production of stock and delivery mechanisms, vital to the timing of the Setareh Doctrine's initial introduction.

He lay back in bed and tried to relax, but it was difficult. It was all becoming incredibly exciting. He could feel the momentum gathering. It was close, so close he could almost taste it.

Chapter 28

Arlington National Cemetery, Washington, D.C.

Woods sat down on the bench facing north toward the Tomb of the Unknown Soldier, a cool, light breeze rustling the trees in the early morning dawn. He unfolded the morning's *Wall Street Journal* and feigned an interest in the news of the day. Through the reflection of the glistening dew, his eyes surveyed the endless rows of gravesites, marked with uniform rows of white gravestones contrasted against the rolling hills of lush green grass, and felt the full weight of the sacrifice on display. There were hundreds of bodies buried within these hallowed grounds ranging from acquaintances to dear friends. It clearly tugged at him.

A few minutes passed, and his solitary thoughts were interrupted by a voice from behind him. "Morning Jake, fancy meeting you here."

"Good morning, Dan. Care to join me," replied Woods patting the open space next to him on the bench, his gaze still fixed on the tomb in front of him.

Dan Elliott, Deputy Director of the Central Intelligence Agency's Directorate of Operations, shuffled around to the open seat of the bench and sat down. "I think I will."

"How's the world at Langley, Dan?"

"Spooky as usual Jake. The world is a fucked-up place, so lots of job security. But I'm pretty sure I'm preaching to the choir. You haven't been out of the game for all that long, and from the song of a little birdie, I understand you may not be completely removed."

"There might be some truth to that bird whistle, Dan, but in my best legal reply, I can neither confirm nor deny that statement."

A short moment of silence followed.

"I believe you invited me here, Jake, you mentioned something you might have for me."

"Someone," said Woods leaning back and crossing his legs. "Someone who I think could be most helpful to you."

Another moment of silence.

"Ah ha...I sense a 'but' coming, Jake."

"But...I need something in return, a payment of sorts. Actually, it's more of a trade, a simple barter transaction."

"Is there a value to this transaction? Better yet, what do you need in return for this 'someone'?"

"I need a Chinese CH-4 drone with laser-guided AR-2 missiles and LT-II or LT-III bombs."

An even longer moment of silence.

"That's all? You want a Chengdu J-7 to go with those? I might be able to work out throwing in a PLA pilot to go with it."

"Good to know you haven't lost your sense of humor, Dan. Look I know you have the best connections into the Saudis and they have all of what I need. I can even pay for it, but I think you might be willing to offer it up no charge when I tell you what I have. Sorry, who I have."

"Okay, you have my attention, what do you got?"

"Are you familiar with Iranian General Amir Javadi? He's attached to the Ministry of Defense and Armed Forces Logistics and is well connected to the Iranian nuclear and chemical military programs."

"I've heard the name. From what I know, he has some clout, well entrenched and in the know on a lot of top-level programs."

"If I told you we have him locked away inside Iran, compromised, and willing to cooperate, would that be of interest?"

Dan Elliott leaned perceptibly closer to Woods, "I see the little birdie was whistling a real tune. I'm all ears."

Woods spent the next ten minutes divulging the barest details, and just enough information to explain the current status and location of Javadi. He had clearly piqued the interest of his old counterpart within the CIA. He also detailed Javadi's predicament, his current physical condition, and the urgency of getting him back into play, but not until Woods approved of the timing. He also stressed the immediate need for the materials he was requesting in trade. It was time to consummate their agreement.

"Dan, I'm running thin on time and really need to make this happen in the next 48 hours."

"Damn, you don't want much, do you?"

"Do we have a deal, Dan?"

Elliott stood and took a couple steps forward watching the beginning of the famous changing of the guard at the Tomb. "Yes. Hang onto your money, Jake. It sounds to me like you'll need it. I can manipulate this through the National Council of Resistance of Iran. The NCRI leadership owes me a big favor, and it'll give you some cover. Let me confirm, but I should be able to have it disassembled and ready to ship out of Faisal Air Base in the next 36 hours. From there, I want our fingerprints off of it. I'll have our assets inside Iran pick up Javadi within the next few hours and keep him on ice until I hear from you."

Woods stood to join him. He recited Javadi's location, and indicated they would have a private jet into Faisal AB by noon tomorrow and wait for instructions on where and when to pick up his material.

The two men shook hands and remained standing facing the Tomb, just as the 3rd U.S. Infantry Regiment's relief commander and the relieving sentinel met the retiring sentinel at the center of the matted path in front of the Tomb. All three saluted the Unknown. After orders were passed and acknowledged, the newly posted sentinel stepped into position and marched 21 steps down the black mat behind the Tomb, turned, faced east for 21 seconds, turned and faced north for 21 seconds, then took 21 steps down the mat, only to repeat the process for the next hour. After each turn, the sentinel executed a sharp "shoulder-arms" movement to place the weapon on the shoulder closest to the visitors to signify that the sentinel stands between the Tomb and any possible threat.

Woods and Elliott watched the completion and then headed in opposite directions. Woods could feel the immediate threat that was in play and hoped that he could also help stand between it and the world.

Chapter 29

Near Ravar, Iran

Dae-Ho Park stepped out onto the balcony and sucked in a full breath of the cool, dry air. He anchored the brandy snifter of two fingers worth of Grand Marnier on the stone wall in front of him and stared at the lights of Ravar in the distance. With all of the conflicted thoughts perusing his mind, he was able to reflect singularly on his daughter, even more distant and fighting a losing battle for her life in a private residence on an olive farm near Todi, Italy. Regardless of the outcome here, and the aftermath of the horrors to come, he consoled himself with the knowledge she was receiving the best medical and personal care money could buy.

Not far away in the black of the surrounding countryside, Wright steadied his night scope; a large smile arose on his face, as he easily identified Park emerging on the third-floor terrace. *Bingo you motherfucker, we found you.*

* * * * *

Ferguson rolled the Landy to a stop. He was certain they were in the middle of absolutely nowhere. They had pulled off Route 9 nearly an hour ago headed southeast, the terrain nearly lunar in appearance, ranging from flat as a pancake to an isolated subtle contour here and there, sporadic shrubs dotting the hard-packed soil. Margolis had been navigating their trip from a GPS map compliments of her cell phone, conveying their travel sans headlights, the stars generously providing Ferguson enough light to negotiate the desolate wasteland.

"It should be a few miles that way," Margolis pointed through the windshield.

The vehicle came to a stop and they both exited into the dark. Each one lifted a night scope and directed their line of sight off to the east.

"There she blows," muttered Ferguson.

"Yep, I see it also, you can't miss it," said Margolis.

Like a volcanic island rising up from a calm sea, a single, multi-peaked mountain protruded up and out of the flat landscape surrounding it. The satellite images they had received confirmed the mountain's isolation amongst the low-level topography surrounding it. Isaiah's additional info indicated the helicopter traffic and a cluster of housing was at the base of the northeastern facing slope.

"Let's get a little closer and confirm this is it," Margolis said, climbing back in the passenger door. Ferguson followed suit.

Twenty minutes later, after parking and hoofing it by foot the last couple kilometers around the base of the rocky protrusion, with Ferguson halting their progress, they knelt in unison behind a rocky crevice that rooted the ground all around them.

"You see what I see?"

Margolis placed the scope to her eyes again, "Affirmative."

The mud brick structures built into the side of the rocky mountain base were silhouetted in the dim light of the stars' reflection. No lights, no activity, and no security appeared to be present. It was eerily quiet.

Ferguson's hair stood up on the back of his neck, "Something's telling me there ain't anything good going on here."

Margolis' sense of fear was also on the rise, "I concur. Do we dare try to get a little closer, see if anybody's around?"

Ferguson barely heard her question, as he was already on the move. "Stay here," he whispered, advancing forward, squatting every few seconds to survey for activity.

Margolis scanned the area again with her scope to double-check for any movement indicating guards or sentries or some sort of electronic security system. With a slight degree of confidence, she watched Ferguson climb higher up the slope, staying above the roof line of the tallest building. Advancing, stopping, looking for any kind of motion, and then moving forward again. As he reached the back of the closest building, he slipped down and crouch-walked along the side wall.

Ferguson had decided to move closer, believing any type of motion sensing alarms would not be a good option given the wildlife that probably frequented the area. Cameras or motion sensor lighting was another matter. As he neared the first building, he noticed the camera mounted on the corner where the front and side wall met. It was angled out to the lower ground, presumably not worried about anything approaching from the mountainous ground behind. As he reached the corner of the building, immediately below the camera, he peered around to notice an open, flat area of ground leading to a cluster of three buildings. The one opposite of his position had two oversized wooden doors that probably housed a garage of some sort. The structure in the middle had a small portico, covering a recessed entrance that appeared to lead directly inward toward the mountain itself.

The door at the entryway had an unusual shine to it. Ferguson knew immediately it was the glimmer of steel. Bathed in an abnormal greenish light, it signaled what he could only assume was an electronic key pad illuminating the area. Additional cameras mounted in multiple locations and angles blanketed the open space, and he realized he had gone as far as he dared.

He reached Margolis five minutes later, they were back in the Landy in fifteen, and back on Route 9 headed south as the first pinkish colors of dawn began to rise over the eastern horizon.

They contacted Wright when they were passing by Ravar, held their emotions in check when he confirmed "Our HVT has been sighted" and signaled their intent to return briefly to the hotel to remain out of sight until he had time to surveil the morning's activities. They agreed to radio silence until Wright was ready to move.

Ferguson and Margolis were pulling into the parking lot of the hotel as the morning prayers were sounding in the center of Kerman, the first rays of sun signaling a new day. Neither communicated it, but both had the same ominous feeling…time was of the essence.

Chapter 30

Themis Cooperative Offices, Alexandria, VA

Per Isaiah's instructions, Woods ascended to the top floor of the newly minted office building of the Themis Corporation and stepped out of the elevator into a sparse, but tastefully adorned foyer area. Utilizing the key card he had been given as well, Woods placed it up to the reader on the wall just outside a large steel door, with the rich appearance of stained oak wood. Upon acceptance of his security clearance, the door produced a dull knock indicating a lock release, gave a slight hiss, and allowed him entry by a turn of the single handle. Once inside, eyes adjusting to the low-level lighting, he had the distinct impression he had entered a miniature replica of a NASA control room.

Employing most of the entire upper floor, the space occupied nearly 800 square feet, broken into three distinct areas, all facing a long wall spanning approximately 30 feet, and incorporating a large bank of video monitors assembled into one screen. The three individual zones were essentially large, two-seat work stations, aligned in a single line facing the large screen, each segregated by a single step up to their respective raised platforms. Two of the stations appeared identical. Each contained a pair of keyboards and six large monitors mounted next to each other across the front of a large desktop, allowing for a line of sight visual over the individual monitors to the large, wall mounted one beyond. The other station looked very much like a dual seat airplane cockpit with an array of four monitors facing each seat, a center console between them housing a variety of gauges and switches. Directly in front of each of both seats were joystick consoles with additional levers and keyboards. The entire floor looked like a very high-tech gamer's convention.

Standing tall in front of the big screen, while Elaine Scruggs and Sheri DeHavilland manned two of the three stations, Isaiah gave a quick salute, "Hello Chief. What do you think?"

"I think you may have blown our budget," replied Woods, scanning the room. "You got a serious amount of gear in here. Please tell me you know what everything does."

Scruggs and DeHavilland both gave a hushed laugh together, and stood up to face Woods, as Isaiah stepped up to join them and stretched out his arms, "We pretty much have everything we need boss. With many thanks to Mr. Cromer's bottomless pockets, and your help with the spooks at Langley and the DOD, we have some serious support options we can offer Adina, Blake, and Clay in the field. And yes, we definitely know what we're doing. Let us show you around."

DeHavilland stepped forward and gestured to her space, "General, this is our Unmanned Combat Aerial Vehicle Control Center. I've been brushing up on my flying skills with the RQ-1 Predator Mr. Cromer so thoughtfully purchased and the Chinese CH-4 you finagled from our friends across the river. We just took possession of them yesterday after they were flown into MOB Kandahar, where Elaine's friends were able to get everything assembled and stored out in the Special Ops hangar. I've been able to run them both through a couple of test flights with the assistance of some flight boys at Holloman."

"No crash and burns I hope?" Woods asked sarcastically.

"No sir, quite the contrary," replied DeHavilland. "They're actually quite easy to fly once you get the hang of it. The Chinese model is very similar to the Predator, so the operation and control is very compatible."

Woods nodded his approval, "That's what I needed to hear Sheri. We only get one bite at the apple with these pieces of equipment, so take care of them as best you can, please."

"Roger that, General."

"Thanks to your backdoor acquisition from General Huang, the Chinese AR-2 missiles are in flight to Kandahar as we speak, General, and should be ready to arm and deploy the CH-4 by early this evening," added Scruggs. "We also have full comm's capability to the field, and with our satellite and drone oversight options we can offer top-shelf tactical ISR support immediately."

"Chief, I don't know who you spoke to at JSOC, but dude you got some weight," interjected Isaiah. "We wouldn't have any of these capabilities without their help, and they bent over backwards to get us on board. They set us up with an encrypted mirror operation on their Intelsat Epic high-throughput satellite platform, and we have it tied into our two UAVs if needed. Our Predator is already tricked out with a variable aperture camera for main eyes, a variable aperture infrared for low-light and night viewing, and synthetic aperture radar for seeing through haze, clouds, or smoke. It's a sweet ride. Now that Sheri has the feel of the wings, we should be able to have secure eyes and ears on our boys and girl within the next eight hours."

"The biggest question, General, is do you want us up with the Predator or utilize an armed CH-4?" asked Scruggs. "I suggest we get the Predator up immediately within range of Ravar for the ISR. We can break comm's silence with them, get their 20 and sit rep, assess mission status, and that should give us an idea of need and timing for introducing the CH unit."

"Agreed," replied Woods. How soon are you ready to make that happen?"

"We're ready now, if you are?"

"Let's do it. I'm getting that gut feeling that time is of the essence."

Chapter 31

Villa Behesht, Iran

Ibrahim Abood sat in an Adirondack chair enjoying the same cool evening air and star-filled sky as Park, comfortably located on the same sprawling, wraparound terrace level at the far end the villa. A stone firepit blazed in front of him, warming his body and soul from the chill of the nighttime.

His peace was interrupted by Dae-Ho Park, as he rounded the corner. An uneasy feeling gripped him as Park sauntered up to greet him with a nod of the head and a tip of his glass in salute.

"Good evening, Doctor," Abood acknowledged Park's silent greeting, "beautiful night, is it not?"

"It's a peaceful place tonight, but one I fear will not remain so in the very near future, given the nature of our endeavor," Park replied, staring off into the distance.

An uncomfortable silence ensued for another minute, both men motionless, the pop of burning wood mixing with the strange sounds of the evening's wildlife.

Park finally turned to Abood, "Who are you?"

Abood feigned confusion, "I'm sorry?"

"I asked who you are."

"I don't think I understand what you're asking me?" Abood replied with a slight tone of indignation.

"I'm familiar with Abbas Abdul-Mahdi's reputation and abilities. I've never met him, he was a known recluse, but you don't remotely display any of the expertise or competence I would expect from him."

Abood began to stammer and was saved by Park's interruption. "I understand you're here to apply pressure on my work and to advance the timeframe, and you've accomplished your mission, but I fail to understand why the false pretense."

Abood stood, and stared confidently into Park's eyes, belying the gut-wrenching that was taking place inside, "I have no idea why you question me and insult me, but I don't need to be a party to your insolence. Your performance was lacking and not meeting with the standards that were expected of you. They enlisted my help, and I was happy to provide it. It obviously has worked given the sudden ability to produce the requisite solutions they were expecting. If you'll excuse me, Dr. Park, I think I'll retire for the evening, I'm tired, and there's still much work to be done tomorrow."

Abood brushed past Park and never looked back. Just as he reached the door to his room, he could hear Park turn to address him.

"Whoever you are, it doesn't matter...we're both dead anyway. The world will soon be on fire, and we will be engulfed in the conflagration."

Chapter 32

Near the border of Kerman and South Khorasan Provinces, Iran

The Landy bounced through the same tortuous path it took the previous evening en route to the 'Close Encounter', as Ferguson had come to call the mountain out of nowhere. It reminded him of the infamous alien landing area that Richard Dreyfuss had found in the movie bearing the same name, *Close Encounters of the Third Kind*. Margolis had no idea what he was talking about and thought him crazy as usual.

The two of them had left the hotel and gone on the move nearly an hour earlier, after getting confirmation from Wright that a party of four, including their HVT, lifted off in the helicopter for parts unknown. They caught a visual of the chopper in the distance, off to the west of them as they traveled north again up Route 91, clearly on a heading toward their same destination. With daylight already upon them, it was agreed not to get too far off the main road this time, in case there was any overhead surveillance. After negotiating a few kilometers into the wasteland, Ferguson hopped out of the vehicle with the exact same tactical gear Wright had bundled for his evening of surveillance, but added enough C-4 and accessories to take a good chunk out of the mountain if it proved necessary.

Margolis returned to the main road and headed south to rendezvous with Wright, who was hoofing it from his position near the villa.

Margolis keyed her bone mic to the predetermined frequency for the day, "BF...CW, this is Adina...comm check, over."

Wright chimed back, "AM, this is Charlie Whiskey, read you five by five, in route to same rendezvous as drop. 20 mikes out, over."

"Copy that CW, I'll circle and grab you headed north. Wait for traffic to clear, over."

"Roger, out."

"This is BF, copy all. I'll be in position in another 30 mikes. When I arrive, I'll forward sitrep and action plan for you two, out."

As she bounded south, Margolis could make out a helicopter in the distance headed into the same vicinity Ferguson was navigating toward. "BF, be advised, the bird that was headed your way, is about to land in your nest."

"Copy that, I just saw it as well."

Traffic was light and the slight overcast of dawn had given way to another cloudless, sunny morning. Margolis pulled a pair of sunglasses out of the console tray, and as she placed them over her eyes, she was startled when the secure satellite phone sitting in the same console vibrated and delivered a low-level chirp. She adjusted the antenna and answered on the third ring. "Three Stooges Engineering."

"Adina, this is Co-op main office, how's the signal?" came the clear voice of Elaine Scruggs.

"Crystal clear. Why the call, must be important?"

"We are looking for an update on your mining activities and present location. We have some UAV tools at our disposal and presently in your vicinity, that we believe can be of use to your endeavors. If you will go to headsets, we can keep you informed."

"Affirmative, we are all on headsets currently, maintaining daily frequency assignment. CW is about to join me in the vehicle 20 klicks north of Kerman, and BF is approximately 15 klicks east of our position hoofing it toward the large mountainous projection about 30 klicks west of Ghale Zari. Just sticks up out of flatland like an isolated volcano."

"Roger that," replied Scruggs. "Ending this call and going to secure tactical comms."

* * * * *

With Scruggs offering GPS coordination, DeHavilland maneuvered the RQ-1 Predator into position in and around the only large protruding mountain as described by Margolis. There wasn't anything else in the area that looked bigger than a pitcher's mound, so she was confident of the target. As she tightened her perimeter and engaged the multiple camera options available, she abruptly stood up and yelled, "Oh shit! Elaine, get on the mic to Blake, he's walking into a shit storm, a handful of hostiles in mobile vehicles. Tell him to begin flanking south to his immediate right and then work his way east up into the base of the mountain. He's out in the open, so he needs to stay low, but if he can work his way to the base, the rougher ground will offer him some cover and a firing position into the open field."

After Scruggs communicated verbatim the instructions to Ferguson, and received his confirmation, she also advised Margolis and Wright to keep their eyes open and head north until they could find a secure stopping point, and wait for orders.

The cameras had picked up what appeared to be four jeeps or patrol vehicles coming out from a crook in the northern side of the mountain, and they were fanning out to the west in the direction of Ferguson, as if they knew he was coming. Scruggs counted two to four bodies per vehicle, in what looked to be Fath Safir 4x4's, with two units sporting either the 106mm recoilless rifle or the Toophan missile launchers, both common armaments on the military transports. She was communicating her observations out loud through her own microphone headset to everyone on the ground and in the office.

Woods had been standing idly by in the 'Situation Room,' as Isaiah had come to refer to it and sidled up next to the large video bank in front, clearly displaying the unfolding action. "Is that what appears to be a road that comes in from the northwest off of 91?"

"It is, General, if you can call it that," replied Scruggs. "I've already drilled down on that with our satellite feed, and it's not much of anything except an area of matted dirt, probably where there has been some vehicle activity in the recent past."

Surveying the idle helicopter at the end of an open channel, where it clearly met the mountain in what appeared to be a cut-out, or natural recession, he noticed only a handful of bodies milling around in that main area. "Get Adina and Clay headed in the direction of that path or road, whatever it is, in case they need to make a direct assault. Might as well come right down the main pipe as if they owned the place."

"Roger that," said Scruggs, relaying the same orders to Margolis and Wright.

"Do we have any armaments on the Predator?"

Scruggs shifted uneasily in her chair, "Negative, General. It's a reconnaissance only RQ model. We can retrofit it at some point, but we were saving the boom stuff for the CH unit."

"That's what I thought, just wanted to confirm." Woods was contemplating whether it was the right time to utilize the Chinese drone and missiles to assist in the destruction of the lab. His gut said yes.

Scruggs read his gut, and his mind. "The CH is missile ready, should I get that in the air as well?"

"Affirmative, let's get it rolling. What's Clay's and Adina's ETA?"

"One hour at best. This is really out in the middle of nowhere."

"Thus, the helicopter. I'm guessing Blake wasn't expecting a welcoming party. They must have surveillance or ground monitoring around the place. That tells me we're in the right place. Tell Adina and Clay to hurry, we need a diversion and Blake doesn't have an hour."

* * * * *

Ferguson was bent over in a crouch, but doing his best track star imitation. He had jagged to his right per instructions and then motored straight ahead to the uneven ground that made up the immediate area around the base of the mountain. He hopped into a trench of rutted dirt with rocky outcroppings and started unwinding his gear. He shouldered the Remington MSR and wedged it into a crevice for support and adjusted the magnification on the scope to observe the oncoming threats.

Shit. They were headed straight at him. They obviously had spotted him on the move or had some sort of eyes or sensors tracking his location. He pulled the MK18 assault rifle closer to him, pulled out two M406 40mm high-explosive round grenades for the H&K M320 grenade launcher, and took stock of the eight 30-round magazines. He also looked around the area for two additional points of cover and made a mental note of distance between his current location and the others. He would need the fall back options as they closed in and zeroed in on his position. He speculated that in addition to the missile launchers, they probably had automatic weapons and rocket propelled grenades at their disposal, and would decimate the area as they closed in.

His initial thought was he would wait for them to close and could try to knock out the tires and drivers first and hope to leave the remaining stranded long enough to catch them in the open. *What are the chances the tires are run flats?*

The odds would take a significant turn for the worse if they were smart enough to drive outside of his range and then outflank him, particularly from all three sides. He'd never be able to hold them off if they assaulted together.

After about ten minutes of observing their wary advance on his position, his worst fears were realized when Scruggs broke in, "They are splitting up. One is holding position in front of you and the other three are moving west, southwest. I'm assuming they're looking to out-flank and surround you."

"I'm going VOX," replied Woods, opening his mic to voice activated. "I don't need to tell anybody that I won't be able to hold them all off if they attack at once, so if you have any thoughts about the cavalry, now would be the time."

Wright broke a moment of uneasy silence, "Blake, you hit 'em with everything you can, and we'll be inbound with help in 30 minutes," Wright lied. "I've seen you in worst spots."

"I plan on making them very uncomfortable. If I can bloody their nose and force them to back off once or twice, that might be enough time for you to join the fun. Don't be late to the party."

Ferguson pulled two blocks of C-4 out of the rucksack he had loaded and parceled out 4 blasting caps and detcord. He broke two blocks in half and added cord tails and caps to create four makeshift explosive devices. He belly-crawled down the fault line of the ground cover he was hiding behind and tossed the four IED's in a semicircle pattern. They would be his last line of defense if he had to retreat to the fallback positions he had sighted and mentally mapped out behind him. Returning to his original position he lifted the sniper rifle and reversed its position to the south and sighted the closest of the vehicles by his calculation. He was confident Scruggs had the rifle zeroed out before it was sent packing.

There was a slight breeze out of the northeast. Ferguson could see two uniformed soldiers standing on either side talking across the windshield, each with a pair of binoculars in hand. He started his calculations. Using a mildot formula, he processed the estimated range to target at roughly 300 meters. It was pretty straightforward math with the land virtually flat, but shooting slightly downhill from his position. Referencing the ballistic chart shrunken down and taped to the chassis of the rifle, Ferguson rotated the elevation turret on the top of his scope to 1.0 mils up. Finally, adding a quarter value on what he estimated to be about a five mile-an-hour wind, he sighted in on the one soldier on the left, who was searching for him through binoculars. Adjusting for the wind, Ferguson settled the center of the crosshairs on the right lens of the soldier's binoculars, and let loose with a .338 Lapua Magnum round. His range estimation was too conservative for center mass of the head, and with a greater drop than anticipated, Ferguson watched through the scope as the round ripped through the soldier's throat in a misty explosion.

The other soldier dove to the dirt and began crawling behind the vehicle, as Ferguson chambered another round and fired it into the front driver's side tire. It visibly sagged as he was rewarded with a standard tire.

He swung the Remington MSR around to the unit due north and let loose with a round into the back seat that connected with one of the soldiers manning the Toophan launcher, flipping him over on to the ground. He was rolling around in agony, but still alive. Ferguson sent the last two rounds in his magazine, one through each of the front tires, then reloaded the MSR. Before he could traverse his aim to the other two vehicles east of his position, the familiar swoosh of a rocket propelled grenade alerted him to duck and pray. The explosion came above his position and to his right about 20 meters away. The dirt and rock debris rained down on him, as the concussion left him confused and deafened. As he regained his senses, he grabbed his remaining gear and crawled up to the crater left by the blast. It was actually close to one of his fallback positions, but, in addition, he thought when he started firing again, they will understand they missed, assume their targeting was off, and recalculate away from the same coordinates he just settled in…he hoped.

Ferguson sighted the sniper rifle again and focused on the reticle, holding the center of the crosshairs just above the top of the soldier's head to account for the extra range, and squeezed the trigger until the recoil of the shot bucked the rifle into his shoulder sending a round that connected with the soldier sighting in the Toophan missile launcher. Ferguson's scope settled back onto the soldier just in time to see the spray from the disintegrating head and brain matter blow all over his comrade, who immediately vaulted to the ground on the other side.

Another whoosh…another cacophonous dismantling of the ground in front of him. He didn't have time to curl and protect from the impact, and it propelled him backwards a couple meters, his head ringing and covered in loose soil, and Scruggs' pleas for his condition falling on deaf ears.

In what seemed like a disoriented eternity, his vision and balance recovered and he found the sniper rifle intact. He chambered another round and searched frantically for the rucksack and MK18. Clawing away the dirt, he found them buried, but in good shape. He peeked over the cratered ledge of his position to see another flash, as a third missile let loose from the east. This time he had a split second to hunker down and cover his ears. He could swear he felt the air from it zip over his head and bury into the terrain a good 50 meters behind him. *Damnit, you sand lovin' motherfuckers, I'm going to make you wish you never fucked with this snake eater!*

He rolled up onto his left side and fired a round that pinged off the launcher of the last vehicle to fire. He deftly cycled the bolt action rifle ejecting the spent shell casing and chambering another round. Without breaking his focus on the scope reticle, he took aim center mass of the unfortunate soul that was reloading the Toophan. The .338 LM round shattered the man's sternum, as the lifeless body crumpled and rolled off the side of the truck, legs pinned, his bleeding torso dangling over the edge. As one of his compatriots attempted to free him, Ferguson dropped him as well, in a squiggling mass of wounded pain.

His hearing rebounding slightly, he could hear Scruggs pleading in his earpiece for his reply, "Damnit Elaine, I hear you. I'm a little busy here. Clay, where the hell are you?"

"We're still 15 minutes out," Wright lied again. At best, they could be to the entrance in 20 minutes, but they were still 40 kilometers from the action.

"Dude, I ain't got 15 minutes."

Another whoosh, and he buried his head waiting for the one that was going to end this thing. The explosion came, but it was off in the distance. He raised his head to see one of the two jeeps to the east in flames. The other one was trying to back up and reverse position, as the remaining four soldiers were crouched delivering machine gun fire downrange to the northeast. He tracked his scope in that direction and couldn't believe his eyes.

"Blake be advised, I thought you had another hostile show up to your northeast, but I believe you have a friendly that may have just taken out a Tango unit," Scruggs chimed in.

"You won't believe this, but I believe that is one of the People's Republic of China's angels in disguise," Ferguson replied. He had the scope trained on Lie Lau leaning over the hood of a dust-covered SUV, ignoring the rounds kicking up dust around her, shouldering an RPG-7. She had snuck up behind the two vehicles in the melee and got within a hundred meters, deadly accurate distance for a notoriously inaccurate weapon. She let loose with another grenade that found its mark again as the other Safir jumped in the air slightly and was engulfed in the explosion, shredding the remaining combatants that were in proximity with deadly shrapnel.

Without hesitating, Ferguson turned back to the south and could see the jeep limping its way toward his position, with what he could now clearly see in his scope as three remaining soldiers. He sighted the driver first and fired another round that found its mark, splattering the inside of the windshield red, and sending the Safir into a hard turn that flipped into a barrel roll over and over several times.

Waiting for the dust to settle, he turned back to the remaining vehicle to the north that was bugging out, hobbling back toward the entry road to the mountain. As he looked back south, the two remaining soldiers had survived the crash, escaped on foot, and were closing on his position. He jettisoned the sniper rifle, picked up the MK 18 Assault Rifle, flipped the safety selector switch to full auto, and let loose on one of the two running in open ground. As he connected with one, the other knelt into firing posture and splashed rounds all over his position. After taking cover and looking back up, a single crack of fire came from Lau's direction, as he watched the kneeling rifleman pitch face forward into the dirt.

"There's your cavalry, Blake. Better late than never," Scruggs said.

Chapter 33

Setareh Lab, South Khorasan Province, Iran

The IRGC officer emerged from the garage with a portable radio in hand and made no sign of apologies for interrupting Commander Togyani as he was engaged in an animated cell phone conversation, outside the Setareh lab entrance.

"Commander, we have a serious situation with the intruder to the western side of the mount."

"I'll call you back, we appear to have an emergency I will need to deal with," Togyani barked into the phone as he signed off and placed the phone in his jacket. "What seems to be the problem, Lieutenant?"

"Sir, per your orders earlier, our scout forces intercepted the intruder and drove him into the foothills, and determining him to be armed, engaged him."

Togyani nodded in irritation, "Yes, I could hear the blasts from here, Lieutenant."

"Sir, the intruder was able to take out several of our men with long distance sniper fire before we could eliminate him, and he had reinforcements ambush our rear flank from the west, and they took out several of our units with RPG fire. The last remaining unit is retreating to our location with casualties. It appears from our cameras the intruding vehicle has yet to pursue but has linked up with the other intruder. He's still alive. Unit 4 is asking for our remaining squad to be deployed immediately in support."

The incredulous look on the Commander's face spoke volumes to the Lieutenant, who backed away slightly, "Your orders, sir?"

"Get your remaining men out from below to meet our returning cowards and take up defensive positions along that wall," Togyani pointed to an extension of the north to south foothills that rose into the mountain and framed the entrance area to the laboratory. "Then order all lab personnel to remain below ground until we put this little invasion down, and tell Javad to get up here and crank up the helicopter. We may need to exit by air until our reinforcements arrive. Finally, get on the phone to our SS camp and have them dispatch one company by fastest means necessary. They can be here in around an hour. Then call Havanirooz Combat Base, and per my orders, use my name personally, have them keep two attack helicopters on standby. They're not aware of the existence of our facility here, and I would prefer to keep it that way, unless we absolutely need their assistance. Understood, Lieutenant?"

The Lieutenant saluted, and then simultaneously jogged back to the garage area, as he returned to the radio, commanding the remaining squad of IRG troops below to immediately meet him at the service elevator that served the garage from the lab.

Togyani bolted past the helicopter and strutted down the dirt road that led into the mouth of the lab entrance, determined to meet the remaining soldiers retreating from the engagement. He was concerned about the ferocity of the attack, given such a small force but was apparently well armed and had the ability to take out three mobile units of highly trained IRGC regulars. *It would be highly improbable that these are simply local resistance fighters that just happened to stumble upon the lab. Why would they be heavily armed trying to engage something they should have no idea that existed below ground here? Could this possibly be a breach of security and the lab location compromised? If it is, is it also possible this could be a covert intelligence operation? Israelis? Americans? British? A combination?* The questions were coming fast and furious.

His mind raced with the worst possible scenarios. He needed answers. He needed to capture at least one of these intruders to determine how and why the facility had been discovered.

After several minutes, from behind him the rest of the security squad disgorged from the service garage and spread out toward the ridge as ordered. He waved again to the Lieutenant that accompanied them from below.

The officer trotted up the road to meet Togyani. "Sir, 4th company is scrambled and in route, and the air base has been placed on alert." He then pointed to the north up the dirt path, "Sir, there looks like some vehicle activity in the distance," they both looked out at the dust cloud in the distance, "that can't be our SS reinforcements."

"Move four of your men out 200 meters, split them two and two, and have them take defensive positions on both flanks of the path. Do they have any rocket propelled grenades?"

"No sir, they all went out with the mobile units. The returning Safir should have a heavy weapon on board."

"We'll hang onto that here with your remaining four men as a last resort." Togyani dismissed his officer and then pointed at his pilot, "Javad, get to the helicopter and be prepared to fire it up. We may need to get airborne until our help arrives."

As the Lieutenant moved away to disperse his men, the one remaining jeep hobbled into the clearing on two flat front tires and lurched to a halt. The windshield was splattered with blood and dirt, and as the driver came to a halt, he immediately reached over to check on his wounded comrade, who he discovered had not survived the trip back.

Togyani barked at the man, "Get that jeep backed into the rocky crevice on this side of the garage, load that missile launcher and standby for orders. We have insurgents that will be following you in from the west and others coming down the road from the north. Stay alert."

Wearily the man obeyed and backed the wounded jeep and deceased comrade into a defensive position.

Chapter 34

Setareh Lab (below ground), South Khorasan Province, Iran

The urgent commotion of soldiers in their subterranean barracks and recreation area down the main hall, dividing it from the adjacent laboratory facilities, drew the attention of the limited number of other non-military and scientific personnel operating in the biological horror show alongside. The overwhelming concern was evident, and it wasn't assuaged by the Lieutenant's orders to remain underground in the lab until the "disturbance" above was resolved, or by the fact he had orders to take the helicopter pilot to the surface with him. The soldiers themselves couldn't wait to get topside, away from the neighboring petri dish of death.

Abood wasted no time making his way over to the soldiers gathering up for the ascent above ground, and confronting the officer, "Lieutenant, if we're going to be left behind without any security or military support, I'd like to have access to some sort of weapon…a rifle, pistol, anything to give me and others a chance to defend ourselves."

"We can take care of you and the others from our positions above."

"I'm sure you can," Abood said with a touch of uncertainty, "but why would it be a problem to allow us to defend ourselves if necessary?"

The Lieutenant eyed him suspiciously, "Have you ever handled a weapon?"

"I have," Abood replied with confidence. I'm proficient with most pistols and have firsthand experience with the AK-47."

Without hesitating, the officer entered one of the doors off the barracks entrance and returned with two PC-9 ZOAF 9mm pistols, a variation of the SIG Sauer P226, holstered on belts, accompanied with several 15 round magazines. He handed both to Abood with a reluctant stare, and with a touch of sarcasm added, "You can handle these?"

Abood grabbed them and threw one each over both of his shoulders. Retrieving one of the weapons from the holster, he adeptly ejected the magazine from the pistol grip to confirm it was loaded, reinserted it, and pulled the slide to chamber a round. With a smirk, "Yes sir, I believe I can handle these."

"Excellent!" replied the Lieutenant. "You're now responsible for the safety of the rest of your personnel. And please don't shoot me or any of my soldiers when we return." With that, the young officer pivoted, and jogged toward the large service elevator at the end of the hall to join the rest of his men impatiently holding the doors open for him.

Abood's mind went into hyperdrive. *What in the world could be transpiring above ground that couldn't be handled by the reaction force he knew was on guard 24 hours a day? Why would they require the urgent need of the remaining forces, housed below? Are we in danger of being exposed, assassinated, shut down, blown up?*

He walked back into the main lab corridor and assured the handful of staff that everything was fine and under control, including Park who had emerged from his office to inquire of the activity.

"The security staff has asked that we remain below and not access the elevators to the surface until they return. If you have any concerns, please let me know."

"Why the weapons?" remarked a pale and nervous staff technician, pointing at the pistols draped over Abood's shoulder.

"Just a precaution Ashkan, no need to worry," assured Abood. "Let's all get back to work."

Park eyed him curiously, and then returned down the hall to his office.

Abood began formulating options. If everything was going to be fine above, he would return to status quo, if something urgent was about to happen, he needed to make sure he could find a way out, and with the Setareh virus in tow. He watched Park disappear around the corner of the hall. *He has to have the real antidote and live material locked up somewhere. It has to be in his possession, he wouldn't trust it out of his sight. It has to be in his office.*

Chapter 35

Themis Cooperative Offices, Alexandria, VA

In the Situation Room back in Virginia, Isaiah was standing with Woods in front of the real-time firefight that had been unfolding on the theater screens up front. His adrenaline was at full throttle, as he had never experienced anything remotely close to what was transpiring. This wasn't his Call of Duty Xbox game, this was real shit, and the distinction wasn't lost on him. He was marveling at how calm Elaine was navigating the drone for surveillance support and relaying information as if she were relaxing on a lounge at the beach. Sheri was leaning in over her shoulder eyeing the video feeds on the screens in front of them and relaying information in an equally serene but focused voice. He was amazed at their professionalism in the midst of the chaos.

The short silence of radio transmissions, while Ferguson and Lau linked up and Wright and Margolis closed in on the target, came to an abrupt end as Scruggs mic'd in to everyone, "C and A, I show four hostiles south of you heading in your direction from the enclave base area on foot. Do you copy, over?"

"Copy that, four hostiles from the south," replied Wright.

Before he could ask if they were carrying any noticeably heavier ordnance, DeHavilland mumbled into her ear, and she cut in, "hostiles are breaking into two pairs, flanking to the east and west. They are straddling the road inbound and appear to have settled into cross firing positions. You're closing fast, approximately one klick out, over."

"Copy."

"Clay, this is Blake. We're approaching on foot from the west, and will angle out to the rear flank of the western pair. We have RPGs salvaged from the Tango Uniforms Lau terminated, and I can set up cuckoo as you arrive. I know you have sniper gear as well.

"You're going to be sitting ducks if you try to come straight through, they'll see your dust cloud coming and be waiting on you. The ground you're entering from will start to elevate slightly several hundred meters out from the mouth of the mountain. If you come to a stop just before there, you'll see some hilly terrain starting to form on both sides of the approach. With a little help from Elaine and ISR, you can use that for cover to gain tactical advantage on higher ground to the north-northeast of the enemy positions. From there you should be able to engage both for diversion and then concentrate on the two closest to you on the east side. We'll take the western two. Co-Op, advise CW to come to a halt when they are 500 meters out and then update on enemy locations, over."

"Copy that Blake, we're slowing now," Wright interjected.

"Another hundred meters CW and you can bring it to a halt. I have you both on ISR and will advise on hostile movements. CW, prepare to stop and approach by foot. Your set of tangos are approximately 500 meters to your 11 o'clock. BF, your two tangos are 400 meters to your two o'clock," Scruggs replied.

Wright slowed to a crawl, he and Margolis scanning the area in front of them, "Copy that. Stopping now and preparing to advance on foot."

Ferguson nodded at Lau to follow him, "Copy, we're on foot now, going EMCON."

Scruggs understood the Emissions Control brevity code for radio silence, and the request seemed to transmit into the war room as well, as a voluntary hush fell over everyone while they watched the next engagement shake out.

* * * * *

Wright and Margolis came to a halt as they angled the Landy north off the worn path and up to a rocky outcropping, positioning the vehicle sideways to the threat. They both donned bullet proof vests and stepped out on the protected side of the truck. Margolis hunkered down for cover with one of the MK18 rifles, as Wright retrieved the Remington MSR and one of the standalone H&K M320 grenade launchers. He gave her the ten second tutorial on sighting the launcher, slung it over her shoulder, and handed her five grenades out of his sack.

They both crouched down, and with Scruggs guiding their movements over the radio, proceeded on foot into the hilly outcroppings northeast of their position that offered just enough cover and distance to keep them invisible to the threats in front of them. About a hundred meters into the increasingly craggy hillside, Scruggs gave them instructions to halt and provided range and direction to the two separate enemy locations below them. The farthest two, ultimately Ferguson and Lau's targets, were to the southeast, and the pair they were responsible for immediately to the east.

On a rocky ledge in front of him, Wright proceeded to set up a make-shift brace with the half-loaded ruck sack and sighted his MSR rifle on the farthest pair first, both of whom appeared to be kneeling in a low-level trench. He recited to Margolis an approximate range estimate and direction and told her on his signal to drop a grenade round in front of their position, but not to go long as Blake and Lau were coming up from behind. He pivoted to the other two closer targets, performed some mental math, ciphered his calculations, and made adjustments to the scope. He would acknowledge he was not as good a shot as Blake, but this was well within his abilities. These two were in a better position as the ground was slightly steeper and had some craggy outcroppings. They were nestled together behind a large rock, but both were exposed from chest to top of head. He was confident that would be enough.

As Ferguson and Lau crawled to within 100 meters of their targets, they heard a faint thud and a grenade exploded to the front and right of the two IRG soldiers, startling both but not doing any significant damage. The second, third, and fourth grenades were more front and center, but still harmless. However, the diversion was perfect, as both men looked up and kept their eyes forward. Lau covered Ferguson from his right, as he leapfrogged his way forward during the noise, and from about 30 meters away, before either one knew what hit them, he leveled his MK 18 Assault rifle and put multiple rounds into both from behind.

"Two western tangos down. I say again two tangos to the west are down," Ferguson broke radio silence.

As the third grenade exploded, Wright let go with his first round that found the chin of the soldier on the left, nearly decapitating him and sending the other soldier scrambling down the short incline to the road where he was in a full sprint retreat when Lau stood up and sent a burst of approximately ten rounds, three of which found their mark, lethally stitching his torso and dropping him to the ground in a heap.

"Remaining two tangos are down," Wright said.

After launching her grenades, Margolis had already climbed back down to the Landy, started it up, and was ready to move as Wright removed his sniper set-up and climbed back down to join her. They began moving forward again as Ferguson and Lau were in a sprint back to Lau's jeep.

"Additional activity in the mountain enclave ahead," Scruggs interjected. "I say again, there's additional armed hostiles gathering in the open area around the entrance ahead. Recommend you exit vehicles again safe distance and approach on foot from original positions on both sides of the road inbound, over."

"Copy that,'" came replies in unison from both Ferguson and Wright.

All four were in visual contact with each other as they approached to within a couple hundred meters of the mouth of the mountain facility, and exited the two vehicles. They all could see the movement of soldiers on the ground and the helicopter centered in the semi-circular opening. Ferguson waved off Wright and Margolis to the eastern edge while he and Lau took up positions in the rugged western-facing foot hills of the mount, the same area he had reconnoitered the night before.

Scruggs was the first to notice, as she broke in, "The bird is starting up. It looks like they may be looking to evac."

Woods turned from his position up front and screamed at Scruggs loud enough for his command to transmit through her headset to the rest of the team, "Don't let that bird off the ground!"

Chapter 36

Setareh Lab, South Khorasan Province, Iran

Javad acknowledged Togyani's spinning of his upright index finger and cranked over the engine to the idle chopper. Realizing the four men he sent out to meet the incoming vehicle were no longer responding to the lieutenant's radio inquiry, Togyani felt it was clearly time to get airborne and wait for the additional reinforcements to arrive. This was a well-trained and extremely proficient force that was decimating his troops, and their advance on the lab's position was undoubtedly going to overwhelm the remaining men. It was time to evacuate.

He barked at the young officer over the growing roar of the rotors and the ensuing dust storm, "Pull your men back into defensive positions around the garage area. I will fly out to meet our incoming reserves and lead them back into the fight. Do not let the intruders into the lab below…understood?"

The lieutenant nodded and saluted his acknowledgement and headed toward the remaining men assembled around the disabled jeep and missile launcher, trying to come to grips with the spinelessness of his commanding officer. Togyani took one last look back at the entrance to see if anyone had breached the area and climbed into the co-pilot seat next to Javadi. With a thumbs-up motion signifying it was time to elevate out of there, Togyani was greeted with a splattering of blood mist and brain matter as Javad's head jerked slightly and his body lurched forward against his seat belt and slumped over.

"Dammit!" a shocked Togyani blurted aloud. He threw off his own seatbelt and rolled out of the chopper onto the ground. He recovered quickly and ran toward the garage area for cover.

"Lieutenant, spread out your four men into defensive positions covering the entrance area," yelled Togyani over the still swirling blades of the helicopter. "And tell them to take as much cover as possible, the intruders have snipers and they're picking us off. You join the other man at the launcher and send a couple of rounds out toward the hills guarding the entrance. We need to keep them pinned down."

The officer barked into his radio, and the last of his soldiers dispersed into the rocky crevices and on top of the garage roof, while the young lieutenant joined his comrade on the launcher. Within seconds they had it loaded and let loose with one missile out toward the western flank of the road. A second missile was fired shortly after and exploded on the opposite side of the entrance way.

Togyani took refuge inside one of the garage doors that was open and noticed the Fiat Ducato, a large panel-style van, that had been used for transporting test subjects to their ultimate fate in the test lab below. Tucked into the back of the first of two garage bays, it smelled like any other gasoline powered vehicle, and yet it reeked of death. As it was unlocked, he opened the driver door and examined the empty key slot and looked around the console for any keys. He turned to the walls of the garage for any visible key storage.

A duo of back-to-back explosions could be heard outside as another pair of missiles were expended. Togyani, cautiously stepped outside, and hugging the front of the closed garage doors, he made his way over to his Lieutenant, who was busy with a pair of binoculars, trying to find any sign of the enemy they were blindly firing at.

"Lieutenant, the truck inside, where are the keys? We may need to make a run for it with you and your men," Togyani lied.

"Sir, if they're not in the Fiat, they should be on a key station located inside the barracks below. It's on the wall to the right as you enter. Do you know where the barracks…"

Togyani had already pivoted ignoring the officer's question and was headed back to the garage area and the elevator that would take him below. "Keep up your fire, Lieutenant," he yelled as he disappeared into the open garage door in the first bay.

Chapter 37

Setareh Lab (below ground), South Khorasan Province, Iran

Abood was rummaging through the weapons bin inside the barracks when he was startled by a fatigued Togyani entering unannounced and in a hurry. His uniform was covered in dirt, and he had blood spatter on the side of his face and neck.

"What in the hell are you doing in here?" Togyani spat at him as he tried to catch his breath.

"Trying to find anything I might be able to use to save me and the staff in case whatever is going on above us goes bad. From the looks of you, it appears we may be closer to that outcome than we were led to believe by your officer who abandoned us a short while ago."

"We have a problem on our hands. There is a well-armed attack taking place above, and we will not have reinforcements here for another half an hour. I'm not sure we can last that long, so I'm looking for options to evacuate everyone," Togyani lied again.

Togyani looked to the right at the wall that housed a set of empty hooks.

"Are you looking for these?" Abood held up a set of car keys.

He shook the keys back and forth in a come and get it motion and conveniently exposed his other hand, clearly in possession of the PC-9 pistol. "These would be to the straight truck above, Commander. I assume you're here to help us out of here?" he replied sarcastically. "Why didn't you take the helicopter and leave us to make do with the truck."

Togyani inhaled deeply regaining his composure, "There is no helicopter, Javad has been killed, we are down to our last half dozen men, and I fear they will not last much longer. You, me, and Park need to find a way out of here. I don't care about the others," he confessed.

"Well, at least we arrived at the truth."

"Can you locate Park?"

"I know where Park is, and I suspect he has in his possession a stash of the virus and antidote. If I'm correct, I'm going to assume you would like for that to go with us."

"How do you know this?"

"Commander, when you brought me here to obviously help pressure Park, it became clear very quickly after I arrived that he has had the answers all along. He's been stalling, and he doesn't hide it well. I know where both are. Give me five minutes, and I'll bring you both. Help yourself to some of the weapons, it sounds like we may need them. Just don't shoot me when I return, I'm actually pretty proficient with firearms, and it won't end well if you attempt anything crazy Commander."

Abood left Togyani fuming. He hadn't been threatened by anyone in a long time, and the arrogance of Abdul-Mahdi giving him orders left him speechless. He quickly recovered and realized they were in a tough spot and if he could deliver the virus and the antidote, they could move the operation elsewhere and replicate from the samples of both. He may even need them to help fight their way out of this. After that, to hell with Park and Abdul-Mahdi, he would deal with them in due time. They are merely pawns in the much greater good of Setareh. First things first, they had to get out of the area to safety.

The door to Park's office was closed, and Abood offered no courtesy knock as he turned the handle to enter and found it locked. He hammered on the door with the butt of the pistol, "Dr. Park, it's urgent we evacuate the lab immediately. The trouble on the ground above threatens all of us in the lab facility below, and the Commander has personally asked that I escort you out of here."

There was noise from within and Park replied, "Give me a minute Abbas, I will join you up front in the entry hall."

Abood slammed on the door again, "Open the door doctor! I won't ask again. I will shoot the door open if you don't join me now."

The door handle rattled at the sound of the lock turning and the door opened slightly to reveal Park peeking out through the crevice, "I told you I would only be a few minutes and will join you up..."

Abood shouldered open the door with enough force to send Park sprawling to the floor on his back as the open door swung fully open, banging off the wall behind it.

"What in the world is wrong with you Abbas?"

A startled Park was attempting to get to his feet as Abood leaned down and pistol-whipped Park across the face, gashing his cheek and nose, sending him back to the floor. He took a glance around the office and noticed all he needed to see in order to confirm he was correct in his assumptions.

On the credenza to the side of the desk was a stainless-steel briefcase opened at a right angle, the custom-cut foam inserts exposed and clearly empty.

"Dr. Park, shut up and listen carefully to what I have to say," said Abood, hovering menacingly above him, the gun pointed right between his eyes.

Park wiped at his face and looked up at the man with a growing hatred, evident in his angry glare.

"Where are the samples? And don't tell me you have no idea what I'm talking about. I'm not stupid doctor. It's abundantly clear you have known and have had the virus and antidote all along, and it now appears you are in the midst of getting ready to transfer them." Abood walked over to the open case.

"I do not have any idea what you are talking about Abbas…or whoever you are."

Abood took two long strides over to the door, kicked it shut, and then added a roundhouse kick to the side of Park's head, nearly knocking him unconscious. He reached up and pulled Park's lab coat off the hook on the back of the door and began wrapping it around the pistol in his hand. He leaned down, placed his free hand over Park's mouth, shoved the gun into Park's left shoulder and fired a round that tore through his shoulder and pinged off the tile floor as it exited behind him.

Park screamed a muffled cry behind Abood's hand, and regardless of his attempt to suppress the noise of the gun, the load report of the shot echoed off the sterile walls. Abood realized the noise would bring unwanted attention, so he leaned in close to Park's ear.

"Where are the samples…Doctor?"

Abood let off his hand slightly from Park's mouth, as he allowed him to gasp at some much-needed air. Abood also saw the slight movement of Park's eyes to the wall behind him.

Park was silent as he worked to catch his breath and grimaced as the intense pain from the shoulder wound gnawed at him.

Abood stood and walked over to the wall that had nothing but a tall cabinet. He opened the doors and surveyed the nearly empty contents. He began pulling out the books, files, and miscellaneous medical accessories that were stacked neatly inside, giving a quick inspection and tossing them randomly to the floor. Nothing. He looked back at Park who looked as if he might be going into shock.

"Doctor, don't make me to kill you. Where have you hidden them?"

Park slumped over as if he were about to pass out. Abood was furious. He kicked at the cabinet as it scooted across the wall slightly. He walked over to Park and put the gun to his head, and after a few seconds debating whether to shoot him in the other shoulder, he had another thought. He slowly stood up, walked over to the side of the cabinet, leaned into it, and pushed it across the wall until it had moved several feet. That was plenty, as the cut out in the wall revealed a small stand-alone safe about the size of a large piece of luggage. He looked at the panel on the front, and saw that it was a biometric lock.

He walked back to Park and dragged him over to the safe. He engaged the power button and grabbed Park's hand, placing his finger against the exposed sensor. The lock released. Abood slowly lifted the door and found what he was looking for. Two small identical cases, each about the size of a cigar box and constructed of some kind of hard-shell composite material, both sealed with three spring loaded latches and each was labeled with a green and a red dot sticker.

His adrenaline rushing and heart beating out of his chest, he laid his gun down, knelt on one knee, and delicately opened the green one and found inside a row of five full 10mL glass serum vials sealed with green caps. A smile slowly took over his face. *This is it!*

He repeated his examination of the red marked case and found the same, but sealed in red caps. Careful not to handle the vials themselves, he closed up both and walked them over to the briefcase, where each fit perfectly into the hollowed foam protective inserts. As he was preparing to close the lid, he heard a throat clearing behind him, and he realized his gun was no longer in his possession.

"Slowly Abbas, or whatever your real name is, turn around."

Abood did as he was told, and as he pivoted, he found Park leaning against the door with the PC-9 leveled at his chest.

"I don't know who you are, but maybe we should have a conversation with the Commander and find out. You're obviously not who you claim to be, and your motives are equally as unclear."

"You don't need to know who I am Doctor Park, Abood needed to stall for time. "My motives are pure and come only from Allah. There's nothing you can do to stop what's coming. I'm just here to help make sure the process is enabled correctly and the infidels are part of the conflagration. It's out of both of our hands now. Call the Commander, he knows who I am and why I was brought here. Names and identities are irrelevant at this point. The only thing relevant now is that the virus is alive and well, we have the means to employ it, and you have had an antidote formula from the very beginning. It's now only a matter of where, when, and how Setareh is deployed."

Park looked at Abood with a mix of contempt and confusion.

Suddenly, the door burst open as one of the lab personnel called out, "Doctor Park, are you alright in here?"

Park's right arm was caught by the swinging door, and he fired off a round that was now aimed into the ceiling. The noise again was deafening and sent the lab technician retreating into the hallway. Abood lunged and grabbed Park at his gun wielding elbow and forearm, driving him into the wall and to the ground. Slamming Park's arm down across his thigh, the pistol fell to the ground, and as Abood picked it up, Park retaliated by throwing a backhanded elbow to Abood's jaw and barrel rolled on top of him as he fell backward. As they grappled each other for possession, the muted cough of another round went off between their entangled bodies.

They both stared face-to-face as the wrestling subsided. Once again, a smile creased the face of Abood as he pushed Park off to the side and slid out from under him.

As he was rising to his feet, Togyani rushed into the room, his pistol drawn as well.

He pointed the gun at Abood, "What in the hell is going on in here?"

He tried to kill me Commander. I asked him for the samples I knew he had been hiding, and after he showed them to me, he accused me of sabotaging his work and then tried to take my gun away from me and shoot me. We struggled, and he lost. I have what we need, Commander," Abood nodded in the direction of the steel case, "the coward had everything we needed all along."

Togyani took one look at Park, his life bleeding out in a crimson pool against the white tile floor, looked at Abood and felt the vibration of an explosion emanating from above them.

"Grab the case, and follow me," said Togyani.

Abood holstered the pistol and stepped over to the briefcase. His smile returned one last time as he closed and locked the lid, his hand trembling as he picked it up realizing the power of what he knew was one of the greatest destructive forces the world has ever known.

Chapter 38

Themis Cooperative Offices, Alexandria, VA

Woods paced the front of the war room, rubbing at his chin in thought.

"Elaine, expand our ISR visual. There is no way in hell that some sort of alert has not been issued by now. Reinforcements have to be in motion."

Before following his order, Scruggs zoomed in to include the positions of the remaining five hostiles on the ground. She copied the screen over to another computer and asked DeHavilland to relay the positions and help create a manual firing solution for them on the ground. It was becoming increasingly difficult to see through the dirty air the helicopter blades were still churning up, and even though that was hampering their visibility from the air, she thought it was likely to offer some cover for them on the ground as they moved into position to initiate a final assault on the lab itself.

After receiving an affirmative reply from DeHavilland, Scruggs elevated the altitude on the drone and expanded the camera angle to take in significantly more geography. It was a desolate area, and there was nothing of concern happening around the lab area that was showing up, just some isolated car traffic on the Routes 91 and 68 north and west. She held steady at the distance, focusing on the inbound path to the lab and points of entry surrounding it.

"BF, this is Co-op, I have remaining tangos sighted for firing solutions," DeHavilland keyed in.

"Go for BF, standing by," Ferguson replied, and then interrupted, "I see the two knuckle heads on the launcher by the garage. We're sighting them now and should silence that shortly."

"Other than those, you still have one located on the roof of a building at 130 degrees from your position, what looks to be right above the launcher. Two more in the clearing 195 degrees from your position, crouched and kneeling behind some cover, looks like a set of oil drums."

"Copy Co-op. We have clear line of sight for the launcher, if you can get me a good range to target, we'll have then scoped and silenced. We'll use our RPG on the two at the oil drums. We'll advance by vehicle for the remaining single, and any others stragglers."

"BF, your range to the launcher is 345 meters."

DeHavilland glanced over to Scruggs, who read her mind and shook her head.

"CW, ISR shows you are clear of any reinforcements for now. We are monitoring approximately 75 kilometers out, will advise, over."

"I want a reconnaissance inside that lab ASAP. Grab any intelligence they can and then turn that place into a pile of rubble," interjected Woods, staring directly at Sheri.

Before a reply came, DeHavilland added, "CW, once you are clear, beat feet for recon inside of lab, gather whatever intelligence you can, and then nuke the place, over."

"Copy that."

Approximately one minute later, Ferguson broke the silence, "One tango down on the launcher, the other is di-di into the garage.

The one above the garage hopped down and is joining him. Prepping the RPG for remaining two, stand by."

Another minute passed before Scruggs interjected on the conversation, "Okay, enemy cavalry has been sighted. I see what looks to be three...no, five vehicles just exited off of 91 at Nay Band, to your northwest. They are a couple klicks to the dirt entryway, then approximately 70 klicks to you position. They are definitely in a hurry. ETA is 45 minutes."

"Copy that. We're inbound on the facility in two minutes."

Chapter 39

Setareh Lab, South Khorasan Province, Iran

After Ferguson had neutralized the launcher with a headshot to the soldier who was manning the weapon system, and with the word reinforcements were inbound, Margolis and Wright had returned to the Landy, driving it up to within a hundred meters of the front door to the facility.

Wright hopped out, and using the vehicle for cover, laid down covering fire while Ferguson joined them on foot. Lau had gone back to retrieve her vehicle. The two remaining soldiers that were still sending sporadic rifle fire at their positions were the only remaining impediments to their advance.

Ferguson slung the RPG off his shoulder as he arrived at the Landy, made a couple of mental calculations, and triggered off the last round they had. A little high, but close enough, as it slammed into the rocky crevice directly behind the two soldiers, shrapnel igniting a fireball that consumed both of them.

They all piled into the Landy and drove straight into the clearing, which was now blanketed in a haze of smoke, dust, and debris still being churned up from the rotors, all eyes mindful of any activity around the garage. As Margolis pulled to a halt, Wright jumped out left and Ferguson exited to the right, both letting off rounds in the directions of the garage and what was left of the two smoldering bodies consumed in the explosion from what a had been a cache of fuel drums. Margolis exited last and took refuge behind the jeep. As Wright reached the garage doors, somebody stepped out from behind the opposite garage wall and took aim, but before he could pull the trigger, Margolis dropped him with three rounds from the MK18 she was still wielding. Wright turned at the sound, gave a wink in appreciation, and in a crouch, slid along the garage doors until he reached the slumped body and added another bullet from his own MK18 as a dead check.

Ferguson, having confirmed all quiet on his side of the open area, trotted over to the still running helicopter, peeked in for any occupants other than the deceased pilot slumped over the controls, and joined Wright at the garage doors.

"Adina, look in the back for the box of grenades. There should be some flash bangs in there."

Fifteen seconds later, Margolis joined them, as Lau appeared with her vehicle and came screaming in to a dusty halt behind the Landy.

"Look what Elaine packed for us," Margolis smiled as she jogged up to join them with one flash bang in each hand.

Ferguson grabbed one, opened the only pedestrian entry door to the garage, pulled the pin, and tossed it in. With weapons shouldered, Wright led the way in, with Ferguson on his shoulder, just like they had trained for and executed dozens of times over the years. Even Margolis marveled at the no flinch, no fear, trusting precision of the entry.

"One down, I have him," came a shout from within.

"Clear," came a response.

Another announced "Clear," followed by an invitation to enter, and Adina cautiously entered through the same door. It was dark, but she could make out Ferguson checking the inside of a van, the only vehicle remaining inside, while Wright was kneeling on the back of a prone body, securing his hands with what looked like the man's own belt.

After another cursory look around, Wright grabbed the still-stunned Lieutenant by the back of his collar and dragged him out the door and into the light and open air. Margolis and Ferguson followed, while Lau joined them, surveying the damage and carnage all around.

After he seated the prisoner on the ground in a crossed legs squat, he turned to Margolis, "Adina, can you use your best haji on him and see if you can find out how we get into this place?"

Margolis began interrogating the nearly deaf IRGC soldier, elevating her decibel level enough to be heard over the noise of the helicopter rotors. Wright and Ferguson walked over to the cockpit and pulled the dead pilot out to the ground. They both looked at each other with the same "I don't have a clue" expression. As Ferguson leaned into the dashboard of controls, hopelessly looking for an On-Off switch, Lau tapped him on the shoulder, motioned him away from the controls, and then reached in flipping the precise switch to kill the engine.

"Damn girl, what is it you don't do?" Wright howled, looking at Ferguson who was shaking his head in disbelief.

Wright turned to go back to their prisoner and froze. Turning back to face Lau, "You wouldn't know how to fly that bird by any chance?"

Lau took one look at the sleek Italian Augusta-Bell AB 212, covered in a layer of settling dust, and smiled, "I don't have a lot of hours in that version, but I can definitely get us from point A to point B."

Wright and Ferguson looked at each other and nodded.

"You get comfortable in that cockpit and get ready to fire it up again. That will be our escape route out of here," said Ferguson.

"Check to see what kind of fuel we have left, we'll need to try to get as close to the Afghan border as we can, if not over it. Adina has a map, you two plot the shortest course you can find and work on an estimate on how far we can go. We're going below, if we can find a way in."

Just as the two reached Adina, one of the garage doors exploded outward as a white van burst through into the opening just missing Adina and swerving into the clear. Margolis dove to the dirt as Wright and Ferguson both let loose a hail of bullets directed at the fleeing vehicle. Nothing found the mark to prevent the escape.

"Shit, where did that come from, there wasn't anybody in there?" Ferguson screamed at the van disappearing into a cloud of dust.

Adina popped up with a helping hand from Wright, "I have an answer for that. Our young jailbird here gave me directions to the back door," she pointed back at the garage, "service elevator in the back disguised as a cabinet."

* * * * *

Abood punched in the access code to the elevator and held the door open while Togyani ducked into the armory to see what kind of weapons were still left. He returned with two KL-7 .62 assault rifles with accompanying bandoliers incorporating six additional magazines and ordered the remaining mill of confused and concerned technicians to remain where they were.

Another explosion rocked from above as the elevator closed and ascended to the ground level. Abood and Togyani held their weapons at the ready aimed at the doors as they opened to a darkened garage.

"Take these and get ready to drive us out of here," Togyani barked at Abood as he handed him the keys to the van and covered the only door leading outside while backing toward the vehicle. "Don't start it until I get in."

Abood obliged the command and reached the driver side door, opened it, climbed in, and closed the door as quietly as possible while readying the key in the ignition. Togyani circled in front and climbed in on the passenger side. Abood cranked over the van.

Togyani pointed straight ahead, "plow through that door and be prepared to turn hard right after you clear it. Don't stop for anything."

Abood shifted into drive and punched the accelerator as the blew through the door and nearly ran over one of the attackers as he cleared the wreckage, steered the vehicle to the right, and accelerated full speed down the dirt road that led away from the laboratory, the dull thud of bullets entering metal reverberating over the roar of the engine.

After the rifle fire subsided, Abood slowed down just enough to alleviate losing control of the van as it bounced over the rough surface. "Where are we going?"

"Straight ahead, we'll meet with our quick reaction force that should be arriving any minute."

Abood noticed the strain in Togyani's voice and looked over to find the commander slumped over and blood pooling in his lap.

"Commander, you've been hit."

"How observant of you." Togyani pressed his left hand into his limp right shoulder. "Keep going, they will have a medic in the force that can help."

Abood returned his eyes to the road and considered their course of action. If he were to meet up with the QRF, he would be stuck with having to remain with the soldiers tending to Togyani or possibly have to return to the fight. Neither options would offer an opportunity to keep the briefcase from being removed from his possession. He'd come too far to give up the prize now, but there wasn't enough time for him to evaluate his options. He would need to play along until another opportunity presented itself.

In the distance he could see a rapidly approaching convoy of multiple vehicles closing in a hurry. He slowed and then came to a stop. He placed the rifle on the floorboard and removed the pistol belt he still retained and stepped out raising his hands in surrender. The lead vehicle, a jeep with four soldiers in it, ground to a halt immediately in front of him.

As they directed a slew of weapons at him, Abood screamed, "Please don't shoot, I'm unarmed. I have Commander Togyani in the front seat with me, he is badly wounded and needs immediate assistance. He said you would have a Medic in your group that could help him."

A grizzled Captain stepped out of the jeep covered in a layer of dirt, as the remaining canvas covered troop trucks stopped behind him. He withdrew his own pistol and keeping a steady aim at Abood walked to the passenger side of the van. It didn't take long for him to open the door and reach in to attend to the wounded Togyani. His head popped back out immediately, yelling orders at the jeep, where a sergeant responded by leaping out of the jeep and running toward one of the trucks. A few seconds later the sergeant and a young medic were in a full sprint to the van.

With the threat from the soldiers subsiding, Abood walked over to join them. Togyani was heading into shock, but still had enough of his faculties to offer up to the Captain, who was obviously familiar with the lab facility, a situational report with estimated number of assailants and commanding the officer to attack and re-take possession.

Abood interrupted, "Captain, I assume he will need to be taken to a hospital immediately. If you want to lay him down in the back of the van and leave your medical tech with me, I can drive him to the nearest facility while you and your men take care of the insurgents."

"Who are you?' the Captain inquired with disdain.

Before Abood could answer, Togyani provided him with Abood's identity as Dr. Abdul-Mahdi and confirmed that he had helped get them to safety. He also conceded that Abood's offer was a wise one and to put him in the back of the van so they could get to a hospital as soon as possible. The medic, who was already administering emergency aid with intravenous plasma while applying a compression bandage to the wound, verbally agreed to the suggestion.

With a touch of new found deference, the Captain complied and ordered two soldiers to lift Togyani out of the passenger seat and assisted with opening the double passenger doors on the side of the van, laying him down in the first-row bench seat.

With orders to the medic, who acknowledged they would take the Commander to the nearest hospital in Birjand, the Captain then waved a young soldier from the jeep and ordered him to drive the van with Abood, the medic, and Togyani to Birjand.

Abood noticed Togyani mumble something to the medic, who in turn eyeballed the stainless-steel briefcase situated between the driver and passenger seat, and he quickly retrieved it to Togyani's side.

After a brief discussion between Togyani and the Captain, a radio was left with the Commander and the medic, to keep the Captain apprised of the situation. The Captain was instructed that if they could not handle killing or capturing this little band of intruders, their orders were to keep the attackers pinned down in the lab area and call up additional reinforcements from the SS camp to quash it. If any of the assailants were captured, they were to be retained for his personal interrogation.

Chapter 40

Setareh Lab, South Khorasan Province, Iran

Ferguson took stock of the ruck sack of explosive charges he had retrieved from the Landy, led their prisoner to the keypad next to the garage service elevator, and instructed him to enter the code to access the facility. When he refused, Wright placed the muzzle of his rifle to the kneecap of the lieutenant, who immediately recognized in his eyes the clear intent to dismember his knee and obligingly tried to control his trembling hand long enough to enter the seven-digit code.

As the doors opened, Ferguson and Wright stepped in with their fireworks accessories and the weak-kneed lieutenant and waved off anybody else to join them.

"Bull shit!" Margolis chimed. "You two are not going down there alone."

"We have no idea what's down there and how bad the situation is, and we need you two to monitor the incoming bad guys. If we're not back up here in," Ferguson looked at his watch, "ten minutes, you and Lei get the hell out of here in that chopper. It's gonna be less than a half hour to the Afghan border in that bird, so get it moving."

As the elevator door began to close, a smiling Wright leaned along as he spoke through the dwindling opening, "Otherwise we'll see you shortly."

Once underground, they stepped off the elevator with rifles aimed along their line of sight. They stepped into and "cleared" a number of rooms that ran opposite each other along a hallway about 40 meters in length in what appeared to be a pseudo barracks, armory, and cafeteria area complete with a kitchen. The last room they came to was a lounge, and their entry startled a number of white-coated lab technicians clearly unnerved from the activities that were transpiring above them. Cups of tea hit the floor as Wright and Ferguson both yelled for everybody to put their hands on their heads and lie on the floor.

"Is there anybody else here?"

No response

"Does anybody speak English?"

A small woman crying in the back raised her hand from a prone position.

"Stand up, I'm not here to hurt you. Do you understand me?" Wright asked.

She nodded her head, sniveling.

"Who else is here?"

"Nobody else. We were all told to stay here until whatever the disturbance above ground was finished. There are some patients that may still be alive in their test rooms, and Dr. Park, I believe, is dead in his office."

"Dr. Dae-Ho Park?"

"Yes, he's in his office, but everybody was scared to leave here to go check on him."

"Take me to his office."

"It's down the next hall to the left, I can show you."

As Wright followed the female tech down the hall, Ferguson placed the lieutenant on the ground with the others and began to place a couple of charges, but held off on any detonators.

Wright stepped into the office, where it was obvious a struggle had taken place and found a man on the ground. He checked for a pulse, and it was faint, but still there. He carefully rolled the man over onto his back, his torso soaked in blood from a gunshot wound to the abdomen. He had nearly bled out, and he wasn't long for the world.

He knelt down and leaned in close, slapping the man in the face trying to rouse him. "Dr. Park, can you hear me?" He slapped and shook him again. A slight groan and a flutter of his eyes. "Dr. Park, my name is Clay Wright, and I work for a man named Jake Woods. I believe you would remember him from your brief stint in Cambodia. Dr. Park, I need to know if you can help us?" He gently slapped and shook him again. "Dr. Park?"

Park extended his hand toward the desk, and Wright looked up to see the clutter of the desk, the empty hole in the wall, and finally the open safe. He stepped over to look in to see it was empty. He returned to Park, whose eyes were open, but looking at nothing. Blood was oozing from his mouth, and he coughed, spitting blood into the air.

Wright grabbed his head and lifted it, alleviating the choking slightly. Park was trying to say something to him and he leaned closer.

It was faint, but Wright heard him say, "My phone. Track it on my phone."

"Track what, Dr. Park?" Wright lifted his head higher.

Park coughed again, and then a pronounced exhale as his eyes rolled back and his body went still.

"Shit!"

The female tech, who had been standing behind watching, began sobbing as she covered her mouth and fled down the hallway.

Wright took out his own cell phone and snapped a couple of pictures of Park. He then frantically began to look for a phone in the office. He grabbed an iPad that was lying on the floor and looked at his watch and realized he was running out of time. He looked all over the desk, on the floor, and into the hole in the wall. He reached down and patted the blood-stained jacket of Park and then his pants. In the back pocket, he hit something. A wallet? No, it was a cell phone. He pocketed it and ran down the hall to join Ferguson.

"Blake, I found Park." He shook his head. "Got some intel, but we need to light this place up. Let's put it on 15-minute timers. That gives us five to plant and ten minutes to get the hell out of here. Hopefully, we can time it so the rest of their cavalry comes charging in to taste the dust."

"Roger that. I'll take this hall and escort all these non-coms out of here. Our little lady tech says there's a lab entrance at the end of the hall on the right opposite where you went. She said not to go past the first air lock, we could all be infected. She also says forget all the test subjects, they're all infected, highly contagious and soon to be dead anyway."

"Copy that, I'm on it."

Wright bolted out with another ruck sack and disappeared down the hall.

* * * * *

"CW, this is Co-op, over. Do you copy?"

Margolis activated her mic, "Adina here, I copy." She dropped the rest of the equipment from the Landy into the back of the chopper.

Scruggs looked at her screen and did some best-guess math in her head. "Adina, you have maybe five more minutes before there are more bad guys than you can handle arriving at your doorstep, over."

"Roger that. We're going to take the chopper out of here. Just waiting on Blake and Clay to exit the lab. They've been below for about ten minutes, and they are due back up any moment."

Margolis gestured a thumb up to Lau, who had strapped into the cockpit of the Bell helicopter and had the engine running and the rotors underway. She looked back at her watch and mumbled under her breath something that sounded like, "you two knuckleheads need to get your asses up here, now."

As she wandered away from the dust of the helicopter and looked out at the road to the approaching cloud, Wright busted through the door of the garage, followed by a gaggle of men and women dressed in white coats along with the lone IRGC lieutenant. She held her breath, and then exhaled, as Ferguson came out a few seconds behind them. Both men were relieved to see the blades turning on the helicopter.

Ferguson yelled into the ear of the female tech, and she in turn translated the message to all of her fellow tech and the lieutenant. All at once they turned and started running up the road as fast as their legs would take them.

Wright grabbed Margolis and trotted them both toward the chopper. He looked at his watch, "We have about seven...make that six minutes before this entire complex turns from a mountain into a crater." He could hear Ferguson talking to Scruggs back at the co-op, giving her and the gang their flight plans and a heading toward the border.

They all hopped into the bird, and Lau expertly lifted it off and away from the mountain clearing. She headed north and then due east on a heading to the Afghan border.

* * * * *

The captain and the remaining QRF slowed as they could see the helicopter lifting off in the distance about a kilometer away, and a small group of what looked like laboratory technicians and workers running down the road. As they reached the lead jeep, the Lieutenant came forward to the Captain, who spun him around to remove the belt binding his hands. He tried to salute, but the captain slapped his hands away.

"What's happening here Lieutenant?"

"Sir, they are escaping by the helicopter."

"Are they now? I see you put up quite a fight, taken prisoner by your own belt."

"Sir, they have the facility rigged with explosives; it's set to go off any minute."

"What?" The captain turned and started yelling commands, motioning for his men to turn the trucks around, while everyone on foot started running again. As he climbed back in his jeep, the ground shuddered dramatically, the earth lifted and rolled toward them, and then the entire mountain erupted into the air. The blast wave came next as an intense burst of compressed air buffeted bodies and vehicles, followed by a driving wind propelled dust storm that covered everything and everyone in a layer of Iranian soil.

From a distance, the occupants of the exiting chopper looked back at the awesome spectacle of a mountain disintegrating in a nebula of exploding dirt, rock, dust, and smoke.

Wright, channeling his best Sundance Kid impersonation, looked at Ferguson and laughed, "Think ya used enough dynamite there, Butch?"

Chapter 41

Themis Cooperative Offices, Alexandria, VA

"Elaine, how's our CH vehicle doing?" Woods asked, while looking over Isaiah's shoulder. The two were studying a map on one of the computer screens, calibrating the area from the lab to the Afghan border. Woods tapped at the screen running his finger north away from the border, "Isaiah, plot me a distance from the lab area to that camp."

"Sir?"

"Do it young man!"

"The CH is hovering over the border. I can have it fully armed and over the area in 20 minutes," Scruggs replied.

"Do it now...and get our Predator down and under radar and back over the border. I'd like to salvage it and not have any American made equipment left behind." Woods motioned to DeHavilland to pass him her active communication headset. He slipped it over his head. "Clay or Blake can you hear me over the chopper noise?"

"Affirmative," came Ferguson's response.

"How much fuel do you have?"

Ferguson tapped Lau on the shoulder, "how much petrol?" He followed her pointed finger to the fuel gauge. "A little over half a tank."

Woods turned to face Isaiah, who, after looking at his screen of specifications for the Bell AB-12, gave thumbs up. "Good, I need you to head due north, we're going to take a 10-minute detour and then get you out of there."

"You're cuttin' it close General, if they scramble anything supersonic, or any tactical birds out of Birjand, we're not gonna be able to fly our way out."

"Understood. But I want to make sure we address the training camp just north of you and clean up that nightmare as well. It's 75 kilometers to the border from the camp area, about an hour by helicopter. On your current heading you're 20 minutes out from the camp. I need you to put down just short of there. Hoof it within laser range of target and paint everything in that camp. We'll have you in and out in less than 10 minutes, copy?"

Ferguson looked at Wright, who was busy fishing out from the stack of equipment Margolis had salvaged from the Landy, the box labeled *Survey Equipment.* Inside he removed a SOFLAM PEQ-1C Laser Acquisition Marker, a hand-held laser designator model favored by special operations forces in rugged field conditions, and passed it over to Ferguson. He thumbed the *ON* switch to make sure batteries were still operational, and gestured a thumbs up. "Roger that Co-op. We're good to go."

Isaiah rattled off coordinates to Woods, who said, "We have the camp at 32° 53' north and 59° 15' east. We are discontinuing ISR and will have hot missiles standing by for your delivery, copy?"

"Roger that, Co-op. We're inbound now and will alert when we are on the ground and moving to target."

Lau punched in the coordinates and veered slightly northwest. The rest of the group looked out on the horizons for any possible incoming hostiles and prayed that no alerts had been issued yet.

Scruggs was busy bringing the CH drone over the Iranian border in the most desolate area she could find, flying it toward the camp low over a pancake-flat plateau that gave way to mountain valleys and ravines. DeHavilland, still learning how to navigate the drone on the fly, was piloting the Predator back over the border into Afghanistan.

Woods had just hung up from his cronies at the Defense Department, politely asking if a possible training sortie could be flown into western Afghanistan. Without any hesitation or fanfare from the other end, two F-16 Fighting Falcons were scrambled out of Bagram Airfield headed southwest at Mach 2. Both pilots told to be on the lookout for a commercial Bell helicopter possibly making an emergency landing in the wasteland west of Anar Dara, and to make sure they were not being tracked into Afghan airspace by any other foreign aircraft.

Isaiah was monitoring commercial air traffic on Flightrader24 global flight tracking system, and monitoring General Commercial, Emergency/Distress, and Air to Air frequencies, for any deviations requested in Iranian airspace that might indicate any new military aircraft activity inside Iran.

Returning to Scruggs at the controls of the Chinese UAV, Woods asked, "Are we ready to launch the AR-2's on target?"

"Give me a five-minute warning and I can have the CH close enough for missile launch." She was instructing Isaiah on how to program the same camp coordinates into the firing computer. All she had to do was get them close and they would home in on the lasers for pinpoint accuracy.

"Thank you, Elaine. Standby, this is going to be close. We need to get them out of there. All hell is going to break loose in that area within the next hour."

Chapter 42

Near Zenowghan, Iran

The young soldier behind the wheel was aggressively steering the white van over the dirt road towards Route 91. From there they would connect to 68 and a two-hour drive to the hospital in Birjand.

In the back seat the medical technician had Togyani stabilized, well sedated, and was monitoring his vitals, when a noticeable ground trembler could be felt outside and the rumble of an explosion in the distance behind them.

The driver pulled to a stop, and he and Abood both stuck their heads out of the windows simultaneously to witness what looked like a small volcano erupting into a mushroom cloud behind them.

Abood stuck his head back into the van, as the medic stepped out of the side door to see the destruction in the distance. This was it. Opportunity knocked. Abood reached down to the floor board and retrieved one of the holstered pistols. He stretched over the console and shot the driver through the back of the skull, spraying blood and brain matter into the desert air, his shoulders and what was left of his head slumped over the open window.

Without hesitating, he opened the passenger door, stepped out, and emptied three more rounds at the stunned medic facing him, two of the bullets finding the man's chest and stomach. As the dead man dropped to the ground, Abood reached in the open door and grabbed Togyani by the boots and dragged him out of the seat and onto the ground, his head bouncing off the floorboard on the way out. In a sedated and bewildered state of confusion, the commander struggled to come to his senses, only in time to gather enough of his faculties to glare up at Abood, staring down the barrel of a pistol. Two more rounds exploded point blank into his face.

Dragging the dead bodies of Togyani and the medic off the dirt road and to the nearest stand of scrub and rock, he retreated to the van and returned with the driver to the same area. He attempted to scrape dirt over the three corpses and, dripping of sweat, decided it faster to forage some more random brush and thickets, placing them over the pile as camouflage. Hopefully, he thought, the buzzards or animals of the night would take care of them before they could be found.

Kicking dust and dirt over the blood on the ground, he also wiped clean the blood and tissue from the driver side of the van with one of the clean medical bandages, and then tossed it along with the soldier's gear and medical equipment in with the bodies.

Returning to the van, he opened up his cell phone and plotted a new course. Once he reached 68, he could follow it west to Ashkezar, then continue west on 78 and 55 to the port city of Bandar Bushehr on the Persian Gulf, one of several locations pre-selected with agents of Hezbollah to help him escape back to Lebanon. He picked up the steel suitcase and placed it in the passenger seat in front. He turned the ignition and a smile returned to his face. He had done it. He bowed his head straight ahead westward toward Mecca. *God willing on this blessed day, the 3rd Intifada begins, the beginning of the end of Zionism is here. May Allah help us overcome this monster, protect the innocent of the world, and accept the murdered as martyrs.*

Chapter 43

South Khorasan, Iran

Lau made one pass over the camp, then maneuvered south of the hilltop blocking the site visually from what turned out to be an ideal landing zone. She descended and placed the skids of the Bell on a large, oval-shaped rocky outcropping, sitting below the ridgeline 100 meters in front of them. "Co-op, this is BF, we are on the ground and headed to our perch. We will be in position in five, over."

"Copy that BF, we are armed and standing by." Scruggs brought the CH drone north slightly and then headed it northeast again on the plotted coordinates.

Wright hopped out first, toting one of the Mk46 light machine guns, leading the charge up the hill to the top of the ridge. Ferguson was out a few steps behind hot on his tail. When they reached the top, they both hit the dirt prone, Wright shouldered the rifle and Ferguson activated the laser. They were relieved to be close enough, less than a couple hundred meters, to precisely hit every one of the five buildings in the camp with a definitive laser signal. The PEQ 1C was accurate to within one meter up to 20,000 meters, so Ferguson calculated it would be like shooting fish in a barrel from this distance.

It was mid-afternoon hot, and the activity outside was limited to a dozen soldiers kicking around a soccer ball and a hand full of men in chairs, trying to stay cool under the shade of an awning adjacent to one of the building's entrances. With no immediate concern of threats, there were essentially no guards posted and no sense of alarm.

"This really isn't fair, you know?" Wright mumbled while he surveyed the buildings through his sight.

"That's the way, uh huh, uh huh, I like it," Ferguson hummed quietly, steadying the designator on a rocky fulcrum.

Wright used the rifle scope to survey the area, and they determined their laser sequence to the five targets by number and added a sixth right in the middle. Wright would use the laser on the rifle scope to paint the location, and Ferguson would focus the designator laser onto the tactical laser spot. Once Ferguson was dialed in, Wright would move on to the next target, and Ferguson would follow after each munition made contact. They figured ten seconds was enough time between the shuttle from one target to the next.

"Co-op, we are in position, target is painted…six times. Repeat target is painted by six. We need ten second interval, ten secs between launch, copy?"

"Copy BW, six missiles away and inbound, ten seconds apart." For the next minute Scruggs toggled off six AR-2 missiles from about twenty kilometers away. "First mike is on target in two minutes."

"Roger that."

* * * * *

The first missile slammed into the center of what was the barracks, disintegrating the building and dismembering the adjoining soccer players alongside. Wright had already moved the tactical laser over to the second target. Ferguson found his spot and settled the PEQ on the second target,

"Got it. move to three."

The next missile hit squarely on the cafeteria, resulting in a devasting detonation. Wright had pivoted his laser to what he surmised was probably a command bunker, and Ferguson quickly found it and barked him on to the next. The fortified dugout erupted and disappeared ten seconds later. While a few bodies confused and bewildered were staggering about in the center of camp, a garage and a generic-looking warehouse were annihilated over the course of the next twenty seconds, and as Wright yelled out, "one to grow on," Ferguson locked in, and a final missile hit dead center of the smoking and smoldering encampment, adding an extensive fireball that consumed anything that was left standing.

As the last debris was falling from the air below them, Wright and Ferguson were already both in a dead sprint to the helicopter, the blades accelerating as they climbed aboard.

"Co-op, target is a scorched earth. We are out of this sandbox."

"Roger that. You are cleared for takeoff, please fasten your seatbelts and get the fuck out of there," Woods replied. "You're heading is due east, keep it low, just off the ground if you can. There will be lots of traffic after all the noise you've made, so keep the pedal down. You will have fast mover escorts at the border just to discourage anybody that would foolishly decide to follow you over. Once across, the escorts will direct you northeast toward Herat. Hopefully, the fuel holds out, but if not, I'll have a QRF out to meet and greet and get you back if you have to ditch."

"Good copy."

* * * * *

Major Brook "Smash" Eha and First Lieutenant J.D. "Crusher" Barker piloted their F-16 fighters into a rectangular holding pattern just east of the Iranian and Afghanistan border, taking turns running a north to south straight-line surveillance pass, ten kilometers on either end of Anar Dara, and back. It was Taliban country, so both kept their warning systems active for any surface-to-air threats.

On his second run in the last ten minutes, Barker's APG-66 Pulse Doppler Radar picked up an inbound target to his southwest.

"Smash, check your screen, but I have a target approaching us from the southwest, twenty kilometers. Looks to be moving at a slower speed, maybe 100 knots at 1,500 feet. Still in badlands, but approaching safety. My guess is that's our bird for rescue."

"Copy. Smash also has radar contact. Stay above him Crusher and widen your watch for any hostiles in pursuit. I'll go to 1,500 level, and hold for intercept when he's free and clear."

"Roger."

Eha barrel rolled into descent and circled around to the south of Barker and went into a smaller oval pattern.

Not less than 30 seconds later, "Smash, we have company. I read a pair of bogies 70 klicks out, closing fast from the west. Estimate on our target in under five minutes."

Eha did the math in his head. The helicopter was probably four, maybe five minutes from the border as well. *Shit! This is way too close.* "Crusher close your gap to the border and activate CMDS."

Barker engaged his AN/ALE-47 Counter Measure Dispenser System and brought himself within two kilometers of the border, a dangerously close margin for mistaking international airspace. No doubt the Iranian border radar and missile installations were fully alerted, although he took some small comfort in the knowledge that Iran's strategic SAM coverage was virtually non-existent along the

Afghan border, except for a limited HAWK site out of range north in Mashhad. That still didn't eliminate any handheld or mobile ground units and the air threat closing quickly.

The F-16s crossed each other as they ran parallel in opposite north and south directions. Barker slowed his airspeed to match Eha, descending slightly to close proximity to Smash in case the Iranian aircraft crossed into Afghan airspace looking for a fight. Regardless of the new relaxed Rules of Engagement in the Afghanistan Theater, there would be hell to pay if they downed any Iranian aircraft in Iran, so their hands were tied to ward off the hostiles as long as they remained over the border.

Eha slowed to meet the helicopter as it closed within a couple kilometers of the border and exhaled a sigh of relief as it was going to beat the bogies to the border.

"Smash, I have two missiles away heading for our whirlybird."

Eha looked out to see missiles in the distance, his missile warning receiver sounding as well, and immediately dove level to their incoming path. "Crusher, buzz that bird and force him to take evasive action."

Barker accelerated and dove directly at the Bell that was just crossing the border, screaming past just overhead and to the starboard, forcing Lau to veer off hard left.

Eha ran a perpendicular path two kilometers behind the chopper and in front of the oncoming pair of Fatter air-to-air missiles and manually let loose a cluster of flares from his CMDS while accelerating hard to the south. Simple, but effective, the collection of white-hot magnesium vessels tricked both of the missiles' infra-red tracking mechanisms and deflected both of them away seconds before they reached the helicopter.

"Talley-ho Smash, outstanding…well done. I show both bogies disengaging. I say again, both bogies breaking off and altering course back inland."

The two F-16's both circled around and reduced speed, pulling up along opposite sides of the Bell and setting a course for Herat to the northeast. A crisp salute came from the male in the passenger seat up front in the chopper's cockpit. Barker returned the salute and gave a directional wave of the same hand indicating the way home to safety.

Chapter 44

Casa Leoni, Positano, Italy

The subtle morning breeze ruffled the sheer curtains as a rising sun filtered a soft light into the room. An aroma of breakfast mingled with the circulating airflow. Margolis slipped out from under the white cotton sheets and mounds of multiple body pillows engulfing the king size bed. In her t-shirt and underwear, she reached the large, marble tiled, Mediterranean-style bathroom, splashed water to her face and scalp, and assessed her road weary features in the large sink mirror. Drying both, and running her fingers through her head of full black hair, she donned a pair of running shorts and proceeded out and down the hall, following an open staircase toward the smells of food.

In the open and expansive kitchen, a small middle-aged woman, adorned in a classic Italian red checkerboard apron, was busy preparing a morning meal bounty, spreading her fare out liberally in bowls and platters over a rectangular granite island. Margolis grazed the eats with her eyes and then spotted Woods, Ferguson, and Wright seated just outside on an adjoining open-air patio. Settled in around a large, umbrella-covered wood table, they were admiring the cliffside view out on to the Tyrrhenian Sea and the town of Positano, splattered in a multitude of colors below. She accepted a hot cup of cappuccino offered up by the smiling maid cum chef and stepped through the open French-style glass doors to a distinctly salt infused air.

"Good morning Adina," said Woods first.

The others repeated greetings, and she offered an exaggerated curtsy and sat in an empty chair.

"I've been debriefing Blake and Clay on your adventures. I'm going to take a wild guess and suggest you don't have much to add."

"You're probably spot on," Margolis acknowledged, gingerly sipping at the steaming cup. "Mission half accomplished. Lab and camp destroyed, Park dead, but we missed out on the damn virus. Does that just about sum it up?"

"Yes, but I would say your mission was a bigger success than you're giving credit to your team. I've had to offer the same pick-me-up to your two glum chums here. Isaiah and some of our best IT spooks are huddled together up at Ramstein, and with a little help from one of Isaiah's dear friends at Apple, are wading through Park's iPad and iPhone you confiscated. After breaking in to portions of them late last night, Isaiah called to tell me you guys may have stuffed out the next Middle East Armageddon."

She offered a look of confused curiosity.

"It seems our boy Park was having enormous pangs of remorse. Not only has he meticulously documented his research on the virus with enormous amounts of data for our CDC and other beltway alphabets to wade through, but he also summarized what that IRGC nut job Togyani was up to. I'll let you read his translated notes when we can get everything downloaded off his devices, but the cliff notes read that he was about to start a biological World War III that was easily going to wind up eradicating millions of people."

She looked at Ferguson and Wright, and both shook their heads in acknowledgement.

"You guys did good...REAL GOOD. I even passed along the same cliff notes to my Intelligence folks at DOD for dissemination all the way to the top, and I just received a personal phone call from our newly elected Commander in Chief offering congratulations. He won't take office for a couple of months, but through back channels all indications are he appreciates everything we're doing. Needless to say, everything right now remains "Classified," so there will be nothing coming officially from there.

"Current POTUS is not happy and is looking for answers from his folks internally and our intelligence partners in the region, and hasn't even responded to the Iranians blowing a gasket with the International community over their sovereignty being violated. Everybody is in denial. It seems a military training facility was sabotaged and destroyed by foreign infiltrators, they claim were American, Israeli, or British...in that order, or saboteurs supported by the Great Satan and her allies. Additionally, in a remarkable bit of irony, a small volcanic eruption, initiated by unknown seismic activity, occurred a hundred kilometers to the south.

"All true, but laughable to say the least. It's a shame they have not a shred of evidence to support that, thanks to our Chinese munitions and equipment, and the fact that clandestine biological laboratories and suicide training camps still don't play well with the majority of the international community and press. None of which will be granted access to either of the locales."

Margolis took another sip of her brew as Woods' cell phone chirped and vibrated on the table. He looked at the incoming call and retrieved it and answered as he stood and walked to the railing for privacy.

"Why are you guys up so early?" she asked. "And where is Lau?"

"Internal clock is fouled up I guess," replied Wright.

"Lei is still asleep in one of the lower bedrooms," added Ferguson. "I got six hours in, slept like a baby. I don't need as much beauty sleep as you two do, and boy does he need it," a hard finger jabbing into Wright's shoulder.

After their narrow escape back into Afghanistan the day before, having landed their stolen chopper at Shindand Airbase in Herat Province, the four weary souls grabbed food in the base cafeteria, managed showers, and the base cobbled up some fatigues for all. They waited out another hour before Cromer's Gulfstream G550 touched down, refueled, and flew them out of the desert headed west. Just over six adrenaline-decompressing hours later, they touched down in Naples International airport and were met by a couple of silver Peugeot SUV's. A one-hour harrowing ride west and then south over the mountains via Amalfi Drive, they skirted back east and up into the cliffs above Positano to the 6,800 square foot villa of Casa Leoni, one of several Cromer's cottage hideaways in the world. It had been just after midnight local time when they were finally able to hit the hay for some long overdue sleep.

"Well, well, well," Woods signaled as he hung up the call and returned to the table. "It appears that our good friend Dr. Park threw us another bone, a big bone." He hesitated for a few seconds for effect. "That was Isaiah on the call. They broke into the phone earlier this morning and found a most interesting app. A tracking app. Park had live samples of the virus and the antidote stored in a metal biohazard briefcase and secured in a safe in his lab office. The suitcase, according to Park's notes, was specifically designed with a GPS tracking chip built in. According to the phone, it's active...and Isaiah says he's about 99.9 percent certain that it's the virus, and it's made its way over to the western coast of Iraq."

"Makes sense, that's exactly what Park was alluding to before he passed," interjected Wright. "No case in his office. What looked to be a safe in the wall emptied out. Somebody has it, and some of it is still out there."

Ferguson nodded. "The van that came out of that garage as we arrived. Whoever was in that van has to be the one in possession."

Woods sat down, completed a text, and sent with a press of a button. "DOD has been alerted, and they have assets being diverted to the area to attempt an interdiction if that case makes its way out of Iraq and into international waters or airspace. I thought our mission was over, but I've been informed that our little black operation may be extended. If that case doesn't move for a while, we've been placed on standby for possible re-insertion. I've been told that it's imperative we recover that case."

His phone vibrated with a text in reply.

"Exactly where is it currently, General?" asked Margolis.

"Well, good question, and this response from Isaiah just now indicates it's headed into the Persian Gulf...it's on the move again."

Chapter 45

Persian Gulf, west of Bandar Bushehr, Iran

It was unusually overcast, a salty layer of clouds confusing the transition from morning to afternoon. The winds were calm, only a slight chop to the waters of the Persian Gulf. Abood was aboard a 15-meter fishing dhow, chugging north along the Iranian shoreline, staying well within the 22-kilometer Iranian territorial limit. Trolling lines were out and nets at the ready for the severely depleted and overfished waters, simply a disguise more than anything else. The real mission for the craft was smuggling a high paying stowaway up the coastline and into proximity of the sliver of Iraqi coastline at the northern mouth of the Gulf, south of Basrah.

Having shed the nom de guerre of Abdul-Mahdi and traveling under his given name Ibrahim Abood once more, he was hoping the Hezbollah chain of allies operating in Iraq and up through Syria would have the discreet ability to get him home to Lebanon. He was hoping that as far as the Iranian leadership was concerned, until they located Togyani's body, or spoke to the soldiers he encountered fleeing the lab, they would no doubt have believed that Abdul-Mahdi perished in the destroyed laboratory or had simply disappeared. He didn't have much time.

After the nightmare that occurred nearly 24 hours ago, the trek west in the confiscated van had proved non-eventful. Two fellow

Lebanese comrades operating in Iran, one of three teams of Hezbollah operatives that had been dispatched in the hopes Abood could accomplish the impossible, had met Abood in a designated dockside hookah bar in the western Iranian port town of Bandar Bushehr. The two operatives had prearranged for marine transport and provided a backpack of enough Iraqi Dinars to trade for passage and anything else Abood would need once he was in the hands of Iraq's Asa'ib Ahl al-Haq or Khazali Network, a fiercely loyal Hezbollah ally.

Still funded and trained by Iran's Quds Force, the Khazali Network was a Shia paramilitary group active in the Iraqi insurgency and Syrian Civil War fighting against the Islamic State of Iraq and the Levant. As a part of the Popular Mobilization Forces, the group would have the knowledge and clout to get Abood safely through Iraq and Syria to his final destination. The irony of a direct link to Iran helping him back to Lebanon with their prized, albeit missing and presumed destroyed biological asset was not lost on Abood. He needed to be extremely careful in the nature of his travels.

He had thought that maybe transferring the virus from the distinct stainless-steel suitcase into something less remarkable might lessen his concern for discovery, but after deliberating the change, he decided to use the obvious to his advantage. If anyone inquired, he would suggest he was on mission sanctioned from the highest authorities in the IRGC and under no circumstances was he to travel commercially or his journey be made known publicly. If necessary, he could allude to the true contents of the mysterious metal case containing radioactive waste material for purposes unknown even to him, and explain they needed to remain unopened for fear of radiation leak. He felt that would be enough to discourage anyone from getting too close.

After nearly ten hours of creeping along the flat sandy coastline of western Iran, Abood was awakened from a deep sleep in the makeshift berth in the back of the boat. Evening was closing in as the resurgent sun had just disappeared behind the western horizon of the watery expanse of the Gulf.

Once darkness had settled in, the vessel moved closer to shore and within a few kilometers of the Arvand Rood waterway that ran north from the Gulf to Basrah and acted as the border between Iran and the Al-Faw Peninsula of Iraq. Out of the obscurity of nightfall came the sound of a small motorboat that flashed a quick burst from a spotlight and was answered in return by an on-and-off flash from a handheld high beam flashlight in the dhow. The open bow runabout, powered by a 150-mph outboard motor, powered to idle and slid up parallel to the fishing boat on the north side, while ropes were exchanged to hold her steady. A rope ladder was thrown over the side, and Abood slipped over the railing and climbed into the bobbing speed boat, a backpack and metal brief case securely strapped to his back.

A quick wave to indicate he was safely on board, and the two crafts drifted far enough away for the smaller boat to engage the throttle and speed off to the spillway that would take them north into Iraq.

* * * * *

Two hundred kilometers to the south of the rendezvous, the USS Boxer had been monitoring the fishing junk since it left the port of Bandar Bushehr, waiting patiently for it to make the fatal mistake of entering international waters. Navy Seal Team 4, currently assigned to the Middle East, had been helicoptered on board earlier in the day from Naval Support Activity Bahrain and outfitted with a Mark V Special Operations Craft with four Combat Rubber

Raiding Crafts extracted from the hold of the Wasp-class amphibious assault ship. Their orders plotted a high-value target capture-or-kill operation with the mission goal of recovering a stainless-steel briefcase and to secure any prisoners if possible, but not required. They had been dispatched from the mothership late in the afternoon and had been drifting patiently 25 kilometers to the south of the target, standing by for orders to proceed as light faded to night.

Tensions in the area were on high alert, worsened recently when a US surveillance drone was shot down by the IRGC, in what America correctly claimed to be flying over international waters. Naturally, the Iranian government vehemently disagreed.

Captain Arthur Bradley, at the helm of the 5th Fleet's flagship of Combined Task Force 151, was frustrated that the vessel they had been meticulously tracking would not come out to sea and play. His orders were specific...*Do not engage target if in Iranian waters*. As the dhow mirrored the coastline northward, and when it stopped along the northern most shores of Iran, his suspicions of a small craft transfer were confirmed when he received secure word from the Defense Intelligence Agency that tracking of the briefcase indicated it leaving the coastal waters and was on the move, inland.

Reluctantly, he issued orders to recall his Seal Team. He commanded his XO to send a secure message to SOCOM that his mission had been aborted and the target was transferred to land in the vicinity of the Al-Faw Peninsula. Given the importance and immediacy of their mission, he was afraid things just got significantly more complicated.

Chapter 46

Casa Leoni, Positano, Italy

A bright sunshine, intermittently interrupted by a handful of lazy clouds, was the perfect medicine for Lau and Margolis, as they both lounged topless on the upper deck of the little bit of paradise they found on the Amalfi Coast. Lau in only a thong and Margolis sporting black bikini style underwear, unabashedly never moved when Ferguson and Wright took turns delivering two cold bottles of a local Pinot Grigio, deliberately hovering longer than necessary with feigned struggles in uncorking and pouring said vino into long stem glasses for their pleasure. The two waiters were in agreement on the main deck below, both ladies could stop a clock.

The rest and relaxation were both welcome, and they all knew that given the circumstances of the virus still on the loose, it was likely they would be called back into action. Wright and Ferguson both had no illusions that the danger was still very, very real, and they were doing their best to unwind until Woods came back with groceries and an update from Isaiah.

After another trip to the sunbathing deck to check if more wine was needed, Ferguson met Woods entering the kitchen, returning with more rations

"Assemble the group, we've got news on our virus courier," said Woods, as he began to sort and place items into the pantry and refrigerator.

Wright stepped into the kitchen following the noise and heard the command. He beat his partner to the steps and feigned volunteering over Ferguson's objections, beelining up the stairs to retrieve the two ladies.

By the time Lau and Margolis had freshened up, attired themselves with t-shirts and running shorts, and reached the kitchen, the boys had already created a lunch of deli meats, breads, an assortment of cheeses, along with a cluster of grapes, and were retreating back outside to the patio table. After everyone was seated, followed by some incoherent banter about no need to dress up for lunch that eluded Woods' comprehension, he addressed Lau first.

"Young lady, we have not had the pleasure of officially being introduced, but I'm here now to say hello, and thank you. Not only from me, but everyone on our team, and most certainly from Blake for saving his bacon."

She acknowledged his greeting and praise with a slight bow of the head.

"Given your natural political leanings you may not actually like to hear this, but the United States of America thanks you also. You're one hell of a skilled fighter and operator, just as rough and tough as you are beautiful."

There was a consensus of shaking heads as Lau showed the faintest signs of blushing from the compliment.

"However, this is not your fight anymore, you've sacrificed enough. Unfortunately, you've blown your cover in Iran, and in the process, you may have blown your life and career back home in China. I'll leave that up to you and General Huang to work through, but I'm going to assume your Ministry of State Security is not going to be feeling very secure about you if you set foot in your homeland again. That's a problem for you in a number of ways, but I have already spoken to the powers that be, and they have assured me that because of all of your help, if you are interested and willing, they can help you disappear and be well taken care of financially. The one caveat is you'll be asked a lot of questions, and they will want a lot of answers as the tradeoff, but your incredible support and cooperation in this matter is understood by those same powers...all the way to the President."

"Thank you, General. General Huang mentioned I could trust you, even if you were American," eliciting a chuckle from Woods, "and unfortunately, you are correct in part of your assessment, but not all. Yes, I'm afraid my career is probably gone...destroyed, and there is no way I can return to China to retrieve it. My life, on the other hand, is not over and appears to have received a new beginning. You say that this is not my fight anymore, but I think and feel that it is. Adina has told me that the virus is still out there. It needs to be stopped, and I am more than willing to join the new friends in my new life," gesturing to the table with both arms wide and palms up, "to finish what we started...if that's alright with you and your team."

Woods eyed her intensely as the other three stooges eyed him. "I was kind of hoping you might say that. We can certainly use your help. Call me presumptuous, but I've already received approval, from the same damn powers, for you to continue along with our merry little band."

"Hooah."

"Outstanding."

"Awesome."

"Well, it seems everybody else is in agreement. Welcome aboard."

Lau's face blushed more significantly, and she mouthed a "thank you" as she scanned all of the smiling faces staring back her.

"With that, let's get down to what we've been tasked to do. Everybody enjoy lunch and then a few more hours of downtime. We fly out of Naples to Be'er Sheva, Israel in five hours, we'll be leaving the villa in four."

A murmur of groans exuded from around the table.

"Understood, and if it's any consolation, I wholeheartedly agree. Regardless, we will be flying in to meet with the DIA's Deputy Director of Defense Clandestine Service and an FSO with the CIA's Directorate of Operations to understand what assets they have available that can help provide for covert support in Iraq.

"Adina, I'm going to need you to reach deep down into your friends in Mossad and have somebody meet us at the IDF Defense School airbase. Let them know you'll need to brief them in person when we get there, nothing broadcast over the air. Remember, it takes a village in that hell hole of a sandbox, and we're going to need all of the help we can cobble together in Iraq to hunt this bastard down. Whoever he is, we need to get him quickly, before he does something catastrophic that we can't stop."

Chapter 47

Near Be'er Sheva, Israel

Cromer's G550 touched down on the runway of the Hatzerim Airbase near the Old City of Be'er Sheva in the northern Negev region of Israel just as the sun began to engulf the Land of the Bible desert. Famous since the dawn of history, home to nomads, Canaanites, Philistines, Edomites, Byzantines, Nabateans, Ottomans, and Israelis, the airbase also boasted the legendary Flight Academy, operating training courses for the Israeli Air Force. Additionally, it offered the seclusion and security demanded by the occupants on the plane and those in a large, black Mercedes SUV driving out to meet the jet as it taxied to the far corner of the base's airstrip.

As the Gulfstream pulled to a halt, the air stairs dropped down and the Co-op team of Woods, Ferguson, Wright, Margolis and Lau exited in an effort to stretch their legs after the four-hour trip west from Italy. They were greeted by the vehicle parking in front of the jet, disgorging three men that all approached and engaged in the greeting ritual of introductions and hand shaking all around.

After a brief respite, the entire group reassembled inside the luxury aircraft. DIA Deputy Director Bart Baum and CIA officer John Early sat in the booth opposite Woods and Colonel Daniel Switow, Deputy Director of Operations in Mossad's Collections

Department. The rest of the team seated themselves on the couch and individual club chairs that flanked the four-top. The diminutive, but solidly built Baum produced a laptop and opened it up on the table, swiveling it outward for everyone to see.

As the computer powered up, Baum removed his glasses and addressed the group. "Thanks to everyone for being here, and a special thanks to the incredible operation you folks performed in Iran." Early and Switow nodded, acknowledging their approval for a job well done. "The threat, however, as we all know still exists. The President elect, and everyone in the know at the US intelligence and defense agencies, as well as Israel," Baum gestured to Switow, "have this as highest priority and have offered their full support to track this threat down and neutralize it. Unfortunately, until they take office, we have some ongoing bureaucratic handwringing and pushback, and the parameters for using your group General Woods remain the same.

"Albeit, for National Security reasons, and the fact we've broken a few international laws and rules of engagement getting to this point, this operation continues to be fully black, and off the books. This is now falling into the realm of Hezbollah, and the fact that these damn terrorists have allies and proxies all over the region, including the Russians, complicates things significantly. Speaking for the US, Israel, and our other regional allies, lest we ignite World War III, we have been ordered not to use our military to encroach on the sovereignty of Iraq. So bottom line is we can't be involved directly from our own military standpoint unless this little group of present company fails, and we're left with no other way to take this threat out. We can utilize available American military units in Syria as forces in support, but for now we have a pissing match going on at the highest levels back home and the responsibility on this whole operation lays squarely at our feet. If we fail, outgoing POTUS has deniability and we all get the gallows.

If we succeed, you can damn well bet he and his admin will take the credit.

"I have been given assurances from the top, that if we fail, as a last resort the White House will authorize SOCOM, along with Sayeret Israeli Special Forces on alert, to solve the issue and deal with the fallout if it comes to that. That, General, is why we still need to enlist your team's services."

"Understood," Woods raised his hand in recognition.

"Thanks to Colonel Switow and his assets in Baghdad, Mossad has managed to identify our HVT in possession of what we still believe to be the virus we have all been briefed on." Baum tapped a few keys on the computer and up popped the image of a Middle Eastern male with the caption below him identifying the man as Ibrahim Abood.

"Charming," snickered Ferguson.

"Quite…and dangerous as they come," Baum replied. Born into a wealthy Lebanese Muslim family, who made their fortune in real estate, Abood has a chemical engineering degree from American University in Beirut and an accounting degree from Long Island U. He initially went into the family business after college, but then disappeared in the early 2000s, believed to have been radicalized shortly thereafter. We're confident he was involved in combat operations with Hezbollah against the IDF during Israel's incursion into Lebanon, and then for certain we know he was promoted into their infamous Unit 133 as a senior officer, we think sometime around late 2010 or early 2011. Sources indicate he probably took over command of the unit a few years ago. He went off the grid 16-18 months back, and we have no intel on him since then."

"Do we know if he's still in Baghdad?" Wright stood up and leaned in for a closer look.

Switow reached over the table and began scrolling through to the next image on the computer, pointing out a location on a map of Baghdad. "Our eyes on the ground have him still in Sadr City. The convoy that brought him north from the gulf has holed up in a warehouse courtyard off Qouds Street. No way to get to him in that hell hole, but we were able to sit on his location and get a peek at him from a couple of our local operatives, and pictures allowed us to get a facial recognition match." He scrolled to a series of telescopic still photo images of Abood and the convoy vehicles parked inside a walled compound.

Woods stood up and leaned on the corner of the club seat and scratched at his chin. "Okay, so we know we can't get to him in Sadr City unless we have an all-out military operation in to get him, and that's not going to happen right now. We do know he still has the case. The signal is still strong and according to Isaiah matches this location exactly, but how long will it be working. We don't know if there's a battery life on that unit, or maybe he's figured out the case is our means of keeping tabs on him. We can definitely wait him out for his next move, unless he plans to use that location as a base of operations and then we have to assume he's going to get into the virus from there and do something with it. Frankly, we don't know shit. Anybody have a thought as to next steps?"

Early, with his tall and lean frame stuffed into the booth, joined the conversation before anyone could react, "I've been noodling on this for a few hours, and I keep coming to the same conclusion any which way I look at it. We know from the notes that General Woods shared with us from Park's iPad that this was an Iranian doomsday virus meant to generate a swath of destruction across a predetermined geographic landscape in the Middle East, from which Iran would come to the rescue and create a greater Persian state from the wasteland that it would naturally fill. However, thanks to the great work you folks have done," offering an open palm acknowledgment to the Co-op members, "I'm convinced we're past that operational scenario.

"Abood is Lebanese and Hezbollah through and through. I'm going to take a wild, but educated guess, and say he hates Israel. He appears to have gone rogue from the Iranians and managed to get from Iran to Iraq with the virus in tow, so I think that takes him out of the operational theater and security of Iran, and the greater Persia scenario is well off his mind. If I were a betting man, and I'm not, unless I'm confident in the result, I would lay a big wager that he's headed back to Lebanon and this is all about Israel now."

"I couldn't agree with you more," Baum chimed in.

Woods nodded his head in agreement, "My first reaction also."

A chorus of agreement mumbled throughout the remaining group.

"So, where does that leave us?" Woods posed.

Wright looked at Ferguson, again both seemingly on the same mental wavelength. "Take it away Blake."

Ferguson accepted the invitation. "I'm going to make an even bigger wager and say he's coming out of Baghdad straight for Lebanon. Strategically and operationally, it's the best launching pad they have into Israel, and I also agree that will be his target. He has all the tools and manpower he needs to unleash it from there. Somewhere from Syria would be his backup plan, but I wouldn't count on it, it's even more volatile and unstable."

"We need to try and stop him before he gets there," concern in the voice of Margolis.

"If he gets into Lebanon, he will be heavily guarded and secluded, and a very tough op to dig him and the virus out of there," added Wright. "I say we wait for him to run, and when he gets into the open, we run a Hellfire up his ass and vaporize the son of a bitch. Why didn't we make that move while he was on the run north through southern Iraq?"

I'm thinking the same thing," added Ferguson. If we can track him, Clay and I can go in wherever and whenever he breaks cover, and we can paint him up for disposal."

Baum shifted in his seat and glanced at Woods, "Good question and suggestion, care to elaborate General?"

Woods took a deep breath, "Same thought the higher-ups had, simple and straightforward. However, the consensus among the folks that are privy to this nightmare came up with a multitude of other concerns that void that solution. What if Abood has split the virus and vaccine? What if he knows about the tracking mechanism in the briefcase, and could he be playing us all along? Could he have transferred some or all of the virus and vaccine from the briefcase along his route or in Baghdad? These are all questions that prevented us from taking him out on his way out of Iran and all through his trek up from the Persian Gulf into Baghdad. Unfortunately, we've come to the conclusion that we have to get our hands on the briefcase to make a determination that the virus and vaccine are intact and all of it is there. We need to get all of it, hopefully before he gets someplace where he can duplicate it, or use it, or both."

"Whoa, that's what I call throwing a wrench in the gears," said Margolis.

Ferguson looked at Wright and then to the computer screen with Abood's face prominently displayed, "Well, if that's the case, then I think we better start making interdiction contingencies if he makes a break for it, wherever he's headed. I presume it will be on his way into Syria toward Lebanon. If he goes airborne, not sure there's much we can do except to blast him out of the sky, but then we're back to our problem of securing the briefcase. There wouldn't be much left to secure. If he stays on land, we try to take him out in the remotest of places and either capture or kill the turd, please note I opt for the latter, and secure the briefcase if possible. If it's exposed, at least it's in the remotest of areas, and we can take a page out of Park's description of the Iranian's Setareh Doctrine playbook and blame it on the damn Syrians. We know they haven't hesitated to toss bioweapons around already, so maybe it just might be the one thing that would finally take Assad out in the process. Just my humble opinion."

"Damn good one, though," Ferguson offered up a fist bump to Wright, who exploded his on impact.

Baum nodded his head in approval, "I concur. I've taken the liberty of pulling in three local operators that are familiar with the area and can assist. They will be on site here within the hour. I also have a couple of Humvees and a stealth Black Hawk on standby for any insertion or extraction that might be required. I'm working through some backchannel contacts at JSOC to have Delta's A Squadron and a platoon of Rangers on standby in Syria to support any operation from this side of the border that you guys might initiate in Iraq. Given that we need to keep their movements under the radar, it may take a little bit to pull them out of their current operations, so hopefully we have a few days to get that squared away. If Abood goes on the move quickly, all bets are off getting them in position to assist."

"Yes, agree. We'll keep eyes on Abood and can alert you to any movement or if he ventures into any other locations in and around Baghdad," affirmed Switow. "I, too, have one of our best agents to assist. He handles and has been monitoring our men in Sadr and will have the latest intel for you if anything changes. Adina, you might remember Benji?"

"Benji Saunders?"

"One and the same."

"Awesome! He's superb, it'll be good to see him again.

"Well, that makes three of us throwing assets on the fire," said Early. "I brought Baker Thompson with me, he's in a hangar back by the terminal. He's my go-to guy here in southern Syria, and he's well-schooled on Lebanon as well. He assisted with training the Free Syrian Army rebels, and has supported our covert ops on Hezbollah. He's been operating in both areas for nearly ten years, so he knows a few nooks and crannies about the theater here."

"Excellent!" Woods exclaimed with a clap of the hands. "We need to get together and meet these folks and start putting some contingency plans in place."

As he sensed the meeting was coming to an end, Baum stood and offered one last word of warning, "Gents… and ladies, I can't tell you how critical it is to get hold of this thing. It was one thing to obliterate the population of a third of the Middle East and congratulations for thwarting that plot. However, our work is not over by a long shot. If we're guessing correctly, the stakes have changed, and the threat is directed at one of our closest allies, which could potentially be the obliteration of Israel. We can't let that happen."

Chapter 48

Western Iraq, near the Syrian Border

Blake Ferguson and Clay Wright flanked Sergeant Major Thomas Trent of the 1ST Special Operations Detachment-Delta, along with Baker Thompson and Benjamin "Benji" Saunders. They were all fixated on the road 25 meters in front of their position. The rundown two-lane Route19, situated in northwestern Iraq near the Syrian border, ran parallel to, and south of, the bigger and better conditioned Route 12, leading to and from Haqlaniyah 75 kilometers to the east of their position and Al-Qa'im 60 kilometers to the west. It was a remote and isolated area in the region and ripe for springing a surprise for one Ibrahim Abood.

Baker Thompson, a paramilitary officer from the CIA's Special Activities Center operating in Syria, and Benji Saunders, a Mossad Katsa officer stationed in Baghdad but performing double duty with the Kidon unit, the elite department of assassins operating under the Caesarea branch, just crawled up to join the party. That seated party constituted the masterminds of the occasion, all leaning against a mud brick wall surrounding the pile of rubble that was once a gas station. The blackened, burned out abandoned remains were symbolic of the entire region...the geographic and societal casualty of war that engulfed this area of Iraq after the US pullout, the ISIS takeover and caliphate, and then their subsequent eviction and demise a year later. Pockets of the ISIS thugs still roamed outside the cities, and all the men were on a keen lookout for any activity around them. They had the benefit of overwatch eye-in-the-sky surveillance keeping watch over them as well.

Behind them, seated in the roofless, pockmarked walls of a once two-bay auto service center, delighting on a cold meal of MREs, the army's notorious Meals Ready-To-Eat, were Adina Margolis, Lie Lau, and Delta operators Sergeant First Class Christopher Campbell and Staff Sergeant Jimmie Lewis, who were both hydrating and recuperating from their run back to the current southern location. Lewis was engaged in an animated discussion with Lau in a Chinese Mandarin dialect, trying to impress her with his abilities honed from a previous army billet in Taiwan for two years. She was impressed but, nonetheless, was still forced to help him with some profound deficiencies.

Both Deltas were still trying to come to grips with why two women, non-military, all kitted up in black uniforms like the entire group, were on a covert operation in the middle of nowhere, Iraq. If they happened upon ISIS, and the probability was high in this area, and things didn't go their way, the tyrannical ISIS treatment of captives was notoriously brutal and horrendous, but for women it would be nothing short of savage. The goal was to avoid any roving bands of the bastards. Regardless, they had their orders and were told both women were highly competent and deserved to be a part of the operation. For their part, Margolis and Lau understood the terrain, and had improved their bona fides when both had indicated to the other members of the team that under no circumstances were they to be left alive if the situation became dire and untenable.

The operating group had been quickly assembled within the last six hours, a diverse mix of black ops and intelligence officers, joining with the contracted services of the Co-op personnel. They were shorthanded, but the movement of Abood from Sadr City had happened much sooner than they had anticipated and pulling additional resources in to address the situation was not an option. Unfortunately, they needed to move now and utilize every person they had available. Baum and Woods were trying to cobble together behind the scenes a blocking force from the 75th Ranger Regiment to be in position in time to support their operation, but they were finding the timing was terrible and potentially unrealistic. Having arrived at the interdiction site via helicopter roughly an hour ago, with a clear evening sky punctuated with a million stars, the team set up shop and went to work on the operational plan hatched in the hangar before they left.

They had decided to give the impression of an ISIS ambush. A half dozen radio-controlled improvised explosive devices were constructed using confiscated Iraqi artillery shells and packed with enough C-4 plastic explosive to take out a vehicle, but not deliver an excessive blast zone. The idea was to set the RCIEDs along multiple locations of the roadside to take out the front, and hopefully the rear convoy units, and leave the core vehicles in between intact. If Abood and the briefcase were in the lead vehicle, they would look to wipe out the middle and rear vehicles with multiple blasts and sniper the driver and tires in the lead unit.

They would set up a triangle "kill zone," two firing positions located to one side of the road roughly spaced at the front and rear of the blast area, and a single firing position on the other side of the road, positioned in the middle facing the core of the convoy. It would effectively cover front, rear, and center with each location being out of direct line of friendly fire from the others. Each position would have two operators spaced slightly apart, one with a Precision Sniper Rifle with night scope and the other outfitted with an M4A1 assault rifle, also with night optics.

Once the explosives were detonated, the front position would take out the driver of the lead vehicle, if it contained Abood and the case and was not targeted for detonation. If not, the lead vehicle and then the rear vehicles would be targeted for detonation, and all fire would be directed to the middle avoiding the vehicle with the high value goods. They would tackle that vehicle last in a process of elimination. Consensus among the operational group believed the plan simple and effective, but contingent on not letting the remaining fighters gain a foothold that would drag out the operation any longer than necessary. The longer in country, the more problems the commotion and any other traffic might present for a timely interdiction and extraction.

They had chosen six potential sites based on the intel they had received indicating the convoy was on the move west out of Baghdad. Once they went airborne and they received confirmation that the vehicles turned north onto Route 12, it narrowed the selection down to two locations, and they were dropped into the night in a desolate area between Route 12 and Route 19.

In order to be on the safe side, Lewis and Campbell split off and hoofed it three kilometers north to plant explosives on 12. The rest of the group, in an educated guess, surmised that the convoy would take the less traveled southern Route 19 and located there. If it were a wrong decision, they would have to cover nearly ten kilometers back north in a little over an hour. No one looked forward to that effort.

Wright had a laptop spread out in front of them, a towel hovering over the screen to deflect the light emitting from the ISR image of their surrounding area being transmitted from a Predator drone high overhead.

He pulled the towel back slightly, "Okay fellas, now that we guessed correctly and they are taking this route on the south, we have their convoy just past Haditha switching off 12 north onto 19 headed west. They're maybe an hour and fifteen out."

"Roger that," Sergeant Major Trent picked up his Modular Sniper Rifle. He headed off to find Staff Sergeant Lewis and let him know they were going to take the single position on the opposite side of the road, clearly the more dangerous of three.

"Blake, you and Lei take the western point, and Campbell and Margolis will go to the eastern spot. Sergeant Campbell is going to get a revelation when he sees Margolis grab the PSR. He doesn't have a clue that she probably is the best shot in this entire group."

"Copy that," sounded Ferguson, as he stood and also exited to go find Lau.

"Benji, you and Baker will stay with me to spot and detonate. Once we blow shit up, we'll continue to spot and act as overwatch for the others and remain in support in case someone needs help. Understood?"

Thompson and Saunders nodded in unison.

Wright checked the screen one more time and looked at his watch. He mentally calculated about 70 minutes 'til show time.

* * * * *

"Charlie One, requesting comm check."

"Co-op reads you loud and clear, Charlie One," replied Elaine Scruggs to Wright's inquiry. She, along with Woods, Director Baum, and Isaiah Taylor were in the Situation Room back at the Co-op offices in Alexandria. Isaiah was monitoring the Predator drone's live video feed coming from the Army's Las Vegas pilot center and had it displayed on the forward screens. It was a pre-programmed flight plan to give all the appearances of nothing unusual, but the "Special Instruction" assessment during the shift briefing had been discussed with the pilot to reflect the secure nature of the targeting package and the potential need for manual adjustments.

The red-eye back to the United States for Woods and Baum had them still sucking down copious amounts of coffee, as sleep had been restricted to what they could get on the plane. Baum had opted for the Co-op's facilities versus the Pentagon in order to keep the covert mission...covert. His impression of the Co-op facilities in the war room had been overwhelmingly positive and only added to the confidence the operation could be coordinated from their current location.

"This is Charlie Two, in position, over," Sergeant Major Trent replied.

"Copy Charlie Two. Charlie Three?"

Ferguson answered on cue, "Charlie Three is in also in position. Standing by."

Before he could inquire, Sergeant Campbell mic'd in, "Charlie Four is ready."

"Charlie One, this is Co-op, we show five tangos eight klicks out and closing, you are cleared for intercept. Be advised, we have confirmation both HVT packages are together in the third tango. Repeat, the third and middle vehicle in convoy," Scruggs' calm, but deliberate voice replied. "Also be advised, your blocking force has been delayed out of Raqqa. They are on alert in support of SDF operations and won't be available to move until 09:00...tomorrow."

"Copy that Co-op. We have a visual." Wright massaged the focus on the night vision binoculars westward on the advancing trucks. *Shit...on our own now with no support. Damnit.* "What is it about Toyotas and this fucking part of the world? Every terrorist must own stock in the damn company." He looked to Saunders and Thompson, "I count two technicals up front," a descriptive term for a light improvised fighting vehicle, in this case pickup trucks with a machine gun mounted in the bed. "Two Land Cruisers following, and another technical bringing up the rear. The technicals look to have multiple tangos in the beds, and I expect the SUVs to have additional bodies as well.

"Charlie Two, you have the rear Cruiser if it isn't detonated, and then advance on the HVT Cruiser when able. Charlie Three you take the second technical after contact. Charlie Four, the rear technical is yours and back up Charlie Two on the rear Cruiser. They're a little spread for the IEDs, but hopefully we can explode the last Technical cleanly. If not, that will be our target from here as well."

"Copy that."

"Affirmative."

"Roger that."

Wright spoke to Thompson, who held the remote detonator for the front IED, never taking his eyes from the binoculars, "Baker, you ready?"

"Ready," as he wiped away a bead of adrenaline induced sweat and flung it into the cool desert air.

"Benji, once Baker detonates the first, I'll tell you which one to blow," he looked at him and confirmed which of the two detonators was in each hand. Pointing to each hand, "the left one is the rear of the convoy, and I'll say 'rear,' and the right is just in front of that, and I'll say 'front.' Copy that?"

"Got it." He held up both hands, and shook the left, "rear" and then the right, "front."

"Excellent. I may ask you to blow both, so be ready for anything." Wright swiveled his binoculars back to the east and refocused the night vision's greenish-hue field of view to the three small rock formations he had placed next to each of the explosive charges along the road. He confirmed the convoy spacing and his selection of the rear IEDs he gave Saunders and tried to find his partners in the field, but they had done a remarkable job of camouflaging themselves into the barren terrain.

It was quiet for about fifteen seconds, as the night sounds of the desert were slowly overtaken by the noise of the engines from the oncoming vehicles.

"Steady everyone."

"Charlie One, this is Co-op, we have a problem. We just picked up multiple tangos coming east from Syria, headed in your direction. I say again, multiple tangos headed onto 12 north out of Al-Qa'im."

"Holy Shit! Baker, on my mark...three...two...one...mark.

Thompson, pressed on the switch and the dark night erupted as the IED exploded just in front of the first technical, tearing off the front end and sending the rest of the carcass flying into the air, landing ten meters to the left of the road.

"Rear!"

Saunders thumbed down on his left hand and the IED erupted several meters behind the last vehicle killing everyone in the bed of the pickup throwing it forward into the Land Cruiser ahead of it."

As all three firing positions opened up on the remaining vehicles and men, the stunned Iraqi manning the Russian made PKM 7.62 x 54mm machine gun on the second technical immediately recovered and was spraying rounds on automatic in a wild arc to the side and front.

"Co-op, it's too late, we are engaged," yelled Wright over the noise. "Can you identify tangos, and are they headed our way?"

"There are six...no check that, eight vehicles filled with tangos, and they have exited onto Route 19 and headed your way. ETA in twenty minutes. Not sure of nationality, but consider them hostile, repeat they are not friendlies." Back in the war room, Woods leaned into Baum, straightened up, looked at Scruggs and raised his hand with five fingers displayed and then slashed at his throat.

"Copy Co-op...damnit!"

"Charlie One, if you can't secure target in five minutes you need to evac to LZ Bravo. Five minutes is all you have, then rendezvous LZ Bravo for extraction. Do you read me Charlie One?"

There was a hesitation as the chatter of AK-47 and machine gun fire exploded in the air.

"Charlie One reads you Co-op. Five minutes."

Ferguson and Lau were peppering the last Land Cruiser, as men were spilling out of the doors, with the upside-down pickup truck in flames crushing the rear. They killed three instantly as the dazed soldiers tried to find some cover outside the smoldering heap of the SUV, each firing blindly into the night. Another man stumbled off in agony as he was engulfed in flames, with other screams coming from the inferno that was the technical. Two more exiting on the other side were picked off by Trent and Lewis. Several others managed to find some cover as they hit the ground or crawled up under the burning metal, a dust and smoke cloud forming over the area. It was probably only a matter of time before the gas tank ignited and the whole thing was going up in a ball of flames.

At the front of the caravan, nobody survived the lead truck disintegrated by the front IED explosion. A similar haze of dust from the blast enveloped the forward field of action as well. Combatants from the second technical and Abood's Cruiser spilled out onto the ground, while the one man on the machine gun continued to lay down random rounds all over the area to the south side of the carnage. After about thirty seconds of sustained fire, Ferguson nearly decapitated him with a single round from the Remington MSR to the back of his head. While the big gun went silent, the driver of the first SUV pulled off to the side of road and stopped parallel to the second pickup, creating solid cover for many of the surviving men between the two vehicles.

The smoke, dirt, and debris in the air was working to the advantage of Abood and the fighters still engaged, as it helped camouflage their positions and inevitably was going to prolong the engagement. Wright knew it and cursed under his breath. The other surrounding teams, aware of the inbound hostiles and understanding the same five-minute warning, sensed this was going to take too long to finish off the remaining fighters and capture or kill Abood.

"Charlie One, this is Charlie Two, our area is still too hot to advance."

"Copy that, Charlie Two."

"Charlie Three and Four, can you advance?"

As soon as the question left Wright's lips, an RPG round slammed into what was left of the garage behind their position, raining dirt and chunks of brick on top of Wright, Thompson, and Saunders, and propelling all three into the wall that they were using for protection. A few seconds later another grenade let loose and exploded in the open field, twenty meters north of Trent's and Lewis' position.

"Shit that was close," screamed Wright as he surveyed Thompson and Saunders to make sure they were alright. They were all stunned, but regained their senses quickly. Another brave but stupid fighter stepped up into the bed of the technical and cocked the PKM for more action. He didn't even get his finger to the trigger before Ferguson put a round between his shoulder blades, exploding outward from his chest before he slumped into the bed of brass casings.

"Charlie One, this is Co-op. Be advised the bad cavalry has picked up speed and will be on your position in fifteen minutes or less, you need to exfil immediately, we have recovery helo inbound to LZ Bravo. Do you copy, Charlie One?"

Wright was busy raking the remaining vehicles with his M4 on full auto. Returning fire was still heavy, rounds popping all around them. "Roger that Co-op. We are disengaging and repositioning to LZ Bravo. All teams confirm, we're bugging out to LZ Bravo. Charlie One will maintain cover fire for two minutes."

"Copy that."

"Charlie Three copies all."

"Roger that."

Hearing confirmations from all of the other teams, who were now working their way west and then south of Route 19, Wright, Thompson, and Saunders were all taking turns laying down automatic fire across the entire burning convoy. Ferguson and Lau rejoined them a minute later, and another minute after that, the gunfire subsided as the entire Co-op team scooted off into the night. Fifteen minutes and nearly five kilometers later, a stealth Blackhawk piloted by Matt Woods touched down in the barren and deserted no man's land of western Iraq. His exhausted, dirty, and pissed off passengers climbed aboard and were in no mood for small talk. It was a silent ride back to the safety of Israel.

Chapter 49

Western Iraq, near the Syrian Border

The cacophony of explosions and gunfire mercifully came to an end and an eerie silence was punctuated only by the crackle and pop of flames from the fires of burning vehicles and the groans of wounded and dying men. Abood rose from his crouched position between the Cruiser and pickup truck, slung an AK-47 over his shoulder, and with adrenaline laced hands double checked the condition of the pack on his back, physically examining the contents of the steel case of viral Armageddon. Everything seemed to be intact, including his nerves, the sensory overload of combat slowly dissipating as his mind and body returned to a better neurological and physical balance.

Commander Hassan Bashara, an apparition out of the blackened smoke, approached him from the rear of the tangled havoc of automotive metal and inquired of his condition. After affirming he was fine, the commander walked nonchalantly away to take stock of the dead and attend to his wounded men. Along with Abood and Bashara, only a half dozen other soldiers had survived the ambush, thirteen were killed or dying.

A single shot pierced the air, startling Abood, a mercy killing from Bashara on a suffering comrade. One of Bashara's deputies was on a cell phone clearly reassuring and directing an approaching convoy of vehicles. Abood could now see the headlights in the distance to the west. He knew, from conversations that had taken place on the drive over from Baghdad and before the ambush, they were soldiers from the Haidar al-Karar Brigades, the Syrian branch of the Khazali Network, dispatched from Aleppo to help escort Abood through the virtual minefield that was all of Syria. Sympathetic to Hezbollah and the Iranians, they were more than willing to lend any assets available for the sensitive nature of Abood's mission.

Bashara was shaking his head and arguing with his subordinate in phone contact with the relief convoy, and instructed them not to come any closer to the wreckage. Concerned about additional IEDs that might still be in the road, he was expressing his doubts to the man that it was ISIS that had just hit them, as most of his remaining soldiers were muttering similar suspicions. He suggested it was too sophisticated and skilled for the imbeciles from the Islamic State. Abood couldn't disagree with his assessment, but if not ISIS, who would it be and how would they know his whereabouts?

As the Haidar al-Karar commander approached on foot from his convoy parked a half kilometer down the road, Bashara told Abood to get ready. They were going to transfer him over to the Syrians and be done with him. He had certainly caused enough grief and damage for him and his men, he mumbled under his breath as he walked to greet the oncoming Brigade leader and facilitate the exchange.

A few minutes later the two men hugged in the middle of the road, and Bashara waved at Abood to come forward. With all that had happened and the uncertainties of who just attacked and tried to kill him, Abood's head was buzzing with concern, and his senses were on high alert. His trust of this process to get home was creating angst and confusion. He picked up his backpack and gun and warily made his way down the road.

"This is Mustafa Aziz. He will provide safe passage to you back to Lebanon," Bashara extended his arms out toward Abood and the Syrian in a gesture of introduction, and promptly turned to walk away. He stopped and gazed back, "As salaamu alaikum wa rahmatullahi wa barakatuh, *may the peace, mercy, and blessings of Allah be upon you.*"

Chapter 50

Themis Cooperative Offices, Alexandria, VA

The overcast day, coupled with the intermittent showers, mirrored the gloomy mood Woods was struggling with, as he stared out onto Founders Park and the Potomac River from his office window. He swirled the freshly brewed cup of black coffee in his right hand in a futile gesture of mixing, when in reality there was nothing to mix. Futility seemed to be the order of the day, and mirrored their latest op, which had been an unmitigated failure. Abood and the virus were still on the loose.

He feared they could have potentially alerted Abood to the fact that he was being surveilled and tracked and would drive him to have the presence of mind to evaluate and understand why. If he considered the suitcase to be bugged, and decided to ditch it and transfer the virus to something else to transport it in, they would be screwed. The only good news from the desert ambush was nobody on his team was injured, and they were all evac'd safely.

His concerns, echoed by Director Baum, were that the trouble brewing would soon reach the current President's ear, who was suspicious of the backchannel covert activity all along and had been given significantly more background personally last night. According to Baum, POTUS had hit the roof and had washed his hands of any knowledge and thrown the entire mess and responsibility onto the incoming President and those on his National Security team. Needless to say, if we don't get this shit under control soon, and this gets out in the public domain, the entire incoming administration is going to be thrown into an international and domestic crisis they will never recover from. They all have plausible deniability, but that likely won't be enough to weather the shit storm that would ensue. Baum had indicated he would be following up with the Israeli Prime Minister to discuss the next course of action. Unfortunately, Woods had also been designated the fall guy, so it was his and the Co-op team's asses officially on the line, as Wood's had known all along.

"General, I have the team on secure video conference, do you want me to connect it to your office?" Isaiah broke in over the phone intercom.

"Yes, thanks Isaiah. Route it to the TV please." Woods returned to his desk, picked up the remote, and turned on the wall mounted 65" flat screen television monitor located opposite the window. He plopped down in the couch and waited for an image to appear.

"You'll need to be on HDMI 2 General, and they should be with you in a couple of minutes."

Woods selected the appropriate input source and made himself as comfortable as possible, given the most uncomfortable of circumstances.

A little over a minute later the somber face of Blake Ferguson popped up, "Morning General. We're really sorry, boss. Another 20 minutes and we would have had the son of a bitch."

"Blake, don't apologize, we thought about the possibility and should have planned on the damn Syrians showing up to escort Abood out, and we could have controlled that with help, but we couldn't get a blocking force for support in time. That's my responsibility…and screw up. My apologies to you and the team. The timing on it all was fucked up. Quite a rough evening, all in all, but everybody is out of there and safe. If you had waited them out, you would have wound up in a firefight I'm not sure any of you would have survived."

"Yes sir, no scratches here, but still a colossal pisser is what you might call it. That sentiment is echoed by everybody involved. They're all here, by the way, seated behind me listening in." A chorus of mixed introductions could be heard in the background, as Ferguson leaned back from the screen to let the group be visible on screen.

"Pisser is a good word for it. Again, my responsibility, but I was thinking of something more like cluster fuck."

"That works, too."

"We should be hearing from Director Baum and the Israelis shortly, but suffice it to say our job is not over. I suspect they are working through scenarios now. Nobody else is in the loop except Mossad, us, and both POTUS and POTUS elect are aware, but we've been chucked like a hot potato. Baum and all of us are being prepped as the sacrificial lamb, to be served up to the wolves, and I'm quite certain it will remain that way unless we can find a solution to our current dilemma. Everyone is scrambling for deniability. Understood?"

There were pronounced affirmative responses in unison, and Margolis could be overheard adding, "Yes, Benji is confirming Baum has already spoken to Daniel and both sides are working on contingency plans."

"Good, we should have some direction shortly, but let's be prepared to offer up suggestions from our end. My guess is we're going to need to get eyes on Abood as he gets into Syria, and I'll hazard a guess and say he's ultimately headed back to the comforts of Lebanon and his Hezbollah brethren. My biggest worry is Abood and the cabals escorting him around don't assume this is just another ISIS shit show. If they have their suspicions, it's conceivable we've tipped him off to the fact we've had eyes on him all along, and he'll start to wonder how we found and targeted him. If he thinks it through, and comes around to believing, or discovers the case has a tracking device in it, he'll ditch the case, and then we've lost him. Holy shit, then we're in a world of hurt. That's why I'd like to hear any ideas from your end?"

"Well, funny you should mention it, but at the risk of stepping over all the bodies running for cover, we're already ahead of you on that," replied Ferguson.

"You have my permission to step over anybody...as long as it makes sense and doesn't turn our life sentence in Leavenworth into a firing squad."

"We think it does. Let me explain."

"I'm all ears."

"We agree he's headed to Lebanon. He's actually half way there according to Isaiah, who updated us on the tracking before we joined this call. They made a brief stop in Damascus, but are now headed toward the Masnaa border crossing. Hopefully, your concern has not been realized, and the virus is in transit and still in the case.

"We all know Hezbollah has always coveted a weapon of mass destruction for as long as they have been in existence. This is it. They are doing everything they can to get Abood back safely and control the virus for their own purpose, whatever that may be. The Iranians had a different goal, a greater Persian empire, and it included the tactical decision of taking Israel out of the infection zone. They were confident that a larger and empowered Persia could dominate and deal with Israel later.

"Hezbollah only has one goal, the literal obliteration of Israel. We are unanimously convinced the ultimate target is Israel. How they strategically go about it could be any number of scenarios. That's why we need to get to Abood now, before the virus gets into the hands of the Hezbollah leadership and decisions are made to return it to Iran, replicate it, weaponize it, or God forbid, both."

"Couldn't agree with you more and those are similar discussions we've already had amongst Director Baum and myself. I'm sure those same things are being discussed up the chain as we speak. We believe the concern is how they handle the Iranians, who still are the major funding source for Hezbollah and would be furious to know that the virus had mysteriously made its way from their home turf all the way to Lebanon. They either have to have a remarkable story, or they run the risk of seeing their funding cut off or reduced, or at the very least severely punished. Given the fact that Hezbollah remains the number one proxy for the Iranians in that region, the Ayatollahs will opt for the latter in order to keep the organization alive and viable. Given that theory, the virus will either make its way back to Iran and then we're back where we started, or they will allow it to be in play. Either way is a non-starter in our minds."

"General, that's why we still think we need to be in place now, before he gets a chance to do any of those things. We either stop him on his mission to bring it to Hezbollah, or we prevent him from being forced to return it, which in that instance I would suggest they will attempt to replicate it before it goes back. The worst-case scenario in the short term is actually unleashing this across the border into Israel. We need to get to Abood before he has a chance to fulfill any of those possibilities.

"Benji and the Institute have assets all over southern Lebanon that can get us across the mountains into the Habaya region of south Lebanon with local transportation waiting for us. Baker is working up documents for the Associated Press and Xinhua News Agency, and we'll use those credentials, under the guise of interviewing Chinese peacekeepers stationed in Lebanon, as cover. We'll have camera gear for the four of us. Lau and Clay will act as journalists, I'll be the cameraman, and Adina will be our interpreter. Hopefully, we don't have to use any of it, but the goal is to intercept Abood wherever he decides to light, place him under 24-hour surveillance, and look for any opportunity to do a snatch and grab. We can make decisions for exfil once we have him and the virus in possession."

"Go for it. I'd say I'd get clearance from the higher ups, but I'm it."

Wright interjected, "If it's possible, permission to snatch only the virus and grab a bullet I can put between Abood's eyes?"

"Normally, I would grant that request, but he may provide a wealth of intelligence if we get his ass into the hands of our folks. I'm sure they would be most grateful, if you get my drift, if we could make that happen. We can't be responsible if he has a non-life-threatening accident or two on the way back."

"Copy that, General. We were hoping that was your answer, since we've already made arrangements for everything we discussed. As an FYI, we're talking to you from a hotel room in Nazareth, we've been on the road for hours already, and we're about 125 klicks out from our crossing point south of Mount Hermon. We have a helicopter on standby to fly us in-country, and we just received our press credentials and equipment for cover. Benji was also kind enough to supply us with all the requisite firepower we'll need as well. He will join us only as far as our connection in Halta. From there, we're on our own."

"Update us when you're crossing and when you are secure enough in Lebanon to do so. We can then provide you with an updated tracking location and keep you abreast of Abood's travel plans. Good hunting ladies and gentlemen."

Chapter 51

Beirut, Lebanon

A warm, salty afternoon breeze from the Mediterranean coastline drifted lazily into the once remarkable city of Beirut. One of the earliest cities in the world, inhabited for more than 5,000 years, it continues a regeneration of physical and social transformation from the civil war of 1975 to 1990. Urban revitalization and reconstruction in the areas devastated during the war have restored anew the city center. However, the largely unaffected but densely populated and politically and socially diverse neighborhoods that surround it, continue to sow the seeds of discontent and future conflict.

A black Audi A8 pulled to the curb outside of the Patchi Office Building, located on the corner of Mazraa and Tallet El Khayyat Streets in the Madi neighborhood of southern Beirut. It was lunchtime in the invigorated commercial and residential high-rise area, and it teemed with people exiting the multi-story office buildings and apartments in search of food in the cafes and restaurants, scattered in abundance just a few blocks east on Mar Elias street.

Sheikh Imad Mugniyah, along with two muscled bodyguards, exited from three separate doors of the full-size sedan, and made their way to the front entrance, as the remaining driver pulled away. The Patchi housed several legal and finance related business offices, but the primary tenant was the Deputy Secretary's executive office of Hezbollah's Shura Council. As the controlling leadership of Hezbollah, the Shura Council oversees all military and sociopolitical levels of the organization. Comprised of nine members, seven of whom are from Lebanon and the other two Iranian, only three would be attending today's meeting. Hassan Nasrallah, Secretary General and top commander of all Hezbollah, and Secretary General of the Shura, sat patiently with Sheikh Naim Qassem, Deputy-Secretary and host for today, enjoying tea and dates as they awaited the arrival of Mugniyah. As head of the Jihad Council, also known as the military council, Mugniyah and the Jihad Council are responsible for Hezbollah's terrorist operations in Lebanon and worldwide, and were the mastermind behind Abood and his infiltration into Iran as Abbas Abdul-Mahdi.

Upon his arrival into the plush third floor council offices of Qassem, Mugniyah was escorted into a small conference room adorned with mahogany furniture and Byzantine influenced oil paintings. After cordial greetings of As-Salam-u-Alaikum, *Peace be unto you,* the black turbaned and robed trio sat silently, signaling an immediate end of pleasantries and a commencement of the meeting.

"Congratulations again to you, Imad, for successfully bringing our brother home. I understand it was not without a violent struggle in Iraq," Nasrallah kicked off the discussion with an appreciative bow. "However, we are here today, not to bask in adulation for our successes, but to address the residual issues that will certainly arise when our Iranian brothers learn of our deceit and theft of their most precious Setareh weapon."

"They will not be happy," offered Qassem. "They will want retribution. The head of somebody…or somebodies will certainly be requested."

Mugniyah nodded in understanding. He only hoped it would not be his.

"Yes, I think we can all agree," Nasrallah continued as he sipped from his cup wiping a hand at his full gray beard and mustache to remove any residue, "that we will need to offer up a sacrifice to quell the anger that will certainly be visited upon us. I assume you have reaffirmed with Abood he will be it?"

"Abood understands his role and has made peace with martyrdom," confirmed Mugniyah.

"It is clear we have to be confident in our complete ignorance of this whole unfortunate mess, a mess created by a rogue associate, clearly acting outside the Council's knowledge and without any coordination from the Shura, other than our offer to assist in his return from Iraq. We can clearly disavow any knowledge of him having ever been in and escaped from Iran, and maintain we were unaware that he carried with him a doomsday virus when we assisted in his return from Iraq through Syria. We need to be clear, concise, sincere, and unanimous in our lack of knowledge."

Both men nodded back at Nasrallah as he eyed them with a questioning look of understanding, and then gestured with an open hand at Mugniyah to speak.

"I understand and agree. I have gone to great lengths to disguise any knowledge in our records of Abood's whereabouts for the last few weeks. We have actually included several field reports of him going missing and losing all contact. The only limited contact he had while in Iran was with me by an anonymous cell phone routed through Syrian towers on my visits across the border, and we have destroyed that phone now that our mission is complete. It will be critical to obtain his phone, which he continues to have and has agreed to relinquish to me for its destruction. I believe it to be nearly impossible for the Iranians to determine any links to us, and we have left a physical trail in Syria...." Nasrallah eyed him with a contemptuous look, "I'm sorry, Secretary...I meant me, not us...me alone. All tracks and trails lead to Syria."

"Correct, Imad. It will be you who I will offer up to the Supreme Leader if any of the fallout should shake past Abood and come back on us. You need to be clear about that."

"Yes, al-Sayyid, I fully understand that it falls on me, and me only, if Abood's actions are associated in any way with the Shura. I will kill myself before you hand me over to the Iranians. I only ask that you offer me that choice."

"I will grant you that request if it comes to that. It would be preferable for everyone that you end it that way, rather than be handed over for interrogation and implicate any of us in that process," Nasrallah calmly slipped a date into his mouth, followed by another sip of the now cool tea. "Understand, they will want their virus back...immediately. Do you have a final solution for Abood, the virus and our ultimate goal?"

"I do," replied Mugniyah mustering a shaky confidence, sweat clearly visible on his forehead and temples below his turban. "I have created a connection in Abood's historical record with Commander Togyani. The commander's death after the lab incursion removes any opportunity for rebuttal on his part to the fabrication we've created. We can easily exploit the link between the two to foster the likelihood they were known accomplices in the construction and the testing of the Setareh virus. We don't have to overstate the implication of Togyani, as I understand he was respected, even if he were not liked by the Ayatollahs and military leadership. However, it does suggest that Abood was at the underground facility by invitation or Togyani's knowledge, and gives plausibility to why he may have come into possession of the virus after the attacks and destruction that took place to the lab.

"Regardless, I have instructed Abood personally to rendezvous at one of our secure port warehouse facilities in Tyre.

We have constructed a temporary biohazard facility there, where we have two of our top experts who will separate the material into small portions of the virus and antidote for replication. A larger share of each will be segregated for the mission and held in reserve for any issues that might arise. We will utilize the remaining material, more than half, as what we were able to recover from Abood's lapse of sanity and return it to the Iranians.

"As a part of that lapse of judgment, we will kill the technicians once they have completed the separations and place the blame on Abood. We will also blame him for the missing material and issue an arrest citation for him dead or alive. That should give Abood time to assemble the twenty-two martyrs in the Shahid, inject himself and the others with the virus, and let them loose on the southern exit into Israel. They should all be able to spread their virus through contact with their assigned handlers in Israel and make their strategic locations for infection without difficulty within 24 hours. Abood will martyr himself as a diversionary distraction."

"And how do you propose handling the situation if there is an unforeseen leakage of the virus into our community?" a concerned Qassem inquired.

"If we have a release and can contain it with the antidote, we will do so and continue with the mission. If we fail, and the virus is exposed in Lebanon to an uncontrollable degree, we have the antidote and the Iranians have the antidote, so we will need to implicate Abood again as a rogue agent that we have clearly been trying to hunt down and reign in or eliminate, and in his death released the virus within Lebanon. We will acknowledge we have a solution to treat, but we will welcome the international community for assistance and expertise in handling the resultant exposure, but that is a risk we knew could exist. Just as the Iranians were prepared to do in their Doctrine, we can focus the blame on Abood having discovered the virus in Syria, a holdover cache of the

Iraqi WMDs smuggled out during the Iraqi conflict, and repudiate any knowledge on our part.

"If we succeed…when we succeed…we will follow a similar script, except we will not reveal it to the world until the virus has taken fully hold, and in the name of Allah, the glorious infection and certain obliteration of the State of Israel will be realized."

Chapter 52

Tyre, Lebanon

The warehouse district in the coastal city of Tyre consisted of a dozen cream colored, sun baked concrete buildings running parallel to the L-shaped wharf, located just east of the main fishing harbor. Both the wharf and harbor make up the northern hook of the ancient city, one of the oldest continually inhabited cities in the world.

The last two buildings, distinguished from the others by the lack of windows and the recently installed chain link security fence and cameras, had seen a flurry of activity from several straight trucks over the last few days, delivering to the three loading dock doors fronting Senegal street on the south side, opposite the main entrances facing the waters of the Mediterranean. A white panel van had entered the building itself through a ground level garage door sandwiched between a stairway pedestrian entry and the other dock high doors.

Across Senegal Street, a large open-air park area dotted with stands of magnificent tall palm trees swaying in the breeze stood buffer to a city-wide block of residential towers to the west and several blocks of commercial and retail buildings to the south and east of the greenspace. In a two-bedroom rented apartment, paid for in cash, on the seventh floor of a populous residential dwelling on the corner of Senegal and El Awkaf streets, Joel Greenberg ran his hand through his head full of wavy salt and pepper hair and focused his Nikon Prostaff 7S binoculars out the curtained window on the two warehouses he had under surveillance for the last twenty hours.

The knock on the door startled him, but the hushed voice of Benji Saunders on the other side of the door calmed any apprehension, and he opened the door to a big hug from his old friend and teammate from Metsada.

"Good to see you my friend," Joel ushered in Saunders along with a man and woman, disguised by a traditional Shemgah head wrap on him and hijab on her. They all hustled inside as Saunders took one last survey of the hallway to determine no one saw them enter and ducked back inside, closing and bolting the door behind them.

"Good to see you also, Joel," Saunders gripped the arm of Greenberg. He gestured to the two masked strangers, "these are two of the four operators that accompanied me, Clay Wright and Lei Lau," both in the process of unwrapping their head scarves. "This is Joel Greenberg, with Metsada, our Special Operations Division. He's been our best man in Lebanon for nearly a decade."

Wright extended his hand, "Nice to meet you Joel, Clay Wright," the admiration in his voice indicating an appreciation and understanding of the well-heeled reputation of highly sensitive assassinations, sabotage, paramilitary and psychological warfare the Metsada conducted throughout the world.

Lau offered her hand as well, "Lei Lau," her oriental ethnicity clearly causing Greenberg to do a double take as her wrap was removed.

"Chinese?"

"Yes sir. Call it a co-operative venture with American operators. It's been a rather unique experience," Lau turned and grinned at Wright.

"They have press credentials to get them this far, and she helps fit the narrative," interrupted Saunders, "Lau is a PRC intelligence officer, and I've seen her in combat…she's one tough cookie and can easily handle her own."

"Excellent, never doubted it."

Clay stepped over to the window and pulled back slightly on the dust covered curtain, "We have two more of us below and down the street in a bistro."

"The Al Koohk?"

"Yep, they have direct line of sight across the park. They will take a stroll by the warehouses and wharf shortly to get a closer look."

Greenberg pointed to the worn maize colored couch and two frayed canvass directors' chairs, "Have a seat, and let me catch you up with what's been going on over there. You can tell me what you have in mind and how I can help."

"Perfect."

Greenberg sat in a folding camp chair by the window, reached into a plastic cooler and retrieved several water bottles and offered them to anyone interested. All three of the visitors took him up on the offer. He took another glimpse through the binoculars and faced the group seated and now hydrating.

"Your man showed up," Greenberg looked at his watch, "almost four hours ago. He's in the last building, the one with the three dock doors, and nobody has been in or out since then. I've spoken to a couple of boat captains down in the harbor this morning, and nobody knows anything about the current occupant. It used to house an import distribution company bringing inbound food and commercial goods.

"Was a little concerned to get too close to have a good look inside, but from a distance along Senegal Street, I got a glimpse in one of the doors as a truck pulled away. Very open floor space inside, a few clusters of stacked crates and boxes, but nothing filled to the rafters. I believe there's office space and an entrance opposite of the dock side."

Wright acknowledged Greenberg and gave him the ten-minute abridged version of what had transpired over the last two weeks and what exactly the present threat appeared to be.

"Shit, this is a fucking calamity waiting to unfold," Greenberg ran a hand full of fingers through his wavy salt and pepper hair and scratched at his stubbled chin.

Wright pulled a Toughbook laptop out of a canvas shoulder bag, flipped it open on his knees, and punched up the power button, "Well summed up. The good news is we're still getting a hit on the tracking right in that building, so we hope and believe all of the virus is in that warehouse, along with Abood."

Out of the canvas bag also came tactical comms units for all four of them, and after Lau passed them around, everyone clipped on their throat mics and inserted their ear buds.

"We are connected with our Co-op operations group, and I'll have ISR overwatch pulled up on our location in a few minutes. We are also connected to Blake and Adina downstairs in the café. We'll go with first names as call signs for everyone, 'Co-op' is home designation, and this operations team on-site is 'Rescue.' We parked the truck behind this building in the adjoining lot, and we are expecting hazmat suits and a biohazard storage case to arrive by a fishing boat to the harbor within the hour. Joel, you're familiar with the area, and you will actually recognize the boat captain as one of Mossad's assets from Sidon, Jasar?" Greenberg nodded his recognition. "You will meet the boat, advise me of his position in the port, and tell him to sit tight. Let him know that three of us will come to him at dark. We'll suit up in the boat while he transfers us by water to a beach area on the eastern side of the wharf, so we can advance on the front of the warehouse. You good with that?"

"Yes, sounds good so far."

"Any other questions or anything else you can add to the current sit rep of the warehouse?"

"No. I'll assume you'll tell me what you need from me after I get back with your equipment. As far as recon of the warehouse, there are still several people inside that were with one of delivery trucks and a cargo van that arrived late yesterday. The truck is gone, but the van is still parked inside there. I also counted six heavily armed men with AK47's that entered with Abood upon his arrival, and they are also all still inside, along with Abood. I have spotted what I believe to be eight others on guard duty outside the building, two in front and two by the dock doors and two pairs outside the warehouse area. Two have been sitting in the white Renault sedan in the food Market parking lot on the south side of Senegal, and the other two have been taking turns strolling through the park on foot. They're not very discreet. The four of them have traded out positions once over the last few hours."

"Excellent work, thanks Joel," Wright acknowledged, placing the open computer on the round rattan wicker stool masquerading as a coffee table, the streaming video of overhead surveillance of the warehouse and surrounding area visible to all on the screen.

"So, what is the ops plan for taking this guy out and recovering the virus?"

"Good question, Joel. The five of us have been noodling on that during the drive over to Tyre. Before this asshole decides on his next course of action, which we believe he's doing as we speak, it's time critical to hit him right here in Tyre, in the warehouse. We'll do that at dark. As soon as the hazmat gear arrives, Blake, Adina, and I will suit up to breach the warehouse from the front. You and

Benji will be responsible for taking out their overwatch help in the park and the car and prevent anyone from leaving the warehouse if they attempt to run. Lei will set up overwatch and sniper help from this window and take out the dock door guards and any threats as they emerge outside the building. You will back up Lei on taking out the guards on the back side.

"Once the roaming lookouts and guards are neutralized, the three of us will breach the front door. We will flash bang entry and take out the armed threats inside. If we can take Abood alive...great, but not necessary in our opinion. Once we have control, we will secure the virus in the biohaz box and exit.

"We have two options depending on any local response. If there is no immediate response, Lei will bring up the truck, and we can all exit by vehicle for helicopter extraction at the same rendezvous as our infil. If we get local police or military interested in our activities, we will go out on Jasar's boat, which will be on standby in the fishing harbor, and Shayetet 13 has a unit in place off the coast to assist in our exfil into international waters and into the hands of the USS Stockdale from our Carrier Strike Group 3."

Greenberg scratched at his chin again, "And if we're not successful?"

"We don't believe in failure," Wright eyed him intently and cracked a wry smile, "however, we do believe in contingencies. If Adina, Blake, and I are not successful on the breach and contain," Wright pointed with both forefingers at Greenberg and Saunders, "you two are cleared to enter through the dock doors and assist taking this bastard out, unfortunately hazmat suits be damned for you guys. Last resort is Lei has the laser and can send a 500-pound JDAM, loaded on our Predator in overwatch, and take out most anything that resides on this wharf...including the wharf. Quarantine alerts will go out, and the hope is no contamination will occur. No guarantees."

"Sounds like fun," Greenberg stood rubbing his palms together. "Do you have keys to your truck? I'll head down to the waterfront to catch up with Jasar."

As the ignition key was exchanged, a voice over the comms chimed in, "CW, this is Blake and Adina, we're on the move for recon from the café and will stroll through the wharf. We will advise of any unusual activity we don't know about and see if we can pick up any additional intel on target."

Wright replied, "Good copy, be advised of tango watch dogs off premise. Two in the park on foot and two in white Renault, sitting idle in parking lot in front of the market."

"Roger that, have a splendid afternoon."

Ferguson and Margolis stood up from their outdoor lunch table, wiped their mouths simultaneously and disposed of their napkins into their empty seats. Ferguson dropped a handful of lire onto the table, reached over and took Adina's hand in his and proceeded to stroll down El Awkaf Street toward Senegal and the harbor, like two lovers on a romantic walk in the setting sun of a warm Mediterranean afternoon.

Chapter 53

Khater Distributing Company Warehouse, Tyre, Lebanon

Inside the abandoned warehouse, Abood observed the stark contrast of the dark and dingy interior, with stacks of old rotting pallets and bundles of used corrugated cardboard that occupied the side wall of the open floor space, and the halogen light stands encased in a clear and white plastic walled mobile biohazard lab tent, that offered the look of safety, but probably would never contain a spill of any kind if it occurred.

The irony was that it didn't matter. As far as he was concerned, he would be infected and dead soon. However, he did not want to unleash this disaster on his home country, so he was praying that Allah would oversee the successful transfer of the virus from several of the vials in the suitcase to the 24 Mumford Autoject subcutaneous self-injection syringes he would take with him. The actual transfer would take place in a biosafety cabinet, which had been installed in the far corner of the tent, so the risk was actually being significantly mitigated, but his concerns were not.

When the transfer was completed, the deadly syringes would go with him in a biohazard case specifically designed to protect and carry them to the infiltration site just south of their location, where the other twenty-two jihadists who had prepared for martyrdom would be easily infected by lethal injection and released into the land of the corrupt infidels. Of no future concern to him, the remaining vials would go to the Shura Council and Nasrallah to do with what they want. He was certain it would be returned to Iran as planned, and he would be delivered as the scapegoat for the missing portions. He had made peace with his name being implicated. That was fine. It would be Allah he would ultimately answer to, not the remaining mortals left to dissect his legacy. He was comforted in the knowledge that for his efforts in the destruction of the Zionist occupation of Palestine, he was certain a magnificent place in paradise had been reserved for him.

The transfer was close to being completed, and he would leave shortly in the van parked at the rear garage door. Everything was on schedule, and the final solution for him and his mission was at hand. A peace began to wash over him.

As dusk began to fall outside, he called for two of his most trusted men, Hamal and Tarek, to join him in the old office structure in the front of the building. In the gutted walls of what once was a thriving business environment, he instructed them that thirty minutes after he departed the warehouse this evening, they were to take possession of the stainless steel suitcase, execute the lab technicians with the pistol wrapped in a towel he handed to Tarek, with instructions not to put his hands and fingers all over the grip, and leave it at the scene. Then they were to take off from Tyre immediately afterward, do not stop for anyone or anything until they delivered the case to the Shura Council in Beirut, and put into the hands of Kalil Badr Al Din. Their arrival would be expected, and that both would be handsomely rewarded.

His two confidants listened attentively, and when Hamal asked if they would ever see Abood again, he reached over and hugged both, "biniemat allah sa'arakuma fi aljana," *By the grace of Allah, I will see you in paradise.*

Chapter 54

Open Air Park, Tyre, Lebanon

Benji Saunders strolled down the crooked, centuries-old sidewalk running adjacent to the open-air market parking lot, the evening humidity still strong enough to enable beads of sweat to stain his linen shirt. He wore it untucked to conceal the IWI Jericho 941F pistol, a silencer screwed to the muzzle, situated in the appendix inside the waistband holster of his pants.

The market, teeming with shoppers earlier in the day sat eerily quiet, save for a couple leftover vendors still packing away some of the raw vegetables that went unpurchased. Saunders pulled out his wallet and transferred a gold American Express card into a clear identification window on one flap, creating a makeshift and unofficial law enforcement badge. He approached the white Renault from the front so as not to startle the inhabitants in the front seats. He waved casually at the two Lebanese men sitting in the open-windowed vehicle, cigarette smoke billowing out windows on both sides.

In Arabic, Saunders called out to them from ten meters away, still approaching at a causal walk, "Excuse me, what are you two doing parked here all afternoon?"

The driver looked at his companion with a puzzled look, and then back at Saunders and with a wave of his hand, ashes from his cigarette falling into the air, "Go away, it's none of your business why we're here."

"I believe it is my business," Saunders flipped open his wallet and flashed the gold AMEX card toward the pair, then flipped it closed almost as quickly, never breaking stride. "This is my jurisdiction, and...." Before either man could react, Saunders had pulled the pistol from out of his pants and sent four rounds into the front seat of the car, striking the driver in the left cheek and neck, and his passenger taking the other 9mm parabellum bullets to his forehead, above his left eye, and the other striking him square in the chest. The silenced rounds, never really ever silent, were still muffled enough not to arouse any suspicion. Saunders made an exaggerated display of coughing loudly as he put one round each into their skulls.

Saunders remained by the car window casually speaking to the two dead men as if having a normal conversation, "It's a very nice evening gentlemen, don't you think? Rescue, this is Benji, the car team is down, I say again the two in the car are eliminated."

Nearly simultaneously and in coordination with Saunders, Joel Greenberg rose from one of the several stone benches that flanked the cab stand runway about fifty meters west of Saunders and the market parking lot. He folded a magazine awkwardly under his arm, tucking his identical Jericho pistol inside it, shook out a cigarette from a pack and placed it unlit in his mouth and began walking north through the grass and pebbled dirt of the park. From the east side, he approached a string of wooden benches encircling a stand of palm trees just off Senegal street. His two sentries had just made his job a whole lot easier. Instead of splitting up, they had both nestled on to the same bench fronting the street and warehouses in the distance and had spent the last ten minutes talking intermittently amongst themselves.

Greenberg approached them from the right side of the bench, snapping at a lighter as if he couldn't get it to light. As he got within fifteen meters, they both turned to notice him, and he slapped the lighter in his open hand and then tried unsuccessfully again to ignite it with his thumb.

In French, he spoke to the pair as he closed the distance to the pair, "Can either of you spare a light?"

They both looked at each other, and staring back intently at Greenberg, the closest one to him reached into an upper shirt pocket with his right hand. It was all the diversion Greenberg needed. He dropped the lighter and reached in between the folded magazine and found the trigger. He shot the one farthest away twice in the face, sending the man slumping down the back of the bench. Before the other man could react and get his hand out of his pocket, the gun turned on him and coughed out three rounds, two to the chest and the other right through the nose. The man sat frozen in an upright seated position for a brief moment, already dead, his body finally toppling over to the left onto his companion. As a car advanced down Senegal and the headlights approached the bench, Greenberg had already sat down with the two dead men and quickly pulled both back up into seated positions, carrying on a mostly silent but animated conversation with both.

"Rescue, this is Joel, the park pair is neutralized, you are clear from here."

Greenberg thumbed the lighter again and it ignited immediately. He lit one cigarette and pulled another from the exposed pack in the top pocket of his second victim. After lighting the second, he took the left arm of the same man and placed it around the shoulder of the other one. He puffed hard on the cigarettes and placed one in each of what was left of the lips of both men. He stood and walked toward the wharf.

After hearing the "clear" from Greenberg, Lau took one last look around the park and parking lot and then studied her scope on the two guards on the back side of the warehouse. Thankfully, they seemed to be operating on the same pattern they had started earlier in the day. They both would spend time chatting on the steps to the rear entry door by the docks, and then every fifteen minutes, they would both perform a sentry walk. One would go east around the side of the building to the front, disappearing for a couple of minutes, and then returning the same way. The other one would go west, reach the end of the building and look through the connecting fence on the corner and return to the steps. It would be easy to take both when they were together.

The timing on the "all clear" was good, both guards were both just returning to the steps. She waited another fifteen seconds to give time for Greenberg and Saunders to meet up and cross over to the north side of Senegal Street, finding a bench that fronted the beach wall facing the Mediterranean. They were in a good spot to provide her emergency backup in taking out the rear sentries, but she was confident they wouldn't be needed.

Having spent the better part of the last hour working her wind, distance, and elevation calculations into the scope, it was now show time. She slid the bipod ever so slightly to the left and focused in on the one guard to the left, sipping from what looked like bottled water. As soon as he pivoted to present his body full frontal, she exhaled and held, pulling the trigger on the SR-25, sending the 7.62x51mm NATO cartridge hurtling at the head of the unsuspecting man.

The top of his head disintegrated into a mass of blood and tissue that splattered against the light-colored wall behind him. His lifeless body slumped to the hard tarmac while his rifle clattered to the ground next to him. His shocked companion froze for a couple of fatal seconds, while Lau reacquired him in her scope. He added to his demise by standing still and looking around him for the threat, as if he might see what it was that just decapitated his buddy. Lau aimed marginally lower to offset her subtle miscalculation on bullet drop and squeezed off another round. The other man's head also plastered the wall with blood, brain, and bone fragments on the other side of the steps.

"Rescue, this is Lei, both guards are down in the rear, you are clear to breach."

Nearly simultaneous to her last trigger pull, the rear garage style dock door opened, and a white van pulled out into the lot. As it began to turn toward the exit, the garage door began to close. Lau watched as a stunned Abood brought the vehicle to a stop, and looking behind him, eyed the one guard crumpled on the ground, a pool of crimson surrounding his body. He poked his head out of the driver's door until he saw the other guard also in a heap by the steps. He ducked reflexively and hit the accelerator as Lau reloaded and let loose another shot that shattered the passenger side window and impacted into the dashboard, just missing Abood's forehead.

As the van careened through the chain-link gate, tearing it off the hinges and carrying one of the two doors on the hood of the van, Lau growled in anger, "Rescue, we have a problem. Abood just left the building by the rear dock. He's escaping in a white van. I've lost visual for a shot."

A half hour earlier, Jasar deposited the hazmat suit ensconced trio of Margolis, Ferguson, and Wright onto the three-meter-wide rock beach that formed the erosion control base of the sea wall. Nearly 100 meters east of the warehouse, they traversed east down the football field length of the rocky waterfront under cover of the ancient stone wall protecting the storage facilities and beach from the waters of the Mediterranean. Accessing the wall's right angle turn toward the open water, they spotted the two guards in the front of the warehouse entrance, sitting together in folding chairs, eyeing the beautiful views of the placid water. At Greenburg's pronouncement of "all clear" Ferguson and Margolis delivered two silenced rifle rounds each into both guards from 20 meters away.

"Two front Tangos are down," announced Wright.

Advancing immediately over the parapet into the front parking lot, they found the outside front door to the building's office had been left open. Quietly entering, Ferguson quickly found the interior door accessing the warehouse locked. He accessed a wired charge from his rucksack and applied it to the door. They waited for Lau's signal confirming her guards were neutralized.

"Go!" Wright yelled at Ferguson, who triggered the hand-held detonator. The interior metal door blew off its hinges and landed inward to the open warehouse. Wright and Ferguson tossed through the opening two flash bang grenades, and Margolis followed right behind with a third one in the middle of the open space. As all three covered their ears and averted their eyes, the explosive devices did their job, effectively disorienting everyone inside the warehouse with blinding flashes of light and a deafening sound.

All three, doing their best imitation of the Michelin man, and armed with IWI Black Tavor X95-S SMG assault rifles including suppressors and a MARS sight on the upper receiver, stood, and Ferguson and Margolis followed Wright as he led through the door first. His weapon up and on his shoulder sighted in front of him, Wright turned immediately to his right searching for targets. Ferguson similarly went through next and turned to his left, while Margolis followed them both, charging into the middle.

Before any of the armed men inside could react, Wright took down two of them with center mass shots, both kneeling from the concussion, just outside the lit tented area to the side of the wide-open interior. Margolis also took out two more, both standing by the rear dock door that was in the process of still closing, each of them clutching at their ears.

Ferguson nearly ran right into a fifth man that had been just inside the blown door. He was on all fours, trying to regain his senses. By the time Ferguson shot him twice in the back of head and was already advancing. He acquired his last target standing up on an elevated dock platform, but before he could engage, the remaining gunman was able to let loose with his AK-47 in the direction of Wright and the tented lab area. Running directly at the shooter, Ferguson cut him down quickly with a volley of body shots that continued until he reached the lifeless body.

One of the random shots had torn through Wright's safety suit, catching him in the ribs, but deflected by the Outer Tactical Vest that had thankfully come with their suits, but his protections was compromised. Once his breath returned, he raised to one knee, grunting from the pain of the hit, nothing lethal, but a bitch of a bruise nonetheless. One of the hazmat suited lab technicians was not as lucky. He was squirming on the floor in pain, while the other tech was crouched behind a bank of equipment. Margolis reached her first and pulled her to her feet shouting in Arabic, "Is the area secure?"

The stunned women didn't respond, she just kept looking at her colleague screaming and writhing in pain.

Margolis shook her violently and noticed that she had no mask or gloves on, looking directly in her eyes through her own mask, "Is the area secure? Is there any danger of bio hazard leak here?"

"No, it is safe," replied the sobbing woman.

Ferguson checked on Wright to make sure he was okay and then made his way toward Margolis. The two of them were looking for anything resembling the stainless-steel suitcase.

"Wright coughed to regain his breath, "Co-op, this is Rescue. We have secured the warehouse. All tangos are down, but Abood is gone. He got away again right before we breached."

"Copy that Rescue, we heard transmission from Lau. He hasn't gotten away. We have re-tasked ISR and have his van under surveillance," Woods replied over the chatter of Isaiah in the background. "Isaiah says the case is not with him, it's still in the warehouse."

Lau chimed in, "Clay, I'm in route with the truck, I'll be at the warehouse in less than two minutes."

"Meet us at the dock doors," he replied.

Margolis and Ferguson had ahold of the female tech and were busy interrogating her, when she pointed behind her and walked them over to the large bio safety cabinet and workstation area further into the tented area. Lying on one of the open tables was the stainless-steel case.

"Is it safe to open?" Ferguson said in his best butchered Arabic, applying the muzzle of his gun to the side of her head."

"It is safe."

Margolis popped the latches and looked inside.

"Shit," they both said in unison.

"Co-op, we have a problem, not all of the material is here. There is room for what looks like ten vials. Only seven are here. Three appear to be missing. Give us a minute."

Margolis asked the tech where the other material was while Ferguson turned and emptied three rounds into the groaning body of the mortally wounded tech on the floor.

As she screamed, the remaining tech yelled, "Please, please don't kill me. We transferred three of the vials into auto-injection devices. The man who just left has them."

Ferguson turned to Margolis, "We have to get to Abood." He took a couple of steps out to where Wright had been and noticed the outdoor spotlight illuminating through the back door left ajar.

"Already on it," Wright closed the passenger door to the already rolling truck, as Lau hit the accelerator. "You guys get that material out of here. Co-op, please tell us where our good friend Abood is headed."

Chapter 55

Southern Lebanon, near the Israeli Border

Speeding south on the Tyre-Naqoura Highway, Abood couldn't contain his frustration at another near miss from someone attempting to take him out. *How could they possibly know where I am, seemingly all of the time? Who are they?* There was an element of fear picking at his senses as well. Not fear as to his personal safety, his fate on this earth was sealed long ago, but the fear that his dreams of destroying Israel, the elimination of the occupying entity, would not be realized.

He instinctively looked skyward outside the window, with the stars brilliant against the black backdrop. Nothing to see, but he could almost feel the drone he felt certain was part of his vulnerability, high above, tracking him as he slowed his speed to keep from being cited by a patrolling policeman.

Roughly thirty minutes into an hour's drive south from the Tyre warehouse, Abood pulled another burner phone from the nylon backpack he had accompanying him on the passenger seat of the van and punched up the "power" button. He slowed the van to the side of the road, punched in a number he had seared in his memory, and selected the text option. His fingers calm and resolute, he typed…

الحل النهائي علينا .لواء الشهداء إلى نقطة الفجر .بدء في 06:00 اليوم. السلام
عليكم ورحمة الله وبركاته. Final Solution upon us. Martyrs Brigade to
dawning point. Commencement at 06:00 today. May the peace
of Allah be upon us all.

He set the phone down into the console and pulled back onto
the road, virtually no traffic at this hour of the evening. One more
glance skyward as he asked for Allah to watch over him to
complete his glorious mission. He obviously had been shepherding
him all along, as he had survived much to get to this point...surely
his mercy and strength would guide him to the conclusion.

His phone chimed a reply. He picked it up in anticipation...

في الموقف عند الفجر ، في انتظار وصولك .الحمد لله. In position at
dawning, waiting for your arrival. Praise Be to Allah.

He tossed the phone back onto the pack and settled himself
backward into the seat. His mind at peace, he smiled.

Chapter 56

Marwahin, Lebanon

Abood arrived at the designated jump off point on the south side of the ancient border town of Marwahin. He drove the van through a double-door wood gate, pulling into the courtyard area of a walled residence, two figures standing guard closing the doors behind him. He parked, exited, and met a large husky man in a red checkered keffiyah with a hug. The pleasantries and conversation ended quickly as Abood pointed skyward, and watched as the man turned away and quickly barked orders, rallying nearly a couple dozen men from inside the one-story mud-bricked home. They all filed out and separated into three separate groups, each man sporting a full backpack, and climbed into three dirt covered vans backed up against the eastern wall of the compound.

The entire convoy, led by Abood returning to his van, set off for the rugged and hilly land just southwest of the ancient city. They negotiated the east-west main road paralleling the terraced hills to the south of town, eventually going off road to a fingered plateau heavily covered in rocks and trees. Rolling the caravan to a stop as far as the vehicles could travel, Abood stepped out with his backpack and an AK-47 in tow, organizing the two dozen martyrs into a single file line and instructing them to wait at the edge of the clearing. He retreated to the men remaining with the vehicles, all offering up hugs to Abood, as each returned to the vans and drove them away the same way they had come.

Turning back to the group, he had them all have a seat on the ground, as he explained the trail they were about to navigate and the dangers of traversing it in the dark. He had wanted to wait until there was enough light to help with the climb, but he felt a heightened sense of urgency and thought it best to push forward and lead them in the dark. The clear night and three-quarter waxing moon, as well as the pinkish hint of dawn intruding on the eastern horizon, would offer some relief to their challenged visibility.

Mustering the group to follow him, and each man to remain within shoulder touch of the man in front of him, he pulled a flashlight out of his pack and found the narrow walking path he was very familiar with from his brief time spent leading the development of Hezbollah's best kept secret.

Approximately eight years ago, Hezbollah created a special forces unit, known as the Radwan Unit, specifically tasked with crossing into Israel and causing as much mayhem and destruction as possible both for the sake of the destruction itself and for the "symbolism" of having troops carry out attacks inside Israel. As a part of that directive, significant effort was given to the creation of multiple cross-border tunnels on its southern border with Israel.

For years the Israeli Defense Force had covert monitoring equipment in place and was in possession of a number of sites where Hezbollah had been, or was actively digging underground infrastructures. Some had yet to cross into Israeli territory, others having already penetrated well into the country. In late 2018, Israel launched Operation Northern Shield to find and destroy Hezbollah cross-border attack tunnels, and a month later, the IDF announced it had found all of the passages and was working to demolish them.

"All" is what they thought. Unfortunately, a natural cavern that required very little additional construction had been in existence for centuries just south of the city of Marwahin, with a single indigenous and undisturbed passage threading nearly 80 meters deep, over two kilometers long, and penetrating nearly a kilometer into Israel's Nahal Bezet nature preserve. Hezbollah's concern was that the IDF could effectively survey the noises involved in digging and developing tunnels, so the Radwan, under leadership that included Abood, had initiated a man-made endeavor to the east of the native Marwahin underpass. The infrastructure improvements to what they referred to as the "Hole in the Wall", were masked with the coordinated deceptive excavations of an unnatural burrowing that led toward the Israeli border town of Zar'it, located several kilometers away in the adjoining Hurbat Kecham Preserve.

Descending the steep footpath that wound back and forth across a sheer rocky slope, thick with trees, the group dropped nearly thirty meters below the start of the path, where they eventually reached a small clearing that exposed a fissure angled back into the vertical cliff. Removing small piles of limbs and branches purposely placed to camouflage, Abood located the narrow opening in the wall. Large enough to allow a single adult to pass, he slipped through the cramped cavity for a couple meters and spilled into a larger entryway bathed in a dim artificial light from the advanced infrastructure for electricity, complemented with ventilation and communications systems that had taken years to complete.

He stepped through a larger opening into what amounted to the mechanical room, the steady hum of generators barely audible behind a set of metal doors constructed into the stone. He lifted a phone receiver located on the wall and pressed a button on the accompanying digital pad.

After a couple of rings, it was answered. A brief conversation confirmed the advance team was on site and had secured the tunnel, and his team was clear to move deeper into the cavern. He looked back toward the tunnel entry, a pang of emotion washed over him as he realized this would be his last time on earth in his native land. It was fleeting, as his excitement level surged, understanding all systems were a go. He stepped back out, ushering in the jihadists who had all safely made the descent, and then he turned and began walking down the lit path, disappearing further into the cave.

Chapter 57

Near Marwahin, Lebanon

Once Abood had made a break from the warehouse, and the missing vials detected, it was decided to immediately re-task the US Air Force MQ1-B Predator drone to keep tabs on his movements. Assigned by the DOD for the Tyre Operation, the live feed from the UAV's overwatch was being monitored by Scruggs, Woods, Isaiah, and Director Baum ensconced in the Co-op 'Sit Room' back in Alexandria, scrutinizing Abood's trek south from Tyre to the hills of southern Lebanon

"Clay, the entire group is on foot. They have all left the vans, and the vans are bugging out…stand by. I'm seeing what appears to be a flashlight on the move just to the east. UAV thermal also confirms they are all scaling down the eastern side of the hill below where they parked," Elaine Scruggs' voice crackled through Wright's ear piece.

The same ISR video, as well as the audio feeds from the Co-op and Operation Rescue team, were also being fed to the Mossad headquarters office in Tel Aviv. The Israeli Defense Force units to the north, including a Biohazard Quick Reaction Team along with the Yamam Border Police units stationed on the northern border, were all placed on high alert. The Israeli Air Force scrambled two F-35's and two F-16 jet fighters with a full complement of ordnance and were flying reconnaissance across the entire northern Blue Line.

"Copy, Co-op. We'll follow into the area being vacated by the vans now," responded Wright.

In her haste on the way out of the apartment to pick up Wright outside the warehouse, Lau had fortunately thought to grab the computer. She and Wright had been able to link to the same Predator feed to guide them on the exact path taken by Abood, and Wright had helped navigate Lau into the rugged rural area Abood and his men had just been deposited in. Parked in a grove of olive trees just north of the clearing, they waited for the four retreating vans to head off to the east, back into the center of town.

Ten minutes later, they started up the truck, and with headlights off, slowly maneuvered over the rocky terrain into the woods to the south. Before reaching the same opening in the tree line, they turned the vehicle around and killed the engine. Grabbing an additional IOTV vest for Lau from the storage area in back, and adding additional ammo for both, they grabbed their rifles and exited into the darkness.

"Co-op, we're in the clearing above the HVT, can you provide updated sit rep?"

"Stand by, we've lost contact."

Wright and Lau both took cover behind a stand of trees and knelt in unison while surveilling the pitch-black area in front of them.

Inside the 'Sit' Room,' on a secure landline tied into Tel Aviv, a voice boomed over the open speaker, "Tunnel!"

"Tunnel?" Woods blurted out questioningly.

"They just entered a tunnel. It's the only explanation," replied the alarmed voice of Colonel Daniel Switow from the Mossad office. "We thought we had all of the tunnels tagged, but this is obviously one that got by us. I'm going to make an educated guess, but we have to assume that the end point on that tunnel is in Israeli territory." A flurry of activity could be heard in the background as orders were being disseminated to reposition the forces on alert. "No doubt in my mind, Abood will inject his jihadists in the tunnel and let them out into countryside. If they get out into the population, even just a few of them, it would be enough to create a devastating epidemic. If most of them get loose, it would be catastrophic, even if we can duplicate the antidote we recovered in Tyre."

"Damnit!" Woods stepped over to Scruggs' and spoke into the microphone, "Clay, we believe they've entered a tunnel below you. We need you and Lau to get inside that tunnel pronto and eliminate all threats, repeat eliminate ALL threats. Timing is Urgent Priority."

Wright sighed visibly…*God, I hate tunnels.* "Copy that Co-op, we're Oscar Mike."

Switow interjected, "General Woods, we are moving a QRF to that site now. I don't give a shit about the implications of invading Lebanon. They should be on site in 20-30 minutes."

"Clay, we are moving reinforcements to your location now. Time to site is three zero mikes."

"Copy that, Co-op, scaling the trail now."

Chapter 58

Inside the Hole in the Wall tunnel, northern Israel

Lau had taken the lead and easily traversed the steep trail down the side of the hill. Wright was amazed at her agility as she bounced and hopped her way down to a small outcropping and was waiting on him as he dropped to the ground next to her. She pointed into the wall and loose debris that lay off to the side. With her weapon shouldered she took a few steps forward and found the opening they were looking for.

"Co-op, we've found the tunnel entrance, no resistance. Breaching now…going dark."

"Copy, CW. Good hunting."

They quietly stepped into the void in the rock one at a time, and without hesitating Lau held a finger to her lips, and once again took the lead as they moved gingerly forward. Wright took in a deep breath and followed behind keeping an eye on their six.

After a few minutes of moving deeper into the earth, the natural subterranean passage alternating between narrow and wider areas, Lau stopped and knelt down. Wright mimicked her movement and watched her cup her ear. They could clearly hear the echo of faint voices from further down the path.

* * * **

Abood had tracked nearly half a kilometer into the tunnel until he reached a large cavernous room with multiple, large cascading stone floors encircling most of the grand opening. He ordered his men and women to have a seat on the rock in order of a prearranged numerical assignment. He removed two dozen envelopes, numbered one through twenty-four, and then positioned on a rock ledge, removed and opened the secure case of syringes. Additionally, he removed a suit vest comprised of several pounds of Semtex bricks and ceramic ball bearings stitched in between the lining and the outer fabric. A release trigger detonator, wired from the plastic explosive into a small buckle, was mounted to the front next to the buttons. Abood slipped the vest on, but did not engage the buckle.

As he began distributing the envelopes to the corresponding martyrs by number, he addressed the group, "My brothers and sisters, we have all volunteered and are about to embark upon a glorious journey in the name of Allah, and through our efforts his pleasure will seal our place in paradise. Inside your envelope are directions and itineraries for where you will proceed once you exit the tunnel into our Zionist occupied territory. I will infect us shortly with an instrument of Allah's conviction, and we will instantly become a contagious weapon from that time forward. I will lead us first and proceed to Nazareth, where I will detonate this vest in the Old City Market center, creating a diversion that will allow you to fade away to your destinations unobstructed."

As he finished handing out the written instructions to his martyrs, who would carry death to all the major cities and populous centers in Israel, he asked them all to stand in a single line. One at a time they started to come forward and receive their injection of terror and destruction.

As he began administering injections, "You will have twenty-four hours before the magnificent tool of Allah will begin to sap the mortal life from you, and your remaining time on earth will not last much more than twelve to twenty-four hours more. By then, the fruits of your efforts will be realized, and the Zionist invaders will not last much longer than you. Allahu Akbar!"

A loud throated reply in unison echoed through the chamber, "ALLAHU AKBAR!"

* * * * *

Approaching the rising tone of a single voice, Wright and Lau reached another right-angled opening and froze side-by-side with their backs against the cold stone wall. Wright took a quick peek around the corner of the rocky entrance into the space and repeated it again a fraction of a second longer. He closed his eyes and processed the image in his mind. He leaned into Lau as they both listened to the preaching going on from around the corner of their position. From inside one of his vest pockets, he pulled out one last flash bang that remained from his breach of the warehouse.

"Listen Lei, this is as far as you need to go with this, you've done far more than any of us would have expected. This isn't your fight. The area is likely contaminated, and I can manage this myself," reaching down to his weapon and setting it for full auto. "They're all grouped together in the center of a large open chamber, with two armed guards flanking each side. Once I toss this in, it will be like shooting fish in a barrel. I need you to head back outside and guide the QRF to this location."

Lau smiled broadly, "Nice try, but this is my fight," her smile transforming into a gritted, steely-eyed determination. "You don't understand why I'm in this to the end, and we don't have time for an explanation or an argument, so let's get on with this, finish it, and get out of this together."

Wright stared at her with a puzzled look and recognized the intensity of her resolve and then broke into a huge grin and nodded his acceptance and approval. He poked her in the chest and pointed to the left of the opening in front of them and then tapped his own chest and extended his forefinger to the right. In a hushed whisper, "Guards first, and then work inward on the group." As they heard the loud exaltation of the Muslim declaration "God is most great," Wright winked at Lau, pulled the pin on the grenade, and launched it through the crevice as they averted their eyes and covered their ears.

Once again, the grenade worked its magic, the loud bang and blast of brilliant white light making a mess of the visual and auditory senses of everyone in the room. Wright led Lau through the dusty entrance, and each peeled off right and left and immediately cut down the rifle toting guards, both bent over in disoriented postures, bookends to the mass of bodies between them. Both of their weapons on full auto, there were no hesitations as they sprayed 9 x19mm slugs into the rest of the dazed men and women, all in various stages of kneeling, bent over at the waist, or on all fours on the floor.

Neither Wright nor Lau had the luxury to second guess the grisly act of gunning down the helpless and defenseless crowd, but in reality, they were anything but. They were without a doubt, hideously weaponized monsters, and there would be no remorse in their killing. They emptied their magazines, and were in the process of reloading, when a volley of return fire from an AK-47 pinged off the wall to the left, continued across their front until Lau fell to the ground.

Wright slammed the fresh mag of ammo into his rifle and pivoted to his right and started to pull the trigger, but through the dusty haze he froze, keeping his aim center mass on Ibrahim Abood. *Shit! Dead man's switch.* Standing tall and still, the AK rifle dangled from the strap over his shoulder. His left arm was clearly elevated outward, the hand wrapped into a fist, and his thumb protruding slightly as it rested on a red lever. By depressing the lever, he had armed the suicide vest he had strapped around his body. If anything forced him to be incapacitated for any reason, simply releasing the lever would cause the device to detonate.

"Freeze, motherfucker!" Wright shouted as he instinctively took a step backward. "Lei... Lei, are you all right?" no response except for the moans and groans of several bodies emanating from the stone floor in front of him, one mortally wounded man clawing toward his feet.

"You infidel monster, you have ruined everything," cried Abood in a polished English.

"Lei, are you okay?" Wright called out again.

"You will pay for this. Allah will avenge your intervention, and you will die."

"From the looks of things, we're all going to die. Ironically, it looks like Allah turned the tables on you and enabled us to ruin your pathetic little quest. Lei...answer me?!"

"I'm here," Lau's reply was barely audible. "I'm hit in a couple places, vest caught some of it, but not dead yet."

"Can you move?"

"Yes, I'm crawling back to the tunnel."

"Good keep moving."

Abood spit with anger, "I'm leaving here, and you are not going to stop me. As I'm sure you know, if you try, I'll blow us all up," as he began to slide to his right.

With his rifle still trained on Abood, Wright knelt down in front of the mangled body of the man that had managed to inch his way to his boot before expiring. "Honestly, you piece of shit, you're not going anywhere. Lei, where are you?"

"I'm out here," the faintness of her response indicated she was back in the tunnel. It's all he needed to know.

Abood continued to shift to his right, stepping over his dead martyrs.

Wright continued tracking Abood with the MARS sight on his Tavor M-95 as he moved further away, but clearly in view, "I told you to FREEZE! You're not listening very well."

"Neither are you," screeched a venomous Abood.

"Well, then I guess this conversation is over."

Wright triggered off two quick rounds in succession entering Abood in the throat and chest, and for a spilt second while his decimated nervous system provided just enough pressure on the lever, Wright dropped to the floor in a ball and yanked the dead man next to him over his body, as the ensuing detonation annihilated Abood's body and engulfed the immediate surrounding area.

The pressure expanded supersonically outward from the explosive core, sending a hail of ceramic balls in every direction and driving a concussive shock wave outward through the two escaping tunnel passageways. Outdoors, dust and debris visibly exited the openings at each end of the cave into the morning air, while rock and dirt collapsed into the internal corridors.

* * * * *

Woods backpedaled from his stance in front of the video bank in the war room, "Did anybody else just see that?"

"Affirmative," replied Scruggs, slumping in her chair.

"Shit," exhaled Baum.

Everyone saw the ISR video display plumes of soot and smoke coming up from two different locations emanating from the border area in and around the Nahal Betzet nature preserve. One of them was clearly the entrance locale that Wright and Lau had accessed.

"General, we're getting reports from our troops on the ground of what appears to be an underground detonation. You can obviously see on the video feed the expulsion of exhaust from multiple points that we believe are coming from a natural underground channel or cave," interjected the Mossad office.

"We see it, we definitely see it," Woods fell back into an office chair that rolled backwards to a stop against one of the computer consoles. He placed his head in his hands and in a subdued monotone addressed Scruggs, "Elaine, can you raise Sheri please."

* * * * *

Wright was pretty sure he never left consciousness, but his hearing was gone, and his head ached from the trauma of a concussion. He slowly pushed the mangled body off of his and felt the pain in his left arm and lower leg that had gone uncovered. It was pitch black. With his right hand he reached into his outer hip pocket and retrieved a KROV compact tactical flashlight. He punched the ON button and shone it at his feet.

His left boot was shredded from the ankle up and pain was shooting sharply from the lower calf to the heel. The right leg had fared better. He reached down to determine the damage and winced at the excruciating pain from his left bicep and elbow that were a bloody, pulpy mess. Managing to move the left leg, he realized it was probably broken but a quick visual confirmed no bone exposed.

Arising to a seated position, he noticed he was covered in blood and body tissue, but quickly understood the majority of it didn't belong to him. *Damn, if I wasn't infected before, no doubt I am now.* The air was thick with dust. He choked and coughed as he inhaled and brought his healthy right forearm to his nose and mouth, the light shining out into the darkness. No blood came up from his lungs, which he took as a good sign there was no upper body contusions. As he struggled to stand, stone fragments dribbled off him, joining larger rocks and rubble covering the ground and multiple body parts strewn about everywhere.

With limited visibility, he sent the beam to his left and limped carefully across the uneven piles of human and natural debris back toward the opening they had come from, his head, arm, and leg pounding from the pain. With his audio sense completely disabled, he hobbled forward in an eerie silence. He reached the opening and panned the light back and forward until he saw Lau seated on the ground, legs splayed forward and her back against the wall. She rolled her head to the side slowly and smiled and mouthed words that Wright could not hear. He pointed to his ears and shook his head as he tumbled to the floor next to her.

She leaned her head into the shoulder of his wounded arm, and the initial pain dissipated as he welcomed her warm and wounded body next to his. They sat together in a silent stillness. After few minutes, Wright's hearing slowly began returning, albeit in a very limited capacity, and he angled the flashlight beam around the narrow passage stopping on the structural collapse from the path in which they entered. They looked at each other with a resigned understanding. Between their wounds, the cave in and diminishing oxygen, and the certain infection of them both with the virus, they would be lucky to survive a few more hours.

Wright chuckled, "This is fine mess I got us into. It seems we have a little time on our hands now, is there any chance you want to explain to me why you felt the need to fight this to the end? No argument, just an explanation?"

Lau giggled slightly and grimaced from her injuries, probably broken ribs, to go along with bullet wounds to her shoulder and thigh, "It's the virus."

"Okay, what about the virus?"

"It started back in my homeland…where it was created by a very evil man. It destroyed my heritage. It annihilated the village of my ancestors, many villages. My grandmother, barely a teenager, managed to escape by becoming a 'Comfort Woman,' a sex slave, conscripted into sexual service by and for the invading Japanese Army. Somehow, she survived, but all of her family members, all of her relatives, and entire villages that surrounded hers, were virtually erased by this madman, General Daichi Arakawa, and his insidious virus.

"I was fortunate to hear all about it directly from her when I was a little girl, and she made me promise I would never do anything to perpetrate evil upon the world. I told her I would go one better; I'd try to eliminate it. It's part of the reason I went into the military. I thought I could help prevent evil, but it became very clear the military in my country, my military has been and continues to be responsible for many evils perpetrated upon my people.

"This was my one chance to get clear of my relationship with my army, and when General Huang presented the opportunity to me, I jumped at it. The beautiful irony was it also gave me a chance to right the exact wrong that directly destroyed my family. It was fate, and it actually offered a chance to right a lot of wrongs personally, while keeping a promise I made so long ago."

Lau met Wright's eyes as he looked down at her, "Sounds silly I know, but it's true."

Wright took her dirt covered hand in his right hand and squeezed it tight, "No, it's not silly, and I believe you. Better yet I understand it. There is a lot of evil in this world. I've spent the better part of my life trying to defeat it wherever it reared its ugly head…and for the most part, I've been pretty successful. Today you and I scored our biggest victory over evil. I believe you have fulfilled your promise and can rest easy."

"Thank you," she whispered, and squeezed back on his hand, "I believe you can, too."

They both closed their eyes and leaned into each other, reconciled to the inevitable.

Epilogue

USS John C. Stennis, Mediterranean Sea...three days later

The well starched Lieutenant led Woods through the gunmetal gray bowels of the USS John C. Stennis, Nimitz-class nuclear-powered supercarrier and flagship for U.S. Navy Strike Group 3. They finally reached entry into the stark contrast of the sterile, white-walled medical department, where Woods was introduced to the Senior Medical Officer, Major Christopher Crockett. Accompanying the Major and adorned in full scrubs was Sheri DeHavilland. Woods shook hands with Crockett while giving a left-handed hug to DeHavilland.

Crockett spoke first, "We're bringing him back out of the medically induced coma now General. He'll be fine and should make a full recovery. However, he's pretty banged up and his system has been seriously traumatized from the antidotal regimens, so it will be several months before he's feeling healed."

"Thank you Major...for everything you've done."

"My pleasure General, but it would've probably been a different outcome if it weren't for Sheri's retrieval and intervention. The timing was critical, and her efforts really were probably the difference maker."

"I would whole-heartedly agree Major. Sheri, thanks for risking it, it obviously paid off," Woods extended his hug to both arms, adding a little muscle to the squeeze.

DeHavilland reciprocated the embrace, "Thanks to the helo crew on board here for jumping on it, and Blake for making the transfer at sea a reality. We were fortunate that everything fell into place and we were able to get through."

* * * * *

Wright opened and blinked his eyes as if a pair of quarters were weighing on his lids. Gradually he regained focus and found the faces of Woods, DeHavilland, Ferguson, and Margolis, all staring back down at him. It took several seconds for his brain to process that he was in a hospital bed, immobilized, but obviously very much alive. He managed a smile and received four larger ones in reply.

Woods moved from the group at the end of the bed to Wright's side, "Welcome back!"

"Thanks! Good to be back I think," surveying his body to make sure all of his limbs were accounted for.

"You had us a little worried," Margolis squeezed on his good foot.

Wright's brain and memory continued to process, and he cringed as the concern became clearly etched on his face, "Lei?"

A slight hesitation from everyone, as Ferguson leaned over the foot board of the bed and raised a thumb up, "She made it. Still out of it for now, but they plan on bringing her out of la la land and into the present a little later today. She'll be just fine. She's right next door."

The relief washed over Wright. *Thank you, God!*

* * * * *

Winston Cromer, Themis Co-op's patriotic financier, turned his magnificent Italian villa into what looked like a physical therapy ward. Wheelchairs, a walker, Star Trac stationary bike, and a NordicTrack were all interspersed among the multiple Deco chaise lounges and side tables of the outdoor patio on the sprawling main level of the cliffside manor. There was nothing like the warm breezes and views of the Amalfi coast to help with Clay Wright's and Lei Lau's convalescence, and it's the reason they both were airlifted into Salerno Costa d'Amalfi Airport after six days aboard the John C. Stennis and driven up to Casa Leoni.

It was also a pretty sweet vacation venue for Blake Ferguson, Adina Margolis, Elaine Scruggs, Sheri DeHavilland, and Isaiah Taylor. After a complete accounting through multiple briefings with Woods and Mossad officials, and an unpublicized visit to the see the President elect to receive the personal thanks of a very appreciative future Commander-in-Chief, the entire Themis Cooperative received some well-deserved R & R and time off for good behavior. Much to the delight of Woods, they decided as a group to enjoy together the open-ended offer of lodging at Casa Leoni and arrived three sun splashed days earlier.

Wright and Lau arrived at the villa mid-afternoon by a handicap accessible taxi and were shown to two of the three bedrooms on the main level by the local housekeeper, each with balcony access to the large wraparound main patio, cum rehab space, that led to the infinity pool a few steps just below. The others were housed among the five additional bedrooms and adjoining bathrooms on the second and third floors above.

It was truly a communal affair, and Woods was the only one missing, but was due to arrive any minute after flying in from a follow-up gratitude and recognition visit to Tel Aviv, and would occupy the remaining bedroom next to Wright and Lau. His current mission was restocking provisions from the depleted food stock on his way over from Naples. Ferguson and Isaiah dispatched themselves for more liquor and wine and then down to the beach to retrieve DeHavilland, Scruggs, and Margolis, the three ladies having spent the day collecting rays along the waterfront, along with a stack of phone numbers from the local Positano male population.

Woods realized you could never punch the delete button when it came to the effects of mission trauma and some of the events that would haunt the depths of your brain, but you could definitely ease the impact on the mind, body, and spirit with some requisite time to forget. He was thrilled the whole team decided to spend that time together.

Nearly four hours, and multiple showers later, the entire group assembled at the long teak wood dining room table adorned with ten wicker and teak chairs. The floor to ceiling windows on the south and west walls overlooking the surrounding hills and cliffside village of Positano were open, allowing the soft breezes off the southern Amalfi coast to envelope the room.

Grilled Caesar salad with artichokes and parmesan, onion soup with crostone, bucatini, with butter-roasted tomato sauce, and torta caprese smothered in fresh strawberries occupied the next two hours, enhanced by eight bottles of 2015 Verrazzano Chianti Classico Riserva and the conversation of good friends growing into family.

After the plates had been removed and Amaretto laced coffees distributed to accompany the still flowing wine, the question that had been gnawing at Wright since his awakening on board the Stennis finally found an opening, and he took it.

He turned to Woods appropriately seated at the head of the table and spoke loudly enough to silence the collective confab and grab everyone's attention, "General, I assume you know that my curiosity is nearly killing me, and I suppose Lei as well, but nobody has taken the time to tell me...sorry Lei, I mean us...how in the hell are we still here? We were both toast. Wounded, bleeding out, surely we were infected, the tunnel was clearly caved in, and I suspect oxygen was going to be in very short supply...so how in the hell did we survive that?"

Woods eyed the now totally silent table and shifted his chair backward slightly in order to cross his legs, "You can thank Sheri for making that happen."

Wright and Lei both shifted their gaze to DeHavilland.

"It was her idea," continued Woods. "With her expertise from her time at the WHO, she recommended, and we agreed, to reposition her to Tel Aviv right before your operation in Iraq. Since there was mutual concern by everyone that there could possibly be a contamination from that attack, we needed somebody on the ground to help coordinate an Outbreak Response team and work on containment efforts. The Israelis had provided the personnel to make that happen if necessary.

"Well, it wasn't needed then, but when you guys recovered the virus and antidote vials in Tyre, but discovered some of the virus went missing, the alert went out to the same OR team with Sheri accompanying. We dispatched them to the northern border when you and Lei took off after Abood. Sheri wanted some of the antidote recovered to be immediately diverted to their location. Once Blake and Adina met the Shayetet 13 in open water, we already had an SH-60 Sea Hawk bird in the air that rendezvoused with them about thirty minutes later over their boats. About two hours later it was in Sheri's hands.

"She went in with the IDF when they initiated a search and rescue operation after it was determined an explosion had occurred. Lucky for both of you, the blast expelled a dust cloud out the other end of the tunnel from where you entered, otherwise, we would have never known to go there. It was about a half kilometer into Israeli territory, and the real fortune was the passageway through that entry, to your location, was structurally intact. The other entry, the way you two got in, had a significant cave-in. They reached you about an hour and a half after the explosion. Both of you were unconscious and in bad shape, you'd lost a lot of blood. Another hour or more and I doubt either of you would probably have made it.

"Sheri was on site with the first group in and not only triaged you both, but provided antidote inoculations to both of you, which was critical to the timing of preventing the virus from getting traction. The same bird that brought Olivia the antidote exfilled you to the Stennis. The rest is history."

With a tear streaming down her soft white cheek, Lei looked at DeHavilland and whispered, "Thank you."

Wright raised his half-full glass of wine and gave a subtle nod of his head in her direction, "Thank you Sheri."

"My pleasure, to you both. I couldn't be happier with the results. Additional thanks go to Isaiah for digging out enough info from Park's iPad to know the parameters of how to apply the antidote. Those details were also critical to getting it right the first time."

A silence dominated the next few seconds as everyone absorbed the gravity of what had just occurred over the last few weeks.

Woods stood from his chair and raised his glass of wine, "I'd like to propose a toast to everyone for a job well done. I thank you, the incoming President thanks you, the Israeli Prime Minister thanks you, and frankly...the world thanks you. It's a better place, and a lot of people are alive today, due to all of you. Mission accomplished."

Lots of clinking glasses ensued, along with a loud "Hear, hear."

As everyone took a seat, while Ferguson was busy filling empty glasses with the ninth bottle of vino, Woods held up a hand, "If I may, I do have one bit of bad news."

"Buzz kill," replied Ferguson.

"Yes, Blakie, unfortunately it is for you. While you've been off helping save the world, the bank repossessed your boat. It was brought to my attention a couple of days ago, and there was nothing I could do. However, thanks again to Isaiah, we may have a remedy." Woods offered the floor to Isaiah, who leaned back in his chair.

"Well...long story short is I found some additional information on Park's pad. It seems his adventures with Iran were predicated on money."

"Shocking," muttered Margolis.

"Yeah. He had a sick daughter, dying from a unique form of cancer at a private treatment facility in Italy, not far up the road from here actually, and he was spending money hand over fist trying to keep her alive with every treatment money could buy. The Iranians paid handsomely for Park's secret and his services in making the virus a reality so that he could accommodate the pricey medical spend. Unfortunately, after a little digging around, I found out she passed away nearly a week ago.

"Not sure they might be headed in the same eternal directions," Ferguson mused.

"No telling, but fortunately, there's a BIG pot of money still sitting in Park's Swiss account...actually was sitting in his account. Per the General's suggestion, and with no objections from anybody else, through about a half dozen cut-outs I managed a transfer of all said funds to the Themis Cooperative, and its affiliated partners all present in this room tonight…to the tune of $24,890,505."

The entire table sat stunned and silent, glances amongst each other circled around.

"It gets better," smiled Woods.

Isaiah continued, "I was also able to track back the deposits to Park's account from a shell energy brokerage company being financed through an oil and gas production entity based in France. Pretty simpleton stuff really, but after some additional drilling down, it was rather obvious the whole operation was being controlled by the Mullahs. Ironically, there was still $15,000,000 and some change sitting in it. Not sure if that was due to Park or anybody else, but I took the liberty of making that due to his account and then drained that to the Themis account as well."

Wright whistled and then looked at Ferguson, "Captain Blake, old boy, I believe this might make up for the loss of your damn boat. Hell, you can buy a fleet of boats."

"I would tend to agree."

Woods stood again and raised his glass one more time, "Ladies and gentlemen, here's to the Themis Cooperative, and a $40,000,000 pay day for our services. To coin a phrase…this looks like the beginning of a beautiful friendship."

Acknowledgements

Many thanks to my wonderful and beautiful wife Ann for allowing me the multitude of personal moments and downtime to pursue my passion for creating stories. I love you.

I can't say thank you enough to two people who gave of their time and expertise in spades, and truly had a dramatic impact on the narrative. Their assistance was invaluable.

My Aunt Boodie, English Professor extraordinaire and creative writing guru, dissected my word mangling and provided me an education in grammar and punctuation, while making me rethink and reimagine words, paragraphs, characters and plots.

Wade Wilson took his own background as a "real" hero to all Americans for his service to the nation, lending his accomplished technical expertise and unexpected talent for gifted prose. Characters, content and action became not only believable, but accurate in detail.

I would also be remiss for not extending an appreciative thank you to Doug Keeney. His abilities as a successful author with a number of published works to his credit, along with his willingness to read *Setareh Doctrine*, offered an unvarnished assessment of the conceptual flaws in the opening of the original manuscript and an encouragement to return to "my style" of writing, making the story significantly better.

Lastly, many thanks to John Clark at Old Stone Press for taking on the assignment of elevating the publication of *Setareh Doctrine* to another level I was not aware of. Simply put, it was another major tutelage as to the inner workings of the publishing world, and the significant efforts required in promotion, marketing and distribution to make my work as successful as it can be.

About the Author

Blessed…and cursed with the creative gene, Mark Downer has always found writing to come naturally, a trait inherited from his father, whom he touts as a truly remarkable wordsmith. Having always felt the urge to write and attempt to produce commercially successful prose, the dictates of another career path and raising a family of three children sidetracked his writing ambitions.

Children grown and financial security earned through ownership of a successful and self-sustaining business make that predilection a reality today. With a life full of study and interest in history, particularly the military variety, and a reading library full of some of fiction's greatest novelists, Downer now pursues his passion, drawing upon those resources and upon his conviction that good always triumphs over evil.

Ghosts of the Past was his first endeavor, created over several years of being drawn back into his creative awakening. It has been the catalyst for his second novel here, *Setareh Doctrine*, which is the first book in the Themis Cooperative thriller series. Look for *Caracas Connection* to follow shortly.

CPSIA information can be obtained
at www.ICGtesting.com
Printed in the USA
LVHW041143110621
689906LV00006B/615